Homecoming

HOMECOMING

Sue Ann Bowling

iUniverse, Inc.
New York   Bloomington

Homecoming

Edited by Carla Helfferich.

Cover image credit: Prof. J.P. Harrington (University of Maryland, College Park); Prof. K. J. Borkowski (North Carolina State University), NASA.

iUniverse books may be ordered through booksellers or by contacting:

iUniverse
1663 Liberty Drive
Bloomington, IN 47403
www.iuniverse.com
1-800-Authors (1-800-288-4677)

Because of the dynamic nature of the Internet, any Web addresses or links contained in this book may have changed since publication and may no longer be valid. The views expressed in this work are solely those of the author and do not necessarily reflect the views of the publisher, and the publisher hereby disclaims any responsibility for them.

ISBN: 978-1-4502-1315-8 (sc)
ISBN: 978-1-4502-1317-2 (dj)
ISBN: 978-1-4502-1316-5 (ebk)

Library of Congress Control Number: 2010902204

Printed in the United States of America

iUniverse rev. date: 3/15/2010

CONTENTS

CENTRAL

SNOWY

12/1/33

The living sculpture could no longer control its body, even to blink its eyes or turn them away from the horror in the mirror … No, Flick thought. His eyes. My eyes. I am still I. I am he. He could still hear and feel—if only he could stop hearing, and feeling, and even seeing! His master's body stepped behind his own in the mirror, and the ice and silver eyes of his sculptor's reflection traveled lazily over his distorted body. Zhaim was a handsome creature—oh, yes, with black hair braided into an elaborate crest above the smooth, bronze face, and a body that might have been designed by a far saner sculptor than the owner who had made a distorted mockery of his own body. Flick hated his owner with a passion that verged on madness, but while Zhaim had no qualms about invading Flick's mind, he never seemed aware of his young slave's hatred. Unaware or uncaring? Flick felt despair sting his unblinking eyes. What did it matter if a statue loathed its creator?

The R'il'noid sculptor walked around his latest artwork, and Flick fought desperately to move, to scream out his hatred—

"Snowy, Snowy! Wake up!"

For a moment Snowy was lost, trapped in confusion between the horror of Flick's emotions and awareness of his own identity. Then the feel of Flame's arms around him, and the concern and caring he picked up from Timi and Amber, and most of all the fact that he could move his own body to burrow

3

closer into Flame's embrace brought him back to himself. "Nightmare," he muttered. "Sorry to wake you all up."

Behind him, he could hear Timi yawn. "You do less of that than most of us," Amber reassured him. "Go back to sleep. We've got a busy day tomorrow."

"Right," he mumbled. "G'night." He readjusted his position against Flame, and closed his eyes. He felt the physical comfort of his friends, bodies jumbled together like a pile of puppies. What had happened was no nightmare, and he knew it. His sensitivity to the thoughts of others, though it had increased greatly in the last year or so, was under at least crude control. His ability to share emotions had also increased—but that was something he could not block without constant, conscious effort. When he slept, those blocks went down. And he was most sensitive to those he cared about. Like Flick.

He owed Flick. Without the older boy's encouragement, he would never have started dancing with Flame, back in the days when he was a ten-year-old catamite and she a slave-bred concubine of the same age. That had led to a blessed respite from the worst of the abuse and more, to a realization on the part of their owner at the time that they were worth more together than separate. Later they had integrated Timi and Amber, both captives, into their dancing group. For the first time in his life, Snowy had friends he had some hope of keeping with him. For that matter, it was the first time he had had a market value high enough that he had some hope of surviving into adulthood.

Sure, he was good looking, with his bronze skin, snow-white hair, and golden eyes. So was Timi, with his black silk skin, matching, loosely curled hair and flame-amber eyes. And the two girls—Flame with her copper hair and alabaster complexion, and Amber with blond hair, blue eyes, and creamy-tan skin—set them off beautifully. But attractive young pleasure slaves were easy to find, here on Central. It was the dancing, and the increased value that gave the group, that had kept them together for over two years now.

Flick—the first real friend Snowy had found since being sold away from his mother—had been sold even before Snowy and Flame had fully developed their teamwork. Snowy forced himself to lie quietly, not wanting to disturb the others again. He didn't know how to control the linkage between himself and Flick, and he didn't dare ask the Masters who might know. His odd talents weren't supposed to exist in a slave. *He* wasn't supposed to exist—his mother had made that clear enough. He'd be killed without mercy if the Masters even suspected his abilities. He couldn't even discuss the situation with his friends—he trusted them, but he did not trust their ability to keep their thoughts shielded from the Master, and he didn't trust the Master at all.

It wasn't the first time he had shared Flick's emotions, and distance seemed no barrier. He was pretty sure it was daytime where Flick was and night here, yet he had experienced everything Flick had felt. Snowy cared about his dancing partners, even more than he had dared care about Flick. Would he share their pain, as he now shared Flick's, if they were sold apart?

He suppressed a shudder, and forced his mind away from that path. Flick's situation was the immediate problem, and not entirely because he knew he would continue to share Flick's agony. He owed Flick whatever help he could give. But what help was that?

He chewed on his lip, sharply aware of the chill darkness around him and the hardness of the floor beneath his body. Sharing a single covering with the other three, though, was definitely preferable to sharing a warm, soft bed with their Master. It didn't bother him or Flame, both slave-bred, nearly as much as it bothered Timi or Amber, but they were all happier in their corner of the slave quarters than in the Master's bed.

So what could he do about the situation with Flick? Maybe nothing—but just maybe …

He didn't dare leave anything Zhaim could read in Flick's mind. He remembered something Zhaim had once said, while showing off his living sculptures to a visitor. "I am not Lai's property, and I do not agree with his soft-headed treatment of Human slaves as people! As the last of the pure R'il'nai, he deserves respect. But his ideas are outdated. When I, as the ranking crossbred, take his place, the Jarnian Confederation will be run as it should be, for the benefit of R'il'noids such as us. I left the Enclave because my father refused to grant me the artistic freedom I needed. He is not welcome here. But he can hardly refuse me the mental privacy he grants even to slaves!" Clearly Zhaim never even thought of granting mental privacy to slaves.

Snowy took a deep breath and released his blocks against sensing emotions. He hadn't actually tried to tap into a specific person's feelings before, and it took a certain amount of awkward fumbling before he could ignore the sensations of his three friends. Once he reached Flick he had to brace himself against the intensity of the older boy's agony and hatred, even worse than they had seemed before. He couldn't leave Flick like this!

He hated going into another mind, even to read thoughts or emotions. It left him feeling sick, as if he'd been swimming in garbage. Actually affecting another's thoughts or emotions was even worse. He'd done it—twice to save his own life, and once to save Timi's—but those experiences had left scars that were still painful. And the only way he could see to help Flick was to go into his friend's emotions deeper than anything he had tried before. He didn't think that what he had in mind would be reversible, either.

Clamping his teeth on his lip, Snowy tried to build an image of what he intended in his mind. No words; Zhaim might be able to detect those. Only emotions. What remained of Flick's personality to be separated entirely from bodily sensations, and sent dreaming. Not of the last few months, or even the last few years, but of the time before his capture, when he had been part of a group rebelling against an unjust and arbitrary planetary government. Only the body left tied to physical sensations, so that changes in heart rate and breathing would convince Zhaim that his captive still felt his manipulations. A shallow smokescreen of the mental reactions Zhaim would expect. But no way of returning from the dream. When he had the emotional message complete, Snowy tried to transmit it to Flick, with a sense of question.

The response was immediate, overwhelming, and positive.

Snowy hesitated an instant longer. It wouldn't work if Zhaim went deeply into Flick's mind, but he rarely did that, not any more. Snowy was a slave himself; there was no possible way he could get Flick away from Zhaim physically. And Flick hadn't really understood that he was being offered a choice; his response had been more of "if only this were possible." What frightened Snowy most, though, was his mother's remembered warning. Could the interference with Flick's emotional state, if Zhaim ever recognized it, be traced back to Snowy?

But the alternative was leaving Flick in his current state of suffering.

Carefully, Snowy went deeper into Flick's emotions. He knew what he wanted to do, and he was pretty sure it was possible, but he was working by trial and error. Several times he had to back up, realizing he had made a wrong step, but finally he had the configuration he was after. He attuned himself to Flick's changed emotions for a moment. Not peaceful, no, but hopeful, excited, looking forward to a better world. A world that would never come, now, for Flick—but Flick didn't know that, and never would. I still owe you, he thought, if there's anything I can ever do. Then he made the last move of his scheme, cutting himself loose permanently from Flick's emotions. The hatred dropped away as he felt his own body around him again.

Not all of the pain dropped away, though. His lower lip was throbbing, and he tasted blood. A quick inspection confirmed that he had bitten it through. Again. Hastily he opened to his friends' emotions, confirming that they were all asleep. And with his head buried against Flame's shoulder, the injured lip wasn't likely to be on any of the monitors. Guiltily he reached for the damaged tissues, and began Healing the injury.

✳   ✳   ✳   ✳

Flick's situation and the minor annoyance of his own bitten lip were by no means the only things Snowy had to worry about. The following day was more than just "busy." Master Kuril had guests that evening he was determined to impress, and the dancing group was a large part of his entertainment. Not just as dancers, either—he had made it clear that he expected them to entertain his guests in more—personal—ways after the dancing.

"I think—Ow!—he's losing interest in us," Snowy commented after the guests had left, while Davy, the overseer of Kuril's slaves, was massaging his sore muscles. His scalp hurt, too—there were times when his hip-length hair had him envying the kitchen slaves, who were kept hairless to protect the Master's food.

"Sorry," Davy said absently, his hands continuing to knead the boy's shoulders. "But you'd all be a lot stiffer tomorrow without this."

Snowy sighed and tried to relax muscles that still wanted to knot with tension. "I know. Davy, you're the best overseer we've ever had. You won't get in trouble for this, will you?"

"Not 'til he trades in about fifty pounds of fat for muscle and quits thinking he can get away with things that'd strain even a fit body. He needs me too much. I don't know how you kids got off as easy as you did. I saw some of the roughing up those guests gave you."

Snowy didn't have to be reminded of that. His ability to Heal his own injuries, and to some extent those of his friends, had allowed him to take care of the worst damage. But quite aside from the care he had to take not to be suspected of doing anything unusual, Healing took energy—lots of energy—and while he had eaten everything he'd had a chance to that evening, he had been ravenous and shaking by the time Davy arrived.

"They weren't all bad," Timi giggled drunkenly.

Timi, admitting that any slave user on Central was less than an ogre? Snowy turned his head slightly so that he could see his friend. He'd already scanned Timi enough to know that his only serious problem was from the level of alcohol in his blood, and he suspected that Timi had cooperated fully in that particular bit of abuse. As far as he could remember, he had seen Timi with only one of Kuril's guests, a slender but fit-looking man whose hair, skin and eyes were all the same shade of golden brown. Snowy had found himself dealing with three at once, and he had barely managed to protect himself without revealing his talents.

"Who'd you get, Timi?" he asked.

"Guy called Derik," Timi caroled happily. "D'you believe it? Saw I didn't like it and he just had me rubbing his back 'n talkin'. 'N shared freshments." He hiccupped.

"Obviously," Davy said sourly. "I hope you remembered how to do a back rub properly."

Davy had drilled them all on that, Snowy thought. One more skill that increased their chances of survival. He'd been too busy himself to pay much attention to Timi's partner, but if Kuril was losing interest as fast as Snowy suspected, they'd likely be sold soon. He turned his head a little farther, and rolled his eyes up to where he could see Davy. "Know anything about him?" he asked, knowing that the overseers, slave and free, had a loose communication network.

"Don't like his overseer," Davy replied. "Derik Tarlian himself—well, he's way above our Master. High R'il'noid—Inner Council level, half brother to Lai himself, and supposed to be a top esper. Number two to Zhaim, I think. Overseer complains he spoils his slaves—but that overseer sure doesn't. Doesn't let Derik know half of what goes on in the slave quarters, either."

Davy wouldn't name someone he disapproved of, Snowy had observed. The fact that he used Derik Tarlian's name without hesitation, while refusing to name either the overseer or his own owner, told Snowy more than his explicit comments had. And if the overseer was really hiding what went on in the slave quarters, Derik Tarlian was probably not in the habit of probing unwilling minds. Snowy had tried to avoid owners who might suspect his abilities in the past, but he had a fair degree of confidence in his own ability to project an image of a normal slave mind. Owners completely lacking in esper talents certainly existed—most Human slaves had Human owners—but they rarely had the credit to buy a group as expensive as theirs. And if this Derik did not try a deep probe ... He looked back at Timi. "What did you talk about?" he asked.

"Dancin'," Timi yawned. The slur in his voice was increasing. "An' music, 'n food. Wanted t' know who did our cho.. chor—uh—'rangements. Tol'm you did." His eyes closed, and he began to snore gently.

Snowy chewed on his lip. Timi was hypersensitive to esper probes and hated them. Unlikely this Derik had probed him. Maybe it would be safe enough. Kuril was far from the worst owner he'd ever had—Colo Kenarian, who'd owned him briefly even before he'd met Flick, had been far worse, and from what he'd learned from Flick, even Colo was not the worst possible. But if Kuril was going to sell them, this guy might be worth encouraging. Carefully. Staying open to the R'il'noid's emotions might give Snowy the information he needed to act in a way that would attract the man, and without alerting Derik that there was anything unusual about Snowy. If Derik visited again, Snowy decided, he would check the man out himself. Davy's attitude toward Derik's overseer bothered him a little, but overseers could sometimes be maneuvered into getting rid of themselves. And it was owners, not overseers, who generally had the final decision on buying or selling a slave. Yes, he decided as his muscles finally relaxed under Davy's manipulations, bad overseer or not, this guy looked like he might be a better owner than Kuril. Snowy hoped Derik would come again before Kuril sold them.

Derik

1/30/34

Four five-beat measures in a row—no, the fourth measure had only four beats, followed by one with—seven? Derik shook his head ruefully. He'd heard that particular piece a dozen times or more, but the rhythm still took him by surprise now and then.

He didn't generally like Kuril's taste in entertainment, but then he wasn't here for the entertainment; he had work to do, of a sort. Derik was an influential member of the Inner Council, the R'il'noid body that handled interplanetary affairs and at least in theory had no influence at all in planetary matters. Kuril, technically Human since less than half of his active genome was R'il'nian-derived, was a leader in the Planetary Assembly—part of the fifth of that body with obvious R'il'nian traits. In practice, people varied from pure R'il'nian to pure Human on a continuum, with the Çeren index providing a legal separation only. And the Councils had to work with planetary governing bodies, not just on Central, but throughout the Confederation.

Kuril was relatively new to his high position, and still seemed to think that he needed to ingratiate himself socially with the Council members. Derik couldn't actually refuse his invitations without appearing to insult the man, but he personally considered this by far the most boring part of his job.

Now, Derik, he chided himself, the man keeps an excellent cook, and the musicians are well above average, even if you don't care for their music. From the glazed look on his host's face, Kuril didn't care for it either. This composer's—Fisan's—music was currently fashionable, but Elyra's half brother Loki was the only person Derik could think of who actually *liked* it.

Thinking of Loki, one of Central's outstanding choreographers, reminded him of Kuril's dancers. Quite young, no more that thirteen or fourteen, but easily the best he'd seen for their age. At least Kuril had learned a little from Derik's reaction at the last of his parties the High R'il'noid had attended. The young dancers should have been resting or limbering up between their performances. Kuril still hadn't caught on to that, but at least this time he had the youngsters serving food rather than being pawed over by his guests.

Derik glanced over at the young slave kneeling at his side, offering a platter of pastries. He'd intended to take the same slave he'd had last time—the boy had seemed so pitifully grateful that Derik wanted only to talk and have his back rubbed, and he'd been good at the massage. Instead, Derik had found himself with the white-haired boy his previous companion had indicated was the group's choreographer. Just as good a masseur, he decided, but at the moment the youngster appeared totally absorbed in the music, fingers moving slightly as he tried to follow the beat. "Going to make a dance out of that one?" Derik whispered, trying to keep the grin off his face.

"Not for the group," the boy whispered back. "It might make a solo, though." His fingers continued to move with the music.

Derik stared at the boy. He'd asked Loki about dancing to Fisan's music once, and been treated to a lecture on the impossibility of what he'd suggested. He felt his lips twitch with the urge to call the boy on such an outrageous statement. And why not? It wouldn't really hurt the youngster. He grinned. "And just what part do you think you can make a dance to?" he whispered.

The boy tipped his head to one side, thinking. "About eight minutes after the start there's half a minute of silence and then a great crashing discord," he said. "The five minutes after that. It won't be polished and I might fall flat on my face, but I do have the rhythm."

Which is more than I do, Derik thought. He pushed his request for a repeat of the section the boy had described toward Kuril, getting the man's puzzled agreement. He'd liked the black, but he hadn't seriously considered trying to buy him—Kuril wouldn't want to break up the group. This one, however, promised to be every bit as much fun. Outwardly, the boy's demeanor was perfect—eyes lowered, head bowed, responsive to Derik's slightest whim. Inwardly—Derik would not probe an unwilling mind, but that claim of accomplishment was unusual for a slave. "Show me," he challenged.

The boy rose to his feet, eyes still lowered, and walked gracefully to the raised center of the floor. Silence fell, broken by the crashing chord, and then the boy began to move. Watching, Derik suddenly felt the rhythm not as bars and beats, but for the first time as an organic whole. Other faces in the room stayed glazed as ever or even annoyed, not realizing what they were seeing.

Derik wanted to applaud as the boy finished his improvisation and walked back to his lounge, but that would have been a shocking breach of manners. One did not applaud a slave; one thanked its master. Stupid. He would not probe an unwilling non-esper, but he could and did use his conditional precognition to check if bringing the youngster into his own household would be safe, and was astounded at the strength of his own positive response.

"Want me to buy you?" he asked as the boy, breathing deeply from his exertions, returned to his side.

The eyes, golden as honey in the bronze face, flicked briefly to Derik's and then slid away. "The others—we dance best together. Oh! That's our cue." Still gasping, he moved to join the other three.

Kuril, Derik thought angrily, did not deserve the group. At the very least, he should have given the boy a few minutes rest after his unplanned dance. And the boy hadn't protested that he did not want to leave Kuril, as would only have been proper slave manners, he had wanted to stay with his friends. Loyalty was a trait Derik prized. And bringing the whole group into his household raised no more warning flags than buying the boy alone. Derik narrowed his eyes, watching the group dance, but this time trying to estimate their fair market value. *How much would you take for them?* he finally 'pathed Kuril.

Kuril might be a borderline telepath, but his shielding technique was leaky. His struggle was clear to Derik—run the price up for the obviously interested R'il'noid? Lower it, and hope the favor would be returned? In the end, the price he named was close to what Derik had already estimated the group was worth, a little more than a dealer would have paid, but still less than the amount that dealer would have asked. Good. Derik had no intention either of accepting a bribe or being cheated. He knew Kuril would expect a little bargaining, so he added, *That would include costumes and props, of course.* Kuril agreed, and by the time the group finished their dance the sale was final.

He'd call the boys Noon and Midnight, he decided, and the two girls Sunrise and Sunset. He could hardly wait to show them off to Loki Faranian.

"I've bought all four of you from Kuril," he told Noon, now visibly gasping for breath, as he came back to the lounge. "Tell the others, will you? My overseer will be picking you up tomorrow morning."

Relief flooded the boy's features. "Yes, Master," he said as he turned away. And was there just a hint of—smugness?— in his expression?

I've been manipulated, Derik thought in astonishment, and not by Kuril, either. He watched as the guests dispersed and the other three slaves rejoined Noon, and his smile widened still more. That boy's got a brain. This bunch is going to be *fun*!

Maybe even more than fun, he added as his eyes followed the boy. He disapproved of the casual use of slaves, but in the thirteen centuries since he'd settled down from the wild excesses of his first two centuries he'd had a number of long-term slave lovers. The last, Janna, had died in his arms five years before. Old age had been beyond even the Healers, back when there were R'il'nai who could Heal. He was ready for another lover, and while most of his lovers had been female, it had always been the spirit within that really mattered. Could this boy be the next?

Wait and see, he told himself. Wait and see.

Lai

2/20/34

As a party, it was low key to the point of boredom. Fine. Lai had avoided social functions since his father had died years before, leaving him the last survivor of the R'il'nai, and he had no desire to host a party in the usual sense. A casual gathering of a few of his and his partner Elyra's R'il'noid relatives, however, he could tolerate and even enjoy. He leaned back against the angle of the pool walls, letting his legs float while he sent his mind beyond the weather shielding over the enclosed patio. Good, his weather sense was accurate as usual; the clouds were lifting and the sunset should be magnificent.

Beside him, Elyra's half-brother Loki chuckled. "Sure no problem telling them apart when they're side by side." He nodded toward the two women examining one of the plants in the atrium, and Lai smiled slightly in agreement. The two, niece and aunt, shared the same delicate features and milk chocolate coloring—skin, eyes and hair. But Elyra, who'd shared his home and bed for the last year, would fit easily under his outstretched arm. He had to look up at her aunt Kaia when they were both standing.

Lai's own half brothers, Derik and Nik, were racing the length of the pool, Nik slightly in the lead. Loki applauded. "Thought you were the athlete, Derry."

Nik grinned, shoving his red hair back from his freckled face. "Advantage of living on a tropical island. Derry spends his time on horses and gliders instead of swimming."

"Don't forget the sailing, diving and caving." Derik stretched out on his back in the water.

"Try dancing," Loki replied. "Believe me, that works every muscle in your body, and takes perfect coordination, too."

"No argument there!" Derik said. "Loki, you've got to come over and see this new dancing group I've bought. They're all athletes, but the leader is incredible. Don't think he ever saw a horse before I got him, and he's staying with me cross-country. First time I've had a rider good enough I can have him try out my obstacle course designs."

"But can he dance?" Loki challenged.

"Improvised a solo to one of Fisan's pieces. And he actually had me feeling the music's rhythm—I'd have sworn it didn't have any."

Lai hid a frown. It sounded to him as though Derik was falling in love again. Most R'il'noids had fairly short-term relationships, with neither party continuing the relationship much beyond pregnancy. Most of those few R'il'noid women who were fertile at all shifted their interest rather sharply from their partner to the unborn child—and they simply were not interested in men who could not give them children. Those of both sexes who were infertile varied between Nik's total disinterest in sex to total promiscuity. A few—a very few—had an interest in sex that went beyond the merely physical to the inner essence of the partner. This had been the R'il'nian pattern; an interest that lasted long enough to see any child of such a pairing reared to adulthood. Since a pure R'il'nian woman was fertile only about once a century, and the R'il'nai never aged, it made sense for them.

Derik had that desire for a long-term relationship, coupled with near-sterility. He was non-aging—still youthful at fifteen centuries of age—and no non-aging woman would agree to stay with him for the century or more he wanted, either because they wanted children, or because they wanted variety. His solution had been to buy Human slaves as lovers. Such a slave would have a long, full and luxurious life, but no choice. Lai supposed it was a better fate than most slaves could hope for, but it still bothered him, as did Elyra's purchase of slave nannies for her children. Granted, the nannies were well educated during their time of service, and freed when it was over, but he still didn't like slavery. Not that he had any say in what was legal on Central.

"Looks like it's clearing off," Elyra called from across the atrium. "Let's go out on the lawn and watch the sunset."

"Put some clothes on; it'll be cool outdoors after this rain," Lai warned as he levitated himself out of the pool, teleporting away the water that clung to his dark bronze skin and black hair almost without thinking. The atrium was large and open to the sky, but it was also weather-shielded and climate-controlled. When they walked through the entryway to the lawn beyond, the wind was cool against Lai's skin.

A line of light had opened along the western horizon, between cloud deck and sea, and the sun was a scarlet ball almost too bright to look at, its upper edge still hidden by the westernmost edge of the clouds. Slowly it dropped as the clouds lifted, and the flame color on the underside of the clouds brightened and flowed eastward. Then the eastward surge slowed and reversed, the color fleeing westward with the sinking sun, reflecting from the metallic eye veining of the watching R'il'noids.

His beloved Cloudy would have found inspiration in the sunset, Lai thought. She would have retreated for a few days to brood in her workroom, and come out of her seclusion triumphant, the beauty of the sky captured in tangible form. She might have carried a vase with the colors of the sunset in its glaze, or a delicate mobile of spun glass. More than fourteen years, and the pain of her desertion was as sharp as on that day he had returned from nearly a month off-planet to find her gone, and a note begging him not to try to find her. It seemed he missed her more with each passing year.

Colors were dimming to violet as the sunset faded, and the wash of autumn gold on the foothills to the east slipped away. The computer touched his mind, lightly. "Supper's ready," he said. "Shall we go in?" He herded the others to the foyer, pausing to admire the crystal bird among the fountains and flowering plants. He'd received it as a legacy from his great-aunt, but it was far older than that. Faran, one of the handful of R'il'nians with the spark of creativity in their souls, had carved it. Loki probably traced some of his talent to Faran, though most of it undoubtedly came from his Human ancestry. Was that what Jarn had seen in the primates he had encountered when he was stranded on Earth, over a hundred millennia ago? Certainly his crossbred descendents, both those who had followed him back to the stars and those who had stayed behind to become the planet-bound Humans of Earth, had far more creativity than the R'il'nai had. And Lai had more than a suspicion that was the reason the R'il'nai had welcomed the Humans among them, and agreed to guide and protect them.

Dinner was spread on small tables scattered through a corner of the atrium. Finger foods, mostly—seasoned meats on skewers or wrapped in tender pastry, crisp vegetables in bite-sized pieces, berries and cut fruits and small frozen confections in stasis. An assortment of dipping sauces was beside each lounge. Mental and physical conversation ceased briefly as the guests took the edge off their hunger, but Loki's eyes kept returning to Elyra's waist. *Lyra,* he finally broadcast, *You aren't eating for two, are you?*

Elyra managed to suppress her laughter long enough to swallow the bite she'd just taken. *Told you one of my relatives would figure it out,* she thought at Lai. Then, more generally, *Yes, we're expecting. Close to the south solstice. Lai thinks a girl, healthy, and probably R'il'noid.*

Too early to tell for sure she's R'il'noid, Lai added. *But most of the genetic material the embryo's shed is Human-derived.*

Nik swallowed a bite and looked accusingly at Elyra. "The Genetics Board …"

"I'm the head geneticist," Elyra replied. "Are you arguing that Lai and I aren't compatible?"

"Of course not. But you never came in for the Çeren procedure." He looked bewildered.

"We did it the old fashioned way," Lai replied. "And yes, I know the statistics. One child a century per R'il'nian father. Jarn was stranded on Earth for three millennia, and he had just twenty-seven children to proto-human mothers. Twenty-three of those were fertile, and the modern Human race is descended from them. And when I checked his *Journals*, I found something else. Those twenty-seven had just seven mothers, and they were the seven women he really loved. I think he wanted those children. And without even realizing it, he did something with esper that was similar to the Çeren lab procedure. I *think* I've figured it out, but it'll be another seven months before I'm sure. And if I'm right, it'll do some things the Çeren procedure doesn't."

"How?" Derik demanded eagerly. "Can any of the rest of us use it?"

"Ask me again in seven months," Lai replied. "For right now, I'm hoping it'll stop the birth of more like Colo."

"And Zhaim," someone muttered almost inaudibly.

"Lots of decent R'il'noids start out wild," Lai protested. "Look at Derry."

Derik winced, but made no attempt at denial. Elyra sighed. "Derry was irresponsible, yes. But not cruel. Zhaim was, and I'm not positive he's changed. Sorry, Lai. I know he's your son and you love him. But I think he's very careful that some things don't get to your ears. The rest of us—well, we worry about him being your heir."

Why couldn't they get off his back about Zhaim? Yes, he'd had to slap Zhaim down pretty sharply a couple of centuries ago—but that was over with now. He'd seen nothing since then to suggest the problem had not been taken care of, and much to be proud of in his heir. Look at the genetic engineering he was doing. No one else had done as much to make borderline planets habitable, but some people could not forget Zhaim's early years, even as they could not forget Derry's. Of course Derry's wild years had been before Lai was born, but still …

"How long are you going to stay with Lai, Lyra?" Loki blurted into the awkward silence.

"Until our child is weaned, at least." Given Elyra's firm commitment to the idea that a woman should not have more than one child by the same father, that was actually more than he should have expected, but Lai still wished she would commit to staying longer. Cloudy would have. But Cloudy could never have borne him a child. Healthy herself, she had carried the gene for the Coven syndrome, and one in four of her children would have had the dominant Coven gene but lacked the other dominant that suppressed the neurological effects. Coven itself was bad enough, but Coven combined with projective telepathy … No, he couldn't argue with the Genetics Board's refusal even to consider Cloudy for the cross-breeding project. But how much part had the Genetics Board's attitude played in her eventual decision to leave him?

They had certainly reinforced the idea that no woman should have more than one child by the same father. They claimed to be following the R'il'nai in that practice, but how much did he really know about R'il'nian society? The only women left alive by the time he had been born were his mother and his great-aunt. He knew that R'il'nian women were physically incapable of more than a child a century, and his own desire for a lasting relationship, together with the records his ancestors had left, suggested that in his species the parents had stayed together to rear that child. Certainly that was what he wanted. He looked at the others. Elyra, her aunt and her half brother were discussing her child to be, Nik was angled toward them and occasionally offering a suggestion, and Derik was sampling the various sauces—no doubt hoping to find something new to his gourmet palate. All R'il'noids by Çeren index, all well over half a millennium old, and five of his closest friends. He'd have included Zhaim as well, but Elyra did not get along well with Lai's son, so he'd timed the announcement party for a time when Zhaim was off planet.

The stars came out overhead, and he dimmed the atrium lighting to a soft glow over the food. Nik was obviously fighting sleep—he lived eight time zones away, and was the only non-teleport present. "Want a 'port home?" Derry asked him.

"I'd appreciate it," Nik mumbled around a yawn, and the two made their farewells to Lai and left. Kaia and Loki followed, leaving Lai and Elyra alone.

"Well, they know now," Lai said.

Elyra chuckled. "Only thing that really surprised them was that we did it so fast. Even the Çeren procedure can take a couple of years. We did it in what? Six tries?"

"Four. First couple I was trying to figure out what to do." He instructed the computer to clean up, then walked with Elyra towards his private quarters. His eyes went automatically to the tri-dee of Cloudy in the niche above his wall screen. She hadn't been a great beauty—washed out, even, with her pale skin, white hair and light brown eyes. But the love and caring that shone out of those eyes had captivated Lai, and the tri-dee somehow captured that aspect of her personality. If only she hadn't taken the Genetics Board evaluation so personally!

Beside him, Elyra caught her breath sharply, and he realized he hadn't been shielding his emotions that strongly. "Lai, we never meant to hurt her. Even less to drive her away. She was good for you. We were so worried about you, when your father died …"

"You had reason to be—I didn't want to live until Cloudy pulled me back from the edge." He forced down the tightness in his throat and looked questioningly at Elyra, not trusting himself to try more direct contact.

She w as no longer driven as she had been before her pregnancy began, but she clearly felt his need. "Come," she said softly as she led him into her sleeping room.

3/2/34

"Damn it, Colo, don't you have any sense of responsibility at all?" Derry's voice, and his frustration was clear to Lai's empathic senses. Lai paused, eavesdropping shamelessly. From the sound of it, Derry was having the same argument with Colo that he'd had all too often himself, but would Colo pay any more attention to a fellow R'il'noid than he did to a R'il'nian?

"For Humans? Derik, we're R'il'noids. That's where your loyalties should lie, not with mere animals."

"The Confederation, in case you've forgotten, is a Human creation, from a time when there were no R'il'noids. When the Kharfun epidemic had killed them all, along with most of the R'il'nai. And without the R'il'noids that had been their leaders, and the R'il'nai as backup, the Human planets couldn't defend themselves against Maung infestations. Not to mention that some planets started attacking each other without R'il'noid leaders."

"Or that they couldn't foresee natural disasters or epidemics, or identify choices that would lead to disaster?" Colo laughed. "I don't deny they need us and they need the Confederation, though they don't always realize that. But we certainly don't need them, except as slaves. Wake up, Derik." Lai felt him teleport away, and resumed his own progress.

Derry's face was dark with anger, and his jaw was set. "Losing your temper won't help," Lai said sympathetically.

"I know. Doesn't stop me from wanting to throw him through a wall. Lai, I've known Humans who were worth ten of him."

"So have I. But without the R'il'nai there wouldn't be any Humans, and certainly not off of their home planet. We're responsible for them. And you're right, Colo has no sense of responsibility."

"You can't blame it on youth, either. He's almost as old as you and Nik. There weren't any adult R'il'noids that way when I was growing up! That's why they made such a fuss about my being wild."

"And you'd outgrown that by the time I was born, or my parents wouldn't have let you teach me the basics of using esper. Ah, well, Colo's Colo. I can't get through to him, either. At least his Çeren index puts him as barely Inner

Council level, so he doesn't have that much influence. Thanks for trying, Derry."

Why did the Humans put so much emphasis on Çeren index? he wondered as he continued down the corridor. It was objective, but it didn't really identify the traits the Humans needed most. He'd have said Kaia was the best choice if he had to pick a successor, then Derry, then Zhaim. Çeren index put them in the opposite order. Oh, well, they were all competent High R'il'noids. And he had no premonitions about his own death at any time in the near future.

Snowy

3/5/34

Derik, Snowy rapidly decided, was easily the best owner he'd had. The R'il'noid seemed to keep slaves as much for company as for service, and he'd introduced them to everything from simply being outdoors to horses and hang gliding. "Explore the estate," he'd urged them once they'd had a quick tour. "See if you can find some novel backdrops for your dancing."

He even noticed that Flame's skin, and to a lesser extent, Amber's, was red and painful after he'd first taken them outdoors, and ordered Brak to provide them with a cream they were to rub into their skin before exposing it to the sun. Brak. Snowy sighed and glanced again at the rain pouring down outside the door.

It was generally wisest not to catch Brak's eye when the overseer was in one of his foul moods. As he was today. Helping the horsemaster with the horses or following Derik's orders to explore outdoors to find new backdrops for their dancing generally kept them out of Brak's way, but between the rain and the horsemaster's being away with Derik ... "We could look for places to dance indoors," Timi suggested.

"We've already checked most places upstairs," Amber said thoughtfully. "Why don't we go down, for a change? Where the wines and cheeses are stored."

"They're locked up," Timi said.

"Not the corridor they open off of. We don't know what's farther down that."

Flame frowned in concentration. "The far end was kind of dark. We'd better take some glow sticks. And it was pretty cool, too."

"Snowy and I'll get jackets, and you girls get the glow sticks," Timi said. Jackets were beginning to be needed outdoors, but none of their previous owners would have provided them.

A few minutes later, the four of them were running down the stone stairs to the underground corridor. There was a lift shaft, but it wasn't for slaves, and they knew it. They looked wistfully at the food and wines stored in stasis behind locked grills, but their goal was the darker end of the corridor. "The walls are getting rougher," Flame said in surprise.

"And it's getting cooler," Amber remarked as she took a jacket from Snowy. "It reminds me … Oh, I'm being silly."

"What does it remind you of?" Snowy asked. Then he froze as he heard heavy steps around the curve of the corridor behind them. "Hide," he whispered, tucking the glow stick he carried inside his jacket and ducking behind a part of the rugged wall that stuck out a bit. Farther along, he heard a gasp from Amber, and then her hand was pulling at his. A moment later, he realized she had actually found a slit in the wall.

"It *is* a cave!" she whispered excitedly. "My parents showed me one once, before the slavers came. And there's no way Brak could get through that slit!"

Any of the four dancers could get through, Snowy thought, but Brak was far too wide—and the width wasn't muscle, either. Blocking the entrance to the slit with his body, he held the glow stick deeper into the darkness. The light was dim, but it was enough to show him that the slit, twisting a little, continued for a considerable distance. "Timi, Flame," he leaned back to whisper. "Here." A moment later all four were looking wide-eyed at a narrow path, walled and roofed by stone that looked like candle wax, leading down to a small stream.

"We need to be careful we don't get lost," Amber warned, but her eyes were shining with excitement.

"Leave one of the glow sticks to mark where we came down," Snowy suggested. "There's a sort of path beside the water. Let's go the way it's running, for starters."

The path was easy to follow, though they had to duck rock formations often. Long points of stone, sheened with water, hung from the ceiling, with stumpy pillars rising beneath them. The glow sticks didn't reveal much color, but Snowy thought the rock was mostly cream-color or reddish. Like the cave Derik had led him through on horseback, but much narrower and with a slicker floor. What had Derik called the rock formations? Stalactites from the ceiling, and stalagmites from the floor, that was it—but these were far more extensive and varied in appearance. Here and there the path crossed the stream, and where the stream was too wide for a single step, there were stones in the water.

"Oh, look," Flame said softly as they rounded a bend to see a cluster of fine, hollow pipes hanging from the ceiling.

"Brak'd never find us here," Timi commented.

"Yeah, and we'd get pretty hungry and cold after a while," Snowy replied. "It's a great place for getting out of sight for a few hours, though. Let's see if we can find a place we can sit down."

So far there had been only one path, but the dim light of the glow sticks revealed a trickle of water ahead, flowing into the stream they had been following from the right. "Let's see where it comes from," Amber said. "I'm starting to feel closed in." She'd left her glow stick as a marker, which left her hands free to scramble up the tumble of rocks the new stream flowed down. Snowy held his glow stick to light her way as well as he could as he climbed behind her. "It's drier than below," she called back. "There's a little spring, but not much room. And it's a dead end."

Snowy followed, with Timi and Flame close on his heels to find a small, sand-floored cavern with a spring at one side. There was barely room for the four of them to sit, but as a secure hiding place from Brak, it was ideal.

"Wonder where the main stream winds up," Timi said.

Amber shook her head. "Not today. I don't want to risk getting lost. Maybe we could come back with a long piece of string or maybe that heavy thread they use to repair the horse gear. But if we need to get out of sight for a few hours, this place looks ideal." She looked around and shivered. "I feel like it's closing in on me," she added. "I don't think I'd want to stay here very long. But at least Brak won't be able to find us here."

No, Snowy thought, he wouldn't. But they needed an excuse to be in the corridor above, in case they were caught on the way. Maybe his earlier idea, of the corridor as a dance backdrop? Not the cave itself, of course, that was their secret. He stared at the glow stick in Flame's hand, but what he was seeing was the corridor, squared off with some white stuff at the end nearest the stairs, but dwindling away to roughness and the color of pale stone as it grew narrower toward their end. Not too high—they'd have to limit the height of their leaps. But the grills fencing off the storage areas—they could use those. Maybe combine their dancing with food service? A sort of dance of plenty, showcasing the food and wines stored here? Gradually the excuse grew into a real dance in his mind.

Southward Equinox, '34

They didn't spend all of their time, or even a large fraction of it, hiding from Brak. A few months later Snowy was leaning against a horse's shoulder, putting his weight into the strokes of the brush against the silky bay hide.

The horse leaned into the brush, eyes half closed and lower lip twitching in pleasure. Timi sighed theatrically in the aisle. "You know, the robot groomer could do that."

"I like doing it," Snowy replied. "The autogroomer doesn't scratch the itchy spots, and it's no good on cowlicks. Besides, think what else I could be doing, with any other owner we've had." He stood back, looking the horse over. The bay shook himself, disarranging his carefully combed mane and tail. It would be a lot easier, Snowy thought, if Derik didn't prefer flowing hair, on slaves as well as horses. He punched the button to lower the suspended saddle and pad onto the horse's back, controlling the final fingerwidth or two by hand to be sure the pad sat smoothly on the animal's coat.

He bridled the horse, and then glanced at the time display on the stable wall. Twelve minutes. Time enough to clean himself up. "Watch the horses, would you, Timi?" Snowy shucked off his coverall, felt to be sure his hair was still tucked under the loose waterproof cap, and stepped into the stable sponge cabinet.

"Well, learning to sail's fun," Timi conceded from the aisle. "And a couple of those new dances you've put together are really great. Horseback riding … It beats the alternative, but I'm just as sore afterward. Jumping off cliffs holding onto a sail I want no part of, and Brak … Well, at least he doesn't care for horses so he stays away from the stable." Snowy could imagine his shudder. "But I still don't like not having any choices about things."

Timi's voice faded out briefly as Snowy twisted under the rinsing jets and then stood, arms out, as the remaining water was blown off his body. He wasn't sure if Derik was too lazy to find out just how his overseer treated his slaves, or so busy he simply trusted all slave management to Brak. Of the five months they had been here, Derik had been off planet for at least two, mostly a few days at a time. And Brak wasn't a slave himself, like Davy. The one thing Snowy really held against Derik was his refusal to listen to any complaints about Brak.

The cabinet finished its cycle, and Snowy stepped out and began pulling on riding clothes. "Wonder how long he's going to stay interested in us," Timi commented.

"A good long time, if I can manage it," Snowy replied.

"Sometimes I think you aren't even interested in being free," Timi accused.

"Free to starve, or be kidnapped and sold by an illegal dealer?" Snowy replied as he settled his riding jacket into place. "Not that kind of free. But I think we've got a better chance of freedom, long-term and knowing enough to stay free, with Derik than any other owner we've had." He shook his hair out of the cap, released the loose braid that had kept it from tangling too badly, and began combing the hip-length white silk.

"Work from inside the limits again, huh?" Timi commented as he began working out a snarl Snowy couldn't quite reach. "Well, I don't like being a pet. Better watch out he doesn't seduce you. He's interested."

Snowy shrugged. "If that's what it takes to keep him interested. Can't say I like it, but seduction's better than rape, and I'll take physical rape over mind-rape any day. It just doesn't bother me the way it does you, Timi. I've been a slave, and taught that was what to expect, since I was born. You were free 'til you were eight."

"And it makes me sick even to think about it," Timi said. "Just don't get to trusting him too much.

"I'm not *that* crazy." Snowy wondered if he could get away with tucking his hair under his jacket collar. Probably not.

"Who's the third horse for?" Timi asked as he stood back to give Snowy a final check.

"Some friend of Derik's," Snowy replied. He glanced back at the time display on the wall. "They're due. You'd better get back out of sight."

The friend turned out to be a boy, only a couple of years older than Snowy, and the young slave looked sharply at the newcomer's neck. No slave chain, and the youngster displayed none of the subservience Snowy was careful to show in his own movements. Not a slave rival, then. Snowy dropped to one knee and bowed his head to his owner. Derik might not insist on formality himself, but it was always safer to follow slave protocol scrupulously in front of strangers.

"Hope you've picked a good mount for me, Father," the newcomer said as they approached and Derik signaled the slave to rise. Derik's son, then? Interesting. Snowy had thought the dancers were being treated as substitute children themselves. And family members could be even more dangerous than slave rivals.

"Oh, I think you'll find Sundrop frisky enough, Coryn," Derik replied, "even though you're used to helping your mother train." He didn't wait to be handed the reins to his gray but checked the girth and swung up onto the eager animal.

Coryn took the reins of the chestnut when Snowy offered them, but checked his own girth and waved off the young slave's offer to give him a leg up. Snowy hastily mounted the bay he'd just finished grooming, knowing how Derik hated to be kept waiting, and they all walked their horses toward a door that opened into a blaze of sunshine as they approached.

The sun made Snowy's eyes water, and the light breeze kept blowing his unbound hair into his eyes. He looked at Derik's hair, tied back for riding, and Coryn's, braided under the protective helmet he wore, and wished he dared braid his own. Still, squinting and an occasional mouthful of hair were a small price for the sense of freedom he got from the wide sky overhead and the surf pounding against the cliff to his left. It was a freedom few pleasure slaves ever tasted, and one of the reasons he was determined to stay with Derik as long as he could.

He followed the others inland, along a trail that wound through stands of resinous woodland and finally entered a broad meadow, crisscrossed with fences, rocks, trees and streams. "An obstacle course," Coryn exclaimed delightedly. "And a good one, from what I can see."

"I've been working on it," Derik replied. "Thought you and Noon might enjoy a race."

Coryn turned in his saddle, really looking at Snowy for the first time. "Not fair," he said. "I've got to wear this stupid helmet."

Derik turned to look at Snowy just as the breeze blew the boy's hair into his eyes again. "I'm not sure that's an advantage to him, but we might as well even things out," he replied. His eyes took on a closed, inward look for a second, and a helmet appeared in his hand. He passed it to Snowy. "Put that on, and tuck your hair into your collar."

"Yes, Master," Snowy said politely, trying to keep the relief out of his face. He'd have to make sure he lost to Coryn, of course, but he'd just as soon not lose because he was blinded by his own hair.

"I'll use the beacons to mark the course," Derik continued. "Show Coryn the tunnel and slide, Noon. They're not very visible from here. And Noon, you ride to win. That's an order."

This time Snowy couldn't quite keep the consternation out of his face. Defeating a member of the master class was dangerous for a slave. But so was disobeying a direct order. And while Derik's order gave plenty of room for Coryn to defeat Snowy in an honest contest, Snowy thought his owner was astute enough to detect any attempt on his part to lose to the older boy. The most he could do was to counter the very real advantage he had in knowing the two horses and the course.

"Sundrop's faster on the straightaway," he said quietly as they jogged over to the tunnel, a natural cave they would have to race through, dodging stalactites. "KoKo isn't as fast as Sundrop, but he has more endurance and he's more maneuverable. I'll walk through the cave with you now—it's easiest if you come in on the left and then cross to the right about two thirds of the way through. Footing's good that way, and you don't have to duck as many stalactites."

Coryn nodded, looking ahead as they exited the cave. "There's the next jump—yes, you'd want to come out on the right for the best approach. And then the slide ... I don't believe this! Is that a jump halfway down?"

Snowy looked down the seemingly vertical cliff and nodded. "It's not a very high jump, and both horses are used to it. But Sundrop'll try to fly it, and the water's swimming deep if she lands out away from the bank. Fine if you were crossing the stream, but the course doubles back and comes up the same bank you slide down. There, upstream, where the sandbar peters out. See?"

The beacon was easy enough to see, next to a break in the streamside vegetation. Coryn leaned far out, studying the entry to the climb. "I forgot Father makes a hobby of designing courses for the big competitions. Thanks for the information, Noon. And don't worry about beating me. I want an honest race." He grinned at Snowy.

The young slave lowered his eyes. A free man, thanking him? He didn't dare try to initiate eye contact with his owner's son, but he did reply, shyly, "Thank *you* for the helmet. I thought I'd be riding blind with my hair in my face."

Coryn threw his head back and laughed as they rode together back to Derik.

Coryn and Sundrop surged ahead at the start, which was fine with Snowy. The faster Sundrop wore herself out, the better chance he'd have. Snowy held KoKo to a pace he knew the bay could hold for most of the course, with some reserve for a sprint at the end. Vertical fence first, then a spread, both narrow enough that he had no desire to try them shoulder to shoulder with Coryn. A four-rock weave, and he made up time on that one. A shallow stream that could be jumped or splashed through, and he asked KoKo for a jump as he looked ahead. Sundrop was slowing under a firm hold from Coryn. Try to pass now? The tunnel, the slide, the weave through nine trees and the pen jump had to be negotiated one horse at a time, and the lead horse in a tight race had an advantage. He asked KoKo for a little more speed, and saw Sundrop speed up in response. Evidently Coryn had listened to his advice. Intellectually, that was fine and losing honestly was the best possible outcome of the race for Snowy. Emotionally, Snowy discovered with some surprise, he wanted very badly to win.

Another jump and then the tunnel, with Snowy flattening himself against KoKo's neck to avoid the stalactites, and the two jumps after the tunnel. The second jump was a spread and he took it fast, urging KoKo to increased speed. Coryn must have known that he wasn't really trying to pass this close to the head of the slide—but Sundrop didn't, and started down the slide fighting Coryn's control. Snowy started down the slide just in time to see Sundrop jump out and land in the stream. He took KoKo down fast but under control, popping the horse over the low jump onto the sandbar and asking for an immediate right turn.

The maneuver put him in the lead, but not by much. Coryn was no more than a length behind him going into the weave through the trees, but KoKo had the advantage on that obstacle, and gained a good three lengths. Just the pen jump to negotiate now—check a stride or two ahead, pop the first fence well to the left, one stride to recover balance, with the reins warning the horse of the pivot to the right, then one stride and jump out at right angles to the entry. Finally the straight run to the finish line where Derik waited. Snowy saw Sundrop's head from the corner of his eye, and dropped against KoKo's neck, for the first time urging the horse to top speed.

The chestnut's head dropped back and then returned, creeping up until the nose was almost level with KoKo's shoulder. But KoKo's superior endurance was beginning to tell. Sundrop began dropping back again, and they crossed the finish line with KoKo clearly in the lead. Snowy felt a brief thrill of triumph that rapidly abated as he realized what he had just done. I did what Master Derik told me to, he thought rebelliously as he eased KoKo down to a walk and circled back toward his owner.

But would that be enough? He could hear Coryn as he returned to Derik: "Can I borrow him, Father?" Snowy's mouth felt dry, and KoKo began to dance under him in response to the boy's tension.

Please, Snowy thought, tell him no, but Derik only said, "I'll have to think about it, Cory." Then he lifted he head, saw Snowy, and smiled. "Good riding, Noon. Better walk them both dry."

Snowy was already sliding off KoKo, and he quickly loosened the girth and slipped the bit out of the horse's mouth. Coryn was a little slower to dismount. "I've only got another two hours before I have to head back to school," he said.

Derik raised one eyebrow. "You could ride back double behind me if you'll promise not to tell your mother," he suggested. "Noon, you can lead both horses back, can't you? They should be cooled down pretty well by the time you're back to the stable."

"Of course," Snowy replied, reaching for Sundrop's reins. Unfair, something inside his head screamed. Unfair? That was Timi's complaint—but slave life *was* unfair. You took the unfairness for granted, while trying to make it affect you as little as possible. So why was he thinking this way?

Sundrop rubbed her head against his shoulder, trying to scratch the sweaty skin under her bridle, and he pushed the uncomfortable thought away. Better use the fact that Derik generally *was* fair toward the horses. "Could I have a rag to rub them down a bit?" he asked.

Two rubbing cloths appeared, draped over Snowy's arm. Derik must be in one of his show-off moods, he thought. I could do that, but sooner or later I'd get caught. He didn't trust Sundrop quite enough to take the bit from her mouth, but he did wipe under the bridle before beginning to lead the two horses along the trail back to the stable. At least he'd be free of Brak for a while. The one place the overseer almost never came was the stables.

Derik

10/20/34

"So my whole trip was a total waste of time," Derik concluded. "And why is it that I always wind up twelve hours off my home time zone when I go off planet?" The sun was rising over the mountains behind the Enclave, but Derik, whose home was in the same time zone, was ready for a long, relaxing massage and bed. It didn't help that Elyra was laughing openly at him, and even Lai was fighting to keep back a grin.

"It wasn't a waste of time, Derry," the R'il'nian soothed. "Sure, it was just a communication problem. But if you hadn't straightened it out now, it would have been a lot more than that ten years from now." Tactfully, he didn't mention the time zone problem, at least not beyond adding, "There's nothing scheduled for the Inner Council meeting today you need to be there for. I'll brief you on what happens later."

"Better have some breakfast," Elyra suggested. "Even with Lai's help, teleporting back here's bound to have run your blood sugar down." She placed a loaded tray on Derik's lap, and then left the room. When she returned, she had a baby on each arm. "Breakfast time for them, too," she commented as she settled both to feed.

"Two?" Derik asked in astonishment.

"Ania's ours and we expected her," Lai said, "though we were delighted when her Çeren index identified her as a probable future Inner Council member. Wif was a total surprise, and we're still trying to figure out where he came from. But his Çeren index is a hair higher than Ania's."

"Eat," ordered Elyra.

Derik took a bite, more out of politeness than any sense of hunger, and blinked a time or two in astonishment. "Two? Çeren index a hundred twenty or more? That's hard to believe. Who was the last—Tethya? Ramil before her, and then Zhaim, and he's close to four centuries old." He took another bite, and suddenly realized that he was ravenous. Elyra, he thought, was better at spotting the cause of his bad temper than he was.

"An average of one a century above a hundred and twenty," Lai replied, "three times what it was before the Çeren technique came into use. High R'il'noids have gotten more frequent, too—several a year over a hundred and eight, now. And we're getting more than we can socialize properly that qualify as R'il'noid, with half the active genes R'il'nian-derived."

Derik swallowed another mouthful, thinking. Three times the number of those testing at the highest level on the Çeren index, yes. But of the three youngest members of the Inner Council he'd named, only Ramil had what he considered a normal attitude toward Humans. Some of the older members were even worse. Colo was openly a monster, making no attempt to hide his depravities. Zhaim—well, outwardly he'd straightened up since the shocking incident that had upset Lai so badly three centuries ago. Derik was not so sure. He suspected love still blinded Lai to many of his heir's deficiencies, though he did not agree with Lai's emotional certainty that Zhaim's attitude was due to poor parenting and too much love on his part. As for Lai's daughter Tethya, Derik reserved judgment. She was barely a century old, and thinking of himself at that age was enough to make Derik cringe. She might yet become a responsible member of the Inner Council. "Think your new technique'll do better?"

"One's hardly a valid statistical sample, but yes—if I'm doing what Jarn did, I think so. And I think some R'il'noids can use it—you, maybe."

"Maybe," Derik said skeptically, "but hardly likely. Who are the boy's parents?"

"That," Elyra replied, "is what we'd all like to know. His mother's a kitchen slave, badly scarred. I have her, now. She's not well, and I've got far more milk than Ania can use, so I'm feeding him right now. She'll take over eventually, with help from Lai and me—the baby's a little too strong an esper for a Human mother to cope with. Her former owner called the Genetics Board in a panic. *He'd* decided not to bother raising the baby. Luckily Wif has a very strong sense of self-preservation."

Derik ducked his head, trying to hide a grin. It wasn't really funny—a threat to an esper baby, when they needed good espers so badly. But the mental image of a slave owner who'd let a baby die, trying to cope with what that baby might be capable of in the way of self defense, tickled his overdeveloped sense of humor. "Who's the father?" he asked.

"We don't know," said Elyra grimly. "The girl goes practically catatonic at the memory. Apparently it started out as a sex show, but the owner and his guests were high on drugs, and there were gatecrashers, and the upshot is that no one remembers who had her after the slaves who really had no choice in the matter, and who couldn't have fathered Wif, anyway. She certainly didn't know them all. At this point I'm going on karyotype—who could have contributed Wif's R'il'nian chromosomes? I've ruled out all of the High R'il'noids in my database, even those who were off planet or dead. And all of the R'il'noids Kuril even thinks might have been there, and I've checked most of the rest. Right now I'm trying to get karyotypes on all known latents."

"So far," Lai commented, "the only possible match is me. I'm beginning to wonder if someone managed to steal some of my semen from the Genetics Board."

The baby did look like Lai, Derik thought. But from what Elyra had said, that didn't square at all with the mother's experience. "Kuril?" he asked aloud. "Uh—Lyra ..."

"Yes, you were there, and in about the right time frame. But not that night, I don't think you'd have been involved in something like that, and the karyotypes definitely rule you out. Sorry, Derry, I know you'd love another child, but Wif's not yours."

Thank all the gods worshipped on all the planets that he'd gotten the dancing group out of that! Kuril wasn't as bad as Colo, but Derik could not approve of a slave owner who'd simply let an unwanted slave baby die.

The little girl ...

Elyra had confided to Derik that she hoped raising another child of his own would help Lai deal with his feelings of inadequacy over Zhaim. If Lai was letting himself love his daughter, Derik could not detect it. If only Lai and Cloudy could have had a child, he thought. Elyra was a good friend, but Cloudy would have been a far better mother, and might well have led Lai into learning that he could love a child without doing damage.

He shifted position, preparing to rise, and flinched as his back muscles spasmed painfully. Elyra looked worried, and he forced a smile. "Don't need back muscles to teleport. I think I'd better get home for a massage, though." Noon, he thought. I'll have Brak send him up as soon as I get back.

But it wasn't Noon who arrived, but Midnight. A Midnight who looked flustered, out of breath, and generally worried. He'd have to get after Brak about sending up the slave he asked for, Derik thought, but then Midnight was a slightly better masseur than Noon. Not as good company, though. He relaxed and let the boy get on with his massage, and gradually the cramps released. "Where's Noon?" he finally asked.

Midnight jumped, his eyes wild for a second. "He, he had a hard day yesterday," he stuttered.

Derik turned to look at the boy, puzzled. "Hard how? I wasn't even on planet." The boy was silent, but his appearance of upset increased. "Midnight, answer me." Derik would not probe an unwilling mind, but he could and did open himself enough that he would pick up a deliberate lie.

"Noon asked us not to bother you, sir," Midnight replied. "But he's really not feeling well."

The boy wasn't lying, Derik decided, but he was terribly worried. Worried enough that his usual half defiant attitude was totally missing. "Has Brak called in a doctor?" he asked, and the boy shook his head.

"Says he's just malingering. He's not. But he didn't want you bothered."

Damn. Derik wanted to stretch the final stiffness out of the muscles that were beginning to relax under Midnight's manipulations, and then go to sleep. If it had been any of the others, he thought, that was exactly what he would have done. But Noon …

He simply could not picture Noon faking an illness. Sunrise or Sunset, possibly. Midnight, probably. Noon? He groaned and sat up. "Come on," he told Midnight. "I'd better check on him." He didn't have much medical training, just the minimum given every R'il'noid who had to work off planet on short notice. He could diagnose his own problems, but he didn't know much about Human diseases. Still, he could at least tell if Noon needed more medical help than he could give. He'd call on Nik if the boy was really sick, he thought. He had somewhat less faith in most doctors who would bother with slaves than he had in those who attended his horses.

He'd ordered Brak to give the four a room to themselves with comfortable sleeping mats, and his first reaction on coming into that room was amusement that the four had pulled the mats together to make a single large sleeping area. Then he got a good look at Noon, with Sunrise and Sunset sitting on the mat next to the young slave, and all thought of some mild childish ailment disappeared. The boy's face was flushed and oddly rigid, and when Derik lifted a fold of skin on the back of Noon's hand, the muscles beneath felt almost unbearably tight. Nor did the fold of skin snap back.

"How long since he's had anything to eat or drink?" he asked the girls, concern sharpening his voice.

Sunrise swallowed hard as she brushed back the golden hair that had fallen over her eyes. "About two days," she responded shakily. "It's been that long since he could swallow. He was still able to talk a little then, and he didn't want you bothered when you came back."

Dehydration Derik could deal with, but it would be easier in his own quarters. The rest … Brak stuck his head in the door, and Derik turned to him. "Get a cocoon with a levitation circuit down here. I'm taking Noon up to my quarters, and the other three to nurse him." He turned back to the girls, scowling a little as he tried to remember what little he knew about Human ailments. "Did he say anything earlier, when he could talk, about how he felt?"

he asked as he triggered the levitation unit on the cocoon and started guiding it back to his quarters.

"Pain, to start with," Sunset replied. "Fingertips and toes, and then working in toward the body. Dancing started to hurt him two or three fivedays ago, not long after you left. I don't think the pain ever stopped, but pretty soon the muscles started knotting up and cramping where it had hurt a few days earlier, and massage didn't help at all—just made the pain worse, he said. After a while he couldn't control the muscles at all, but they kept on twitching."

Not a minor ailment, he thought as he eased the cocoon with its helpless occupant down on his own bed and hunted through the emergency supplies for dilute saline. But not a Human disease he was familiar with, either. He reached mentally for the computer, feeding Noon's symptoms to the medical program even as he set up the rehydration. Nothing quite matched.

Derik's estate was set on a cliff facing the western ocean, south—poleward—of Lai's home, which faced the same ocean. The sun, high in the northern sky this close to the solstice, was beginning to touch the balcony rail outside his window. Not quite noon, he thought. Nik would still be awake, though it would be an hour after sunset for him. There was no doubt in Derik's mind that he needed Nik, but if he could tell his half- brother what was wrong with Noon when he made the initial contact, it might save an additional teleport to bring in whatever medical supplies Nik would need. Nik, though an outstanding physician and respected member of the Genetics Board, was not quite able to manage a teleport by himself. And Derik had not replenished his own reserves enough to do much more than assist Nik in teleporting here.

He turned back to the boy lying immobile in the cocoon. He could describe Noon's symptoms to Nik, he decided. Easy enough. Classic Kharfun symptoms, if the young slave were R'il'noid. But Kharfun in Humans was a mild disease, self-limiting and often unnoticed. It had just about wiped out the pure R'il'nians and the early R'il'noids, and led to the modern crossbreeding program, but it simply did not make Humans particularly sick. And while many Humans were not slaves—there were far more Human slave-owners than R'il'noid—R'il'noids could not be slaves. Noon was Human.

Wasn't he?

He'd bought the group from Kuril, who'd owned Wif's mother, and at about the time Wif was conceived.

Noon was too young—not even fourteen at the time.

Not outside the limits for a Human—and crossbreds showed up with every possible maturation pattern. No correlation with Çeren index, either.

He turned to Sunrise—youngest of the four, but he thought the brightest after Noon. "Did you know a girl, a kitchen slave with a scarred face, at Kuril's?" he asked.

"Feline? Of course. She and Noon were good friends."

"I understand Kuril once used her in a sex show. Was that while you were there?"

All three faces hardened. "A couple of fivedays before you bought us," Sunset answered.

"And the boys?"

Midnight's face showed both anger and surprise. "We cooperated or they put the harnesses on us. The girls say it's easier without."

"Lots easier," Sunset confirmed. "Especially Sn—uh, Noon. He's really gentle. Feline asked him to be first."

R'il'noids weren't always physically distinguishable from Humans, and crossbreds who didn't have many overt R'il'nian traits often went right back into the Human gene pool, lost within a few generations. Noon wasn't an obvious crossbred, but … Derik reached for the boy's head, and gently pulled back one eyelid. The eyes were rolled back, but he could see enough of the iris to confirm the color. Honey gold, as he remembered, but when he looked closely, there were metallic gold flecks almost hidden in the gold. Not as obvious as his own gold-veined brown, but just as sure an indicator of R'il'nian genes.

He reached for Nik's mind, letting his anxiety show, and got a "what's up?" response almost at once.

I think I've found Wif's father, he sent back. *Bought him from Kuril as a slave, but he's got all the symptoms of a bad case of Kharfun, and if you look closely enough, he shows the eye veining.*

He felt Nik's shock even as his half brother grabbed an emergency kit and began hunting a few extra items. *Telepath?* Nik sent in reply.

Haven't tried. He's in no shape to ask if he's willing.

You'd better check. Confirm the symptoms, at least.

Double damn and a few swear words he wouldn't say with the kids listening. He started to speak the name he'd given the boy, then caught himself and turned to Sunset. "You started to call Noon something else," he said. "His own name? The way he thinks of himself? What is it?" Panic bloomed in the girl's eyes for a moment, and he added, "Not to hurt him. Only to get his attention, if he's conscious at all."

The redhead's eyes flicked back and forth between the other two slaves. Finally, reluctantly, she answered his question. "Snowy. He said it's what his mother called him."

Snowy. And fifteen years ago Lai had been in love with a white-haired, brown-eyed woman nicknamed Cloudy. How had he failed to see the resemblance? "Snowy," Derik said gently, cupping the boy's face in his hands, "it's all right. I'm not going to hurt you. Just relax and let me have enough contact to check how you're feeling." He kept the contact light, ready to pull back if he felt any resistance, but all he felt was thirst, pain, and half delirious thoughts of water. *It's all right,* he thought at the boy. *We're taking care of the thirst, and we'll help you with the pain.* Before he could get a response, Nik's *Ready* echoed through his mind.

He broke contact with Snowy and made full contact with Nik, blending his mind with the physician's for the teleport to his room, remembering only after he heard gasps of dismay that Snowy's friends would not be used to people appearing out of thin air. Or to Nik's hasty blood typing, which involved touching his tongue to a drop of the boy's blood.

"Nik's a very good doctor," he told the three, "and he's going to fix what's wrong with Noon. You've all helped a lot, but I don't think there's anything more you can do. On back to your quarters, now."

The three closed ranks almost audibly, turning to him with identical angry, stubborn expressions. He couldn't teleport them away, and he *would* not force their minds. "He's getting the best medical care on this planet," he told them, and began pushing them toward the slave quarters telekinetically. They weren't far from the door, and he had them well on their way before they had a chance to react. Then he turned to Nik.

He didn't have to ask if his diagnosis was correct. The vial in Nik's hand was choked with fluorescent green crystals, and for the first time Derik felt really frightened for the boy. "That bad?" he asked anxiously.

"I've never seen a case so advanced. When were you last boostered, Derry?"

"Couple of years ago—titer says I'm good for another half century, at least. I'm not worried about myself, dammit."

"Neither am I, but the boy's blood type matches yours."

And the first line of defense against a severe Kharfun infection was passive antibodies. Derik hastily peeled out of tunic and shirt, and held out his arm to Nik. "I'd still better contact Lai," he said. When Nik raised an eyebrow, he added, "Cloudy."

Nik continued setting up the transfusion, but his eyes went to the boy on the bed. "She was sterilized, but reversibly," he said slowly. "Lai could have reversed it, maybe without even realizing what he was doing. But the boy's not Coven affected. Not with that skin tone. Too bad we can't get a Çeren index with the Kharfun, but let me run a karyotype to confirm. Lai's going to be livid about this, you know."

Livid, Derik thought, was an understatement. He, Lai and Nik all shared the same R'il'nian father, Tarl. Derik was the oldest, by some three centuries, and he'd given basic esper training to both of his younger half-brothers. He knew Lai as well as anyone did—including Lai's deep attachment to Cloudy. Lai had grieved for Cloudy when she had left him. How he would react when he found out she had probably left him to give his son a chance at life … Well, Derik wasn't sure, but he was reasonably certain that his own close relationship with Lai would see some major changes when Lai found out he'd owned Cloudy's son as a slave. He could only hope the changes would be temporary.

"Do you have a birth date on him?" Nik asked.

"He was registered a little after Northern Solstice in '20. Makes him fourteen and a half, now."

"Conceived a couple of months before Cloudy disappeared, then. Well, he's definitely half-bred. And he has both the R'il'nian chromosomes that've been driving us up a wall in Wif. I should have listened harder to Lyra. She felt when Ania was conceived that Lai was rediscovering something he'd done before. We put it down to his 'rediscovering' Jarn's technique."

Derik swayed a little, and Nik moved to cut off the blood transfer. "He's stabilizing," he added. "I can start second stage treatment in half an hour or so. He's going to need pain blocking for that."

"I'll contact Lai," Derik said, but his eyes went to the boy's face. Not a slave, but Lai's son. His nephew. He wasn't sure how to handle that, and he rather doubted that Lai would give him much chance to handle it himself. But the next stage of treatment would be agonizing for the boy without pain blocking, and Lai was a lot better at initiating that than Derik was. *Lai*, Derik reached out, *I think you'd better come out here. Emergency.*

Lai

10/20/34

Lai was rarely caught off guard by events. He had in full the R'il'nian talent of conditional precognition—the ability to foresee how his own actions would influence the probability of future events—and he used it regularly. He had used it, he remembered now, when Cloudy had left him. But he had used it in his usual mode, for the welfare of the Confederation as a whole. His own happiness, and Cloudy's, had evidently counted very little against the birth of the child now lying before him.

Would he have gotten the same answer if he had tried the same question a year after Cloudy had disappeared? Probably not. It had just never occurred to him.

"We used Derry's blood for immune serum," Nik said, "But we need to start the second stage of treatment. He's going to need pain blocking for that, and you're the best around."

"And he's my son," Lai said sharply. "Stay away from him, Derik. You've done enough harm already."

Derik backed away, his face paler than Lai had ever seen it. "There's no way I'd hurt that boy, Lai. I love him."

"As you've loved slaves in the past? No way, Derry. I don't want you even seeing him." He moved to the boy's side.

Derik was visibly struggling to control his response. "In the long run," he said finally, "that's going to be his choice. For right now ... Be gentle, Lai. He's not used to mind touch. I tried earlier for very light contact to check his symptoms, and I think he's using a smokescreen shield. I don't know what his mother may have told him, but I think he's been trying to hide. He didn't even want me to know he was sick."

Lai ignored Derik, laying his hand lightly across the boy's forehead. Physical contact wasn't necessary, but it would make the mental contact easier. He reached for his son's mind, and picked up the boy's pain and thirst, both linked to a myriad of painful memories of slave life. He wasn't quite deep enough for effective pain blocking. He traced the sensations, trying to reach the youngster's current awareness, and the fear in the memories seemed to increase. He pressed harder, and abruptly there was nothing. Startled, he pulled back, shifting his fingers to feel for the pulse in the boy's throat. A little fast, and the breathing was labored, but no worse than would be expected for an advanced case of Kharfun syndrome.

"Problem?" Nik's voice came.

Lai probed again, more carefully this time. He could barely detect the gap where a mind should be. "Mirror shield," he replied, "and a good one. I can't get through enough to pain-block without risking permanent injury."

Derik opened his mouth and shut it again, obviously choking back a reminder that he'd tried to warn Lai against exactly this reaction. Nik's face creased with anxiety. "I've got to start the second stage of treatment soon, and I don't know if he'll survive it without pain blocking. I've never seen a case this advanced."

"Lai," Derik said tentatively, "I know you're not going to like this, but I'm the only one of us he knows. He's obviously too frightened to let any of us contact his mind, but there's a chance he'd initiate contact with me. If he reads in my mind that we're only trying to help him, he might allow the contact we need for pain blocking."

Lai looked at Derik, fighting the impulse to grind his teeth, lash out at Derry, or do any of the other things his frustration demanded. The boy needed help, and if Derik could assist in providing that help … "Try it," he ordered through clenched teeth.

"Snowy," Derik said, and Lai, watching, could only think how much the boy looked like Cloudy. It hurt to look at him. How could Derik have picked a name so like that of his lost love? Well, what the boy had been called as a slave was unimportant. He'd have to pick a proper name. Roi, he thought. That was what Elyra had planned to name their child, if it had been a boy. It had overtones of both love and compassion, and that, in its way, was even more appropriate for Cloudy's child than for Lyra's. As was the name itself—Lai had rarely used it, but Cloudy's real name had been Saroi.

"It's not working," Derik said. "He could be unconscious, or maybe he scared himself into a blind shield. Or maybe he just doesn't trust me as much as I thought he might. Nik, where do you want to treat him? You're welcome to leave him here—I'll even move out if Lai prefers. We can't teleport him if he's resisting contact, but you're welcome to borrow my jump-van."

"My place," Nik said immediately. "I've got the life support system he'll need. Lai, can you stick around for the first twelve hours or so, in case he opens up enough for pain blocking? Derry?"

"Not Derik," Lai snapped. "You and I, yes. There are some other good pain blockers, and I'll contact them. Derik, do you have any information on the boy's mother?" I can try to find her, now that I know why she asked me not to, he thought. Lyra will understand. Meanwhile, he tried not to think too much about the boy, ignoring his own relief that Roi would be at Nik's, not the Enclave, during his recovery.

Snowy/Roi

11/1/34

Snowy didn't know where he was or how he'd gotten there. Every muscle in his body ached and knotted in intermittent cramps. He tried to shift his body to ease the pain, but nothing seemed to respond. Even his eyes would not open.

He had some confused and broken memories, of Derik calling him by his name when his owner shouldn't even have known it, and of a moment of total panic when he'd thought they knew about his odd abilities. But where was he now? A completely paralyzed slave was useless. It made sense that Derik would have sold him, probably for whatever organs remained useful, though the thought hurt. Yet whatever he lay on was soft, so soft that he could not even be sure he felt it, and the smells were clean and pleasant. That did not make sense in terms of a medical parts dealer.

"Awake?" came a cheerful, androgynous voice. "Good. I think the worst is over. You're going to be all right, though it'll take a while. You had Kharfun syndrome, and that's about the nastiest thing going, for R'il'noids. You're over it now, but you'll need help to learn to use your body again. If you'll drop that shielding, I can start showing you how."

Drop his shielding? They did suspect his abilities! And R'il'noid? He'd had R'il'noid owners, like Colo. They weren't necessarily any meaner than the Human ones, but they could do things to their slaves that terrified him. He remembered what Zhaim had done to Flick. He couldn't be one of those—could he? He did share some of their abilities, but he wasn't like them! He wasn't!

"Roi! Get your heart rate under control! Drat it, Derry was right. We don't know what your mother told you about yourself, but from the way you're reacting, it wasn't right. I don't think she would have lied to you," the stranger added hastily, "but I don't think she understood it all, herself. If she had, she could have demanded a Çeren test for you when you were born. Will you try to settle down and listen to me?"

Who was Roi? A new owner's name for him? Snowy couldn't do anything but lie quietly, but his heart felt as if it were trying to shake his chest apart. He didn't have much choice about listening to the stranger. While he had no intention of believing what he was told without proof, it couldn't hurt to find out what they wanted him to believe. As for his heart, the pounding was uncomfortable as well as giving away his emotional state. He reached inside himself, finding the chemicals that were accelerating his heart rate and neutralizing them.

"Better," the voice said, sounding relieved. "Introductions, first. I'm Nik Tarlian. You've met Derik—he and I are both half brothers of your father, Lai."

This time Snowy managed to calm his heart after a couple of violent thumps, but Nik seemed aware of even the brief lapse.

"I take it your mother did not tell you that you are half-R'il'nian—that Lai is your father. And you are not and never have been legally a slave. Quite aside from the fact that anybody with enough R'il'nian genes to get as sick as you got from Kharfun cannot legally be a slave, your mother was free. She thought she had to hide, as she evidently taught you to hide, and in the process she destroyed her identity as a free woman so thoroughly that she could be kidnapped and sold into slavery."

Ah, now Snowy recognized the story. He'd heard it under a dozen different names, but the plot was always the same—the abused slave who was found to be free, and who lived happily ever after as a member of the slave-owning class. He'd had some serious doubts about the "happily ever after" part even before he'd realized that the story was actually encouraged by slave owners. But it gave him a framework—a framework based on lies—for what Nik was telling him. The question was not what they wanted him to believe—he had that figured out, now—but why. And what, if anything, he could do about it.

He listened to the rest of the story with some interest—the details differed from any he had heard before—but absolutely no belief. There was nothing about his real concern—what had happened to his friends? He couldn't feel them, but that could mean that they were in no emotional distress, or that they were dead—he had no way of knowing the difference. He wasn't even sure he could feel them through the new type of shield he seemed to have thrown up.

He was a little ashamed of wanting to know what Derik had to do with his current situation. Nik's only mention of Snowy's owner—former owner? Did Nik own him now?—had been that comment about Derik being Nik's half brother, and Snowy wondered now if that had been a slip. Even if he could work out a way of communicating, he wasn't going to ask any of his questions. Too much chance of putting himself even farther into Nik's power.

"So the first priority," Nik was saying now, "is to work out a way for you to communicate with us so you can tell us if something hurts or you're hungry or thirsty, and start getting your body back under control. They'd both be a lot easier if you'd allow mind touch, but you don't seem inclined to cooperate on that, and there are other ways. This," he touched something in Snowy's hair, then wiggled it so that the boy could feel the band around his head, "is a brain wave pickup. I can't read your mind through it, just tell if you're asleep or awake. But we can calibrate it to let you communicate. Can you think "yes?""

Snowy's first reaction was "no way." He did not want the man knowing every time he thought positively. Still, it would be nice to be able to say yes when he really wanted to. He'd been keeping his surface thoughts chaotic until he decided what to do, but it suddenly occurred to him that this "calibration" might work with something other than words. He thought of yellow paling to white, repeating the image several times. On the fourth repetition, a computerized voice said "yes," and he stopped in confusion.

"That's fine, try it again," Nik said.

Snowy tried thinking yellow to white again, and was rewarded by the computerized "yes." Simple enough, and he wasn't giving anything away as far as he could tell. He let Nik talk him through "no," "hungry," "thirsty," and "hurts."

"Good," Nik said. "Feel up to more?"

Why not? The faster he could find out what they wanted of him, the better prepared he would be to deal with it. "Yes," he triggered.

But Nik didn't have more words in mind. Instead, he began a careful explanation of exactly what the Kharfun syndrome had done to Snowy's nervous system, and what the boy would have to do to repair the damage. About a third of it made sense. The rest Snowy stored for future study—but the third that did make sense told him that Nik knew more about Snowy's abilities than the boy had ever intended. Probably, Snowy thought, from his ability to control his heart rate. Well, he wasn't going to give Nik any more. If he could figure out how to control his body from Nik's instructions, fine. But he was not going to do any experimenting while Nik was around.

Over the next few fivedays he decided that Nik's explanations could only make sense if they referred to moving his own body the same way he could move objects at a distance. It wasn't an ability he had used much, aside from helping the others recover from slips while dancing. It was too obvious to any observer. But small movements, he finally decided, would be put down to the muscle cramps, which were getting worse with time. His first cautious movements of fingers and toes went unnoticed, and by mimicking the effect of muscle spasms he was even able to move his arms and legs.

And he had nightmares. Nothing surprising about that; he'd never met a slave who didn't have nightmares now and then. But his had become almost continuous—he could no longer sleep without dreams. The content of those dreams had changed, too—all too often he was Zhaim or Colo, with his friends as victims. Nik seemed to know he was dreaming a great deal, but obviously had no idea of the content of those dreams.

In the end it was curiosity that betrayed his growing ability to move. For over a month he'd had to rely on hearing, smell and touch to give him a sense of his surroundings, and touch wasn't much help. His sense of perception, together with hearing, told him he was in a room somewhat larger than the one the dancing group had occupied at Derik's, but considerably smaller than Derik's private rooms. Light through his closed eyelids varied more than just being on or off, which argued against a simple on or off switch. It wasn't enough. He wanted to see his surroundings, and he finally sharpened his control enough to reach for his eyelids, opening them the same way he would have moved a distant pebble.

What he saw at first was blurred, and he had to learn to adjust the muscles within his eyes to focus while holding his eyelids open. But when he got all of the adjustments working together, he was fascinated by what he saw.

The size of the room was no surprise, nor was the equipment lining the walls. But the light came from what he first thought were pictures on the walls. Then he realized that the surf breaking on the beach was in motion and even the clouds in the sky were moving, though much more slowly. He reached out with his mind, expecting to find a clever mechanism, and found instead that the depth behind the wall was real. When he turned his attention back to the wall, he found that the transparency was a door, with a simple catch. Mesmerized by the white sand and turquoise water, he reached for the catch and released it. The smell and sound of the ocean came into the room as the door slid open.

His body was not in a bed, but in a tank of some kind of clear gel. No wonder he couldn't feel much. Almost without conscious volition he rotated his body so that he was lying sideways in the tank, facing the open door. The swish of the small waves running up on the shore, and the muted roar of breaking surf farther out, were a welcome change from the mechanical sounds of the room, and he breathed deeply of the warm, salty air. The door opened at ground level. If his body obeyed his will better, he could walk out onto that beach.

As if summoned by his thought, a boy his own age came into view, walking along the beach and kicking at sand and seaweed. Snowy froze. Shut the door? No, he reasoned, the motion was more likely to attract attention than the mere fact of the door being open. He lay very still, hoping to be overlooked.

He thought at first it would work. The boy came close enough Snowy could see the sandy hair and peeling nose, and the sulky expression on the downturned face. Then, just before the stranger disappeared beyond the edge of the door, he looked up and saw Snowy. He stopped for an instant, surprised, then in two quick steps he was in the room. "Who are you?" he inquired scornfully, his tone implying that Snowy had no business at all being where he was.

Nik had expanded his computerized vocabulary significantly, but Snowy couldn't think how to answer the question with the words he could produce. And he didn't like the feel of this boy. Coryn, he thought, had some sympathy with others, and even the imagination to accept that others' thoughts might not agree with his. Derik's son might have tried to avenge himself on a slave who had defeated him, but that was so normal that Snowy could accept it. This boy felt more like Zhaim, hurting others simply because they were there to be hurt.

The stranger took a step forward, his face twisting into a sneer as he saw Snowy's helpless state. Take whatever abuse the other was so obviously ready to give, or try to protect himself and give away even more information about his abilities?

He didn't have to make the choice. Nik's voice came into the room, with an authority it was impossible to ignore. "Florian, what's the first rule around here?"

The stranger lowered his eyes and backed away a step. "Don't bother the patients," he said automatically. "But sir, the door was open. I couldn't just ignore it."

"Next time contact me, or if I'm not here one of my assistants. Got today's problem solved yet?"

"There's nothing out there but seaweed and creepy-crawlies!"

"Both of which include a number of very tasty edible species. Get back to looking for supper. Use the computer to find out what's edible. You may not be hungry, but I am."

Florian backed the rest of the way out of the door and stamped his way back to the beach. Nik turned back to Snowy, an amused grin on his freckled face. "Did Derry ever give you a taste of tanalis?" he asked.

Too late to close his eyes, and why was Nik talking about Lord Derik's gourmet foods? "Yes," he triggered, and his mouth filled with saliva at the memory. It seemed an impossibly long time since he had tasted food, let alone anything as good as the tanalis.

"If you can control your eyes," Nik said matter-of-factly, "then you should be able to control your throat enough to swallow. We'll be having tanalis tonight, if Florian realizes that his despised seaweed and creepy-crawlies are the main ingredients. And once you get the swallowing under control, you'll be halfway to normal speech again."

Nik seemed to be inviting eye contact, and Snowy found it hard to shift his gaze. He'd built up an image of the man in his head, and the reality was quite different. The face was boyish, matching the voice, but he hadn't expected hair as red as Flame's, freckles, or the light green eyes veined with gold. Those eyes were warm and dancing with amusement, with none of the authority that had been in the voice a moment before. "Why?" Snowy triggered, more confused than ever about his status here, but still not trusting enough to allow mind touch.

"Why what, Roi?" Nik replied. "You really do need to learn to talk again, you know. Or at least learn to manipulate individual phonemes with the computer. Of course that'd be faster if you'd learn to read at the same time, now that you can see again."

Read? That wasn't actually illegal for slaves, but it certainly was not encouraged. Timi had known how when he was captured and he had taught the other three, but Snowy had been careful to hide that knowledge. If Nik was really offering to teach him to read, that was one bit of his abilities he wouldn't have to hide. "Yes," he triggered eagerly.

"Good," Nik replied. "Roll back over, and I'll rig a screen over the tank where you can see it, and start teaching you how the characters relate to the sounds. Then you can start catching up on some of the education you've missed."

His "why" had really been aimed at why they were treating him as they were. Snowy still didn't understand that. He simply did not believe Nik's earlier explanation that he was really Lai's son. But he was having an increasingly difficult time finding any other explanation for his apparent status. Better take advantage of it, he thought, even if he didn't understand it. He focused his eyes on the screen, eager to begin the reading lesson.

Lai

3/10/35

Lai looked around, searching for his son in the evening light. The sea breeze had died away, and the scent of the thyme carpeting the paths rose from Lai's feet. "Roi, are you here?" he called aloud, wondering if Nik's guess that the boy might be in the herb garden had been wrong.

"Yes, sir," he heard the reply, and then he saw the white hair above the back of the float chair. At least the boy was sitting up, now, though he still worried about how long it was taking him to recover from the Kharfun paralysis. The chair was rotating as he strode toward it, and by the time he reached it, Roi was facing him.

Facing him, but not looking at him. The eyes were lowered, the head slightly bent, the overall posture that of a slave. He'd have been kneeling if he could. "Roi, look at me," he pleaded, and the white head lifted obediently. So much like his mother in some ways, he thought bleakly, and utterly unlike her in so many others. He'd dropped his mental and emotional shields, but the boy remained a blank, still mirroring. "Can't you at least drop your shields?" he pleaded.

"I don't know how, sir," the boy replied tonelessly as his eyes slid away from Lai's and fixed once more on a bed of purple spikes.

A blind shield, Lai thought. If the boy didn't know how he'd set up the shield, it'd just have to wear off—deliberate tries to break it on Roi's part would only prolong the duration of the shield. Maybe if he tried to get the boy to talk about something that he was interested in ... "Nik says you like the herb garden. Has he taught you anything about the different plants? What's that purple one, for instance?"

"Lavender, sir." No follow-up, just a mechanical answer. Polite, responsive, but with a slave's responsiveness. Could Zhaim be right, that the boy's early conditioning as a slave would never leave him?

"Is that one of your favorites?"

"Yes, sir." The eyes remained lowered, the face expressionless—though that could be due to the paralysis.

"What are some of the others? And what are they used for?"

"Peacemint, sir—it helps with the muscle cramps. And the scent of peacock plant helps, too." The voice was level, as expressionless as the face. And it had taken a direct order to get the "sir" instead of "Master." Lai had encouraged the boy to call him "father", but tried to order as little as he could. Roi had known too many orders in his life.

The sky had darkened from lavender to deep blue, and the first stars were coming out. He'd sat with Cloudy once, on an old stone wall with thyme growing in the crevices. The white hair in the starlight was hauntingly similar, but he had no idea how to reach the person beneath that hair.

The air was cooling rapidly, and the first hint of the land breeze ruffled the boy's hair. "Let's go in," Lai said, "before you get chilled."

3/28/35

Lai looked out at a gray winter drizzle that threatened to continue for at least another day. The weather matched his mood.

"I can't connect with him, Nik," he said finally. "I've been out to visit him half a dozen times now. He is scrupulously polite. He answers my questions. You say he's soaking up what the educational programs can teach him. But he won't make eye contact without a direct order. He won't ask a question. His shields are as tight as ever."

"That bothers me, too," Nik agreed from behind Lai. "I'd feel a lot happier if I could check how he's handling the Kharfun paralysis. But Lai, you're seeing him about once a month. How do you expect him to relate to you? How much of the problem between you is due to your blaming him for Cloudy leaving you?"

Lai turned back to his half-brother. "Blame him? No. But seeing him does remind me of her."

"And you still haven't gotten anywhere in tracing her?"

Lai shook his head in negation. "I've managed to identify five owners since Roi was sold away from her seven years ago. The last was four years ago, and that one apparently sold her to a street dealer I haven't been able to trace. I'm still trying, but this, this planet has no system for tracking slaves. Bad enough that slavery's legal, and that a free woman like Cloudy could be kidnapped into slavery, however illegally. I have less voice in planetary affairs than the Enclave staff."

"Blame our ancestors," Nik replied. "They're the ones that arranged for R'il'nians and high R'il'noids to handle interplanetary squabbles but to have no voice at all in internal affairs. Which includes legalization—or outright banning—of slavery."

Lai sighed and turned back to the gray landscape outside. It might be snowing higher up in the mountains behind the Enclave buildings, but here it was merely depressing. "None of which gets us any closer to the problem of what to do about Roi. You're sure you can't keep him, Nik?"

"I can't keep him and Florian both. It's not Roi's fault—he tries to get along with Florian. But Florian is not ready to share me with anyone. And I'm Florian's last hope. If his parents had asked for help earlier, maybe he'd be able to accept Roi by now. But the bottom line is that one of those boys will wind up killing the other if I try to keep them together, and I think Roi will adapt to a change in guardian better than Florian would. Even after five months Roi's not really relating to me."

Lai was literally unable to use profanity to express his emotions. His fluent use of both Galactica and R'Gal was based on translation from R'il'nian, and the inherited language expressed emotional content via empathy, not in words. The spoken R'il'nian language, he suspected, had evolved in order to allow the separation of logical and emotional communication. But there were times, like right now, when he almost envied the Humans and R'il'noids their ability to swear in frustration.

"School, then," he finally said. "Tyndall, for preference. We all did well there, if you think he's up to the academic rigor."

"He's bright enough, but he doesn't have the standard academic background and he's still very limited physically," Nik said uneasily. "Why don't you and Lyra take him on?"

Lai ducked the question. "Derik's due back," he responded. "Maybe you're right about my needing to listen to him more." He walked over to the interface lounge. If he was going to assist Derik in teleporting back, he would need to tap into an external source of power. Jumps on the planet were easy enough—he needed only to move water to balance any changes in potential energy and momentum. Interstellar teleportation—or communication, for that matter—demanded far more in the way of energy.

He leaned back on the lounge, activating the interface to the computer. From within, the interface was only a faint green-gold tinge to the world, though he knew that to Nik, his head was hidden in a globe of light. He reached through the computer to the fusion generator, setting his mind to draw the energy he needed. Then he reached out for the distant planet where Derry waited.

The response was not as strong as he expected, and Lai looked sharply at Derik after he had provided most of the effort needed to land his half brother on the other lounge. Derik's fondness for gourmet meals had never put excess weight on his slender frame, but now he looked gaunt to the point of starvation. Nik took one look and filled a glass with fruit juice and a generous dollop of honey. "Drink," he ordered, and stood over Derik until the exhausted man had finished the glass.

"Is Lyra around?" was Derik's first question.

Lai reached mentally for Elyra, including a quick request that she bring more food. "She's here," he replied to Derik. "Derik, what happened? You look terrible."

"Not enough time home between assignments, and lots of underwater work and xenotelepathy on this last one." He sighed and looked reproachfully at Lai. "You don't have to keep sending me off planet to protect Roi. I love that boy. There is no way I'd hurt him."

"You wouldn't hurt him intentionally," Nik put in unexpectedly. "But you could sure hurt him without meaning to. Like right now—I don't think he's really absorbed the fact that he's not a slave. Having a former owner around wouldn't help that."

"Oh," Derik said slowly. He looked down into his empty glass. "I—guess I didn't think of that."

Elyra walked into the room, looked at Derik, and set down her tray temporarily to remove the glass from his hand before she placed the tray on his lap. "Eat that," she ordered, "and don't give me any nonsense about not being hungry."

Derik twisted his head to look up at her and managed a sheepish grin. "At the moment, I'd be lying if I tried to. Can you test this for genetic material? And what species?" He removed a vial from a belt pocket and handed it to her before digging into the meal she had brought.

Lai waited until Derik paused in his eating to speak. "I'm sorry, Derry. I've been acting more on emotion than logic, though Nik's right about why you need to keep away from Roi for a while. Report summary?"

"Sentient, aquatic—hard to be anything else, on a planet with barely enough land area to set the ship down—peaceable, and virtually no chance of developing space flight or interest in anything beyond their hydrosphere. Atmospheric oxygen's so high nothing could live on land, anyway—it'd combust spontaneously. I set up warnoff beacons, and I'd suggest leaving them activated and avoid further contact." He began eating again, a little more slowly.

Lai nodded, confirming Derry's judgment, and glanced over at Elyra. She was frowning, seeming puzzled by her analysis of the tissue sample. She looked up, caught Lai looking at her, and turned to Derik. "Where did you get this sample, Derry?"

"Teleported a bit of tissue out of an anoxic mudslide—and believe me, on that planet anoxic sediments are hard to find. Is there enough DNA to do anything with?"

"It's pure R'il'nian and some of the variable sequences aren't in my database. And it looks fairly recent, on the basis of racemization. Any idea of the age, Derry?"

Derik shrugged. "Their time units are based on biology rather than astronomy, and I never did manage to translate them exactly. I *think* four to twelve centuries. They've had humanoid visitors before, and thought at first I was more of the same. They pointed out where one of the earlier visitors was buried by a submarine landslide, and I managed to get that sample."

Lai was staring at both of them, his mind racing. R'il'nian—it must be from one of the other groups that had fled R'il'n in the diaspora close to two hundred millennia ago. He might not be the only one of his species left alive! He reached forward in time, trying to see the future results of his own possible actions. Go himself? Yes! Quickly! And high probability not only for his own happiness, but for the good of the Confederation as a whole. "Derik," he asked, his voice shaking a little with excitement, "the XP ship you were on. Where is it now?"

"On its way back to Murphy for refitting. Lai, you're not thinking of abandoning the Confederation, are you? The waterworld inhabitants—they had no concept of where their visitors came from. They have no concept of anything outside the hydrosphere of their own planet. Their visitors probably came from the hemisphere away from the Confederation, but that's half of space. And have you ever been along when an XP ship was exploring? With unflagged jump points they're limited to short hops—around five light years max, with a day or so minimum of maneuvering between them. More likely fivedays or even months before they pick up a jump point in the direction they want to go. Have you any idea of how long it would take to explore oh, say a half-space a hundred light years out from the waterworld? Even if you limit your goals to the vicinity of stars with the right mass? Sure, push the exploration in that direction. But we need you here. Desperately. Let the exploration specialists do the exploring."

Lai lay back on the lounge, leaning again into the computer. This time he used it as an extension of his own mind, extending his intuitive sense of urgency into the complexities of conditional precognitive mathematics. "There isn't time," he said finally. "Something's been nibbling at the back of my mind for a long time. This has brought it into focus. I have to find whatever other R'il'nai are surviving, not just for my own sanity, but for the future of the Confederation. And it's urgent."

More than urgent, vital. Conditional precognition was above all others the talent for which the Human population of the Confederation trusted the R'il'nai to settle interplanetary disputes. It could be vague. Intuition and imagination were needed to find possible courses of action. The end goals had to be clearly defined. In some situations, the possible outcomes depended strongly on the actions of others, and the results of CP mathematics were fuzzy.

But this case was almost a textbook example. Lai's own choices were clear: do nothing, encourage exploration beyond Derry's planet, or go with the exploration crew. Outcomes? He'd used several. The welfare of the Human race a few centuries and a few millennia into the future. The survival of the Confederation for the same time spans. Even his own happiness—he had learned to include that from his loss of Cloudy. The probability of any of the outcomes being positive was essentially zero if he did nothing or if he simply encouraged exploration without going along. If he went with an exploration ship himself, guiding its selection of directions at each jump point, the probability of a positive outcome was at least even on any criterion of success, with the greatest differences being for the longest times in the future.

"I wouldn't be getting results like that unless it was important that I find them quickly," he ended his explanation to Derry.

"Not to the point that you have to leave today," Derik said flatly. "Think, Lai. The XP-13 is the closest exploration ship in the direction you want to go. It needs servicing, fuel, food, and minimal leave time for the crew. It's going to take at least two fivedays for that ship to get back to Murphy and probably longer than that to get it ready to leave again. No matter how anxious you are, you've got the better part of a month to think about how the Confederation is going to hold together while you're gone."

Lai walked over to the window and looked out at the rain. "You're right about giving the XP-13 time to refit, and doing some thinking about the situation here. I'm not planning to leave for good, but I'll probably be gone for longer than I have before. Months, at least."

"And the chances are you'll wind up going too far to keep in touch," Derik pointed out. "What about Roi? And who are you going to leave in charge?"

"Zhaim. He's my heir; it's time he learned to take a little responsibility." All three R'il'noids flinched. "He's not that bad," Lai protested. "And he won't have my veto power."

"Lai," Elyra said gently, "we all know how much you love Zhaim. And some R'il'noids take a long time to grow up. But right now … At least use your CP to check out the probable effects of leaving him in charge here."

"I'm not sure he has a choice, Lyra," Derik said, his voice troubled. "If Zhaim's here at all, he's going to want to be in charge. And what about Roi?"

Lai returned to the lounge and reached forward again, still concentrating on the welfare of the Confederation, but this time putting more emphasis on how he might prepare for his own prolonged absence. More than likely, he would be in contact range for several months, and leaving Zhaim in charge for that period did not trigger any strong negative reactions. Once he was out of contact, though …

"Blurred," he reported. "Which probably means that Zhaim's decisions control whether leaving him in charge is a good idea or not."

"What about Roi?" Nik demanded.

"Tyndall." Lai had decided that while he had been examining his options with Zhaim. "I know, it's probably not the best place for him academically or socially. But the security system is superb. If I order 'no visitors,' even Zhaim can't bother him. And since we've managed to avoid making his existence public, he should be safe."

"Including from me," Derik said unhappily. "Lai, can't you trust my word? Sure, I was a little wild my first few centuries, and some people are still throwing that in my face. But I've settled down, damn it. And I would *not* do anything to hurt that boy."

"It's not your intentions I question, Derry, it's your judgment. At least when your emotions are involved, and they very obviously are. Forget Roi for now, and concentrate on keeping the Confederation running. Zhaim's got a Çeren of one-thirty-five. You're one-thirty-two, and Kaia's one-thirty."

Derik was already shaking his head. "Kaia and I get along fine, and when we do disagree we can generally work out a compromise. But I don't think Zhaim will accept our joint judgment. And a triumvirate won't work if one member thinks he can overrule the other two."

He shook his head again, this time letting his eyes close as he did so. "I'm in no shape to think about this. If you're planning to travel on the XP-13, you'll be here for at least another twenty days. Let's all sleep on it."

It wasn't that simple, of course. The Inner Council erupted at the very thought of Lai being out of touch for a prolonged period, though they would not argue with Lai's CP. The Outer Council, which Lai found useful as a sounding board on occasion, suddenly decided that matters which had gone for months or even years without any decision being made must be cleared up before Lai left. Even the Planetary Assembly, which in theory had no input from R'il'nians or high R'il'noids except on interplanetary matters, suddenly needed Lai's input on anything that could possibly affect its relations with the Confederation.

Lai did his best to ignore them all, but even so he found himself so busy that he had little time to see to the things that concerned him most. He made time for Zhaim, and grew increasingly uneasy at his son's immaturity and inability to compromise. Arranging for Roi to attend Tyndall kept getting shuffled to the bottom of the things he had to do, and every discussion with Zhaim increased his uneasiness about his younger son. Finally, he made a decision he would have said was unthinkable a month before, and called in Derik, Kaia, and Nik.

"Somebody has to take responsibility for Roi while I'm gone," he told them, "and arrange for him to attend Tyndall. Would you three take joint temporary guardianship?"

Derik's jaw dropped open briefly, and then he gave Lai a hurt look. "You know me too well," he accused. "You're making me responsible for the boy's welfare, and I bet you're defining his welfare to include not seeing him."

"That's part of it, yes, at least until he realizes he's not a slave any more. But I also want his guardian to have clout enough to protect him from Zhaim. I am going to leave Zhaim in charge. But I'll be in contact and emergency teleport range for at least several months—as you said, exploration's a slow process, and teleportation's not possible to someplace you've never been unless you know another teleport at the other end. Can you and Kaia watch the decisions Zhaim makes and let me know if you agree that he's making poor ones? Advise him, but don't try to outvote him. That may give me the information I need to decide whether to leave him in charge once I'm out of contact range."

"What happens if one of his decisions threatens to precipitate a real disaster?" Kaia asked skeptically.

"Contact me and I'll deal with it. Agreed?"

The three R'il'noids looked at each other, then back at Lai. "Agreed," Derik said. "And if I'm going to talk Tyndall into accepting Roi next term, I'd better get at it. The new term starts in a few days."

Roi

5/1/35

Snowy was used to having his name changed every time a new owner bought him, so he had no problem responding to "Roi." He was even beginning to think of himself as Roi. But he still had no idea of whether to believe Nik.

True, the man Nik said was his father, Lai, had visited him several times. But there had been no real friendliness or caring in the man's attitude. Nothing like what he had seen in the relationship between Derik and his son, or even in Derik's attitude toward Snowy. If anything, the man had seemed uneasy in Roi's presence.

Roi understood why Nik wasn't here—Nik was a physician, and the health of his patients always came first. A R'il'noid baby, arriving unexpectedly a week early and with known health problems, had to be more important than Roi was. That didn't stop Roi from wishing that Nik were along to introduce him to his new—owner? Guardian? Jailer? He just didn't *know* enough!

"Here we are," Lukon said cheerfully, and Roi dutifully looked out of the windows of the jump-van. The landscape was depressingly flat, and the grass outside the low, ornamental wall surrounding the complex was browned. Inside the grass was green, but the buildings were an even less appealing shade of dead-grass brown. A handful of boys, mostly much younger than Roi, walked along the paths between buildings.

Heat licked in like flames when Lukon opened the door, and Roi gasped in surprise. Lukon was already sweating, but he showed only a condescending amusement. "Mid-continent in the middle of summer," he said. "You didn't expect it to be cool, did you? Need help to get into the float chair?"

"I can manage it," Roi replied carefully. If the comment had come from any of Nik's other assistants, he might have pointed out that most of his life prior to Derik's ownership had been spent inside of temperature-controlled buildings. It never got this hot at Derik's, and there was always a sea breeze at Nik's. He glanced up at the sky and cringed mentally. Not only was it hot, it was huge. He forced himself to glance again around the flat, distant horizon and decided that the computer's information about the climate and geography of Tyndall had given him no sense of what the reality would be like.

Lukon had been piling Roi's luggage—what there was of it—on a floater as the boy looked around him, and finally commented, "Well, if you're through goggling, let's go," and led off down one of the paths.

Roi followed him, eyes on the floater. Most of the floater load was clothing—what Nik had called "school uniforms," like the gray tunic and trousers he wore over a white shirt. Nik had added a few things Roi would need to care for himself. The most important things in Roi's eyes, two aromatic plants from Nik's herb garden in glazed pots, were perched atop the rest of the load. Roi watched anxiously as Lukon handed over the floater to a robot, following the plants with his eyes as the floater moved away.

Lukon led the way to the nearest of the buildings, and Roi was careful not to react as they passed in a single step from the heat outside to a blast of icy air. No, not icy, he decided as he followed Lukon down a corridor and through an anteroom. It just felt that way after the heat outdoors.

"This is Roi, Schoolmaster Nebol," Lukon said as they entered the inner room where a man sat behind a raised desk. "I believe you have all the information on him."

"Inner Councilor Derik's protégé," the man answered, to Roi's considerable surprise. His eyes raked Roi up and down, and Roi picked up a good deal of resentment in his emotional aura. "You have his luggage in the system? Good. I'll take over, then." He turned to Roi, who kept his eyes carefully lowered.

"We don't normally take new boys your age," Nebol said bitterly, "but I could hardly say no to your guardian. You'll just have to try to fit in. We'll run placement tests this afternoon. For now, get on up to your room and get your things put away, and read the rules. Kim will be by to start the placement tests in a couple of hours. Follow the flashing green light to find your room. Dismissed."

The light was easy enough to follow out of the building, but once on the pathways Roi got a nasty shock. He could manage the chair as well as ever—that was controlled by the brain-wave pickup on his head. But it took enormous effort to lift or turn his head, or to raise his arms. He could do it, but only with far more concentration than usual, and he knew he'd get hungry very quickly, spending energy at this rate. He wondered when supper would be available—he'd been too tense to eat much lunch—and suddenly remembered that Tyndall was not only in the northern hemisphere, but a good four hours west of Seabird Island. Four extra hours until a meal. He'd better unpack the candy Nik had insisted he bring along.

The room was cooler, but otherwise no better than the paths. It was about the size of the cubicle he had shared with his friends at Derik's, with built-in sanitary and cleaning facilities. But the walls were the same depressing dead-grass color as the buildings, and the built-in computer terminal was exhausting to operate. There was an unpleasant buzzing in his head that made it difficult to concentrate. He managed to get his clothing on the shelves and levitate the plants to the windowsill, but he was soon fighting a headache in spite of the candy he'd gulped down.

By the time Kim arrived for the placement tests Roi was too tired to care much about the outcome, though he tried to cooperate. He wasn't sure how well he was doing—some of the questions seemed easy, and on others he was totally lost. What he was picking up from Kim was increasing bewilderment—but he was too tired to attempt to discover whether the man was puzzled by the unevenness of his answers, or by his temerity in trying to enter Tyndall at all.

The final test was the most confusing. Kim flipped the switch on a box he had brought with him, and the buzzing in Roi's head increased to a roar. Worse, his paralysis returned. Well, not entirely. He had discovered earlier that the computer gave him a nasty mental shock when he tried to contact it directly, and tapping small objects against the touch screen had no effect—he had to lift his arm and touch the screen with a finger. But it took relatively little effort—far less than to control his mouth and throat—to manipulate the keys set in the desktop. When Kim asked him which of three sounds was different from the other two, he used most of his remaining energy to levitate his hand onto the number pad, then keyed in "2" telekinetically. Kim looked puzzled, but accepted the answer.

Roi's performance on this test, however, continued to bewilder his tester—and Roi himself, for that matter. Some of his answers—generally those he was sure of—brought a clear positive emotional response from Kim. But Kim seemed to score as errors some of the times that Roi was sure he had given the right answer, and Kim's response to the times Roi triggered "don't know" was also mixed.

"Well," Kim finally said as he flipped off the switch, "no R'Gal for you this term. Probably just as well, considering what else you have to make up. Roi, please don't take this as meaning that you're stupid. You're not. Your ability to apply what you have learned is excellent, and I'm impressed by how much you've managed to pick up in—what, five months of just fooling around with the computer? But you don't have the background for the courses you'd normally be taking at your age, so I'm going to have to put you in with much younger students. You do understand the discipline system here, don't you?"

"Peer pressure," Roi replied promptly. It was basically the same system, under a different name, that he had known all his life. Wise overseers, like Davy, worked within the system, allowing the slaves themselves to handle day-to-day decisions. Brak had tried to crush the slaves' network—stupid, in Roi's opinion. All he'd done was drive it underground and make things much harder for himself. At least one thing here, Roi thought, would be familiar.

But Kim sounded worried, and as he gathered up his equipment and prepared to leave the room, he turned back to Roi. "Please," he said, "don't be afraid to come see me if you have problems. Any kind of problems. My office is here, in the same building as the dining room." He crossed the room to the computer terminal, bringing up a map of the school and highlighting first his office, and then the dining room.

"Of course," Roi replied politely, but he would no more have asked the man for help than he would have asked Brak. He was far more interested in the location of the dining room. His stomach had been growling with increasing urgency throughout the tests, and the schedule indicated it was almost suppertime.

When he slid open the door the corridor, which had been empty six hours earlier, was crowded with boys. Most were about his age, and wore the same school uniform—short-sleeved, square-necked gray tunic over a white shirt, with a colored scarf at the throat. Some of the boys wore shorts instead of trousers, but the majority had dark green scarves about their throats—the same color as Roi's. Roi tried to introduce himself, but the others refused to acknowledge his existence. He caught a few scornful glances at the float chair but for the most part the others looked over his head, and he was unable to maneuver the float chair through them.

It wasn't accidental, he decided. Every time he thought he saw an opening, someone stepped in front of his chair. Surely they were hungry, too. He could hear other stomachs growling. He was hemmed in tightly for a few moments, and when the crush lessened most of the handful of remaining students were blocking the lift shafts. When he finally reached the door out of the building, it was to see the last of the others running down the path to the central building.

Roi sent the float chair after them, but its speed was limited. By the time he reached the dining hall, the others were already seated and eating, and Nebol's withering look made it quite clear that he was in trouble for his unintended tardiness.

Where was he supposed to be? The round tables that crowded the room had colored tops, and the boys seated at them wore scarves that matched the table colors—pastels and young children closest, with deeper colors farther away. Roi located the green tables, almost against the far wall. Aside from Nebol and Kim, he saw only one face he knew, that of Derik's son Coryn— and Coryn, who wore a violet scarf, was very carefully not looking at him. Considering the number of faces turned toward him, that was almost a relief.

The float chair would have fitted between empty tables, but not when the room was crowded with students. Even working his way along the wall,

Roi had to dodge automated servers, and when he finally managed to reach the green tables, it was to find every place filled. He hesitated, hungrier than ever at the sight and smell of roast meat and baskets of crusty bread. The green-scarved diners—mostly the same students who had blocked him in the hall—looked over, beside, or even through him, but never directly at him.

"Xazhar," Kim's voice came from behind Roi, "this is Roi. He's in your year group. Make a place for him, will you? Roi, this is Xazhar K'Zhaim Laian." The boy across the table from Roi looked briefly murderous, and then forced a smile.

"Nys, Malar, make room for that—contraption—will you?" He looked Roi up and down, his expression very much like that of a slave owner evaluating a new purchase.

Roi managed a "Thank you," as he moved his chair into place, but he was thinking of Kim's veiled warning about peer pressure. He'd always found it easy to fit himself into new groups of slaves, but had he been wrong in assuming that would carry over to his fellow students? Didn't K'Zhaim mean that Xazhar was a descendant of Zhaim, perhaps even his son? He looked surreptitiously at the boy he suspected was the leader of his age group, searching for some resemblance to Zhaim.

The features and skin tone were similar. The long, elaborately braided hair was not, but it might have been bleached and dyed—certainly the mahogany top, coppery sides and the twin flares of gold running back from the corners of the forehead didn't look natural. Eyes? Not the ice and silver Roi remembered from his contact with Flick, but a rather nondescript yellow-green flecked with copper.

Roi turned to the plate one of the automated servers had placed before him. Eating the way Nik had insisted on, using telekinesis to raise his hand and the eating tongs, was exhausting, especially when he was tired and hungry and the buzzing in his head interfered with any use of his talents. It would be so much easier to lift the food to his mouth directly. And why not? He reached out for the hot bread on his plate, separated a bite-sized chunk, and began levitating it to his mouth.

Xazhar cleared his throat, not loudly enough to be heard over the buzz of conversation at the other tables, but a clear signal for attention at the one where Roi sat.

"S'Derik," he said, his voice low but intense, "I don't know what kind of a gadget the Lord Derik gave you, but if I catch you using it to play with your food again, I'll take it away and break both your arms."

Roi's initial reaction was shock—not so much at Xazhar's words as at his own carelessness in displaying his abilities so openly. But why had Nik encouraged the much clumsier use of the same abilities? Or had he misunderstood what Nik was telling him to do? At any rate, Xazhar could hardly take away a non-existent gadget, though it was safer for him to think such a gadget existed. The threat to break Roi's arms, however, sounded real. Roi could Heal them, of course, but not without being noticed. Almost by reflex he dropped his head and apologized, letting the bread drop back to his plate.

Resentment came afterward, but why? Six months ago, he'd have responded to "S'Derik"—slave of Derik—with pride. He hadn't liked being a slave, but having an owner of high status reflected that status on him. Besides, Derik was easily the nicest owner he'd had. Somehow, his time with Nik had changed that attitude, even though it hadn't convinced him he wasn't a slave.

Roi glanced around assessing the other boys—not only at his own table, but around the room. Esper talents—and he was sure there must be some— were well hidden. The school uniform did not lend itself to ostentation, but Xazhar's elaborately dyed and braided hairstyle was far from being the most ornate. Kim's veiled warning about the peer pressure discipline began to make sense. Why had he been sent here? To copy the other boys? Well, he wouldn't do it. Learn, yes. But he was glad his hair had been cut short during his illness, unhappy though that had made him when he first discovered the loss. Beauty that enhanced his value, he decided, was worth the effort. Ultimately, it increased his chances of survival. But the kind of competition he saw here had nothing to do with that.

Survival triggered a third, lasting reaction. Levitating his arm as well as the food through whatever field he felt as a buzzing in his head took a lot of effort. So much effort, in fact, that he felt even hungrier after the meal than before it. That wasn't going to work long term. The obvious solution of levitating just the food clearly wasn't going to pass in front of Xazhar. Teleportation?

He hadn't had much chance to exercise his talents as a slave—just a little experimentation on the rare occasions when he could be sure no one was watching. He'd had several months practice in levitating his own body, coupled with moving his limbs telekinetically. Teleporting ... Well, he knew from his cautious experiments as a slave that he could interchange two objects of similar shape and size if they started out at about the same level. The serving platters and his stomach were nearly enough the same height, he thought, but simple interchange wouldn't do here. Somehow he had to stretch his stomach out, teleport food into the cavity, and allow the food on the platter to collapse gently into the vacancy. He'd have to do some experimenting back in his room, he thought. The candy Nik had packed would keep him going in the meantime.

6/17/35

Things would have been bearable if Xazhar had confined his sniping to meals. It hadn't taken Roi more than a few days to work out a modification of teleporting that would keep him fed, transferring food in a steady stream to his stomach. It wasn't fun and his stomach didn't feel right afterward, but it would keep him alive.

Physical education was something else. All of his other classes were graded by what the students knew, which meant that most of his academic classes were with six-year olds. It was humiliating, but he could console himself with the thought that he was learning everything presented in the classes, even if he had trouble getting his homework into the computer. Physical education, however, was graded by age. Trying to make his body look as if he had any control at all was hard enough. But the other students knew he was in baby classes academically, and never let him forget it. Worst of all, Xazhar was in his swimming class.

Roi knew how to swim. Further, it was one of the easiest exercises to perform with his damaged body. If the other students would just let him alone, he thought, he could swim as well as any of them.

They would not let him alone. Xazhar and his followers were after Roi every time the instructor looked away. It never occurred to Roi to say anything to the instructor, let alone to Kim, and having his ankles grabbed and his head jerked under water became an expected and hated part of the class, destroying his one-time pleasure in swimming.

The climax came a month into the term, when the instructor left the pool. Roi was swimming lengths, slowly. It seemed he was always hungry, now that Nik's candy was gone, and he just did not have the energy to move his arms and legs much. He wasn't paying much attention to the other students, and it came as a total surprise when Xazhar and three of his friends shoved him under water. He tried to push them away telekinetically, but he was pushed back—Xazhar couldn't do much through the suppresser field, but with Roi weakened by lack of food, not much was needed.

The previous attacks had never lasted more than a few seconds—long enough to get water in his throat, but never lasting to the point that he was in serious danger of drowning. This time the attack seemed to go on and on, and his lungs were demanding air. He reached out mentally, trying to get the instructor's attention, and realized with a shock that the man was not there.

His vision was starting to close in, and the need for air was becoming overpowering. Could he teleport himself? He'd never tried teleporting a living creature, let alone himself—but if he didn't do something quickly, he'd pass out and probably drown.

Then he heard shouting, and the hands holding him down were suddenly pushing him to the surface. Through his own choked efforts to breathe he heard Xazhar's voice, mock-concerned: "He went under swimming lengths. We thought he was drowning."

Liar! And Roi was having so much trouble breathing he could not even correct him.

The instructor pulled him out and watched as Roi choked up the water he had inhaled. "Got it out? You'd better get back in the pool."

"No!" Roi tried to push himself away from the pool, but nothing seemed to work right. Get back in the water, with Xazhar waiting to drown him? His vision narrowed until nothing existed but the horrible pool, and then he fainted.

There was a good deal of shouting when he awoke in the infirmary, and it took him a while to identify one of the voices as his swimming instructor. The other was strange, but if he listened hard he could understand what it was saying. "Blood sugar almost zero! I don't know what happened, but with that blood sugar level you're lucky he survived and I am *not* going to clear him for any more swimming."

No more swimming? The instructor was arguing, but Roi was aware only of relief. Exhausted, he sank back into sleep.

Lai

7/4/35

For Lai, the first few fivedays of the trip were a welcome vacation from unrelenting responsibility and equally unrelenting labor. He slept most of the first fiveday, until they reached the flagged jump point near the outer edge of the system that held Derry's water world. From that point on, Captain Tova alerted him whenever they made an unflagged jump and needed guidance to the next jump point. Not that he needed alerting—the roughly plotted jumps were more than enough to wake him from the soundest of sleeps. He rapidly joined the crew in calling the XP-13 the Bounceabout.

And the small crew—who at the start of the trip had treated him with exaggerated courtesy and some awe—now reserved their awe for his ability to identify unflagged jump points. Lai could "feel" jump points at distances where the ship's instrumentation could barely detect them. His willingness to put that ability at the service of the crew, together with his genuine interest in each of their specialties, had led to his gradual acceptance in their small society.

An unlatched door meant "come in," so he was not surprised when Cinda stuck in her head. "We're stable," she reported. "Captain Tova says you can tie in to the power plant any time you want. Is this really the last contact with the Confederation?"

Lai smiled at her as he hooked the interface into the fusion generator that powered the engines. "Last one I scheduled with Derry and Kaia, and I understand you lost sublight communication with Murphy a fiveday ago. Any last messages from the crew?"

"Nah, we all sent our farewells to Murphy before we lost contact. Not that we'd mind some recent news. Elik's not at all happy about waiting until we get back to find out who won the regional plasmaball tournament."

"I'll ask Derry," Lai promised as he completed his hookup and lay down, lowering the interface over his head. Even with all the energy they could handle for boosting at both ends and a prearranged contact schedule, he, Derry and Kaia would all be working at their limits. In fact, since they were not even sure this contact would work, it was not on the official schedule. That meant Zhaim had no idea that whatever he had done over the last few days would be relayed to his father—a final test. Lai reached for the ship's energy source, feeling it increase as he drew all of the power it could give him to spin his mind out toward Derik and Kaia.

Derry, he thought as his mind made fumbling contact, was unhappy about something. Kaia as well, though his contact with her mind was entirely through Derry's. That arrangement in itself told him how difficult they were finding the contact. Hastily he sent the results of their last fiveday's flagging, along with a request for the sports information the crew wanted. *What's wrong?* he added.

The Bomban referendum voted down slavery—pretty much along the lines you suggested. Why would Derry be unhappy about that? Then the explanation continued. *Zhaim's been trying to invalidate the referendum. And it turns out he's got a lot more control than any of us suspected over the peacekeepers in that region.*

Invalidate a decision reached by a planetary government, no matter how reached? The Confederation didn't *have* that power. His job—and the job of the crossbreds, now that the R'il'nai were nearly extinct—was to protect against external, mostly non-Human, threats, and to arbitrate differences among Human-occupied planets. *He can't do that,* Lai sent back, shocked.

That's what Kaia and I have been telling him, Derry's mind whispered back. *Legally, he can't. But as a practical matter...*

As a practical matter, if Zhaim controlled the peacekeepers he could do as he pleased. Not for long—holding the Confederation together for the long term required scrupulous fairness. But Zhaim's weakest talent had always been long-range precognition. From the sound of this, he wasn't even looking ahead as far as his father's return.

And up to the point when he would have assumed contact with his father was lost, Zhaim had done a good job—a job Lai had approved of wholeheartedly. The sudden change argued premeditation.

Could Derry and Kaia be angling for more authority themselves? He couldn't rule that out, but on everything he knew of those two and of his son, Zhaim was the one of the three who really wanted power. And if Zhaim actually had acquired that much influence over the peacekeepers, leaving him with the Confederation would mean he was in charge—and he could do irreparable damage in even a short time.

The alternatives?

Lai could not face the thought of killing the son he loved. That was not a viable solution, anyway. Aside from the fact that Zhaim might still develop a better sense of responsibility with age, killing him would only make Zhaim a martyr and destroy Lai's own credibility.

Drug Zhaim? Possible, but risky—and it would make a permanent enemy of his son, as well as a martyr.

Abandon his search? He still wasn't sure why this search was so urgent, but he had no doubts at all that it was vital for the future of the Human species.

Bring Zhaim with him?

It was not a solution that appealed to Lai. The Bounceabout's crew accepted Lai, but he'd had to work for that acceptance. He couldn't see Zhaim working for anyone's acceptance. And the ship was small. Normally it carried only nine people, and the four exploration specialists had been temporarily reassigned to lab jobs on Murphy. That left a crew of just five—Captain Tova, computer and communications specialist Cinda, medic Kalar, navigator Elik and engineer Britt. Lai had turned down the captain's offer of her own quarters, fitting himself instead into the area normally occupied by the ship's ecologist. That left three cabins empty, so there was room enough for Zhaim. Zhaim probably wouldn't think so.

Zhaim would probably not make a good first impression on the other R'il'nai Lai was hoping to find. But ... Lai ran half a dozen different scenarios in his head, looking ahead for the probable futures stemming from each. Little as he liked the idea, having Zhaim with him appeared to be the best solution.

Which left Lai with two purely practical problems: how was he to persuade Zhaim to join him, and how was he to get Zhaim here?

He did not fully understand the urgency that drove him, but he knew that returning to Murphy to pick Zhaim up was out of the question. He reached into the computer memory of the ship, checking the newly flagged jump points. In general, the jump drive could be tuned to travel between any two jump points, provided both were in range and close to the same gravitational potential. Many of the points flagged by the Bounceabout were too far off the gravitational potential of the nearest point to reach, but there was one, flagged three fivedays before, that looked possible.

Derry, he thought, *if I anchor from this end and you and Kaia take the Central end, could we get Zhaim out to this point, a little closer than the one I contacted you from twelve days ago?*

He felt Derry's increasingly shaky evaluation. *I don't want this, Lai. But if he cooperates—yes, I think we can do it.*

I'll have to handle that. Be open for contact in twenty-four hours. Lai felt Derry's agreement, followed almost at once by the breaking of communication.

He stayed in the interface for a few minutes, working out the logistics of moving back toward the Confederation. The ship was no more than twelve hours' maneuvering from the jump point that had brought them here. Return to that jump point, and from there… It took him a few minutes to work out the drive settings that should take them to the jump point he remembered, and for good measure he worked out the reverse settings that would bring them back to the nearby point. Then he removed the interface and headed up to Captain Tova's command post.

She wouldn't be happy to double back, though he thought no more than a day and a half would be wasted. In the long run, she'd be a lot unhappier about Zhaim's joining the ship.

Zhaim

7/5/35

Zhaim had none of his father's inability to swear, and his first reaction after the unexpected contact with Lai had been to damn Derik in twenty different languages. The interfering old R'il'noid had to be the source of Lai's information. He should have known Derik would not have told Zhaim the truth about his contacts with Zhaim's father. He should have waited longer before he started remolding the Confederation closer to his own ideals.

Not that he had allowed any of his anger to show as he arranged for his absence. Bad enough that his father insisted on dragging him along on a wild goose chase. He could at least pretend that the invitation was an honor.

He stalked across the deeply furred floor to the window wall overlooking his private domain. From here, only the outer stretches were visible—untamed sunlight pouring down from a sky so deep a blue that a few of the brightest stars were visible, glaciers and icefalls that were near blinding in their intense whiteness, and rare outcrops of pale rock amid the snow.

Only a chosen few visitors ever saw behind the mountains to the inner parts of the estate, where force shields protected his sculpture gardens from icy winds, thin air, and burning sun. He had learned that lesson early, back when he still lived at the Enclave. His father had seemed impressed with his manipulation of plants, he recalled. Then he'd made the mistake of showing the old R'il'nian his sculptures in living human flesh. He had expected more approval. He still flinched at the memory of his father's outrage.

Why? He had broken no laws. What he had done was a perfectly legal creation of a new art form. Yet all of the elderly R'il'nai still alive at the time had acted horrified.

For Zhaim, having power and not using it was a form of weakness. And the weak neither survived nor deserved to. As far as he was concerned, the impending extinction of the R'il'nai was as well-deserved as it was inevitable.

The fact remained that his father had power, even if he chose not to use it. Zhaim had moved out of the old R'il'nian Enclave and built his own estate here, high in the mountains, shortly after his father had first seen his sculptures. He was careful not to share his hobby with any of the R'il'nai, though now that his father was the only survivor, he had been unable to resist occasional forays to embellish the gardens of his old home at the Enclave. After all, he'd be moving back there when his father died. But he knew too many other things to risk his father's reading his mind. He had no choice but to obey orders. At least those orders had been presented as an invitation and an honor. He would not lose face in the Confederation, and he remained his father's heir. He needed only to wait.

He turned from the window toward his wardrobe. Twelve hours left to conclude his business here and select the very limited luggage his father had indicated he could take. Business was pretty well taken care of. No doubt some of his living sculptures would die, which was annoying, but they could easily be replaced. The only thing that worried Zhaim even a little was the slave brat Lai claimed was his son. The brat had not yet been Çeren indexed—could not be, for a couple of years, at least—and there was a remote chance that it would test high enough to throw off Zhaim's carefully crafted alliances. Not high enough to challenge Zhaim's own position, of course, but just possibly high enough to worry about. He had guarded against that as well as he could, helped by the fact that his father had left getting the brat into Tyndall to Derik. Reminding Nebol of Derik's notoriety as a practical joker had been almost too easy.

So ... Packing. If he were to pretend that he represented the crossbreds at a first meeting with another group of the R'il'nai, a good first impression would be important. Shipboard wear could be casual, though hardly as casual as what his father preferred. Zhaim slid back the door to the huge suite that housed his clothing and personal adornments, and turned into the mirror-walled room that held his selection of casual wear.

He admired his own reflection, graceful and beautiful as a cat, even as he continued to consider his meeting with Nebol. He had been very careful about what he said to the man. But there were things Zhaim knew as an Inner Council member, such as the brat's bout with Kharfun and the high-Çeren son it had produced, that were not common knowledge. He had made quite sure that neither his father nor Derik had thought to acquaint the school with these facts, and he had left Nebol convinced that the brat's paralysis was either faked or due to a spinal injury.

Having his own son at Tyndall, and in the same age group as the bastard, was another piece of luck on Zhaim's part. He ran over the note he had sent Xazhar an hour ago:

> So sorry I won't be here to invite you home for the term break. Derik and Kaia will no doubt be quite busy as well. Glad to hear you are doing so well, and I commend your school spirit.

Innocent enough on the surface, he thought. But Xazhar would understand his meaning. Zhaim hadn't dared to be too explicit with Nebol, but his son firmly believed that the brat was still Derik's catamite, placed at Tyndall as a practical joke on the school. Xazhar's school spirit was quite real, but Zhaim had diverted it to his own ends. The brat would probably survive its time at Tyndall. But remembering the severity of hazing during his own time there, Zhaim thought that any spirit the slave had managed to develop would be quite thoroughly broken.

On to packing. Much as he hated for anyone to see him twice in the same costume, he would have to make an exception for the crew, he decided. Not that they really counted. But his father had been explicit in how little space he would have to store his things on the ship. Things that would pack in little space, he decided, clean easily and shake out wrinkle-free. His own ice and silver eyes, black hair and bronze skin were best set off by jewel tones, accented with silver. He entered those parameters into the wardrobe computer, and looked dispiritedly at the half dozen outfits it offered for his selection. Only that many, of all those in the room? Well, he would pack them all.

Now for the serious selection. He turned into a corridor, its walls lined with stasis display cases. A spectacular creation of green feathers and emeralds caught his eye, but after a moment he shook his head regretfully and moved on. He'd never be able to keep it looking fresh with the limited space he was allowed. The deceptively simple tunic and trousers of liquid silver was a better choice, he decided. He needed at least two more. The patchwork of tattooed slaveskin was one of his favorites, but definitely out in his father's presence.

He worked his way to the first U-turn in the hallway and doubled back. Too bad he didn't have time to design a costume specifically for the occasion. Occasion! He was thinking as if there would really be a meeting, instead of humoring his father's delusions.

And yet …

His father was a sentimental fool where the Humans were concerned, but he had an annoying habit of being right in his long-term prognostications.

Suppose there were other R'il'nai out there, less effete than the ones Zhaim had known?

If there were, he thought, then it *was* important that he make the best possible first impression. He turned and strode down the corridor with renewed energy, searching for exactly the right outfit.

Coryn

7/16/35

"I still don't think it's fair," Ander grumbled as he strode around the room.

"Not fair to who?" Coryn replied, looking up at his wiggling toes. He turned his head on the footrest of the reclining chair, rolling his eyes up until his lanky friend was visible.

"You!" Ander replied. "Cory, you're the top student our year, class head, top Çeren index. You ought to have the top younger student to tutor. And Kim asks you to take on this kid everybody says is your father's catamite! Have you any idea how that's going to look?"

"That's the down side," Coryn admitted lazily. "There *are* plusses."

"Such as?"

Coryn studied the constellations he'd used to decorate the ceiling. "Tutorial's graded on how much improvement your tutee makes, not on absolute achievement. Say what else you like about Kim, he's good at evaluating students' abilities—and he says Roi's about as smart as he's seen. He just doesn't have any background. I can handle that a lot better than stupidity or lack of motivation." Well, he was guessing on the motivation. But he remembered the boy who'd beaten him in the horse race a year earlier. Even if the youngster wasn't cooperative, Cory might at least find out what was going on. His father might be the world's worst practical joker, but this whole mess just didn't feel like him.

Ander made a rude noise and continued to pace the room, obviously not believing a word Coryn had said.

Coryn sighed and capitulated. "Xazhar K'Zhaim has made up his mind that the kid's not going to make it," he said.

Ander stopped short and slowly perched on something that might have served as a chair to some inhuman species. "Now that," he said after a moment's pause, "makes sense. I wouldn't mind thwarting Xazhar myself. Need any help?"

"Maybe after I've figured out what's going on. He's due any minute."

"And you want me out," Ander grinned as he unfolded himself and headed for the door. "Let me know how it goes. Hey!" Suddenly his voice was both angry and concerned.

Coryn did a hasty back somersault off the recliner, spun and headed for the door. One glance showed him an empty float chair bobbing against the wall and two students kicking at a third, who lay curled up on the floor. Ander was already wading into the fight, if it could be dignified by that name, and Coryn followed.

"Malar! Sheeran! A fair fight's one thing, but there's no excuse for this! You're on report, both of you." Xazhar wasn't actually there, but Coryn had no doubt who was really to blame. He took a quick glance at the boy on the floor, once the other two moved away. He couldn't be sure that the deep, freely bleeding cut over the kid's right eye was the only damage, but it looked to be the most serious. "Get his float chair, Ander," he said, "and if I catch you two pulling something like this again, I'll do more than report you to Kim."

"Then tell your father to get his fancy-boy out of here," Sheeran shouted back over his shoulder.

Coryn ignored him, kneeling instead by the boy on the floor. The cut was no longer visible, hidden by blood-soaked hair, and the boy was slowly uncurling. "You all right?" Cory asked.

The youngster raised his head—cautiously—but did not lift his eyes. "I'm all right," he said.

"Sure?" Cory asked dubiously. "Have you got enough feeling to tell?"

"Kharfun doesn't affect the sensory nerves, just the motor nerves." It sounded to Cory like something heard over and over, and repeated automatically. But Kharfun? Humans weren't affected that way by Kharfun. He lifted the twitching form into the chair, startled by how little the boy weighed and the way the bones seemed to be poking through the skin.

The boy gasped as Coryn pushed the chair through the door. "So now what's bothering you?" Coryn asked, fully expecting to hear something about the room's eclectic decoration.

"It doesn't buzz in here," came the shaky reply. "Please, how do you do that?"

Buzz? Could the kid possibly be talking about the suppresser field? "This?" he said, and flipped off the room shield. Roi nodded as the shield went off, but his face remained expressionless.

Coryn was beginning to feel as if he were the one being kicked in the head. Kharfun, and now this? He was sure he recognized the boy as one of his father's slaves, though he'd been careful not to mention that fact to the other students. But there were no more than twenty-five of the three-hundred-odd students at Tyndall who were even aware of the suppresser field as anything other than a barrier against picking answers out of another's mind, and all of that group were High R'il'noids. "Who *are* you?" he demanded as he crossed the room to turn the shield back on manually.

"I don't *know*," came the answer, shaky with frustration. Almost at the same time, Ander spoke from across the room.

"Cory, where do you keep your first aid kit?"

Coryn shut his eyes for a moment, forcing himself to be calm. "Aid kit's in my gym bag," he said carefully. "Now, Roi, would you mind explaining why you don't know who you are? I mean, who we are's pretty obvious to most of us."

Roi's head stayed down as he answered. "I've been a slave all my life," he said. "Then I got sick—I don't really remember much about that—and when I woke up Nik said I wasn't a slave. But a lot of the stuff he told me—things just don't *happen* that way. Not in real life."

Coryn grabbed on to the one thing he recognized. "Nik? Nik Tarlian? Describe him!"

"Red hair, freckles, not very big and he didn't look very old, though I think he was. Eyes light green with a tracery of gold. He said I had to come here because he couldn't keep me and Florian both."

That certainly rang true. Coryn couldn't see anyone but a near-saint like Nik getting along with Florian. "Ander," he called as he walked back over to the computer and began entering Nik's access code, "get him cleaned up, will you? I'm going to ask Nik about this."

Nik looked harried, rushed, and generally disinclined to visit, so Coryn didn't waste time on formalities. "Need to know, Nik. A student here, named Roi. I'm supposed to tutor him."

Nik looked startled and glanced downward. "You're not on a secure line, Cory."

Secure line? That sounded like Roi was a lot more important than just his father's slave—and also helped explain why his father hadn't said anything to Coryn. But Nik was continuing.

"I've been trying for months to get through to him who he is. I'm not sure I've succeeded. Even his father couldn't seem to make any connection with him. If you can help him—well, your uncle, your father and I will all be grateful. And make sure he eats enough. He was starting a growth spurt when he left here." He glanced to the side of the pickup, swore briefly and vanished.

Coryn turned away from the holoscreen. Ander was cleaning the last of the blood from Roi's hair and face, exposing a forehead where no cut was visible. "Roi," Cory said, "who did Nik say was your father? And look at me."

"Bad manners for a slave," Ander commented. "My father would have half killed a slave who looked him in the eye."

"And bad manners for a half-bred not to look another R'il'noid in the eye. Roi?"

Reluctantly, the boy raised his eyes. "He said Lai was. But that's …"

"Unlikely, on the surface. But only two of Tarl's half-bred sons were R'il'noids, my father and Nik. He didn't say "'one of your uncles,'" he said "'your uncle'" as if I'd know who—and that has to be Lai, Tarl's only pure R'il'nian son. Roi, Nik's not only my uncle, one of my first memories is Mom taking me over to visit him. We're neighbors. And I've never caught him in a lie. He doesn't approve of Dad's practical jokes, either. You're exactly who he said you were—Lai's son, a half-bred. And if you're paralyzed from Kharfun, and picking up the suppresser field, you're probably R'il'noid."

Roi was looking at him now. "Coryn," he asked tentatively, "does that mean I'm supposed to ask questions, too?"

"Yes," Coryn replied. "I'm supposed to be helping you learn. I can't help you learn unless I know what you don't know, and I can't know what you don't know unless you ask me about it." He paused, trying to work out whether he'd said what he intended, but neither Roi nor Ander seemed to have any problems.

"If you've been taught to be a slave, there'll be an awfully lot you'll have to unlearn," Ander said. "Starting with looking people in the eye, and asking questions. Body language—right now you're so awkward it's hard to tell, but I bet you say, "I'm a slave" with every move you make. You need to stand tall, and stride out like you expect people to get out of your way."

"That," Roi said, with more spirit than Coryn had seen yet, "can wait until I can walk at all. Did I hear Nik say to make sure I got enough to eat?"

Coryn grinned and reached for a tube of honey. "You used esper to heal that forehead cut, didn't you," he said. Then, as Roi's head started to drop, "No, don't act like you're ashamed of it. But you need extra food if you're using esper. Especially carbohydrates. Eat that—all of it." He watched, still amused, as the boy—his cousin, he realized suddenly—gulped down the sweet, sticky stuff, and then he remembered, with less amusement, how thin Roi was. "Eating with Xazhar spoiling your appetite?" he asked.

"Sort of," Roi replied through a last mouthful of honey. "Mostly it's that—what'd you call it? The suppresser field? It makes it really hard for me to lift the food to my mouth. I've been trying to move food straight from the platter to my stomach, but it's not working very well. Gives me a stomach ache."

This time Coryn couldn't stop his mouth from dropping open in shock. "You're teleporting food right into your stomach?" he managed to gulp. "No," he added hastily as Roi's head started to drop again, "it's not *wrong*. It's just horribly dangerous. How are you *doing* it?" he added, as curiosity overruled his caution.

"I make a very tiny pocket in my stomach and sort of teleport the food into it in a continuous stream. It's hard, especially through this suppresser field. But if the food's at the same height as my stomach, it's easier than lifting my arms."

Ander's face had taken on a speculative look. "Saliva," he said. "I bet that's why you're getting a stomach ache. Digestion starts in the mouth, with saliva, and you're bypassing that."

"No!" Coryn exploded. "Don't encourage him, Ander. Roi, if you need more food I'll get it for you. You can eat in here, where the suppresser field is shielded out. But promise me you won't do any more teleports involving your own body until you've learned how to do it properly. Please?"

"Couldn't you teach me?"

"Roi, all I know about that kind of teleporting is that it's dangerous if you don't have the background training, and I'm not that far yet. And I can't ask my father because he's in over his head trying to do your father's job on top of his own. I'll see you get enough food. Just please, don't go fooling around with teleporting until you know how." He paused to think for a moment. "Uh—if you can't even get food to your mouth, how are you getting your homework into the computer?"

"Mostly I'm not. I do as much as I can, but I can't do very much at a stretch. I get too hungry, and I'm out of candy."

"Use my terminal," Coryn suggested. "It's legitimate, as long as I'm tutoring you, and it'll get you out of the suppresser field. Stupid setup, if you ask me, but Nebol's paranoid about students cheating by picking answers out of other students' brains. As if there weren't other ways to cheat. Anyway, R'il'noids can get shields if they're bothered. What's your Çeren index, and we'll start the application process."

Roi moved his chair over in front of the holoscreen before answering. "I don't know. I don't think Nik does, either. He said the test was no good because I just got over Kharfun. What is the Çeren index, anyway? Everybody here talks about it, but nobody ever explains why it's important."

Coryn snagged the chair he normally used at the terminal and dragged it over beside Roi's float chair. Ander came over to stand behind them. "It's used to rank crossbreds," Coryn explained as he sat down. "Measures the fraction of active genes that are R'il'nian-derived. Pure R'il'nians are one-forty-four. Pure Humans run from about two to eight—all Humans have some R'il'nian ancestry way back. Crossbreds start out with both sets of genes, but they lose some and others are inactivated because they've got two mechanisms for the same process. It's sort of random, so a first-generation crossbred can be anywhere from all R'il'nian to all Human. You never see either extreme, of course. If you score seventy-two or better, you're R'il'noid. If you've got lots of inactivated R'il'nian genes, you could have R'il'noid kids but not be R'il'noid yourself. That's called a latent. They're under genetics board control, like the R'il'noids. One-oh-eight or better's High R'il'noid—automatically on the Outer Council. I'm in that group, and so's Xazhar. Nik isn't, but I'll take him over a lot of the High R'il'noids any day. One-twenty or above—there's less than twenty, and they make up the Inner Council."

"So I could be crossbred but still have a low Çeren index?" Roi asked.

"Çeren's not perfect," Coryn replied. "Father grumbles about it all the time. Says Kaia should be on top, and Zhaim a lot lower than he is. Something about the test not caring whether the R'il'nian genes code for eye color or brain organization. But it is objective, and it does correlate with R'il'nian talents. You won't be low—not if you can teleport food through the suppresser field and if Kharfun affected you that badly."

"Oh," Roi replied. His face was wooden as always, but Coryn had decided that his lack of expression was an after-effect of the Kharfun.

"Now," he said briskly, "do you know how to use a mental interface?"

"I don't want a computer reading my mind!"

Coryn blinked in surprise. "If you've got control enough to use a mental interface, you'd feel any reading it tried, and be able to block it. Has anyone tried to read your mind in the past?"

"Most of my owners. Not your father; that's one of the reasons I didn't want him to sell me. Xazhar."

"It's a moral issue for Father. If you're a telepath, you don't invade another mind without explicit permission. But telepaths can and do 'talk' to each other mind to mind. If Xazhar's trying to read you without your consent, that's immoral by the rules I've learned. But I really think a mental interface would be a lot easier for you." Coryn hesitated. He'd learned telepathic manners as a small child. Roi rather obviously had not, and he wasn't sure how the young ex-slave would react to his suggestion. But he thought that what he had in mind would reassure, rather than frighten Roi.

"Would you let me probe at you?" he asked. "Not to read your mind, just to check how sensitive you are to attempted probes, and how strong your shields are. If you feel me, say so. If I'm pushing too hard, tell me, and I'll back off."

Was there a trace of amusement in the boy's emotional aura? Or was Coryn simply responding to his own frustration at the lack of mobility in Roi's features? "Go ahead," Roi said. "There! I felt you."

Coryn blinked in surprise. That probe had been a preliminary test, not one he had expected Roi to feel. Was the boy guessing? His suspicion vanished as he continued, being careful to keep his timing random and give no physical clues. It was a game he'd played with his father, as part of his own early training, and he thought he was good at it. But he wasn't even sure he felt Roi, yet the younger boy was calling every attempted probe.

"No wonder the suppresser field bothers you," he said after a few minutes. "You don't have to worry about the mental interface reading anything you don't send it. At least not without your knowing it. Mind if I increase the pressure? I want to check your shields."

When Roi gave reluctant agreement, Coryn hardened his probe, reaching for Roi's surface thoughts. No obvious shields. Frustration at his partial paralysis, of course, and anxiety at his problems in keeping up with his lessons. A kind of shy admiration for—Xazhar? Coryn blinked in surprise, then suddenly realized that something was missing—there was no trace of Roi's sensitivity to the suppresser field. Suspicious, he concentrated on Roi's emotions—harder to read than thoughts—and again picked up a faint trace of amusement, this time mixed with a little—smugness?

"That," he said admiringly, "is the best smokescreen shield I've ever seen. If you can do that, you don't have to worry about a mental interface. Want some advice?"

The smugness vanished, replaced by chagrin. "Yes. How could you tell?"

"Well, for one thing, Father's not likely to be attracted to anyone who's dumb enough to be taken in that way by Xazhar. Then I'd just been talking to you, knew how bothered you were by the suppresser field, and I couldn't pick up a thing on that. Finally—I'm hardly an expert empath, but I can pick up emotions a little. Yours weren't matching your thoughts. No!" he added as the chagrin was suddenly replaced by blankness. "Don't turn your emotional broadcast off completely. That's really going to make an empath look twice at you, especially given that unemotional face of yours. Just make the broadcast emotions match the thoughts in your smokescreen. Now, can you read my mind, at least the part I hold open to you?"

"Is that all right?"

"The rules I learned—and don't take it for granted everyone plays by the rules—are that it's all right to mind-share with another telepath if you're careful not to do any damage or go any deeper than they're willing. You don't go into a non-telepath's mind unless you've got clear, unforced permission or it's a life-or-death emergency. In this case it's perfectly all right—we're both telepaths, and I'm asking you to contact my mind because it's the easiest way to show you how to use a mental interface and set up permission for you to use mine."

Coryn was vaguely aware, as he waited for Roi's response, that Ander was moving away to sink into the recliner. Most of his attention was taken up with preparing himself for Roi's contact. Other minds always felt different, grating on his own personality. An experienced and considerate telepath, like his father or Nik, was able to adjust his mind to minimize the discomfort, but a totally untrained telepath like Roi? Coryn was braced, but at the same time he did not want to give the youngster the idea that the invited contact was unwelcome.

Amazingly, it was not. Roi's mind touch was by far the least obtrusive Coryn had ever experienced. "You have an even softer mind-touch than Nik," he said, "and he's really good. Now, just follow my mind and watch what I do. Once you're using the interface properly, we'll call up some of your homework and find out what your problem is."

The next half hour passed so swiftly that Coryn was aware of nothing in the room. Roi was bothered a little by the mental interface—not nearly as much, he assured Coryn, as he was bothered by the suppresser field. He learned to use it quickly, though, and Coryn rapidly decided that his academic problems were due entirely to his inability to get his answers into the computer. "You don't need nearly the tutoring in your classes that you do in not being a slave," Coryn told him when they finally broke the mental bond. "Ander, he's really good. Ander?"

The gangling redhead was slumped in the recliner, eyes closed and a decidedly greenish tint overlying his fair complexion. "One of your headaches?" Cory asked sympathetically.

"Yes." Ander spoke very softly, as if the sound of his own voice might make the headache worse. "Medicine's back in my room."

"Can I help?" Roi asked unexpectedly. "I used to be able to make Flame's headaches go away."

Coryn glanced down at Roi, remembering the healed forehead cut. He couldn't recall even hearing about esper healing, but then there was a lot of esper stuff he hadn't been taught yet. "He's got a really soft touch," he told Ander.

"Anything's better than this," Ander whispered. "And Nik's stuff will put me out for the rest of the day. Go ahead and try, Roi."

"Better eat this," Coryn warned Roi as he dug out another tube of honey. "Carbohydrate before esper work, protein after. That much I *do* know. I'll squeeze it into your mouth; you just keep swallowing."

Roi moved the float chair over to the recliner and laid his hand on Ander's—and this time, Coryn was sensitized enough to realize how much that simple movement cost the boy. Ander's eyes opened wide in brief shock. Surprised by Roi's touch, Coryn thought, and was surprised himself by how fast normal color and a broad grin returned to Ander's face.

"It's gone," the redhead said happily. "No flashing lights, no nausea, no pain. And no sleepiness, either. How long will it last, Roi?"

"Until you'd normally get the next one, I think. There's something wrong with the blood vessels in your head, but I don't know enough to fix that. But you should be fine for the rest of today, anyway."

Coryn crossed the room to the stasis cabinet, and rummaged through it for a container of his mother's custard. Only one left? He hesitated for a moment. The custard was exactly what Roi needed, but Mom's food packages only came once a month, and it was three fivedays until the next was due. He glanced back at Roi, confirming how thin the kid was and the greenish color of his skin, and suddenly grinned. He knew his mother, and he was pretty sure of the effect of a com message about his starving, motherless tutee. "Here," he said as he pulled out the last container. "Better eat this."

Roi

9/7/35

"All right, class dismissed," the instructor said, and added, "Roi, please stay for a couple of minutes."

Now what had he done, Roi wondered as he watched the other five students leave. This was a new math instructor, his fifth in the month and a half since Coryn's tutorials had started, and he didn't yet know the man well enough to judge whether he was in trouble.

"You're putting in all of your homework from your tutor's terminal." The accusation that Coryn's help was beyond tutoring was not voiced, but the suspicion was clear.

Roi relaxed a little. Cory had warned him that this would probably happen, even as he urged Roi to start challenging for more advanced classes. "Yes, sir," he agreed, following the line his tutor had suggested. "I have problems getting stuff into the terminal in my room. I'm still paralyzed from having Kharfun syndrome, and I have to use telekinesis to operate my terminal. And they won't let me have a room shield, because the aftereffects of the Kharfun won't let them get a Çeren index on me. Coryn has a shielded room and a mental interface, so it's a lot easier for me to use his."

The instructor's eyebrows rose, and he blew his cheeks in and out a few times. The buzzing in Roi's head abruptly stopped, and he TK'd what he hoped was a relieved smile onto his face. "Yes, that feels much better," he said.

The instructor looked hard at Roi. "I don't have the same type of interface that Coryn does," he said, "but if you can operate his you should be able to use this. I want you to enter your homework here today." He reached into a cupboard and pulled out a caplike contrivance that suddenly turned into a ball of light in his hands.

Once again, Roi was grateful for Coryn's coaching. He'd never used this type of interface, but he was able to recognize the light ball, and knew that using it would not be too different from using Cory's interface. He allowed the instructor to place the glowing sphere on—no, through—his head and did his best to ignore the golden haze around him.

The first seven problems were easy, and while the new interface felt harsher than Coryn's, Roi had no trouble working out and entering the answers. The eighth took some thinking, and the ninth—*derive* the formula for the volume of a sphere?

Roi knew the formula—they were studying areas and volumes, and he'd learned the formulas for areas and volumes of a good many shapes in the last fiveday. Coryn had told him that the formulas came from dividing the volume or area into much smaller, calculable pieces and adding them up, but he'd been vague about the details. What was the best way to divide up a sphere?

Not cubes. It was easy to calculate the volume of those, but figuring out how many cubes went into a sphere was not so easy. None of the other regular solids would pack well, and—wait a minute. How about pyramids, with all of their points together at the center of the sphere? He knew the formula for the volume of a pyramid—a third of the base area times the height. And—yes! All of the bases would add up to the area of the sphere, and he knew the formula for that! Of course, his instructor might ask him to go a step farther and explain where the formulas for the volume of the pyramid and the area of the sphere had come from.

Instead, his instructor rubbed the side of his nose with his finger and muttered, "You'd think after all the years I've been teaching I'd know when to ignore what students say. That's very good, Roi, and you've already done today's homework, plus a couple of problems I won't be giving the rest of the students. That last one was very elementary calculus, by the way. You don't have the background to handle it without the memorized formulas yet, but your basic approach was correct. I'll put a notation on your record so you won't be bothered by this next time you move up. Dismissed."

Another of Xazhar's pinpricks, Roi thought resentfully as he headed back to his room. He considered heading straight for Coryn's room rather than being any later for his tutorial, but his legs were cramping badly in this rainy, cold weather, and he wanted to rub them with a few of the gold-dusted peacemint leaves. A good whiff of the clean, spicy fragrance of the purple-haired, turquoise-veined peacock plant wouldn't hurt, either—he was still upset by the detention, benign though it had turned out to be.

In fact, the calming odors of both plants were generally a good idea before Coryn's room. He'd thought of some changes he could make in his own room, once he'd found out that such changes were allowed, but he hadn't yet come up with a tactful way of telling Coryn he did not want his help in that particular project. Cory's favorite recliner, for instance, was covered with fake fur in violently clashing shades of chartreuse and magenta. At least Roi hoped the fur was fake. He couldn't imagine any animal tasteless enough to grow such a covering.

He was almost in front of the door to his room before he noticed that it was very slightly cracked open. The cleaning robots. He was sure he had latched the door and toggled the privacy switch when he'd left for classes. Too annoyed to feel ahead for danger, he sent the chair through the door.

Someone had trashed his room. The north window, where the peacemint and peacock plant normally struggled for light, was empty. Shards of their brightly glazed pots were mixed with dirt and torn plant fragments on the floor and bed.

Stunned, he moved his chair forward. He'd never before had anything of his own, even his body. Nik had potted the plants after he'd caught Roi in his herb garden during a near miss by a tropical storm, and then insisted that he take the flourishing herbs with him to Tyndall. For the last month Roi had been fighting the growing dullness of the north window, and fretting over the plants' health. But this!

He was so focused on trying to find some salvageable living piece that the attack came as a total surprise, throwing him out of the chair and slamming his head against a corner of the bed. After that, events were a chaotic blur. He was sharply aware only of his own brain and the need to control swelling and keep the neural network intact. What happened to the rest of his body was unimportant.

By the time he came totally back to himself, he was sprawled on the floor, alone, with a shard of broken pot cutting into his cheek. His whole body ached, and the buzzing in his head nauseated him. He checked out his body, Healing a few bruises with more than the usual difficulty, and realized that he had been raped. That was something he thought had ended with his slavery, and he flung the evidence away in disgust.

His head ached worse than ever after that, and it took him a while to realize that the pounding and shouting at the door were not inside his head. Coryn? He must be hours late for his tutorial by now! But he couldn't seem to figure out how to open the door, or even to tell Coryn to go away.

He must have blanked out then, because the next thing he was aware of was intense sweetness in his mouth, and Coryn's voice ordering him to swallow. He didn't want to—the nausea was worse, and he was sure that if he did manage to swallow, the stuff would come right back up. But his mouth was being held shut, and shoving the sticky sweetness down the tube that led to his stomach was the fastest way to get rid of the taste in his mouth.

"Attaboy," Coryn said. "Keep swallowing. I know. Sweet tastes awful at first. You're in esper shock. Kim's contacted the infirmary, and there'll be a medic here soon. But honey's the fastest treatment, if you can swallow at all."

Esper shock? The world was coming back, and he swallowed another mouthful of honey, suddenly attracted rather than repelled by the taste. His empathic shields had vanished, and he was sharply aware of Kim's anger and concern, and of Coryn's frantic worry. More than that—Coryn genuinely cared about him. Roi wasn't sure how to react to that. He had always assumed their friendship was of the enemy-of-my-enemy variety, and he'd been comfortable with that. The idea that Coryn genuinely liked him, for himself, was new and frightening.

He swallowed another mouthful of honey and opened his eyes as a medic carrying a cocoon came through the door. "Partly esper shock," Coryn told the man. "He's swallowing honey all right, so he should be over that soon. But he ought to be in a shielded room. He has problems with the suppresser field."

"Yes," Kim agreed. "Don't bother contacting Nebol. You know what a fanatic he is for paperwork."

The medic nodded in agreement and ran his eyes over Roi's body. Roi was suddenly aware that his clothing had been torn half off, and his head was in a pile of dirt. And he was *cold*. He'd better rebuild his empathic shields before the medic's presence became intolerable. At least the cocoon the man was wrapping around his body was warm.

✻   ✻   ✻   ✻

"You healed yourself except for that lump on the head, didn't you." Coryn's voice was accusing.

Roi looked up from the infirmary bed, surprised. "You said it was all right."

"Yeah, but you did such a thorough job the infirmary couldn't find any evidence of anything except you hit your head on the bed. Malar and Sheeran, wasn't it? I saw them coming out of your building when I was going in, looking *very* pleased with themselves."

Roi thought back, but felt only a fresh pang of loss at the destruction of the plants. "I was so shaken up by the state the room was in that I don't know who attacked me. They—they killed my plants."

Coryn dropped into the bedside chair, shaking his head. "They raped you—they did, didn't they? And all you're worried about is your plants. Roi, sometimes you are weird."

"I've been raped lots of times—what do you think being a slave is all about? But I've never had anything of my own before."

Cory grimaced and sighed. "I don't own slaves, and neither does Mom. And I think Father agrees with your father that it'd be a good thing if slavery were illegal on Central. But I don't think I ever realized before I met you just how—corrosive—it could be. I'll contact Nik, now I've got a medical report to send him, and ..."

"No!" Roi exploded. It was bad enough that Coryn knew how stupid he'd been, eliminating the evidence of the attack. He didn't want Nik to know, too.

"Please, Cory, promise me you won't tell him. I feel so stupid about cleaning myself up, and now there's no proof anything happened except maybe I fell down …"

"Sooner or later, he'll find out."

"Later? Please?"

Coryn groaned and closed his eyes briefly. "All right," he said finally, "on two conditions. One—you can reach me just about anywhere at school, can't you? Well, if anything like this even starts to happen again, you contact me. Immediately! Agreed?"

He wasn't going to budge on that, Roi sensed. Could he do it? He reached out through the suppresser field, and found he could locate Ander and Kim, and, somewhat to his surprise, Xazhar, in a towering rage. "I guess so," he said. "You'd have to be listening for me, though."

"All right," Coryn said. "Second, how'd you manage to—uh—'get rid of the evidence?'"

Roi looked at him with surprise. "Ported it away. Same as the food, only backwards."

"Where to?"

"Well, I aimed it at Xazhar's bed. Only I don't think my control was very good just then. I'm pretty sure I got his quarters, though."

Coryn stared at him for a moment, wide eyed. Then he began to shake and even choke, and after a moment Roi realized he was trying not to burst out laughing.

"It's not that funny," Roi protested.

"You weren't at supper," Coryn replied. "Xazhar was late, one eye looked swollen, and he was generally disheveled—like he'd had to 'fresh and change clothes at the last possible minute. And he was furious! Started tearing into his own clique like he figured they were responsible. You got his room all right—probably right where he slipped on it. Malar and Sheeran may not have been expelled over this, like they deserve to be, but they sure aren't getting off entirely. Be careful around him, Roi. He'll never believe you could do something like that, but he's in a pretty nasty mood. Lucky he's taking it out on the people he figures have access to his room." He snickered as he rose. "Anyway, I'm glad you have some normal instincts. See you tomorrow."

"Tomorrow" turned out to be late in the afternoon, after the infirmary staff finally decided that Roi did not have a serious concussion. "Not that I got off lessons," Roi grumbled as he guided his chair alongside Cory to the infirmary door. "They got all the class notes to me, and then every one of my instructors showed up to make sure I understood them. And piles of homework, and they didn't have a mental interface at the infirmary, so I just had to do the answers in my head. Can I use your interface this evening, Coryn?" Then Roi saw what lay outside the door, and forgot all about homework.

White flakes were drifting down from a dark gray sky, forming lacy tables on the grass and fluffy balls on the bushes. The paths were clear—part of the same weather shielding that kept them dry when it rained—but Roi sent his chair as close to the edge of the path as he could, and reached through the weather shield to the white stuff. It was cold, and when he pulled his hand back, he found that the weightless stuff turned to a few drops of water in his hand. "It's ice," he said wonderingly.

"Snow," Coryn corrected him. "Rain started turning to snow 'bout an hour ago. Roi, you've seen snow before. Haven't you?"

"I was a pleasure slave, a house slave. I never saw weather 'til your father bought me, and it was never this cold at his place." He looked around in wonder as they moved along the path. It was almost dark, even though it was not yet suppertime, and the flakes were clear in the lights. This was what he was named for? He'd noticed even before meeting Coryn that the oppressive heat was fading, but now he was really glad for the jacket Coryn had brought from his room and insisted he wear. "After I put my homework in, do you think I could find out a little more about this kind of weather?" he asked.

Coryn nodded as he opened the door to Roi's building. "I got mine in early," he said, "soon as Ander and I finished cleaning up your room. Kim let us in. Nik sent you some stuff, by the way. We went ahead and opened it up for you."

"Coryn! You promised!"

"Promised I wouldn't tell him about the attack yesterday. I didn't. But I did tell him your plants weren't doing well in that north window." He moved aside so that Roi could palm the door open.

Roi sent his chair into the room, trying not to look at the empty window. Something different—he looked unbelievingly at the shelf that was supposed to serve him as a desk. Three plants—two smaller and bushier versions of the two he'd lost, and a third laden with fragrant bloom. All three were in a reflective, open-fronted box that shone into the room like sunshine. He moved his chair closer, afraid that the vision would vanish as he approached, but the plants were real, the flowers sending their fragrance though the room. He brushed the leaves of the peacemint and peacock plant telekinetically, and breathed deeply of the mingled scents of mint, citrus, lavender and cloves, with an added sweetness from the flowers. When he turned to thank Coryn, the older boy was gone.

✶   ✶   ✶   ✶

Roi did try to say his thanks that evening, but Coryn was playing a board game with Ander and simply waved him toward the computer interface. "Get your homework in," he ordered, "and then we can talk."

That didn't take long, as Roi had already worked out what he wanted to enter. He glanced toward the older students when he'd finished, confirming that they were both still engrossed in their game. Pattern chess. He went back to the computer briefly, checking what information it had on snow, and then turned back to watch the game. Pattern chess was almost as prestigious a sport among the more intellectual students as plasmaball was among Xazhar's group, and Coryn was one of the best players at Tyndall.

"Gotcha," Coryn said at last, and Ander leaned back and rotated his neck, eyes closed.

"You can't give me enough of a handicap to make it an even game," he said. "Hey, Roi, why don't you learn? Give me a break from getting beaten. Maybe we could even double up against him."

"Why not?" Coryn grinned. "Finished putting in your homework? Come on over, then. I could use a review of the basics, and you've got the abilities."

Ander pulled back the thing he'd been sitting on, and Roi moved his float chair into its place. Cory had shoved most of the colored tiles into a loose pile, and picked out two red and two white pieces. "We'll start with a level one game," he said as he arranged the pieces in a square, the two red tiles on Roi's left, the white ones on his right. "This is the starting pattern. We each have a goal pattern, from rearranging the starting pattern. Yours is to have your lower left and upper right red, and the other two white. Mine is the opposite. It wouldn't even be a game in the non-esper version, with alternate tile swaps—the first player would always win. But in the esper version you don't touch the tiles except mentally, both players go at once, and you have to hold your pattern for three seconds to win. The struggle is strictly for control of the tiles—you can't contact the other player's mind directly. The computer will give us an audible starting tone. Got it?"

Roi reached mentally for the tiles. It sounded simple enough—hold down the two tiles closest to him, interchange the other two. "Got it," he repeated.

When the computer gave its starting ping, Roi shifted his tiles as he had planned, hardly aware of opposition. Coryn cleared his throat and said, "That's good. Now let's try a level two."

Levels two and three—four and eight squares on a side, respectively, went the same way. Coryn looked stunned, and Ander had both hands plastered over his mouth. "Did I do something wrong?" Roi asked uncertainly.

"You're about an order of magnitude better'n either of us expected, that's all," Ander chortled. "Sure you've never played before?"

"I don't think so," Coryn said. "He feels like he's learning as he goes along. But he's strong—well, I guess he'd have to be, working through the suppresser field. Roi, let's try a real level four game, with the computer figuring the starting and goal patterns. It's pretty hard for a person to set up the patterns—unless they're as simple as the stripe-check we've been using—so they come out with equal moves for both players, but the computer's set up to do it, and put the tiles in their starting positions. Can you handle a two hundred fifty-six tile grid?"

"I can try. How long do I get to study the patterns?"

"Five minutes."

Time enough, Roi thought. He identified the teleports he would need to make, felt out the tiles, and set the jumps in his mind. When the computer beeped, he got all but eight of the tiles where he needed them on the first try. The remaining eight seemed glued down, and he had to pry them away mentally to put them into place, exchanging only one pair at a time. When he raised his eyes again, Coryn's mouth was hanging open, and Ander was in the recliner, doubled up in silent laughter.

"I haven't been beaten that thoroughly since the last time I played my father," Coryn said.

"Maybe the two of you together could beat him," Ander managed to choke out between fits of laughter.

Coryn looked thoughtful, but before he could answer, the com buzzed for attention. The holoscreen lit up with Nik's smiling face.

"Go with it, Coryn," he said. "The other two think it's a marvelous idea and why didn't we think of that. I took the liberty of walking over and making sure your mother knew the whole story. She's even agreed—reluctantly—to allow your father on the place if certain conditions are met. Roi?"

Roi moved his chair over in front of the pickup. "I'm here, sir. Thank you very much for sending the plants and the lights and everything."

Nik snorted in depreciation. "Should have realized you'd have problems with the dull winters at Tyndall. Got snow yet? We're having a beautiful late spring here. Glad you hooked up with Cory. I want you to know that what he'll be suggesting is fine with all of your guardians. It's up to you whether you want to see Derry—he's stayed away to let you get used to not being a slave. For that matter, it's up to you whether you accept Cory's invitation. Personally, I hope you do—but the decision is up to you." He winked and vanished.

Roi turned to Coryn, completely lost. "Cory, what's he talking about?"

Coryn looked smug. "You planning on anything special over the holidays?" he asked. "Break's less than a month away, you know."

"Just stay here, I guess. Xazhar's staying, too." That frightened him a little. Xazhar was bad enough busy with classes and plasmaball. Xazhar with nothing to do …

"Well, you're invited to come home with me. Ander most always comes. Anyway, Mom loves company she can mother. I had to wait until I was sure it was all right with your guardians, though. Wasn't much help your not knowing who they were, but I figured Nik would know." He grinned. "Nik is, of course—thought he would be. And my father, and Kaia. You don't have to see my father, of course, but Ander's right. You and me together just might be able to surprise him at pattern chess. Game to try?"

Go home with Cory? Get away from Xazhar, and the constant struggle to look as if he could use his body, and the buzzing in his head? Roi wasn't sure he really wanted to see Derik—but he'd been afraid for months to say anything about his old friends. He hadn't wanted to risk leaving himself open to control through Timi, and Amber, and Flame. Derik already knew of that friendship, and he would certainly know what had happened to the three.

"I'd love to come," he whispered to Coryn, so overcome he could hardly manage the sound.

Derik

9/29/35

"A little more to the left—ai! No, don't stop, that's it." Derik closed his eyes and tried to relax under Midnight's massage. Trouble was, if he really relaxed he'd be asleep in seconds, and he had to think out what to say to the Karlain and Unber delegates. Maybe, he thought groggily, he'd be better off giving up and just letting himself get some sleep. Otherwise, he was apt to doze off during the negotiation session.

He had almost decided in favor of a nap when another mind touched his.

Derry?

Kaia. What now? He ran over a lengthening mental list of possible disasters.

We need to talk.

Face to face? Sure. He sent her his location, and felt Midnight stiffen as she appeared in the room. *Still not used to teleports,* he thought. *I'll have to do something about that.*

Kaia sank into the largest of the room's chairs. She was easily a head taller than Derik, but otherwise she was a perfect, scaled-up version of her niece Elyra. *A chocolate statue,* Derik thought, *set off by a swirl of fabric in shades of gold and flame.* "Well?" he said, switching to R'Gal which Midnight would not understand.

"The Karlain-Unber situation."

Derik relaxed a little. *At least it wasn't a new emergency.* "It's not my kind of problem," he admitted. "You'd do a lot better, if only those patriarchs would listen to you."

"School vacation's coming up in a couple of days," Kaia said. "What are you doing about it?"

"What will I probably be doing, or what would I like to do? I don't see how I'll have more than a few minutes free, when I add the negotiations to my share of the routine stuff. What I'd like to do is spend some time with Cory and maybe with Roi. All we know about Roi at this point is third hand from what Cory's told Nik. And some of that doesn't quite square with some of the things I remember. I need to talk with Cory, and with Roi as well—at least as long as he's comfortable with me. A self-trained esper is always cause for worry. He's carrying enough R'il'nian genes to produce a high R'il'noid son. We need to know what we're dealing with. And with these damned negotiations, I don't know when I'm going to find the time. I'm so short of sleep I've practically fallen asleep over the negotiations twice already."

"If they'd accept me as negotiator, even temporarily?"

Derik jerked his head up, eliciting an indignant growl from Midnight. "You think that's possible?"

"Possible. Maybe even probable. You've been working with the delegates. I've been talking to their wives and checking over their history. You've had a problem because their beliefs are so much alike—and both societies are based on the importance of the nuclear family. It's more of a family quarrel than a war between conflicting belief systems—and I'm better at resolving family quarrels. The wives agree with that. And both cultures have a tradition of dropping everything—up to and including invasions—to clear up family problems."

"So if I tell them the truth—that it's very important that I talk with my son and nephew over the next few days, and that you as co-regent will be taking over the negotiations temporarily—they might agree?"

"No guarantees—but I think probably yes. The wives will be pushing in that direction, anyway."

"Kaia, if this works I owe you."

Kaia chuckled wickedly as she stood. "Let's wait and see if you really have the easier job," she replied.

10/1/35

Maybe easier, maybe not, Derik thought a couple of days later, but it was definitely the job he preferred. Even if it did involve getting up at three in the morning—and his internal clock insisted it was still no more than four—to teleport to Seabird Island, where Nik and Vara both lived, by noon local time. Even if Vara was looking at him with a distinctly jaundiced eye. Even if both boys were out riding one of Vara's horses. At least Vara hadn't run him off the place—yet.

The sun beat down on the deck around the swimming pool, and the turquoise waters of the lagoon were visible over the hedges that surrounded the area around the house. Horses grazed on the green pastures farther along the shore, and upslope, away from the water, trails led into the subtropical forest.

"You've done a nice job with this farm," he said cautiously. "Good stock, and a beautiful setup. No wonder Coryn rides so well."

"Coryn rides well because he likes it, because I got him started young, and because he gets regular lessons at Tyndall," she replied, as scrupulously polite as he was. "Derik, what is going on? First Nik asked me to invite Coryn's tutee for the holidays. Then the school authorities contacted me and warned me he was your catamite. Then Coryn said no, he's Lai's son, and ..."

"They said *what?*" Derik gasped, shaken out of his half doze. "The school, not Nik or Coryn."

She looked at him, a puzzled expression on her face. "The school head commed me two days ago and said that the boy was your catamite. That you'd twisted arms to get him into Tyndall. They didn't know why, especially since most of their students are R'il'noid."

Derik was shaking his head in disbelief. "I got him into Tyndall, yes. Because Lai asked me to. You know how busy he was with preparations for that search of his. I ... Look, you remember Cloudy? About sixteen years ago?"

"Yes." Vara looked down at her hands, lying on the table before her. "She was very much in love with Lai, and I thought he was in love with her. I never understood why they separated, why she just—disappeared."

"We may never know all of the reasons why," Derik replied. "But we do know—now—that she was pregnant. Whatever the genetics board did to prevent that, Lai unconsciously reversed it. We know that she left Lai a note asking him not to try to find her—and he honored that. We know that she tried to erase her identity, and as a result of that was kidnapped into slavery. Roi is her son and Lai's, born a slave, though never legally one. I bought him, as a slave dancer, almost two years ago. He came down with Kharfun syndrome and I called in Nik. That was almost a year ago, and I haven't seen him since."

He looked down at his hands, twisted together on the table. "I won't say he might not have wound up my catamite, if we hadn't found out who he was. I love him, and there are parts of that love you wouldn't accept. But Vara, I'm not the person I was when you first knew me. I'm not even the person I was a millennium ago. I will not betray Lai's trust by seducing his son. And I've never been the person you seem to think me, one who would seduce his own child."

In a way it would have been easier, he thought, if the Genetics Board had not insisted that she bear his child. But he could not find it in his heart to regret Coryn.

Vara lifted her head, her expression brightening as she looked to her left, upslope. "Here they come," she said.

Derik turned to follow her gaze, and smiled. The boys were just coming out of the forest. Coryn was bareback on an aged gray that picked its way carefully down the slope, Roi held firmly in front of him. Cory's friend Ander followed, somewhat over-mounted on an eager bay. Derik watched for a moment or two; then as the riders reached the end of the slope Cory looked up, waved, and urged his mount into a gentle lope.

Derik met the boys where the horse trail ran along the hedge that bordered the deck. "Father! You're here! Roi, swing your leg over. Catch," Cory said as he swung Roi down into Derik's arms. "Mom, thanks. Okay to just turn Cotton out in the pasture? She's cool enough."

Vara was already feeling ears and between the forelegs of both horses. "Yes on Cotton," she replied, "just run a brush over her back. Sponge Trapper and put him on one of the automatic walkers. And *walk* them over to the stable."

"Nik'll be here soon," Coryn called back over his shoulder as he and Ander turned toward the stable. "We saw him starting along the beach path."

Derik had already turned toward the chairs and table by the pool. Roi was limp in his arms, with no muscle tone at all, though he should have some, by now. And he was far too light in weight for his increased length, even lighter than Derik remembered from a year ago. "Aren't they feeding you anything?" he asked, trying to keep his tone light, as he sat and cradled the boy on his lap.

Roi turned his head to face Derik and seemed to be forcing himself to make eye contact. "Coryn's been feeding me. Are you really my uncle?" he asked.

"Yes," Derik replied, "and proud of it. Nik explained, didn't he? About Lai being your father?"

Roi's eyes dropped. "It just didn't seem to make sense. I mean, I remember my mother. She never said anything about that. Just said I had to hide my differences, or I'd be killed."

"I knew your mother," Vara said from across the table. "She was a lovely woman. But I don't think she wanted to think about why the Genetics Board wouldn't approve her for the crossbreeding project. I think Lai would have sided with her if she'd confided in him when she first realized she was pregnant, but she didn't understand the situation well enough to realize that you never had to hide. Once you were born, that skin pigment would have been enough to tell her you didn't have the genetic combination the Board was most afraid of. A Coven-affected wouldn't have had any pigment. You have the Coven gene—that's where your white hair comes from—but you have the protective gene as well."

Roi's body twitched in Derik's lap, more of a spasm than any intentional movement. When the boy lifted and turned his head, there was no movement in the neck tendons. Could Roi possibly be using levitation and telekinesis, skills he had never been taught, to move his body, and even to speak? That he might have such skills was no surprise, but surely he couldn't have learned to use them that well on his own! Derik was getting increasingly anxious for Nik's arrival when Roi spoke.

"Are Flame and Timi and Amber all right?"

Flame? Timi? Amber? Wait a minute. Sunset had said that Roi's name was Snowy, though Derik had called him Noon. "You mean your dancer friends?" he asked.

This time Roi did look him straight in the eye. "You called me 'Noon.' I had one owner that called me Cotton—same as the horse we were just riding. But my name is—was—Snowy. That's what my mother called me. Flame and Timi and Amber were what their mothers called them, too."

Derik flinched. He couldn't just start calling the three by what Roi said were their "real" names, not without explanations he wasn't quite ready to give them. But he'd better start thinking of them a little differently. "They're fine. Midnight—is that Timi?—was giving me a much-needed massage a couple of days ago. I think he's taller than you are, now. The girls—Flame would be the redhead, and Amber the blond, right?—are filling out, too. I've been trying to get them to learn to read and write, but I don't have much time free, and they don't seem very interested."

Roi's face remained still, but Derik had the feeling that the boy was laughing at him. "It's really all right if they learn?" he asked.

"Of course. But they don't seem to be able to get the idea. Roi, what's so funny?"

"Timi taught me to read, long before Nik said it was all right. They all know how. Timi knows most, because he was captured when he was about eight, so he had more time to learn. Amber's mother was a doctor, like Nik, but she was enslaved younger. Flame and I were slave-bred, but we learned a lot from Timi and Amber. They're not going to admit to you they can read, though."

And Derik didn't know because he'd never tried to read their minds. He'd relied entirely on conditional probability for his own safety.

"Can you set it up so they have access to the education programs on your computer behind your back?" Roi continued.

"If that's what it takes," he smiled down at the boy. "Your mother called you Snowy as a reflection of her name, didn't she."

"I think so. But I didn't really know what snow was until last month. I thought just white, like the horse we were riding today."

"Cloudy was a nickname, you know. Your mother's real name was Saroi. So you're still named after her."

Roi looked up at Derik, briefly, then buried his head in the man's shoulder. It still didn't feel right. The pressure of Roi's head against Derik's shoulder should have been balanced by increased pressure on the arm around the boy's back. Instead, it felt as if the boy's whole body was pressing into Derik.

He heard Nik's voice, light against the deeper background of the two boys' chatter, and looked up in relief. The three were coming through the gate, Nik dwarfed by Ander's lanky height and even a little shorter than Coryn. When had the two boys grown so tall? Well, it been almost a year since Derik had seen Ander, and he hadn't had that much time for Coryn last vacation, what with all he'd needed to do for Lai. And they changed so fast, at that age. He *had* to find time for Cory. And for Roi, if the younger boy would accept his attention. At the moment, though, he was more concerned about Roi's physical condition.

Nik, Derik 'pathed, unable to keep all the anxiety out of his mind-voice, *shouldn't he have better muscle tone, by now?*

Nik looked up, startled, and walked briskly across to join them. "Here, Roi," he said as he placed one of his hands on the boy's, and wrapped the other around Roi's upper arm. "Try to lift my hand."

Derik was uneasy, but couldn't analyze why. Nik's face changed as Roi lifted his hand. "Here," he said sharply, "let me see exactly what you're doing."

"Nik, don't," Derik started to say, as his own uneasiness blossomed into real fear, but it was too late. He was thrown backward, chair and all, while Nik went flying toward the house wall and a volcano seemed to erupt inside his head.

He found himself lying on his back in the ruins of the chair, with the noon sun beating though his closed eyelids. Nik? Roi? Coryn? Hysterical sobbing, intermixed with his own name and Nik's, was coming from the direction of the pool. He rolled his head to the side and forced his eyes open.

Vara was coming out of the door, her face white with shock. Nik was huddled on the ground next to the house wall. Derik tried to scramble to his feet, but the ground seemed to be spinning and tilting under him. He managed to pull himself to a sitting position and located the boys: Coryn with his head in his hands, sitting on the edge of the pool, and the other two sprawled on the patio, sopping wet. Roi was shaking violently, but all were breathing. He looked back toward Nik, and gasped with relief as his half -brother made an abortive attempt to rise.

"What happened?" Vara demanded, one hand massaging her temple while she clung to the wall with the other.

"Poltergeist reaction, I think," Derik replied. "We're all in esper shock, Vara. Can you get some food out here?" At least the table was still standing, and he needed its aid on a second attempt to rise. "Ander," he called as he clung to the table and waited for the world to slow its whirling, "why are you two so wet?"

"Figured the water might shock him out of whatever state he was in," Ander called back, "so I jumped into the pool with him. Scared him, though, so I got him back out in a hurry."

"Good thinking. Now get some food into him. Get his blood sugar up," Derik replied. He straightened up cautiously to stagger past Vara, on her way to the service pillar, and dropped to his knees by Nik's side. "How bad?" he asked.

"Broken collarbone, some bruises, and one hell of a headache, but I suspect every esper on the island shares that. Derik, he pulled most of it. It was a brainstem reaction, and the instant he was aware of it he pulled it. And you're dead right about the muscle tone. He's moving his body entirely by telekinesis and levitation—no muscle control at all. I didn't catch on because he wouldn't let me into his mind, I didn't think he was capable of that kind of esper control, and I was giving him some electrical stimulation to keep the muscles from wasting too much until he recovered control. Five months without that—he's a mess physically."

"And he's obviously not properly blocked," Derik added. He was thinking faster than he could move, stunned by Nik's insistence that they'd caught only a fraction of the boy's possible reaction. Like Lai and Nik, he had assumed the boy was a latent—carrying almost the full suite of R'il'nian genes, but expressing only a fraction of them. He'd caught only the fringe of the reaction—not nearly as much as Nik. He'd told Kaia that a self-trained esper was always a cause for concern, but he'd never expected anything like this! None of them had, and as far as he knew none of the boy's owners had even suspected Roi had esper abilities. "I'd have thought he'd have reacted to Florian at some point," he said shakily. "Nik, can you make it back to the table if I help you? Vara's got some food there, and the boys are already converging on it."

Coryn and Ander were both shoveling in food and taking turns feeding Roi by the time the two men made it to the table. Derik considered suggesting Roi and Ander change into dry clothes, but it didn't seem very important in the heat of the summer noon. His own head was still pounding, and he envied the two older boys their resilience. Roi's head was down and he looked absolutely miserable.

"Do you understand what happened?" Derik finally asked.

"Something in my head lashed out at Nik and you. It wasn't deliberate. I thought I'd fixed it so that wouldn't happen again, but somehow it did anyway. I'm sorry, really I am. But I don't understand *why* it happened."

"Again?" Derik asked sharply.

Roi seemed to pull in on himself even more. "I think I killed a man once, an overseer," he said tonelessly.

Derik's first impulse was to shake the boy, more for his defeatist attitude than for the esper reactions. But that would do no good at all. "Roi," he said, "what happened was a poltergeist reaction. They're normal in crossbreds, especially around your age. It's caused by the strength of esper powers increasing at a faster rate than the judgment necessary to control them, especially around puberty. The results can be pretty undesirable—as you demonstrated today—so esper children are normally blocked against using their abilities except in strictly limited self-defense. Then when they're mature enough to use those abilities responsibly, they're taught to take over control of those blocks. I blocked Coryn when he was a baby, and his esper training for the last couple of years has mostly been on gaining control over those blocks. You got missed on the blocking, for the same reason you weren't inoculated against Kharfun syndrome—nobody knew you were R'il'noid. Understand so far?"

Roi perked up a little. "Does that mean you can stop me from doing it again?"

"Yes. My guess is that you've done a pretty good job of blocking yourself, as a result of that earlier episode you mentioned. You just didn't get the keying quite right. I'm going to have to go into that original block and help you change the keying, and for that I need to know exactly what happened—which means you'll have to share what's evidently a very unpleasant memory with me. And you're strong enough I'd better do it with you under HiControl, which will temporarily knock out all your esper abilities. If Nik's right about how you're moving, that's unfortunately going to bring back the paralysis, at least temporarily. Probably this evening—I don't have the time I need right now. But you're blocked. You have to be. Otherwise you'd have smeared Florian all over the walls while you were at Nik's."

"Not to mention Malar and Sheeran, at school," Coryn contributed.

Derik jerked his head up, and winced at the intensification of his headache. "You mean the other kids are giving him problems at school?" he asked. And if the school authorities didn't believe Roi was really Lai's son, he thought, they wouldn't be giving him any extra protection.

"Yes. Uh—Father, if you're going to be doing esper work, shouldn't you do something about that headache?"

"What kind of something? I'm an old man. I don't recover as fast as you youngsters."

Coryn and Ander exchanged puzzled looks. "We didn't 'recover'," Cory said. "We asked Roi to stop the headaches."

"He does it all the time for my migraines," Ander added.

Nik's jaw dropped, and after a few seconds Derik realized that his own mouth was wide open. "He's Healing those intractable migraines of yours?" Nik said.

"I'm not really healing them," Roi apologized. "I don't know enough for that. I just sort of get the inflammation to go away. Is that wrong, too? Cory said it was all right."

"It's all right," Derik hastily agreed. "You just caught us both by surprise. That particular esper talent is pretty rare. The rest of the stuff you've been doing—well, it's not at all uncommon in crossbreds. Healing is very rare. I don't know where we're going to find someone to teach you." Healing had been rare among the pure R'il'nai, and it had never shown up in a crossbred before. Certainly Lai did not have that ability, though his great-aunt Bera had been the last R'il'nian Healer. Bera had stored her skills in the Big'Un—could Roi understand them? Nik couldn't, beyond the simplest concepts. But Derik wasn't going to say more than he had, right now. Coryn evidently had no idea of just how rare Roi's ability was, and Derik wasn't sure if knowing that would be good for Roi or not.

"Can you Heal things other than headaches?" Nik demanded. "Cuts, bruises, broken bones, cancers, other diseases?"

"Cuts, bruises, broken bones, yes, I think. All the time on myself and my friends, anyway. Cancers I don't know. Some infectious diseases, yes, but it didn't work on the Kharfun."

Nik was nodding his head. "Kharfun's invisible to esper. That's why it's so deadly to R'il'nians and some R'il'noids. Think you could put this collarbone back together? Better eat some more first."

"I have to go through your mind to get to your body," Roi warned. "But I'm all right on food. Cory's been stuffing me."

"Can you monitor, Derry?" Nik asked, and after a moment Derik nodded. He'd been uneasy before Roi's mental explosion, sensing something was wrong but unable to pin down the feeling. This time he used his conditional precognition deliberately, and felt no hint of any problem.

He reached for Nik's mind, settling into a mental position where he could watch what went on. He felt Roi's hesitant contact, and then he and Nik gasped simultaneously as they got the feel of Roi's mind. "Nice, huh," Coryn said smugly.

"He's got the Healer's touch," Derik replied softly. "You kids are way too young to remember Bera, but that's who he reminds me of." He watched as Roi removed the inflammation from Nik's head almost without thinking, then TK'd the ends of the broken bone into precise position and removed the inflammatory chemicals from the region. So much he could follow. He could sense the threads of collagen that came next, tying together the torn soft tissues as well as the bone ends themselves, and the growth of microscopic crystals of calcium phosphate. He'd observed and experienced Bera's Healing himself, and he thought Roi was doing the same thing, though a good deal more slowly. But as to *how* the boy was doing it …

"Break," Nik said, voice and mind together.

Am I doing something wrong? Derik's ability to sense emotions was weak and took conscious effort, but he thought Roi was confused and upset.

Not at all; you're doing a great job. But one of the things I learned from Bera was that Healing takes an enormous amount of energy. Until you learn to Heal and eat at the same time, you need to break pretty often. "Coryn," Nik added aloud, "get some more food into him. Roi, that's really enough for right now. You've got everything back in place and tacked together so it'll heal properly, and that's about as far as Bera would go in Healing broken bones. Gives me an excuse to be lazy for a few days."

There's still something wrong. I changed your body some way, so the healing could go faster. When I've done that on myself, I've felt—wrong—until I changed it back.

Good boy! Yes, my body normally reacts against rapidly dividing cells—stops most cancers, among other things. But it also slows healing. It's not a problem for a short time, and Bera used to tack-heal, leave her patients in accelerated healing mode while their bodies finished healing themselves—a couple of days, usually—and then reverse the accelerated healing. "Coryn, he needs carbohydrate and protein both. That stewed grain and nuts is fine, but add some honey. Let's see, Roi—Derik needs to check that block of yours, and you'd better Heal his headache first, but wait at least half an hour. I need to show you how to reverse the effects of the Kharfun properly, but that had better wait until Derik's got your blocks properly keyed."

"Straighten out that ass Nebol," Derik added.

Vara nodded. "You boys weren't here yet, but he tried to convince me that Roi was still Derik's catamite."

Coryn and Ander looked at each other. "That was the scuttlebutt at school," Coryn said, "but the Kharfun, and then the way he could hear the suppresser field, and his healing that cut—"

"Suppresser field? Cut? Coryn, has Roi been physically attacked?"

The three boys exchanged glances. Coryn, looking slightly guilty, did not look directly at his father and spoke a little quickly. "That ass, Nebol—and that's an insult to asses, who are generally sensible and resourceful animals—insists on keeping a suppresser field going at the school because he thinks it'll prevent cheating. R'il'noids can get room and personal shields if the field bothers them—I've got both. But he won't admit Roi is R'il'noid, so Roi can't get them—and he's very sensitive to the field."

"You mean he's been having to use TK and levitation to move his body though a suppresser field?" Nik exploded.

"Until Kim assigned me to tutor him, he was having to feed himself and operate his terminal manually through the field. You think he's thin now, but he was skin and bones that first tutoring session. My mental interface and shielded room helped him probably more than my tutoring did."

"Your mother's food packages helped a lot, too," Roi added shyly.

Vara managed a smile, though she was still massaging her temples. "I must confess I had my doubts about Coryn's 'poor, starving tutee,' but I'm glad now I sent the extra food," she said.

"All right," Derik said, "we need to get him certified as R'il'noid, so he can have shielding."

"Am I?" Roi asked.

"Yes, and we don't need a Çeren index to prove it. The old performance-based tests are still valid, and you've already shown you can pass those."

"Given Nebol's attitude toward you," Nik commented, "it might be a good idea if someone else signed off on the tests, though. Jik, maybe?"

"Jelarik? You should probably meet him anyway, Roi. He's old even by my standards—about four millennia—and he's got some metabolic problems so he hardly ever leaves his own estate. But he's the head of the Genetics Board, and he's taken quite a lot of interest in you. He's halfway around the world—twelve time zones away—but I'll contact him when he's awake. However, Cory, you still haven't answered my question. Has Roi been subject to physical attack?"

"What makes you think that?" Cory replied, but his eyes had flickered to Roi's, and refused to meet his father's."

Derik sighed, massaging his still-aching head with his fingertips. "Roi," he said, forcing himself to be patient, "Nik and I are trying to help you. Your father sent you to Tyndall because he thought it was the safest place for you. If you're in any danger there, we need to know about it so we can protect you. But we can't help you if we don't know what's going on!"

Again the boys' eyes met, and Derik was quite sure they were communicating. I will not, he thought, eavesdrop, but it was hard to trust the judgment of the three youngsters.

In the end he thought Roi nodded, ever so slightly—or was he picking up an emotion of assent? At any rate, Coryn let his breath out in evident relief. "There've been some problems with Xazhar K'Zhaim's bunch," he said.

"Xazhar's supposed to be keeping the students my age in line," Roi added. "But the ones I'm having the most trouble with are his friends. And he's never called me anything but S'Derik."

Nik snorted. "Always did think it was a mistake to let Zhaim raise that son of his. But if a parent wants to raise a kid, the Genetics Board generally goes along. Your father was hoping you and Xazhar would be friends, Roi. All right, all right," he added, fixed with the indignant stares of all three boys. "But he is your nephew."

"And Zhaim's my nephew, and yours," Derik replied. "I prefer Roi, thank you. Roi, how are you feeling? I'm about ready to wrap it up for today—got an Inner Council meeting in half an hour—but my head's getting worse, not better."

The boy's mind-touch was hesitant at first, then more confident as Derik welcomed him. And the headache—it vanished so quickly Derik was startled. *It's easy compared with healing bones,* Roi told him, and then vanished from his mind, going on to Vara.

"I may be back this evening your time," Derik said as he prepared to teleport back home, "but if not, expect me tomorrow morning." This evening if I possibly can, he thought as he arrived at the Council room. And arrange with Jelarik for Roi's testing, and get Nebol straightened out about Roi and warn him about Xazhar, and arrange some kind of physical therapy at the school, and …

Kaia looked pleased with herself when she 'ported into the room, and raised one hand in sign of victory. Yes, Derik thought, she had been right. In some ways he did have the harder job. But he wouldn't have considered trading it back for the negotiations.

Roi

10/1/35

"If you feel like hitting someone, run it off," Snowy's mother had told him. "Just make sure you're running in the direction your owner wants. You're not likely to get into trouble that way."

Snowy had done a lot of running in the six months since he'd been sold away from his mother. *Six months? Wait a minute, that had been years ago.* Not that he'd liked his mother's owner, or the overseers who gave most of the orders. But this new owner, and the brutes he expected to keep his slaves in line, left him half sick with fear. He had learned so early that he could not remember learning that crying, struggling, or any expression but happiness or eagerness to please would bring uncontrollable pain. He knew how to keep this owner happy, if anything he did could manage that.

Still, he hated being a catamite. He wanted to strike out, and kick, and struggle, but he knew better than to think he could get away with it. So he hated and ran, head down and arms pumping as he returned along the balcony to the slave quarters.

Corner ahead—better slow down; one of the guards might be—was!—coming the other way. But neither his body nor the mind inhabiting it responded in the slightest to his concern. Horrified, he tried to rouse himself, knowing to the smallest detail what was to come, but helpless to do anything except to keep running until his lowered head slammed into the guard's groin.

Get away! Keep running! But Snowy was frozen in shock just long enough for the gasping giant to grab his arm and swing him against the wall, hard enough that Snowy felt bones splinter. The guard must have felt it, too, and known he was in trouble for damaging his master's property. His eyes flicked to the balcony railing, and he made a sudden dive for Snowy. Something in Snowy's mind knew the guard's intention and struck out in frantic self-preservation, and at the same instant Snowy was inside the man's mind, somersaulting over the balcony railing and falling, screaming, to the stone-paved floor below, while the slave he had intended to destroy before it could communicate what he had done huddled on the balcony above …

"Roi, Roi! It's all right, Roi, you're safe now. Come out of it!"

He was wrapped in something and being held tight, and he tried to open his eyes, only to discover that he had no control at all over what he thought was his body, that he was as helpless as he had been in the nightmare? Memory? And another mind was touching his—

"Roi! Don't try to shut me out, please. Nik! Where's that antidote? He needs it fast! Roi, you're going to be fine. We had to give you HiControl—remember? The paralysis is because of the Kharfun, that's all. You just can't use esper to move, like you have for most of the last year. Here's Nik with the antidote; it'll put you to sleep and you'll be fine when you wake up. And I know what happened this afternoon; you won't strike out uncontrolled again."

A hand grabbed Snowy's arm and for an instant it was the guard grabbing him again, but blackness descended before he could react.

10/2/35

Roi awoke to tuneless humming and the fragrance of herbs. Peacemint, he thought drowsily, and peacock plant, and something sharper—cinnamon, perhaps? When he reached for his eyelids they opened easily, and the ceiling shimmered with reflected sunlight from the ocean outside. After a moment he turned his head toward the humming. Nik had drawn a small table up beside the bed, and sat stripping the leaves from a stem of peacemint. Behind him, Roi could just see two figures power surfing in the chaos of waves beyond the reef. He couldn't see the sun, but from the shadows surrounding the trunks of the palm trees, it must be close to noon.

Roi drew a deep breath, relieved to find that he could, and Nik turned his head. "All right now?" the physician asked. "You scared us both yesterday evening."

"Scared you? What about me! Couldn't you at least have warned me what to expect? Nik, it's not funny."

"Sorry," Nik grinned as he stood and walked over to the service slot. "I wasn't laughing at you, Roi, but Tyndall and Coryn together have been good for you. Can you imagine saying what you just said five months ago? As to warning you, no two people react the same way to controlled dreaming. Sure, we could have taken half an hour listing all of the possible reactions—and you'd probably have psyched yourself into feeling a few of those as well as the ones you did feel." He retrieved a mug and a brownish stick from the service slot and carried them back to the table, stirring as he walked. "Get this inside of you. Peacemint tea, and I've added orange and cinnamon as well as honey.

Mints usually make good teas, and I tried this when you were so interested in the peacemint. Not bad at all." He held out the cup.

Roi looked at the mug and at the table—about the height of his mouth, he estimated. Lifting the cup and his arms seemed such a lot of wasted effort. "Could I teleport it straight into my mouth?" he asked.

"Can you? Let me monitor and make sure you're doing it right," Nik cautioned. "Mmm—very nice. Where'd you learn that continuous-stream technique?"

Roi started to duck his head, then remembered he wasn't supposed to do that any more. "I had to figure it out to feed myself the first couple of months, going direct to my stomach. Then Cory said it was dangerous and made me promise not to do it any more if he got me extra food. It was giving me a stomachache, too. And I haven't figured out how to teleport stuff up or down without using an awfully lot of effort."

"Counterweighting," Nik replied. "And don't ask me the details, I'm a borderline teleport at best. Ask Derry when he gets here. He's the one who's decided you have to be given at least basic esper training, and as soon as possible. I don't envy him the job at all, especially when your father gets back. But he's right. You've worked out too much on your own not to be taught to use it properly. Thank goodness Coryn had the sense to warn you to go easy.

"Ready for something more solid? You can teleport this into your mouth— it's a smooth custard, so you don't have to worry about chewing it—but it's time you started using your muscles. Use that Healing sense of yours to see exactly what muscles I use to swallow. Then find the same muscles in your own throat. Right. Now, remember how to swallow? See if you can find the nerves—well, ghosts of nerves—that lead from thinking about swallowing down to those muscles, and try to send an impulse along them."

Roi fumbled a bit, but with Nik showing him exactly what to do, he managed a spasmodic contraction of his throat muscles that felt a little like swallowing.

"Good! That's exactly right. Remember that if you do get any food down your windpipe, you can push it out telekinetically. But do the swallowing with muscles, not telekinesis. Finish the custard, and then we'll work on another set of muscles. It'll be at least a couple more hours until Derry gets here. He did some controlled dreaming himself after he left here last night—I monitored for him—and set up an appointment for you with Jik after your supper. And he was going to tackle Nebol before he came here."

By the time Derik finally arrived, Roi had discovered that he had far more muscles than he would ever have believed, and that at least half of them refused to respond in the slightest to his prodding. Muscles he had been using without conscious control, like those involved in breathing, were relatively easy. Those that had been cramping he could get under some control, though the contractions were weak and he had difficulty locating the nerves. Nik remained outwardly cheerful, but Roi's ability to block out the emotions of others was as poor as ever, and he could feel the man's dismay at his poor performance, and the intensity with which Nik blamed himself for not realizing earlier what Roi was doing. It was a relief from more than weary muscles when Derik arrived.

"Lay off him for a bit, Nik," was Derik's first comment. "You've still got most of a month. And set up a glucose drip while I'm telling him some of what he needs to know. Any questions before we start, Roi?"

Most of a month to go, and two hours—well, more like three—had already left him exhausted? Roi cringed inwardly. But he did have a question, one he was almost afraid to ask. "Last night—did you see everything I remembered?"

"Yes, and a lot of connected memories. I had to, Roi, because I had to know what made you set up that block the way you did."

"I think you got some stuff I *never* intended to tell you."

"I suspect I did. But Roi, Bera tried to tell me thirteen centuries ago that I'd get myself into serious trouble some day because I couldn't tell love from lust. I went back to that memory last night. I wasn't mature enough then to understand what she was trying to tell me. I hope I am now. But I think you did me a favor by kicking me into revisiting that memory.

"First, I was right about the keying being the problem yesterday. You keyed the block to fear, and you've evidently gotten over your fear of us enough that you didn't trigger the block, but your response to Nik's dismay did trigger the brainstem protective reaction. I've fixed that, but I'm still worried that you made the block too general. I'd rather wait until your father's back to tackle that, though.

"Now, Tyndall. I talked to Cory and Ander last night, and talked with—well, shouted at—Nebol this morning. Took a bit of shouting to find out why he thought you were still my slave."

"The other students thought so, too—especially Xazhar. But ... I wouldn't be important enough that Zhaim would have any reason to try to fool Nebol about me, would I?"

"Given that he left before we knew just how much talent you had, I don't know what he was thinking. But he is very definitely the person who convinced Nebol that I got you into Tyndall under false pretenses. I strongly suspect he even used covert esper to reinforce the idea—Nebol was much more resistant than he should have been to the idea that you are really Lai's son. That's illegal as well as immoral, and I'm certainly going to tell your father about it when they get back. But Nebol did agree to accept Jik's test results, and you'd really have to work at not testing R'il'noid, from what I've seen."

"You're sending me back to Tyndall, then."

"With a good many more safeguards than your first half term," Derik replied.

"And," Nik chimed in, "with someone along to make sure you get regular physical therapy. Do you really hate school that much, Roi?"

"Not the learning; I like that. I wish I didn't have to take classes with the little kids, though. I'm the same age as the tenth year kids, and I hate being treated like I'm fourth year—well, it's better than first year, like it was to start with. But the ones my own age—I wish I wasn't in the same dorm with them. Derik, I don't have to be like them, do I?"

"Of course not," Derik replied, looking a little startled. "Observe them, yes. They're examples of the people you're going to have to deal with all your life. But you don't have to copy them. And remember that most of them are copying Xazhar, and from what I learned yesterday, Xazhar is just reflecting Zhaim's feelings toward you. Given time, you may even find kids your own age you want to be friends with. You seem to get along fine with Coryn and Ander."

"And I didn't expect to," Roi admitted. Then, sheepishly, "I'd been afraid of Coryn ever since he wanted to borrow me after I beat him riding."

"I think," Derik said, "that he was looking for a riding partner, not revenge. Would you be more comfortable closer to Coryn? He says there's a suite free in his dorm. He and Ander will only be there another half term, of course, and then you'd probably have to go back with your own age group."

"A small suite's a good idea," Nik commented. "That would give room for Lukon to stay with you."

Lukon? Oh, no! Of all Nik's assistants, Lukon was the one Roi came closest to disliking. It wasn't logical, just a feeling that to Lukon, he was a dysfunctional body that inconveniently had a mind attached. As to feelings, he doubted that Lukon had any beyond a preference for efficiency, or that Lukon had ever thought that his patients had feelings at all. "I don't want Lukon staying with me," he said, and braced himself for Nik's anger.

Nik and Derik exchanged glances, and Derik said "Who else do you have, Nik? What exactly would be the requirements?"

"A good practical knowledge of muscular and neural systems," Nik said. "A good masseur. A bodyguard to some extent, since you're worried about Roi's ability to defend himself properly through that block he's set up. Somebody to make sure he's eating enough, and doing the exercises I set up, and help him out on the things he really can't or shouldn't do. Lukon might have problems on those last requirements, but he's the best I've got on all of the others."

"Only Roi doesn't like him," Derik said. "Any suggestions, Roi?"

"Timi?" Roi asked hopefully, but Derik shook his head.

"Timi's got the massage skills, yes, but he's totally lacking in medical background and he's even less mature than you are. Plus he's no good at controlling his temper, and you'd wind up spending all your time protecting him from Xazhar. It just wouldn't work, Roi, though I know you'd like to have him with you."

Roi sighed deeply, remembering to use protesting muscles rather than telekinesis. It had been a long time since he had been so sore, and he knew from his experience as a dancer that he would feel even worse tomorrow. Wistfully he remembered Davy's hands, working the soreness out of his muscles after dancing ...

Davy.

"How about Davy, then? He taught all four of us about massage, and I think he said it was considered medicine where he came from."

Derik and Nik looked at each other, both clearly at a loss. "Davy?" Derik asked.

"He was an overseer at Kuril's—*not* like the one I remembered last night." That one hadn't even been at Kuril's. "He was a slave, too, and he used to help us out whenever he could. He said knowing the massage techniques might help us get better owners. It did, too." He still couldn't manage all the muscles needed for a grin, but he thought one at Derik.

Nik frowned. "What kind of medical background?"

Roi tried to remember everything Davy had told them. "He said the school he went to had been sacked and burned. He was doing his first year's wandering after graduation, and he got arrested and later sold to Central. I think he said it was called Jibeth."

Nik's head jerked up. "Jibeth? Sacked and burned is an understatement! I didn't think there were any survivors at all, and if there is one I certainly want to talk to him! I corresponded with the herbalist there—that peacemint you like so well is from one of the cuttings she sent me. You say Kuril had him? When?"

"When Derik bought us. That was when—two years ago? Kuril used him as a masseur as well as an overseer."

"Not quite two years," Derik answered. "Go on, Nik. I know you've been wanting to find out what some of those Jibeth herbs were used for. We can worry about whom to send with Roi later. Now," he added to Roi, "esper training. Nik will be working with you on recovery from the Kharfun paralysis in the mornings. Part of that work will be on eating normally, so you'll get breakfast and lunch with Nik. I'm running the Inner Council meetings while your father's gone, so I need to leave here late afternoon local time—Seabird Island's about eight hours earlier than the Enclave—but I'll plan on about two hours a day with you after your lunch and hope I can give you the groundwork you need by the time vacation's over. If things stay quiet and Kaia continues to handle the stickiest situation the Council's got to deal with right now, I might be able to give you another session after your supper, but that's going to vary."

"I thought a vacation was supposed to be a rest," Roi said wistfully. "I've got schoolwork to do too, you know. Coryn wants me to be ready to challenge another year by the end of vacation."

Derik smiled sadly. "Roi, you're R'il'noid, almost certainly High R'il'noid. We don't take vacations, at least those of us who are responsible don't. There's always something to do that nobody else can do. Oh, there are hours free, if you're lucky even days. But it's never predictable. The only reason I can even count on being on planet for the next month is because Kaia and I are filling in for your father. And if an emergency comes up I may not even have the time to work with you."

"You make it sound like being a slave."

"Not that bad. Certainly there's a lot more choice, and more things to enjoy when you do have free time. But the main difference is that the discipline is from inside yourself, instead of being imposed from outside. I wish," he added grimly, "that Zhaim understood that."

I hope, Roi thought, that Derik is wrong, and I'm not R'il'noid at all.

10/8 /35

Over the next few days, Roi settled into his new schedule. Mornings, from before breakfast to after lunch, he spent with Nik, relearning how to control his body. Partially relearning, at least. Some of his muscles seemed to be unreachable by anything he or Nik could do. He learned to speak after a fashion, instead of simply vibrating the air in front of his mouth, but speech took an incredible number of muscles, and some he simply could not control.

Esper lessons took less time but were far more intense. Roi hadn't had much physics yet at Tyndall, so Derik insisted he study the basic conservation laws—energy, momentum, angular momentum and mass—on the computer teaching program. "If you can Heal, you may eventually be able to exchange mass and energy if you conserve hadrons," Derik told him, "but you're a long way from being able to do it. And don't even think about trying to put two masses in the same place. I still go weak kneed at the thought of your teleporting food into your stomach. No more teleporting until I teach you how to do it properly. Nik should have known better this morning."

Mostly, he learned that his trial-and-error use of his esper talents was inefficient, clumsy and often downright dangerous. Not that Derik ever said as much. Instead, he concentrated on teaching Roi the basic principles of using esper talents in line with the conservation laws. Counterweighting, for instance, turned out to apply to levitation (which Derik *was* teaching Roi) as well as to teleportation. It was simply a matter of moving a mass down at one location while he moved one up at another. Conservation of gravitational potential energy—obvious enough, once it was pointed out, but not something he would have worked out on his own. There were areas—the landslide areas—set aside for counterweighting and used by mechanical teleports and by some espers, but experts generally preferred to use water.

Jik's testing had turned out to be considerably easier than Derik's training, though Roi was still dubious about Jik's conclusion that he was not only R'il'noid, but High R'il'noid. Even Jik admitted that Roi's highly abnormal childhood affected the test results. Roi found himself wondering what a "normal" childhood would have been like.

Still, Roi had more free time than he was used to. He didn't see much of Coryn and Ander, who were surfing and riding when they were on the island, and visiting friends when they were not. Roi spent much of his free time exploring the riding trails in his float chair.

On the eighth afternoon he found Vara schooling a young horse in the arena, and stayed to watch. Derik's horses had always been well trained, and the process of teaching a horse to accept a rider intrigued him. Vara seemed totally unaware of his presence until the end of the lesson, when she encouraged her mount to walk with a loose rein. Then she raised her head, saw Roi, and walked the horse over to the fence where he sat.

"Coryn's neglecting you, isn't he," she said.

"Not really," Roi replied. "He took me riding again yesterday. And just being here, instead of being stuck at school with Xazhar, and all the help I'm getting—I can't thank you enough, my lady."

"Vara," she corrected. Her horse snorted and shook himself, then stretched out his neck to sniff at Roi's hair. Roi blew back at the horse's nostrils, and smiled as he felt the animal relax. The facial muscles he could control at all were beginning to respond automatically to how he felt—something he had never dared let them do before.

"Could I lead him around a little when you're through training, Vara?" he asked shyly. "I know he needs to be walked, and he doesn't like the robots."

She looked at Roi in his float chair and frowned. "You're right about his not liking the robot walkers, but do you have the mass to control him? Or the strength?"

"The chair and I together mass more than I do alone," he pointed out. "And Derik's been teaching me levitation struts. If I use those at an angle, there's no way he can jerk me or the chair around.

"Levitation struts?" Vara replied as she dismounted and handed Roi the horse's reins. "I thought Derik was just teaching you the basics."

"He's teaching me the basics, but he's making me work out how the stuff I've already figured out fits in with the basics. I've been moving my body entirely by levitation and telekinesis for almost a year, now—don't even think about it much. So he says I have to learn how to do it properly and think about what I'm doing. But he made me promise not to try teleportation at all until he had time to teach me how. I wish he'd make my training a class, with Cory and Ander in it too. At least Cory. I don't feel right about taking all his time, when I know Cory wants to visit with him, too. And I think it would be good for both of us to practice together."

Roi thought Vara grimaced, though he didn't have a very good view of her face through the horse's head. He turned toward the stable area and the horse resisted briefly, the animal's apprehension clear to Roi's mind. The boy sent reassurance along the empathic link, and felt the horse relax a little. "What's his name?" he asked Vara.

"Flight," she replied, matching his speed on the other side of the horse. "Roi, tell me—what is Derik like? Yes, I've known him far longer than you have. I knew him quite well, fifteen centuries ago, and I swore then he'd never get close to any child of mine. I've been trying to keep him away from Coryn, at least as much as I can. He's told me he's changed a great deal since those days, but I didn't believe him. Then—I've been watching him with you. I think he really cares about you, Roi, and perhaps about Coryn, too. And that does not match what I remember. You knew him as his slave. What is he like, now?"

"Kind," Roi replied promptly. "And he won't read another mind uninvited. That was important to me, when I thought I had to hide. He said the other day that Bera once told him he had a problem telling love from lust. Most of the owners I've known had lust mixed up with power and even hurting. I never liked being a catamite, and I wouldn't have liked it with Derik. But the kindness and caring would have been worth it."

"And if he won't read minds, he doesn't know that his—attentions—are unwelcome."

Roi managed to find the muscles to nod his head. "He didn't know how I felt until he helped me with that keying. I think it really shook him up, but he won't talk about it. Just changes the subject."

Vara stepped ahead to open the gate, and waved Roi on through. "Have you asked Derik about practicing with Cory?" she asked.

"No."

"You might ask him about it. He may feel it's not to the advantage of either of you, but if he says I'm the reason, tell him to come talk to me. Can you hold Flight while I get the tack off and sponge him down?"

"Sure. And walk him dry afterward?" he added hopefully. If he couldn't run, dance or ride, leading the horse around and feeling the play of its muscles seemed next best.

"If you like. Roi, how did you know he doesn't like the walkers?"

"I can feel emotions. I wish I could shut them out better. Animals don't reason like people do, but they do feel, and Flight gets scared every time he's turned toward the walkers."

"Any idea why?"

Roi frowned as he tried to understand the horse's emotions. "He seems to connect the walkers with being dragged," he said.

Vara nodded slowly. "My walkers won't, but some of the cheaper ones will," she said. "Something like that could have happened to him before I got him. Oh, Roi, Coryn did remember to invite you to his birthday party, didn't he? I know he meant to, but sometimes he can be so forgetful."

"Yes, of course. I'm looking forward to it." That was a polite lie, actually. Part of his ambivalence was simple jealousy. He doubted that anyone had bothered to make a record of his own birth date. His mother might have known, but it seemed nobody had been able to find her or learn what had become of her. At any rate, it had been close to a year since he'd waked up at Nik's, and nobody had ever mentioned a birthday as if he had one, so he supposed he did not. But he worried also over something else he had just learned about birthday celebrations: guests normally brought gifts, and he had nothing to give Coryn.

"You know," Roi commented when Derik dropped by for a lesson that evening, "this would be a lot easier if I could practice with Cory."

"You mean group lessons?" Derik asked. "I'd be all for it, myself. I think you could benefit from Coryn's help on the basics, and some of the stuff I'm teaching you would be helpful to him. But frankly, I'm here on sufferance and I don't think Vara'd be very happy about increasing my contact with Cory. Not that I'd do anything to harm him."

"Why don't you ask her?" Roi managed to keep a grin out of his emotions, but it took conscious effort. He thought Cory was getting a little jealous of the lessons he was getting from Derik, and this ought to fix that problem—as well as giving him someone to practice with.

"I agreed not to see much of Coryn, but Vara *has* been letting him visit me lately. It's worth asking her, anyway—I'll make a point of doing that before I leave this evening."

"Good," Roi said, thinking that Coryn might have the nerve to suggest the old idea of playing pattern chess with Derik. He hadn't quite dared to do it himself, given Derik's prohibition on doing anything that involved teleportation.

That didn't stop him from fretting over not having anything to give Cory. He didn't doubt that Derik or Nik would help him, but he wanted to give Coryn something from himself. A night's sleep did nothing to solve his problem.

10/9/35

The next morning Nik dumped something into Roi's hands, and ordered, "Squish it." Squish it? It had taken all his strength just to get his hands palms-up on the table, even with Nik's help. He tried to close his hands, not easy since only the thumb and one finger on one, and three fingers on the other, were under his control. And the stuff did squish, taking the print of the usable fingers and pushing the limp ones out of the way. He looked up at Nik, who nodded approval. "Make about half a dozen balls, and then roll them into cylinders," the physician said. "I'll be back in a few minutes—I want to talk to Vara."

The balls and rolls were a boring exercise, and when Nik was slow to return Roi tried to make things a little more interesting by modeling a horse. It wasn't a very good horse—the fingers he couldn't control kept getting in the way. If he could just make it come out like the image in his head, he thought, and then harden it somehow, he might have his gift for Coryn.

"Harden it?" was Nik's response when he asked. "No, but we could certainly make a casting from it." He looked at the crude horse with a dubious expression.

"Not this," Roi assured him. "But if I could shape the same material telekinetically—not as part of physical therapy—I think I could make a decent horse. And I'd have something to give Cory that was really from me."

"I can manage the casting, once you get what you want," Nik assured him, "but you work on it outside of therapy hours." He turned the little horse in his hands, studying it. "You know, Wif might like a couple of animal figures, and I could cast them in something he could chew on safely. His first birthday is coming up."

"Wif?" Roi asked. "You mean that was true, too?"

"Roi, I never lied to you. Neither did your father. You have a son, named Wif, who's almost a year old. His mother's Feline, who's living with Elyra—well, you haven't met Elyra, but you should. Your father and I—Wif's grandfather and great-uncle—have made a point of being foster fathers to him. That party tore Feline up pretty badly, emotionally as well as physically. She wants nothing to do with men. But I really think you ought to meet Wif, at least. Be a big brother to him."

Roi grimaced. He had done his best to forget some parts of his slavery, and that evening at Kuril's was one of them. But that wasn't Feline's fault, or the baby's. He was, he decided, relieved that Feline was safely away from Kuril, and curious about the child they said was his as well as hers. "How?" he inquired. He didn't even know where Elyra lived.

Nik looked relieved. "Talk to Derik," he said. "Just remember that Elyra lives an hour east of Derik. It's two hours before noon here, so it's three in the morning at her place. She should be up by the time Derry leaves this afternoon, so ask him to teleport you out there. I can make it myself, with Lyra at the other end, but I can't take you with me that way. If you ask him nicely, Derry might even set up a patterned teleport you could use to go back and forth. If you could manage teleporting food into your mouth, you can handle a patterned 'port. Meanwhile, let's get back to exercising your hands."

A patterned teleport? Roi was learning a lot from his lessons with Derik, but he chafed over his teacher's insistence that he not use teleporting at all. Even Coryn, who had warned him about teleports involving his own body, had been willing to teach him pattern chess. Derik wouldn't even allow that. Nik obviously wanted him to visit his son. Could he use that to get around the teleporting ban?

Derik was willing enough to teleport Roi to Elyra's for a visit, but immediately balked when Roi suggested that he would like to go back and forth himself. "It's too dangerous," the R'il'noid responded. "You don't know enough about how to use the conservation laws yet. I'll jump you over to Elyra's after your lesson, and leave you there during the council meeting. But you're not ready for a teleport on your own yet, even a patterned one."

"Oh, come on," Cory scoffed. "He does good exchange teleports. I bet the two of us could beat you at pattern chess, if you'd let him play."

Derik's eyebrows rose while Nik settled back in his chair, removing himself from any argument while he prepared to enjoy the contest. "Got your set here?" Derik challenged.

In response, Coryn dived beneath his chair, bringing out the box and hooking the playing grid to the table's computer outlet. "Fourth level?" he asked.

"Fourth level. I know you can't beat me alone, so if the two of you together can, I'll admit Roi is ready to learn a patterned exchange teleport. I'll even go one step further—if the two of you give me a good game, I'll lift his ban on teleporting as far as pattern chess is concerned. And if I clobber you both, you let me teach you both at my speed. Agreed?"

"Agreed," Coryn said. His mind settled into rapport with Roi's.

Is this a good idea? Roi asked. *He's annoyed enough to be pretty hard on us.*

He won't be expecting your playing style. Hit him fast with all the 'ports at once and we've got a good chance this first game. Hard part's going to be holding them for three seconds, but on that I can really be some help. Once he figures out what you can do we've got problems, but this first game we can definitely give him enough of a fight he'll have to let you keep on playing, and maybe enough he'll back down on the patterned teleport.

Coryn triggered the computer, starting the five-minute countdown and putting their goal pattern in front of the two boys. Roi glanced at the starting pattern and worked out the exchanges he would need to make, then reached for the feel of the tiles. Everything at once and fast, Coryn said, and then the two of them would have to hold the tiles in place for three seconds. The countdown seemed endless.

He didn't realize the game was over until Coryn poked him and he opened his eyes to see their pattern, clean and complete, on the grid before him. When he looked up, Derik was looking stunned, mouth wide open, and to one side Nik was struggling not to laugh aloud. "We won?" Roi asked, feeling stupid.

"Thoroughly," Derik replied, running his hands over his face. "I think we'd better revise today's lesson plan. I'll teach you that patterned teleport, but I want you to understand exactly why it's patterned the way it is. Your father beats me, on points, pretty often, but I haven't been clobbered like that in centuries."

"Not since the last time you played Bera?" Nik grinned. "He's a Healer, Derik. Bera broke that down into three talents—empathy, exceptional control, and ability to manipulate a very large number of similar objects—cells, in the case of Healing—simultaneously. The last two carry over directly into pattern chess. Ever heard of a Healer who wasn't a superb player, if they played at all?"

Derik sighed and readjusted the computer, unhooking the game grid and bringing up a physics summary. "All right," he said. "Elyra's place is seven hours west of here, about halfway between the equator and the south pole, and a bit higher elevation than the peak at the center of this island." He gestured over his shoulder at the mountain. "Now what all do you have to do for a balanced teleport?"

Conserve energy and momentum. Energy first. "Move mass down to balance my mass moving up, same as with levitation. The distance down times the mass I move down has to be the same as my mass times the distance I move up, though that's not quite exact for big vertical changes. Water from a high reservoir to a low one's easiest. Momentum—I want to wind up going the same speed as my surroundings, right? Here everything's going like so, moving around the planet." He thought eastward, around the planet toward the sun. "Seven hours west of here, things would be going—uh—up and a little backwards relative to here. So I have to swap momentum, too." He thought for a moment. "Maybe teleport water from a high reservoir near Elyra's to a low reservoir here? I'm not sure how to transfer the momentum to myself, though."

"That's what the patterning will help you learn. Go on."

"Kinetic energy shouldn't be a problem if I'm just changing direction, not speed …" He stopped short as he saw the slight change in Derik's expression.

"Coriolis force?" Cory hazarded.

"What's that?"

"It's a sort of fictional force you have to use in a rotating coordinate system. Like if you go from the equator toward the pole you turn in the direction the planet's rotating"

Roi reached for the computer page, trying to understand Coriolis force. The math was beyond him, but the diagram … "You said Elyra's is nearer the pole than here. So it'd be closer to the planet's axis, and it'd be moving a little slower. So I do have to worry about kinetic energy. But … Wouldn't the water swap I was thinking about to balance momentum take care of that?"

"Yes, if you do it properly, but you have to remember it. Anything else?"

Roi looked at Coryn, who shrugged helplessly. "I can't think of anything else except feeling out my destination to make sure nothing's where I'm trying to 'port to, but I bet I'm missing something." Roi said.

Derik grinned. "At least you know you don't know everything," he said. "Actually, you'd probably survive a teleport using what you've mentioned, but you wouldn't feel very good afterward."

"Something like the stomach aches I used to get teleporting food into my stomach?"

"A little, though I think Ander was right about that being basically a digestive problem. At least once you figured out how to do it. What would happen if you levitated—fast—to the top of that peak?"

"It'd be a little colder, and my ears would probably pop."

"Air pressure!" Cory said suddenly. "The air pressure in your inner ears has to be the same as the atmospheric pressure. You could burst your ear drums if that gets too far off."

"And lungs, and sinuses," Derik added. "Not that you're likely to burst your eardrums 'porting between here and Lyra's, but you could certainly give yourself an ear ache. And you'd create quite a noise if you don't swap air out of the exact volume your body's going to be occupying, and into the volume you leave here."

A lot to think about at once. "Derik," Roi said slowly, "suppose you have to do a fast 'port in an emergency. Like, oh, suppose you were watching a star and it went nova?"

"You die. You never count on teleportation to get yourself out of an emergency situation unless you have all the details of the teleport worked out in advance and stored in your head, ready to trigger with a single thought. Emergency teleports without getting all the conservation laws right have probably killed more R'il'noids than Kharfun syndrome. And if you're watching a star that might go nova, you'd better have a sublight beacon at least a light-minute closer to the star than you are, and get out the second it quits transmitting. Either that or have your perception focused on the core of the star. By the time the front of the light wave reaches you, it's too late."

"I guess it's a little more complicated than I thought," Coryn said. "Are you sure I'm ready for this?"

What Roi was picking up empathically was closer to sheer panic, but Roi had actually done more teleporting than Coryn had, and he wanted to learn to do it properly. "I want to see my son," he stated. "I can learn, if you'll show me how."

Derik grinned at both of them. "You're not ready right now," he told Coryn, "but if you stick with the lessons for the next four fivedays, there's a good chance you will be ready for a patterned teleport by the end of vacation. Roi, you don't have the physics yet to set up your own teleports, but that's the whole point of patterning—I'll work out the physics and integrate conservation into a memorized teleport between two specific points. As a matter of courtesy and because she has blocks set up against uninvited teleports you always contact Elyra first thing. For right now, I want you to depend on her at that end and Nik here to make sure that the area you are teleporting to is clear. Use perception as a backup and to help you adjust air pressure properly. You'll have to switch to it eventually."

When Derik finally teleported him to a small, sparsely furnished room at Elyra's, Roi was startled to be grabbed and hugged by a woman he'd never seen before, a woman so small she hardly had to bend over to reach him in his float chair. "Roi!" she exclaimed. "You look so much better! But haven't they been feeding you?"

"Lyra!" Behind Roi, Derik sounded as if he were trying to hold back laughter. "As far as he's concerned, you haven't even been introduced yet. Roi, Elyra and your father were living together when you were found, and you have a baby sister to prove it. Lyra probably knows everything about you that Lai did. Don't let it worry you. I'll be back for you when the Council meeting is over. Don't try to teleport yourself back; I want to take you back and forth several times and give you more control each time." He squeezed Roi's shoulder and vanished.

Roi gulped and looked uncertainly at Elyra. Now that the meeting with Feline and his son was imminent, he was far more apprehensive than eager.

Elyra looked closely at him. "Roi," she said, "what are you feeling so guilty about? Roi gasped and slammed up his crude emotional shields, and Elyra raised her eyebrows. "You *are* good at shielding. Roi, I'm an empath, probably not quite as good as you are, and not as good at Nik at blocking out other people's emotions, and you are positively reeking with guilt. Why? You had no more choice about what happened than Feline did, and while the evening as a whole was traumatic for her, she's not angry with you—though you may get some spillover from her general attitude toward men. As for the consequences, Wif is a delightful little boy, and Feline is far better off than she would have been slaving in Kuril's kitchen and being thrown to his guests when he was short handed. So what are you feeling guilty about?"

Mostly, Roi admitted to himself, because he had never bothered to find out about Wif—though he didn't see what he could have done earlier than the start of vacation, a few fivedays ago. "I guess I'm over-reacting," he mumbled, and followed Elyra to a room with a padded floor where two small children played and a woman studied a desk screen. Sunlight spilled in the windows, and a half-open door led to a walled, grassy area.

It took a moment for Roi to recognize the woman as Feline. A bronze halo of curls had replaced the smooth scalp he remembered, and the hazel eyes she turned toward him were fringed by unexpectedly long lashes. Her face was still scarred, though the scarring seemed to have faded a little. Most of all, she looked—not old, exactly, but adult. Roi in his float chair suddenly felt that he belonged with the playing children, while Feline and Elyra were grown-ups—on the other side, somehow. His eyes went back to the children, both dark-haired, bronze-skinned, and clad only in diapers, and he wondered which child was Wif.

"Snowy?" Feline said uncertainly, her eyes on his float chair. "Oh, sorry. It's Roi now, isn't it. Wif's the one with your eyes." Her own eyes went to the child happily smearing paint on a large sheet of paper on the floor, and the expression on her face changed to one of total adoration.

"I've put lunch up about an hour so Roi won't starve waiting for his supper," Elyra said from behind Roi, "and I'll be back for Roi after lunch. Ania, if you pull that kitten's tail it will probably scratch you, and it will be your own fault. You don't like having your hair pulled, and the kitten doesn't like having its tail pulled. Feline, if Ania misbehaves, call me," she added as she left.

Roi, watching Ania toddle after the kitten, thought it was unlikely she'd get close enough to pull its tail. Certainly Feline did not look particularly concerned, even when the kitten approached Wif and then jumped into the center of the little boy's painting. Wif looked for an instant as if he were going to cry, then stared more closely at the bright green paw prints leading away from the paper. He placed his own chubby hand in the paint, and then pressed it onto the floor, gurgling at the green handprint that resulted.

"On the paper, Wif," Feline told him, and looked ruefully at Roi. "Everything in here either washes out or can be washed." Her eyes flicked back and forth between Roi and Wif, and she felt increasingly agitated to his empathic sense. "You aren't going to take him away from me, are you?"

Roi's first reaction was an attempt to picture himself caring for Wif at Tyndall. The thought panicked him. He couldn't do it. And his own early memories centered on the mother who had been the one stable, caring part of his life. "Of course not," he said. "He needs you. But I hoped maybe you'd share him with me a little." He looked again at Wif, and realized that he wanted what was best for this child, and with an intensity that surprised him. Was this what Derik felt for Coryn? Was it even possible that his own father might feel this way toward him, some day?

Feline relaxed visibly. "Of course. I'd rather have you than your father, to tell the truth. Wif's too young to really know what a birthday is, but would you like to come to his birthday party? It's the fourteenth."

By the time Elyra returned, Roi was on his back in the grass with both children and the kitten on his chest, all four well covered with varicolored handprints. "Nap time," Elyra announced, "at least for the babies."

"And for me," Feline said, "if I want to keep up with them this afternoon."

Roi glanced down at a painty forearm. "Is Derik here yet?" he asked.

"Probably another hour—the Council has quite a lot of business today. Would you like to clean up a bit before he gets here? Or are you trying to make a new fashion statement?"

Roi TK'd himself to an upright position as Feline removed the children, and looked down at his clothing. "I haven't looked in a mirror, but I hope Feline was right about this washing out."

Feline, halfway to the door, looked back and giggled. "It does. Believe me, I've had lots of opportunity to know. The grass stains are likely to be more of a problem."

Roi levitated himself back into the float chair, wondering why he felt so tired when it was only a little after noon—oops, it must be after sunset on Seabird Island. Teleporting on a round planet brought problems other than conservation of momentum. He did some rapid calculations in his head, and realized that Derik must be getting up very early indeed to arrive for lessons each day shortly after noon, Seabird Island time. He'd known that before, but he hadn't really felt it.

"Elyra," he said as he was coming up for air after she had scrubbed the paint off his face, "do mothers and fathers always fight over children?"

"Are you and Feline having problems over Wif?"

"Oh, we worked it out. But she was afraid I was going to take him away from her."

"And you've been staying with Vara. That's a special case, Roi. There's always some tension because matings among R'il'noids are controlled by the genetics board, and the best matings genetically are often not between the people who would get along the best. Usually something can be worked out so if the genetic parents both want a part in the child's life, they can have it. Vara and Derik was a combination that the genetics board wanted very badly, and Vara would agree only if Derik promised to stay completely away from the child at least until Cory's twelfth birthday. Took us over fifty years to get the pregnancy, and by that time Derik was doing all the blocking. Vara wasn't even happy about that."

"But why did she think he'd be bad for Cory? Cory loves both of his parents. And Derik's about the best owner I ever had."

"Too bad your father didn't realize you felt that way—I think he took it for granted you wouldn't want Derry anywhere around. As for the way Vara feels—she first knew Derik when he was young, and the people I know who knew him during his first century agree he started out awful. Worse than Zhaim. I—Roi! When did that happen?"

Mention of Zhaim had triggered that almost forgotten nightmare of Flick's fate, and Roi suddenly realized he hadn't bothered to rebuild his empathic barriers after sharing emotions with Wif. Elyra must have picked up the image of Flick's distorted form in the mirror, with Zhaim's cruel smile behind him. "A little before Derik bought me," he said.

"He's still doing it," she whispered, her eyes wide with shock. "Your father knew he was, three centuries ago, but he thought he'd stopped it. Lai would never have left Zhaim in charge if he'd known—it was only conditional precognition that made him leave Derry and Kaia with instructions to contact him if they thought Zhaim was making poor decisions. No, Derry was never that bad. He hurt people, yes—he still does, at times. But never for the fun of hurting them.

"Roi, promise me something. When your father gets back, share that memory with him. Not to hurt Zhaim, but because it's something Lai needs to know. Please?"

Roi wasn't sure about sharing a memory with his father or with anyone else. He still wasn't at all certain that his father would even care about him, and he did not want to risk possible revenge from Zhaim. Xazhar was bad enough! "I'll think about it," he said reluctantly.

10/25/35

Roi turned the finished horse on the table before him, examining it critically. It was smoothed and abstracted compared with a real horse, but to his eyes it held the essence of Horse. He and Nik had chosen a hard, slightly transparent black material for the casting, and he was pleased with the results. He hoped Coryn liked it as well as Wif had liked the simple animal figures Roi had created. Those had been cast in a softer, herb-scented material that served equally well for teething or playing, and Nik had made the children a crawl-in colony ship of plastic panels to house them.

Although this was not an important birthday, Coryn's party would still be a little more formal than Wif's. Roi was rapidly outgrowing his clothes not only in length, as had been obvious for some time in the fit of his school uniforms, but in width as well. Now he turned from the horse to the new clothes laid out on his bed, wondering if he could get into them without telekinesis. He was in far better shape than at the beginning of vacation almost a month ago, and while the muscles he could not control remained stubbornly unresponsive, those he could use at all had gained significantly in strength. He could lift his hands a few finger-widths from the table, now. Actually putting on the tunic, however …

Roi had been trying for a couple of minutes to disentangle himself when Nik came into the room and pulled the arm Roi couldn't quite control to a vertical position, sliding the fabric that was blinding him down over his chest.

Roi sneezed, shook his head and looked up at Nik. "I don't think I can do this at school without telekinesis, Nik."

Nik shrugged. "You'll have help at school next half-term, Roi. Better go put your gift on the table."

Help from Lukon, Roi thought as he guided the float chair down the corridor to the small room where Vara had set up the gift table. He wasn't any happier about Lukon than he'd been at the beginning of vacation. He put his horse on the table, moving the float chair back a little to view the whole array. No names of givers—according to Ander, part of the fun was to guess who had given each gift. He knew the bridle and saddle were from Derik, and that Vara's gift—a horse to be boarded at Tyndall—would not be brought in until the last minute. He had a part in that present—convincing the horse that it was housebroken, at least for the few minutes it would be in the house. The rest—well, his little statue did not look out of place.

Coryn's first attention was for his parents' gifts—things might have been rather awkward if it hadn't been, Roi thought as the horse, wearing the new tack, was led out to the patio and tied. But his next selection was Roi's figure, and while Roi was trying not to pry, Cory was broadcasting his delight too strongly for the younger boy not to feel it. "But who's it from?" he asked. "Mom? Father?"

Both shook their heads, grinning, but after five minutes or so Vara, who knew what Roi had been doing, suggested, "Who else knows how much you like horses, Coryn?"

"Roi?" Coryn asked incredulously. When Roi nodded shyly, he exclaimed, "But it's beautiful. Where did you ever find it?"

"I modeled it, and Nik cast it from the model," Roi explained.

"You made this? Roi, you've got an open slot next half term, haven't you? Get into an art class. This—it's better than anything I've seen for sale."

To Roi's surprise, Nik and Derik were looking at each other as if they were considering Cory's suggestion seriously.

"It would give him a break from academics," Derry said, softly enough Roi wasn't sure he was intended to hear.

"And he won't need physical education as much ..." Nik broke into coughing as he caught Roi's eye, and didn't finish the sentence.

Why? But it sounded as if they might really let him take an art class.

Cory's party was not a large one, and the remaining gifts did not take long. It was Roi's first real experience with a birthday party, and he thought nothing of the way Coryn nodded at his father and stepped aside, or of Derik's move to the spot where his son had been standing.

"Officially," Derik said, "this is Coryn's birthday. But he's agreed to share it this year, since we were all too overwhelmed to celebrate Roi's last year.

Roi, we may never know exactly when you were born, but your ID chip was inserted early in the southern winter, and your father decided that for official purposes your birthday would be fifteen days after the Northern Solstice. You have a big one coming up—the official transition from childhood to adolescence at sixteen—in a little less than six months, but Nik and I had something we wanted to do for you—not exactly a present, since he's on conditional manumission, but something I hope you'll like." He glanced toward the door.

And Davy stepped into the room. He was a little thinner than Roi remembered, and had some new scars, but his eyes were more at peace than Roi had ever seen.

"You need someone with you at school, and you don't seem to care for Lukon—Derik, I don't think he's hearing a word I'm saying."

"Yes I am," Roi half sobbed. "Oh, Davy! Are you really going to help me out?"

Davy walked over to Roi's chair, dropping to one knee so his head was on a level with Roi's. Roi reached out to throw his arms around his old friend, and Davy responded in kind, hugging Roi close. "Look at you," he scolded. "No muscle tone at all. Of course I'm going to help you out. Would even if it weren't earning my freedom. But don't expect me to take every order you give. My job's to get you back on your feet and help you as much I can with what Bera left, not to pamper you." When Roi looked surprised at the reference to Bera, Davy grinned.

"Nik had a very partial set of the writings from Jibeth. When I started telling him what I remembered, he realized they were based on Bera's writings. I've spent a good part of the last month with the surviving Jibeth fragments, Nik's translations into Galactica of Bera's R'Gal writings, and my own memories of the Jibeth traditions, trying to make them back into a whole. I wasn't the only student to survive—Nik has three others to help him, now. Some of the teachers may even still be alive, back in the Goodnews cluster, but that has to wait for your father's return. I can't access Bera's stored memories. Nik says he'll try to teach you, though it'll have to be on vacations when you can access the Big'Un. But I can give you as much as I remember of the Jibeth traditions, and Bera's writings."

Roi sighed and leaned his head into Davy's shoulder. An hour ago, he'd been dreading the return to school, now only four days away. But with Davy, and in Coryn's dorm, and with at least the possibility of an art class to relieve the academic grind … Beyond that, even. His father would come back, and this time Roi would have some idea of how to respond. He'd have someone to care about him, the way Derik cared for Coryn; the way he himself was trying to care for Wif. Not that Derik didn't care for him, but there would always be the memory of slavery between them. "I think I might even enjoy school this time," he said.

But underneath, he wondered. Nothing had ever gone right for him before. Why should this time be different?

Riya

MARNA

First Year

"Well, *I* don't know how to fix it," Marna announced, flopping back on her heels and glaring into the entrails of the life support computer. She pushed her copper-gold hair back out of her sweaty face, adding another streak to the grime that almost hid skin the color of ivory buried for millennia. It had been close to two centuries since a R'il'nian hand had touched the system, and even in the closed environment of a sealed dome on a satellite, dust accumulated.

Beside her, Ruby trilled anxiously, and Marna looked ruefully down at the tineral. Huge dark eyes returned her gaze from the catlike face, and small hand-paws twisted together uneasily. The tiny scarlet feathers that covered the face and the thin, monkey-like body were still bright, as were the feathered wings that now served only as a weather cloak, unneeded in the domes. As a juvenile Ruby had flown with those wings, exploring every cranny of the complex of domes and tunnels. Her younger relatives still flew and sang their clear, fluting songs in the dying trees.

Ruby wasn't full-grown. A tineral grew throughout its life, its voice deepening and mellowing as its body enlarged. A really old tineral, like Onyx, would mass over half as much as Marna herself, and have a voice like a bass violin. Ruby was almost breeding age, though no larger than a R'il'nian baby, with a voice that blended clarinet and viola. She had grown too large for her wings to support in the Riya-normal gravity Marna insisted on maintaining.

Marna sighed, feeling as if the station had betrayed her. She'd lived here for two of her three centuries, with only the tinerals for company. "I can't fix it," she told Ruby. "So we're going to die, just as I should have died with everyone else, two centuries ago."

Even now, the memories of that time were hard to face. She was a Healer, and the horror of being ordered to remain in safety on the isolated satellite while the population of her planet was dying had almost destroyed her. Only her mentor, Tyr, could have compelled her obedience, and his dying words still rang as clear as if he had just placed them in her mind: *I do not think we will find a cure in time for this plague. Already half of our people are dead, and most of the rest of us are dying. Someone must live and warn off any who may come, Marna, and as you are where we can hope the plague cannot reach, you are our best hope. You must not return to Riya, even if the plague kills us all and seems to have burned itself out.* How ironic, she had often thought, that she, who had been willing to risk her own life to study a new and potentially threatening pathogen, should be the only and most unwilling survivor of the R'il'nai. The isolation designed to shield the population of Riya from a threat that had proved to be no threat at all had instead shielded her from the death of her planet.

Wearily she stood, brushed futilely at the knees of her coverall, and began wrestling the cover panel back into place. Ruby, always eager to imitate her, caught at a corner just as Marna was snapping the panel home and squealed in pain as her finger was pinched. Hastily Marna freed the little paw and shouldered the panel the rest of the way into place. She held the injured paw lightly between her own finger and thumb, reaching deftly into the little animal's mind and through it, into the damaged finger. Block the nerve to stop pain, first, then reknit the crushed and torn capillaries and remove pooled blood. Check the bone—undamaged—then repair muscle, connective tissue and skin. In less than a hundred breaths she released the nerve block, dropped her hold on the paw, and scratched Ruby affectionately between the wings.

"I wish I could Heal the life support system as easily as that," she said. She had Healed it in the past, when a living part of the artificial ecosystem had faltered. But the satellite station was too small to support a truly self-regulating ecosystem, so computer control was needed to keep it in balance. The computer, unlike the large planetary one on Riya, was not self-repairing. And repairing the computer was totally beyond her ability.

The tinerals didn't understand her words, she knew. They were biddable, easily trained, responsive to her emotions, and glorious singers, but not particularly intelligent. But she needed to talk, and they were the only listeners she had. Ruby caught at the leg of her coverall, and she let the little animal lead her out of the computer room.

Feather trees should have made a green dimness of the large dome but the skeletons of their leaves, drained of life by sap-sucking insects the computer encouraged rather than controlled, crunched dryly underfoot. The tinerals, accustomed to supplementing their cultured diet with fresh fruit and nuts, searched vainly among the dry, increasingly brittle branches. A group of the older ones, including Ruby's mother Sapphire, cried musically as Marna passed them, their voices a chorus of bassoons, cellos, and bass viols.

Marna had lived for two centuries because Tyr had begged her to, and her only grief at her own impending death was that she could not return to Riya. It was the tinerals that worried her, the tinerals and the need to continue the warning. She had long since set a verbal warning broadcast on every communication band known to the R'il'nai. The language was inherited; other R'il'nai—if there were any—would still be warned off, but with no one to answer their questions. And surely there were others! The population of R'il'n had broken up into several groups during the diaspora, when the astronomers had predicted that their home would become unlivable in a few millennia. Surely one of the other groups had found a world as welcoming as Riya, and survived!

She could supplement the audio warnings with the visuals from the last days of the dying, and with a mental recording sent out via mechanical telepathy. It wouldn't be as good as her own direct communication, but she couldn't think of anything more she could do.

The tinerals, though … She traversed a tunnel that looked like a paneled corridor, followed by a group of the hungry animals, and entered a smaller dome. The vegetation here was grain, fruit bushes and vegetables, robot tended. Most of the plants were drooping or covered with masses of fungal spores, though in one corner insects shrilled. Marna wrinkled her nose in disgust at the sour, musty smell. It didn't help that she had to breathe deeply to compensate for the reduced oxygen and excess carbon dioxide in the air.

Would it have made a difference, she wondered, if she had checked the computer, perhaps taken it out of the system entirely half a year ago, instead of trying to deal with each biological emergency that arose in the way she understood, as a Healer? "Not likely," she muttered to herself as she crossed the bridge over an artificial stream. The water was opaque with algae and bacteria, and added its own foul stench to the air.

Two or three varieties of the ornamental plants surrounding the food culture building were thriving, but they were all species too toxic to use as food. Too poisonous even for the fungi, bacteria, and insects, she thought.

She'd switched to thermally distilled water for the food culture vats several months ago, but it hadn't stopped infections entirely. She'd had to destroy all but two of the cultures, and neither of the survivors smelled or tasted normal. The tinerals, whose official function had been to alert her to problems with food or water, refused one entirely and would barely nibble at the other. The group that had followed her and that now clustered just outside the door to the building were attenuated with near starvation, but when she offered them a bowl of the least suspect culture only the youngest would even try it.

"Well, the distilled water's still drinkable," she told them as she filled a second bowl. The tinerals drank so eagerly that they must have entirely stopped using the fouled streams. The still's capacity would barely support her, the surviving cultures, and the fifty or so animals.

Marna took a sample of the less contaminated culture and determined that it was not actually toxic, then dumped a glob into the cooker and set it to produce a highly spiced stew. She wouldn't have chosen the dish normally, but she hoped the seasoning would disguise the foul taste the culture had developed. She laid eating tongs and a bulb of chilled water on a lap tray, noting as she did that the group of tinerals at the door had swelled to over thirty, with more coming across the dying fields. She refilled the water bowl they had emptied. This must be their only remaining source of food and water.

So what was she going to do about them? They had been widespread as pets on Riya, domesticated for so long that even their planet of origin had been forgotten. She had encouraged hers to forage for part of their food, but on the satellite they had no competitors and no predators. The pathogens that were destroying her artificial ecosystem were common on the planet, so she didn't need to worry about contaminating Riya. She could teleport the tinerals home, or could she? It had been two centuries since she had teleported a living creature. Better pull up some of the computer's information on teleporting. She did remember that all kinds of conservation laws were involved.

"Well, you certainly can't survive much longer here," she told them as she added the completed spiced stew to her tray and carried her lunch to a bench outside the door. Two juveniles—the brilliant green male she called Emerald and a soft orange female, Citrine—fluttered down beside her and begged for food, crouching on their folded hindquarters and reaching their hands out in entreaty. She offered them a chunk from the stew and watched their reactions. Emerald sniffed, looked at her beseechingly, sniffed at her bowl as if to reassure himself that this was indeed what she was eating, and took a tentative nibble. After two bites, he allowed Citrine to grab the rest of the chunk. The orange tineral went through the same pantomime before dropping the remainder of the chunk to the ground. No, they couldn't survive here.

"The big problem is predators," she told them thoughtfully. "Maybe one of the vacation islands, where the predators were exterminated?" Against her will, her mind returned to a summer two hundred years gone, and the subtropical island called Windhome. She'd met Win there, a Healer like herself. He slid into her memory—violet eyes, hair so darkly red it was almost black, and a bronzed face alight with laughter or tender with love. She'd been flying through the tunnel of a breaking wave when it had collapsed on her, and Win had TK'ed her out of danger. Later they'd flown together, levitating through surf and over mountains, and made love in a hidden valley dizzy with flowers. They'd planned to rear a child together when Marna finished her research. She'd touched minds with Win often, in the early days of the epidemic, and later done her best to lighten his agony as he himself lay dying. He had been as insistent as Tyr that she not return.

She pushed the memory away, forcing herself to think only of the possibility that Windhome might be a suitable place for the tinerals. Win would approve, she thought as she carried her tray back inside the building. He had given her the four tinerals from whom the population of the satellite descended, and convinced the rather dubious medical council to let her take them with her. She could still see him, his face carefully arranged to solemnity for the benefit of the council, explaining how the animals could serve as a check on the food and water recycling systems. He'd never argued that with her, stressing instead the company they would be. Well, he'd been right both ways.

The computer's communication link to the big planetary monitor on Riya was still intact, and appeared so far to be working normally. Marna walked through empty rooms to the nearest interface and pulled up the planetary computer. She identified herself—silly, she thought, since there isn't anyone else to contact it. <Send available visuals of epidemic two hundred years ago,> she entered.

\Reason for request?\ the computer responded.

<Station life support system in catastrophic failure. Observer lifetime estimated in days.> Drat your programming, she thought. <Videos needed to reinforce an automated warnoff message.>

The computer's silence lasted considerably longer than the light speed transmission time to Riya and back. \My condolences\ it finally replied. \ The station computer has lost control over that section. The life support programming appears to have broken down completely. I suggest you send your completed message back to this facility for broadcast in case there are further breakdowns. Videos are being transmitted on alternate channel.\

That made sense, Marna thought. Now for the next problem. <Request tutorial on teleporting.> The computer responded promptly, and Marna's eyes widened as she looked at all the information. That complicated? She remembered the requirements for energy and momentum balance, but the computer was practically giving her a short course in physics!

She'd known this once, and she could learn it again fairly quickly, but she had over fifty tinerals to teleport, and only a few days to do it in. Exchange teleports were easy, she remembered. Exchanging two objects with the same mass, size and shape automatically balanced energy and momentum. Under normal circumstances she would not have considered bringing anything from the surface up to her isolated satellite, but given the state of the artificial ecosystem that was hardly a problem. But what could she find that was the same size, shape and density as a tineral?

Chewing on a broken fingernail, she brought up the material on exchange teleports, and found that was exactly the problem with simple exchange teleports—sea water and a little air would work as an exchange medium, but the tinerals would wind up in the water, and they were terrible swimmers. Most would drown.

"There's got to be a simple answer," she muttered, and noticed a link to multiple exchange teleports. She absorbed the new information, and suddenly saw a solution. "A triangular exchange," she said aloud. "Take the air out of the volume I'm 'porting you into, put it in the ocean, and teleport the water up here to balance your mass. It won't be exact, but I can add some energy to make the potential energy balance. It won't be any harder than lifting one of you. You might get splashed when the water rushes in to replace the air, but it should work without drowning you." Ruby chirped questioningly from the arm of her chair.

"I've got a new home for you, where there's plenty of food and good water. I might even be able to find you some new friends," she told the three who'd followed her into the building.

It took four days to teleport all of the tinerals except Ruby, Emerald and Citrine to Windhome and to complete her recorded warning. She had already set the station computer to broadcast her message for as long as the power panels would hold out—perhaps for centuries—and the source code for the recorded warning was now being transmitted to the planetary computer on Riya. The air had gotten so bad that she kept an oxygen tank—the last one—by her side. The last culture had tested as too toxic to risk eating three days ago, and she had only one packet of preserved food left.

Ruby and the two youngsters were gasping and struggling for air, and she gave them each a few breaths from the oxygen tank, and then filled her own lungs. "Time for you three to go," she told them, trying to keep her voice calm. "I won't be able to manage a teleport if we wait any longer."

Ruby cried in protest, clinging to Marna's neck when she was picked up, and Marna's careful calm deserted her. "Ruby, you can't live here any more," she sobbed. "And I can't leave. I promised. Tyr and Win both. That I'd stay here and warn people not to land."

Use your head, girl. Your job was to provide a warning. You can't do that if you die here. It's time to come home, love.

Win? she thought wildly. Of course it couldn't be; lack of food and oxygen were making her woozy. She took a few more deep breaths of oxygen. Not Win, but her own subconscious. She'd conditioned herself so thoroughly to her own exile that she hadn't seen that it had become totally meaningless. And the same triangular exchange teleport that she had used with the tinerals should work for her.

"Home," she said aloud. "I *can* go home. I may die, but I'll die with a Riyan wind in my hair." She ripped open the food packet with shaking hands, slung the carrying strap of the oxygen tank over her shoulder, and picked up Ruby and a bulb of water. Emerald and Citrine fluttered to her shoulders. Eating and drinking as she went, Marna ran back to her sleeping quarters. A change of clothing and a portable interface went into her carrysack, followed by an ultra light sleeping bag and a tri-dee of Win. She closed her eyes briefly as she picked up the hair clasp he had given her. A woman trying for a baby let her hair grow out; the clasp had been a promise of the child they had planned. She'd never worn it. She thrust it into the sack and glanced around the room for one last time. Nothing else here of importance but printouts of the breeding records of the tinerals, and she'd be able to access them from the planetary computer on Riya.

Marna took a final deep breath from the oxygen tank and wrapped her mind around the three tinerals and the carrysack. She let Windhome flood into her consciousness: the smell of the breeze caressing her face, the sun bright overhead—no, it was sunset there now, with high bands of cirrus glowing pink against the rapidly darkening sky and surf breaking on the amethyst beaches. Her memories coincided with reality, and she pushed herself through into the warm summer evening.

The plague that had destroyed her world might yet lurk in the green-scented air, but if it did, she welcomed it. A rush of tinerals surrounded her. "Home," she said again. "I'm home."

She had forgotten a lot about planets, Marna decided less than a day after her return to Riya. Rain was hissing through the leaves overhead and pounding her head and shoulders as she tried to squeeze herself closer under a slight overhang. She flinched as thunder crashed no more than a heartbeat after a brilliant burst of light, and envied the tinerals their feathered cloaks.

She glanced downslope to the tree where she had left her sleeping bag and carrysack, hoping she had remembered to seal the computer interface into its waterproof bag and wishing she had thought to ask the computer for more details about buildings as well as wildlife. As far as she could tell, there was nothing left of any of the tourist buildings she remembered but piles of rubble from the lava rock foundations. The tourist brochures, she remembered now, had proudly stated that all facilities were constructed of local, biodegradable materials. It hadn't occurred to her that they would degrade so fast.

Another series of lighting bolts struck, farther away this time. Marna looked back toward the east and saw with relief that there were patches of blue sky showing through the clouds. Maybe the rain was almost over.

She frowned as she considered her situation. From what she remembered of her vacation here, there were seasons when it rained almost every day. It was warm enough, but she was still stiff from sleeping with a couple of rocks and a tree root poking through the sleeping bag, and now she was soaked through as well. She needed protection from the weather and a sleeping area. If no buildings had survived the last two centuries, she would have a choice of leaving the island or building herself a shelter.

The thunderstorm gave a last, tired rumble, the rain cutting off as abruptly as if someone had turned off a faucet. Marna got to her feet and pushed her way through the wet underbrush to her supplies. The sun came out as she was trying to wring the water from her soaked sleeping bag. She shook a convenient bush to get as much water as she could off the branches before she laid the sleeping bag over it, and then got out the interface.

She intended simply to ask the computer for the location of any surviving buildings. As a graduate of the Healers' Center, it was her responsibility to use her Healing talents when needed for the benefit of the R'il'nai as a whole. Most of the time, that was a matter of Healing trauma—actual illnesses had been rare. In return, she could claim food and shelter from the planetary computer. But with no other R'il'nai to Heal? Tyr had told her to live and warn off other R'il'nai, she thought stubbornly, and to do that she needed food and shelter. But would that even be possible on the island? She certainly had no idea of how to build even the crudest of shelters! Perhaps the computer had some kind of tutorial?

<I need shelter,> she said uncertainly. <Tyr asked me to …>

An architectural design program appeared on the screen as the computer replied, \Please state what you want.\

She shook her head in disbelief. Was it just her imagination, or did the computer sound eager, even relieved? <Explain.> she asked.

\Part of my programming is to keep the mainland cities in repair. I am also required to have R'il'nian input on a fraction of the work I do.\

She didn't know much about computer programming—that was a specialty quite distinct from Healing. But she knew enough to see that the two requirements the computer had stated could be in conflict after two centuries with no R'il'nians on planet. She'd been thinking in terms of what she could do to earn shelter, but it now seemed that she would actually be aiding the computer by trying to design the home she wanted.

Marna was still shaking her head in bemusement when the robot surveyor arrived, equipped with interactive architectural programs, an inflatable shelter, and a dry sleeping bag. Computers, she told herself firmly, did not have emotions. Some farsighted programmer had simply inserted a requirement that some small fraction of the buildings built or even repaired by the computer and its robotic extensions have input from a living R'il'nian.

Marna had never designed a building in her life, but with the help of the architectural program, she tried. She wanted the sunset over the ocean to come into her workroom, and the sunrise over the shoulder of the volcanic mountain at the island's core to wake her at dawn. Wide verandahs sheltered the windows on east, west and south from the midday sun and occasional tropical downpours. The outside of the north wall was designed as a tineral city, with sleeping boxes and automatic food and water dispensers to ease their transition to wildness. Then the robots took over, and she stood back and watched as her new home grew into a far sturdier reality than she had expected.

If the plague lingered, it stayed well hidden. The tinerals settled in as if they had been born on Riya, their bellies and then their bodies plumping out rapidly on a diet of the local fruits, nuts and tubers. Desperate for activity, Marna swam, fished, and foraged with the tinerals. Fresh fruit, nuts, fish and some of the milder tubers suited her taste far better than the synthesized food her new kitchen could produce. She transplanted some of her favorite flowers and shrubs to a garden east and south of the growing house. She needed more to keep her busy, she thought, and ordered a sailboat kit from the computer's stores. More robots did the heavy lifting, but other than that she assembled the kit with only tineral aid. At least, she thought as she retrieved a pair of small pulleys from Emerald, the tinerals probably thought they were helping.

The days were shortening as she began assembling the sails and rigging the boat, and the tinerals started pairing off. Ruby vanished for several days.

Marna worried at first, but then she caught sight of her favorite cuddled up on a tree limb with the handsomest of the lavender strangers. Yes, she thought to herself, Ruby was old enough to breed now. She wondered what color the infant would be. Neither purple nor the recessive dilution factor that produced amethyst had been in the satellite gene pool.

With the older tinerals distracted by mating and the younger ones fascinated by the strange antics of their elders, construction of the sailboat speeded up considerably. Marna finished painting the final protective skin onto the hull, and stood back to look at her new toy. Yes, toy was the right word, she decided.

The plague had come at Festival—the worst possible time. Normally, there would have been exploration groups out looking for new knowledge, new planets, even evidence that others of the R'il'nai had survived the exodus from lost R'il'n. There would have been survivors in the few colonies Riya had managed to establish. But Riya was a beautiful planet, and uncrowded, thanks to the low reproductive rate of the R'il'nai. *Everybody* came home at least once during the once-a-century Festival, and if anyone missed coming to Riya, those who came and went back home carried the plague with them. Everybody was exposed to the new and devastating disease.

Everybody except a lone researcher who had to keep herself isolated for the protection of others. In two hundred years, she had not had a single contact to warn off.

On the satellite, that had been bearable. The satellite, she suddenly realized, had been designed to counter any sense of isolation. The computer was programmed with a variety of voices and personalities, and she had to interact with each properly or risk a simulated argument. Random tasks the robots could have done were left for her to carry out. Probably, she thought wryly, that was the part of the programming that had caused the breakdown of the life support system. But it had also kept her sane.

A few months on Riya had already made her see the futility of the task that had kept her alive for two centuries. There were no other R'il'nai left alive.

No other Riyan R'il'nai, perhaps, Win's mind-voice answered. *But we were very isolationist, love. And we know there were other groups of R'il'nai alive a quarter of a million years ago. What if they come this way?*

If they do, the computer will tell me, she replied crossly. *For now, if all I have left is a meaningless promise and toys, then I will play with my toys.* She turned to the computer-generated map of the archipelago that was now her home, refusing to be drawn into the question of just what it was that still spoke to her.

*   *   *   *

There had been a time, two hundred years ago, when Win had taught Marna to sail. Marna had thought of that, with mixed feelings, when she bought the kit. There were times when she sought for anything that would remind her of Win, and other times when the power and immediacy of his presence in her mind almost convinced her that she was going mad. On the whole, though, she welcomed the distraction of sailing again.

She capsized the boat half a dozen times before she succeeded in sailing all the way around Windhome, and twice more before she felt confident about venturing out of sight of land. Luckily the weather stayed fine, with steady northeast trade winds and only occasional afternoon squalls. Eventually she decided that with the option of teleporting herself home as a backup, she could venture on a longer journey.

She'd go northeast first, she decided, tacking upwind to the island of Wavebreak, with its long, sloping beaches oriented just right for huge breakers. She would fly the wave tunnels as she had that day when she had first met Win. It would be a comfortable day's sail out and a good deal less than that returning downwind to Windhome. She might even find more tinerals to increase her little flock. She tucked the inflatable shelter, the portable interface, her sleeping bag, and several days' worth of food and water into the boat before she went to bed that night.

By early the next afternoon, she was beginning to think she had overestimated herself. The winds were stronger than the normal trades, with a swell that was far higher than she had expected. Win had been in her mind most of the day, urging her to turn back to Windhome, and she finally lost her temper at him.

Yes, I know your body was left to rot on Windhome, she snapped back at the voice in her head. *What do you want me to do about it? Teleport it properly into the sun? How could I possibly find what was you? Why can't I explore a little?* Spray caught her in the face as the sailboat bucked beneath her, and she looked up to see herself surrounded by whitecaps. Clouds were spreading over the sky to the south.

Don't be ridiculous, love, Win's voice came back. *Use your weather sense, and remember what time of year it is.*

What time of year? She frowned a little. She had noticed the days were getting shorter when—over a month ago?—and since she wasn't living by clocks and calendars, the actual solstice had probably been considerably before that. Late summer, then. She looked again at the sky to the south, and felt a sudden chill that had nothing to do with the wind. Tropical storm season. She'd forgotten about that, too, living on the satellite. She reached southward with her mind, and gulped at the intensity of the swirling winds she felt. She was only on the outermost fringes of the storm, and already her little boat was close to its limits. If the storm moved north ...

At least the wind was steady so far. She lashed the sheets in place, keeping just enough of an eye on the sail to move it telekinetically if she had to, and groped in the bottom of the boat for the computer interface. Were the weather satellites still operational? she wondered as she asked for a weather briefing.

The storm was south-southeast of her, moving very slowly northwest. The architectural program had insisted on certain design features in her home that she had thought silly at the time, but now recognized as acknowledgment of a tropical storm's destructive power. With the feel of the storm in her mind, she wanted that house around her. She was closer to Wavebreak than to Windhome, but the sailing time downwind to Windhome would be far less, especially with a wind like this. *Teleport home*, Win urged. But she ignored him. It was as if fighting the wind gave her a reason for life she had almost forgotten. She set her course for Windhome.

The sky hazed over gradually, turning the sun first glassy, then diffuse, and finally hiding it altogether. The wind, behind her left shoulder now, seemed at first to have died down, but Marna knew that was because the boat was moving with it, fairly flying toward home. In fact, the wind was rising and becoming gustier, whipping spray into her face when she turned her head to study the clouds. She licked salt from her chapped and stinging lips.

She didn't notice the rain, at first, thinking only that the spray was getting thicker. Then she realized that her lips didn't seem as salty anymore, looked out to see a gray curtain hiding the horizon, and realized that rain was pouring into the boat. She gritted her teeth and sailed on, feeling ahead with her mind for the island.

She didn't actually see the island until she rounded its south side and tacked her boat into the little southwest-facing harbor. It was like sailing into the teeth of a hurricane, she thought, and then had to laugh at the aptness of the cliché as she dropped the sail and TK'd the boat the last few lengths to the boathouse. She was glad now that the architectural program had insisted on the boathouse, and the heavily tied-down roof of the house, and a few other safety factors. Thank the long-dead programmer who had thought to include a natural hazard map as part of the program!

Much later, she wondered why she had insisted on sailing the boat home, rather than teleporting.

*   *   *   *

Win's voice came oftener as the storm season advanced, and Marna found herself thinking more about his presence. She had expected the knowledge that any remaining trace of his body was on the island to bother her, but it seemed more as if Win was still present with her. She would hear his voice, not calling her name or wailing in grief, but simply companionable. He would point out a cloud formation or a bird or a flower she might not have noticed otherwise.

Her job as a Healer had been to prevent death, and she'd been too concerned with that to pay much attention to philosophical arguments about what happened after death. As the storms intensified and she had less to occupy her body, the thought that she might rejoin Win if she died became harder and harder to reject. And she had to reject it. She had promised Win and Tyr both to do everything in her power to prevent any other R'il'nians from landing here, and if she let herself believe that Win would be waiting for her when she died, she'd never be able to fulfill her promise. Eventually she programmed the food synthesizer to feed the tinerals if they came to the house, and teleported herself to the mainland.

The one place she could be sure of reaching from Windhome was the place she'd been born, in her mother's home. Her earliest memories were of falling from the young feather tree that grew in front of the house, and her mother Healing her broken arm even as she scolded Marna for climbing the forbidden tree. Her father, when he returned from troubleshooting a balky computer, had been a good deal less upset—in fact, he'd spent the next day teaching her how to climb trees safely.

The tree was gone, and so was the garden that had been her mother's pride. Even the sapling planted to celebrate her birth was missing. The one planted the day her baby brother was born, just before Marna had left for the satellite, was a towering tree, with broken branches warning that it, too was growing old and must soon be felled. Swallowing hard, Marna walked into the house.

Most of the furnishings had fallen into dust. She wandered through the rooms, finding it hard even to remember which were the family living quarters and which were those where her mother saw patients. Her parents had separated, amicably enough, when she had left for the Healers' Center, and she wasn't even sure where her father had been living when the plague struck. She remembered what the computer had told her that first day—that it was required to keep things in repair, but also to get input from living R'il'nai. The conflict must have resulted in many of the buildings being abandoned.

The cities, unlike the tourist facilities and the private residences, had been built to last and then kept running by the computer and its robot extensions. For a few weeks Marna shopped for a new wardrobe, ate in gourmet restaurants still operated by robots, and visited the great museums, libraries, and entertainment centers. The computer seemed almost pathetically willing to aid her. How much maintenance could it do, she wondered, as a result of her requesting a dress in a specific fabric or viewing one of the rare great works of art? But the cities had been built for crowds of people and their ghosts were far more difficult to live with than was Win's friendly presence on the island, never mind that both were probably inside her head. She replaced her new wardrobe and elaborate hair style with sturdy hiking gear and a short haircut that she could wash in any pool she dared swim in, got a floater and loaded it with an inflatable shelter, sleeping bag, portable interface and spare clothing, and set out to explore her home planet on foot.

It took until well after the fall equinox just to rebuild her muscles and harden her feet. She knew the seasons, this time; after the hurricane she had requested that the computer keep her advised of the sun's course through solstices and equinoxes. The morning of the winter solstice found her following a broad, shallow river upstream from savanna, tawny in the morning sun of the dry season, into the first outliers of jungle.

Marna's skin, darkly tanned by now, was gritty with dust, and the shade of the trees was a welcome relief from the sun. She followed a thread of a trail that paralleled the river, looking around her with satisfaction. Jewel-like winged lizards no larger than her thumb sparkled through the sunlight of the frequent meadows, and when she approached them, she found that they were drinking the nectar of the abundant flowers. Flowers now, in the dry season? She looked more carefully at the little meadow in which she stood, and realized that it must be a pond during the wet season. For land plants, this was the season of growth and flowering.

Back among the trees, she saw movement out of the corner of her eye, and caught her breath in delight as she managed to make out the form of a butterfly cat. The animal was as long as Marna was tall, even without its tail. Its sleek coat was greenish yellow with dark green swirls on its sides, rings of the darker green on its legs and tail, and four angled swirls like butterflies flaring out from its forehead to encircle its eyes and its tufted ears. Butterfly cats were solitary hunters, and rare. Marna felt privileged to see one.

She kept walking, afraid any break in her steady movement would frighten the animal away, and tried to watch it out of the corner of her eye. Its peridot eyes clearly saw her, but the creature showed no sign of fear. It was stalking something, she thought, its movements as fluid as the river and utterly silent. She reached out with her mind, wanting to feel its wildness ...

The beast was stalking *her,* and preparing to spring.

Startled, she stopped short and turned to face the suddenly charging predator. For a moment, caught between its mind and the fluid beauty of its charge, she stood mesmerized. At the last possible moment she regained enough control to levitate herself to a position above the beast. When it stopped and reared up to face her she reached into its mind more forcefully, implanting the idea, once deeply ingrained in every predator, that her kind were not its prey.

She would have to rig some kind of broadcast warnoff that would protect her while she slept, she thought. What was wrong with her, that she had forgotten so thoroughly the dangers of her home? Or was it simply that she was still trying to rejoin Win in death?

Second Year

The spring equinox found Marna moving back to the north, keeping ahead of the rains as she recrossed the savanna and moved into true desert. Furnace winds parched her mouth and throat, and blowing dust caked her eyes. She paused near the crest of a dune, shading her eyes against the glare of the morning sun.

The blue line to the north had become more than a line. She nodded in satisfaction as she turned back to the floater and picked up her canteen for a drink. The map had been telling her for more than a day that the Wind Hills were ahead of her, but this was the first time she had been sure that what she saw was more than a mirage. She sealed the canteen and returned it to the floater, making a quick check of her remaining water containers. A good three days' worth, she thought, and she should reach the foothills and at least one spring tonight. She licked her dusty lips and began climbing down the slip face of the dune.

By late afternoon she had sighted three cabins, all well away from the line to the hills. The fourth, however, was directly in her path, and she paused to study it. It was built of the pale limestone that made up the backbone of the Wind Hills, roofed with red slate, and seemed almost untouched by time. In fact, it didn't look as if it could possibly have been abandoned for as long as the cabins on Windhome, or even for a fraction of that time. Marna's heartbeat quickened as she stepped closer. Could this place possibly be isolated enough to house a survivor of the plague?

She circled the cabin, looking for any sign of life. On the fourth side was a door, propped part way open by a chunk of rock. She ran up to it, her heart pounding and her breath tight in her throat, and looked inside.

The small windows had been sandblasted over the years, and her eyes, adjusted to the glare of the desert sun, at first saw only darkness broken by paler rectangles. Marna closed her eyes and covered them with her hands, willing her sight to adjust but already aware that there was no smell or sound of life. When she looked again, she saw that the room was half filled with drifted sand.

Something dark protruded from the sand to her left, and she thought at first it was a tree branch, oddly shriveled and distorted. She scuffed her way across the room to try and pull it free, and only then realized that what she held was a hand.

Her knees buckled and she collapsed into the sand, still holding that poor, withered travesty of a R'il'nian hand. She stroked it gently while tears ran down her face and the trained Healer in her mind noted the spread, backward-stretched fingers and bent-back wrist. A plague victim, no doubt hidden from scavengers by the drifting sand and mummified in the heat and dryness of the desert.

Gently she dug the sand away, revealing a contorted body that seemed little more than a skeleton covered with stretched, dried leather. Someone tired of the press of crowds had come here for rest and renewal, perhaps, but had brought the plague along and died in agony, far from any help. Elsewhere, the last to die had been reclaimed by the life of the planet, not even their bones remaining. Here, there had not even been a scavenger to accept the poor body.

Logic said she should get away, that the person was long gone and the body might still harbor the plague.

She could not abandon the remnant.

The body refused to be composed into any semblance of rest, but she brushed away the last of the sand and carried it into the sun, now high in the sky. Deaths among the R'il'nai had been rare, and she finally had to ask the computer for the proper words.

"I do not know who you are," she told the body finally, "so I cannot speak of your life and the happiness you brought those who knew you. I can only say the final farewell. Take the goodness and joy of your life with you as you go before, and let all sorrow and evil be consumed with your body in the furnace from which it came."

She reached out to cup her hands around the skull-like face, locking her mind on the body. She gathered herself mentally, reached for the sun, and thrust the body into its nuclear heart.

For a long time after the funeral Marna sat unmoving beside the cabin, tears running down her face and making brief marks in the sand. Finally she struggled to her feet and began pulling the floater on toward the hills, but her pleasure in seeing the beauty of Riya was gone. She might as well go back to the island, she thought. At least there she had the tinerals for company.

*   *   *   *

The tinerals were bearing their young when she returned. Most of the animals chose to give birth on their own, but Ruby preferred Marna's bed. Her lavender mate, still suspicious of Marna, watched nervously from outside the window as Marna patted the garnet-downed infant dry.

"She's going to be a beauty, Ruby, and a color I've never seen before," Marna told the tineral. But there'll never be a child for me, she thought as she handed the newborn back to its mother.

You'll raise a child and bear one too, love. Mine in spirit, if not by blood. She jumped to her feet. Surely that message hadn't come from her subconscious, nor could it have any precognitive content. She left the island again the next day. But if Win's voice on the island tempted her to death, the unheard voices on the rest of the planet drove her in the same direction. And the food …

Even the best of the restaurants served synthesized food. Considerably better than what the satellite had been able to manage, but still synthesized. Marna's mother had grown food, and Marna herself had managed to grow some of her own food, even on the satellite. Once the computer's robot extensions had grown most of the food consumed on Riya, but maintaining the cities had been given higher priority by the programmers, and Marna had no idea of how to reverse that. But why couldn't she grow edible plants, as well as the fragrant flowers and shrubs she had already planted? True, she wasn't trained in agriculture, but she'd learned a lot from watching her mother, and the computer tutorials could teach her more. And spring was planting time …

She had the robots transplant the merely ornamental plants to the west side of the house, where they would be visible from her workroom windows. On the south side she laid out a vegetable garden, with fruit trees against the verandah. She swam as often as she used the bathing facilities in the house, but salt water had to be rinsed off. Why not a bathing pool, with fresh water? But that could wait. For now the important thing was to get the vegetable seeds in the ground.

Her tinerals were fascinated by the planting. Why bury perfectly edible seed? they must have thought, and followed her down the rows, digging up seeds as fast as she could plant them. "You're hopeless," she finally laughed. "Let's let the robots do the planting, and we'll mark out the bathing pool. And I need to check on some of the recipes my mother used to make, and be sure I'm growing all the ingredients." With the aid of the computer and its robotic extensions, she soon had most of the edible plants she wanted poking green shoots above the ground. These included some herbs for flavoring, and that suggested healing herbs to her mind.

The Healers' Center, she thought. They'd had gardens and greenhouses with every healing herb known. She wouldn't want all of them, of course, and there were actually synthetic drugs that were better for some ailments, but she'd more than once wished she had a few liverfrond leaves for a stomach-settling tea, or flybane oil as an insect repellant. She hadn't been there since she was a student, but surely the computer had kept the healing herbs going.

By that time she'd learned that the computer could give her teleport coordinates to anywhere on the planet, so it was no great problem to teleport to the Healers' Center. She'd lived there for sixteen years, learning everything she could about the Healing art, so the place was even familiar. She thought. Only ...

Her mother's home had been derelict, stripped of most of its memories. She'd never spent much time in the cities, but even there she had felt haunted by the ghosts of its former inhabitants. Here she was stunned to see the sameness of the place.

Oh, there were changes. A tree she remembered climbing on a dare now had its lowest branches far out of reach. A sapling planted when an aged tree had been broken by a storm her last year of classes was now a mature tree, and trees she recalled as far too tall to climb were gone, replaced by saplings and young trees. But the greatest changes were the paths, paths she remembered as crowded with other students, her friends.

They were empty.

The laboratories still had their equipment, but there was no one there to argue over who got to use it first.

The greenhouses were crowded with flourishing plants, but empty of people. Only the robots were present.

Marna's vision blurred as she stared at the narrow, waved leaves of a plant her herbalist professor had described as an excellent remedy for localized itching. What had his name been? All the students had called him Squeaker, for his high voice and bouncy personality, and she couldn't even remember his real name. She could see and hear him in memory, though, and remember how to make the infusion that would sooth a rash. The plant grew from offsets, he'd told the class.

And now he was dead, a victim of the plague.

"That one, too," she told the robot at her side when she could speak again. "I'll work out where to plant each of them."

Immediately to the east of the house, she decided, should be a fragrance garden, with the healing herbs beyond it. Unfortunately she did not have climate-controlled greenhouses, and some of the herbs she wanted did not grow well on the island.

"Grow," she snarled at a raindrop plant, and what she thought at it could not be put into words. The little bush was no larger than her hand, with fat, translucent leaves. Those leaves were useful as a wound dressing for R'il'nian and tineral alike, and Marna was determined to have a few plants available. The drought-adapted plants, however, did not appreciate the island's moist climate. Another leaf dropped as she knelt by the raised bed.

She rocked back on her heels and thought. An open greenhouse, perhaps, with a transparent ceiling to let in the sun but not the rain. But if she was going to do that, she would have to limit the time she spent away from the island. She did not want the island to be run by sophisticated robots, and the all-purpose gardening robot she'd brought in once she'd finished her planting and remodeling was useful only for routine weeding and watering. Good for a week or two without her supervision, but not much longer.

She had always wanted to learn snow sports, and she had planned to spend her second winter on Riya at a mainland mountain resort. She had even confirmed that the robot trainers were still functional. But did she need to spend the whole winter away from her island and the company of the tinerals? Did she even want to? Her new home was powered by a small fusion generator, and with that to tap into for energy it wouldn't be hard to teleport back and forth between the resort and her island.

Yes, she decided. She needed exercise, as much for her mind as for her body. But there was no reason not to use her esper talents to get to the best places to exercise. Next winter she would teleport back and forth between the snows of the mountains and her island.

The window was brighter than normal, even set to translucent, and when Marna flipped the switch to turn it transparent, the snow outside was so bright that she squinted and darkened the window. "The storm's over," she chanted, as she leaned her forehead against the window. Brilliant blue skies and snow-covered mountains met her gaze, with even the narrow trees all but hidden in the untracked whiteness.

She'd spent close to a month with the automated trainers, learning to use the thermal suit and forcewebs. She knew how to set the friction of the forcewebs to allow sliding in any direction. She could ski, snowshoe or toboggan, on the level or on slopes, and change the settings as the terrain demanded. She had been ready for the final test, to head cross-country on her own. And then the storms had started.

Three storms, one after another, had battered the mountains. She had teleported back and forth to Windhome, and even considered trying another winter resort area. But that would mean changing the route she had planned, and she found herself increasingly reluctant to change anything she had planned, and more and more short-tempered when things did not go as she intended. This morning, though, the sky was clear and the weather promised to hold for several days. She smiled widely as she turned back to don her thermal clothing and picked up her forcewebs.

She was not pleased when the computer advised against leaving the immediate vicinity of the lodge. <Why?> she snapped back. <Is another storm coming?>

\Weather forecast clear,\ the machine responded. \But\

<Suspend advisory,> Marna ordered. <I'm going.> It was a cheap victory, as the machine was programmed to take orders from Riyans. But it was a victory nonetheless, and put her back into a better humor.

Her good mood remained dominant while she ate breakfast, packed lunch into her light backpack, and attached the forcewebs securely to her boots and the control unit to her belt. When she stepped out into the snow she was buoyant, enjoying the bite of the wind on her face and the prickle of ice in her nostrils. She was almost reluctant to activate the face shield on the thermal suit, and when she did, she adjusted it only to cut the glare of sun on snow and keep her face from freezing.

The first leg of her trip was familiar, up the wide, gentle slope behind the lodge with the sun at her back and her own long, blue shadow before her. She waved at the shadow and giggled when it waved back. When she came to the ridge line she laughed aloud at the fold on fold of whiteness before her, and then turned right, to follow the slightly steeper slope uphill to the head of the first downhill run.

Beautiful, Win whispered at the back of her mind. *But love, don't you think you ought to find out why the computer didn't want you leaving the lodge area?*

Her happiness vanished like snow in the desert. *Will you give me no privacy at all?* she snapped. *Get out of my mind!*

She felt his dismay, but was unmoved by it. *Won't you even try your CP?* he finally asked tentatively.

I said get out, she exploded, and tried for the first time to go after him as the intruder she then felt him to be. How dare he treat her as a child!

I love you, he whispered and then, between one breath and the next, he was gone. For the first time since she had returned to Riya, she felt totally alone.

And about time, she thought as she looked out over the mountains. But some of the brightness seemed gone from the day, and the wind seemed to chill, rather than invigorate her.

It didn't matter, she told herself. She didn't need an imaginary companion, and certainly not one dead long since. She would complete her daylong trek, and tell the computer—what? It would answer only as it was programmed to. Well, she would follow the route she had planned, anyway.

The sun rose higher in the sky, warming her face through the shield. She flung herself down powder slopes with what she told herself was gleeful abandon, and reset her force webs to climb the next rises. Now and then she heard roaring, or saw plumes of white rising above distant mountainsides, and thought that perhaps she could learn avalanche surfing. Not the wild avalanches, of course, but surfing avalanches triggered by controlled use of telekinesis had once been a popular sport. She thought about that as she sat on a ridge crest eating lunch.

She was perhaps an hour into the afternoon, descending a slope in great zigzagging loops, when disaster struck. She was so accustomed to the occasional roar of avalanches by then that it took her a moment to realize that this roar was from uphill, and a further moment to glance over her shoulder and see the snowy hillside falling toward her. With crystal clarity she realized that this was the danger of which the computer—and Win—had tried to warn her. A danger even she had recognized—and ignored.

And she was not prepared.

If she had prepared in advance, she could have teleported herself out of the danger zone. But esper talents were not outside of the laws of physics. To teleport herself, she must balance momentum, energy and mass, as well as making sure two masses did not try to occupy the same space. Given time—even a minute or two—she could have calculated those balances and jumped out of danger.

She did not have the time.

Even as she crouched and aimed herself for a belt of trees that might provide some protection, the leading edge of the avalanche overran her, tumbling her helplessly down the slope. The churning snow caught and twisted one forceweb until she thought her leg would break, but the torsion activated the safety cutoffs and the forcewebs went abruptly inert. She clawed her way upward through the fast-moving snow, and tried to remember what lay downhill. Only her perceptive sense kept her from total disorientation.

The buffeting and spinning as she was carried along reminded her of the time she had been caught in the breaking wave—but then Win had been there to rescue her. Win. She had repudiated whatever was left of Win, but as the slowing mass suddenly set rigidly about her body, she wondered at her own insanity in wanting to be alone. She struggled to move, but felt only the slight snapping of a switch, followed by the growing cold of the snow that held her prisoner. Her struggles must have turned off the thermal suit, she realized with a growing sense of despair. Exhausted and chilled, she could not even visualize a place of safety. *Win,* she sobbed mentally. *Forgive me, my love.*

She thought she heard him sigh behind her, and the embrace of the snow seemed to warm a little. *I can't move you,* his voice came gently, *but I can show you the way.* Slowly a picture grew in her mind, of her room at the lodge and a simple three-way exchange teleport: the air in a small volume of the room to the snow outside at the level of the floor, her own mass in that snow to replace her own body, and her body to the new vacuum in the room. Momentum and potential energy balanced, and while the teleport was not elegant, she thought she still had the strength to do it. If she did it now, before her body chilled any further. She reached for air and snow and made the exchange, falling to the floor in sheer exhaustion as she returned to the blessed warmth of the room.

She couldn't just ignore warnings, she realized as she dragged her bruised body to the bed and wearily stripped off the inactive thermal suit. She still had the job Tyr had given her, of hanging on until the description of the plague could be transmitted to other R'il'nai.

But she wished, as she curled her body up beneath the covers and waited for warmth to return, that she had died in the avalanche and rejoined her people.

Marna asked the computer for information on avalanches the following day, and spent the next two days skimming it. She had intended to concentrate on avalanche hazards, and was initially repelled by the reminder that avalanche surfing had once been a popular sport. At first, with the nightmare of total loss of control close, she was horrified at the idea. She concentrated on recognizing the warning signs as she returned to skiing and snowboarding. But she kept remembering how it felt to surf the waves, so smoothly thrilling above, so turbulent below. Was the same true of avalanches? And it wasn't as if teleportation wasn't a fail-safe, if she was just thinking about the hazards.

By the winter solstice she had expanded her lessons to include avalanche surfing. Not slab or wet-snow avalanches, she didn't feel ready for those yet. She learned to ride small, carefully triggered avalanches of powder snow and found it far more thrilling than skiing or water surfing. Gradually she began to ride larger and larger avalanches, until a day came when the air and snow surface alike were too warm for dry-snow avalanches. The spring equinox and the beginning of the new year had caught up with her.

Third Year

Spring was the time for planting. Herb seeds this year, for the annual herbs, and of course the vegetable seeds. Some of the perennials had died—perhaps they needed a colder winter than that on the island? No matter, there were plenty of small plants at the Healers' Center. Half a month later Marna looked around herself and found nothing to do but pull weeds—which the robots could do perfectly well.

The resort where she had spent the winter still had snow, but it was increasingly soggy. Borderline for skiing, and impossible for avalanche surfing. Marna *wanted* to go avalanche surfing. The southern hemisphere? But she already knew better. Virtually all of Riya's mountains were in the northern hemisphere. Where would the earliest skiing be, next fall? When she asked the computer she was astonished at the answer.

Now! There *was* a winter sports area that still had dry snow, though she would have to give the computer a day or two to get it operational. She had forgotten the mountains near the North Pole, snow covered and below freezing year around and with the sun shining continuously in the summer. What a wonderful place to go while the garden was getting established!

It would be cold, this early in the spring. She'd need a heavier thermal suit, but that was no problem. She teleported to the new ski area a few days later, and within a very few more days was becoming accustomed to the sun being low even at noon, and the sky staying light at midnight. She found rocks—mountain peaks—poking through the snow in places, and other areas where the computer warned her of crevasses under the snow.

<Are they stable enough to levitate into?> she asked once she understood what a crevasse was.

\Some are, but it is not advisable.\ She ignored the second phrase, only asking the computer to find her a stable crevasse.

It took time, but when the computer told her it had found a crevasse that appeared stable, Marna promptly donned her thermal suit and teleported to the rim of the crevasse. She was disappointed at first to find herself in what looked like an ordinary snow field. But when she felt around with her perception, she found that there was only a thin layer of snow bridging a great chasm at her feet. Better have a good look at where she was going, she thought, and teleported the snow away.

No wonder the computer had advised against skiing in this area! The snow bridge would never have held a skier's weight, even with the force webs adjusted to their longest. The sun was shining brightly, making the snow too bright a white to look at without the face shield, but the chasm was an incredibly deep, brilliant blue. As she levitated herself into it, the blue grew more intense as the darkening of her face shield grew less, with the light coming as much from the walls as from the narrowing strip of nearly white sky overhead. She almost forgot the lesson of the wild avalanche. Almost, but not quite. When one of the walls moved, ever so slightly, she teleported herself back to her room at the lodge instantly.

If computers could breathe sighs of relief, she thought, that was what the planetary computer did. That night the incredible blue followed her into her dreams. In its own way, she thought as she woke, the descent into the crevasse had been almost as exciting as avalanche surfing. Not something she'd want to do every day, but she told the computer to find her more crevasses.

She asked the computer for more information, and learned that the crevasses were in a glacier flowing to the warmer lands bordering the sea, and that the color was due to the way the ice had crystallized from layer upon layer of snow. The sea? She went to the foot of the glacier and found that a river flowed from a great cave at its end. She flew above the river, downstream, and after a long day's travel above its forested banks found where it flowed into the sea. The trees seemed quite different from those of Windhome, and she spent several days exploring the new forest.

But the blue of the crevasses and the thrill of riding the avalanches still called her, and she returned to the higher country. She was flying through a more twisted crevasse than most when she saw the darkness in the blue. At first she thought it was a rock, like several others she had seen trapped in the heart of the glacier. But the shape was wrong, and when she reached out with her mind, she realized that she was looking at a R'il'nian body.

The only complete body she'd found until now had been the mummy in the desert sands, but she'd found several skulls and femurs, and once a nearly whole skeleton. She'd sent them all into the sun, with love and regret. She had no thought but to do the same here—but she couldn't manage such a long teleport while levitating herself. She looked upward, to where the blue sky shone as a line of white light, and flew up into the brightness. She walked quickly to a spot she judged was just above the body, and felt downward. There. She locked her mind on what had once been a person like herself, and teleported it to the ice beside her.

A woman, the hair long and confined by the clasp that meant she had been trying for a baby. The body looked—not peaceful, for there was pain and despair in the expression, but far more complete than the mummy had been. As she herself might have looked after two centuries, if Win had not helped her to teleport to safety after the avalanche. Tears blurred her vision as she pulled off her thermal gloves to cradle the woman's face in her hands.

"I'm sorry," she whispered. "I wish there was something I could do to help you." But there wasn't, beyond a decent funeral. She no longer had to ask the computer for the words to accompany the teleport into the sun, but her grief was no less. When the body was gone she stood, brushed the snow from the knees of her thermal suit, and teleported back to Windhome. This time, however, she stayed for only a few days before returning to the clean coldness of the snow country.

MEETINGS

ZHAIM

10/6/35

The jump warning sounded—two dissonances alternating at two-second intervals, impossible to sleep through even if the lights had not gone on when the warning sounded. Zhaim swore and reached for the shock webbing, fastening it over his body on the bunk. Webbing, not a force field. Clumsy but necessary. He swore again, glad that he did not have his father's limitations.

XP ships were notorious for the roughness of their jump transitions. Possible destination points for a jump could be picked up via electromagnetic radiation—but they were picked up where they had been when that radiation was produced. For a five light-year jump, that meant the ship would be aimed at where the jump point had been five years before—and where it almost certainly would not be when the ship arrived. While an accurately aimed jump was smooth, one aimed slightly away from the actual jump point was—to put it mildly—difficult. Artificial gravity and force fields tended to do strange things during such jumps, hence the physical webbing and the fact that exploration jumps were normally taken in free fall. Zhaim had known that intellectually before this trip, but he hadn't realized what it would feel like, even when he learned that the crew called the ship the Bounceabout.

And the jumps were so damnably frequent. His father was very good at conditional precognition, good enough that Zhaim had trusted him—at least briefly. But the old R'il'nian now freely admitted that he didn't know anything at all about the planet they were seeking; he knew only that it was

143

overpoweringly important that he find it, fast. Lai had speculated on the reason—something coming up in the Confederation that would need help from other R'il'nai to handle?—but as far as Zhaim could see, they might as well have been playing the old children's game of near and far. And Zhaim didn't want other R'il'nai interfering in his own plans.

The warning changed to one-second alternation, and the artificial gravity cut out. Jump due within sixty seconds. Zhaim gulped and grabbed for one of the bags he kept in easy reach of his bunk. With only the loss of gravity, he had managed to keep his stomach under control. If the jump was anything like as rough as they had been lately, he'd lose it—and he knew from bitter experience that his father would not allow the crew to clean up after him. Lai even cleaned up his own messes, which Zhaim considered a horrible example. R'il'nians should *never* be seen doing menial work!

The lights went out and his body surged against the webbing, seeming to twist several different ways at once. He barely had time to get the bag to his mouth before his outraged stomach erupted. He was still heaving when the lights came on and the floor gradually became down again. His nausea only subsided when gravity became completely normal. Damn, this was the second jump in less than a day. And his father *knew* how sensitive he was to them.

The lights began dimming again, but he was far too upset to sleep. He started to reach for the light level mentally, then remembered that on this ship the controls were all physical. He had to remember where the damned switch was, and then TK it into the on position. Human ships carried R'il'noids often enough that they should be equipped for telepathic needs!

He pulled the shock webbing aside and looked gloomily at his wardrobe. Nothing there the crew hadn't seen him in a dozen times, but he still took a few minutes to choose. Properly dressed in silver and garnet, he slid open his door and strode firmly toward the control room.

An argument, with his father's voice raised against those of the crew? Zhaim had been frustrated by the fact that the crew members, though young as was usual on an exploration ship, were fiercely loyal to his doddering old father, rather than responding to his own youthful energy. But a moment of listening outside the room told him this was not the opportunity he was looking for. The crew members were arguing with his father, all right, but only because his father wanted to take some risk and they considered that part of their job was to guard him. Zhaim eased into the control room, discovering that every person on the ship was present.

"This is not dangerous!" Lai argued, and even Zhaim had to admit he sounded anything but doddering. "That message has to be from the R'il'nian planet I'm looking for. Yes, they had a disease problem, or did when that message was sent. But that was a light-speed message. We don't know the distance, only the direction. They could have found a cure by now, but to find out, we have to move in that direction. The inverse square law will tell us exactly where they are or were once we know how fast the signal strength is falling off. And a plague isn't going to spread through vacuum! We needn't land on the planet if it's not safe. Could even be Kharfun—the symptoms sound like it—and we have a cure for that."

Captain Tova had to throw her head back to meet Lai eye to eye, but that was exactly what she was doing. "We will not risk you," she said, but there was just a trace of wavering in her voice.

Zhaim wasn't sure of all the nuances of the argument, but he had every intention of being on the winning side—which he fully expected would be his father's side. Besides, if the old R'il'nian wanted to risk his life, that was his own business. Zhaim certainly wasn't going to stop him. "Getting more information is hardly a risk," he suggested politely, and preened himself at the light brush of his father's approval.

Captain Tova glared at them both. "Information alone, no," she agreed. "But if we get more information you're going to want to stick your neck out farther and farther." She backed up a step, apparently realizing that she had gone too far.

What does it matter, Zhaim thought scornfully, next year or next millennium. Father, your species was extinct before I was born, with no females left. And I'm not the only one of the younger R'il'noids to feel that way. Cloning—well, he tended to agree with his father's stodgy conservatism on that. The last thing he'd want to face was a clone of himself.

"Anyone who goes down to the surface wears an isolation suit—including me. But we do need that information."

Captain Tova was definitely wavering now, glancing around at her crew instead of keeping her eyes locked on Lai. "So what exactly do you want us to do?" she asked, her voice clipped.

"Keep jumping toward that signal, with jumps as long and as close in time as we can manage," Lai replied. "We've got a direction now, not just my CP. Listen for the signal at each jump point, and get accurate measurements of intensity and of any change in the message. It'll take at least two or three jumps to get an accurate fix on how far we have to go, but I'm guessing a month to reach the system. Then we worry about whether we're facing a dead system, desperate survivors, or a recovered population."

"And may the Mothers help those with weak stomachs," someone muttered, and Zhaim winced. He'd forgotten that aspect of following his father's wishes.

✱   ✱   ✱   ✱

"I got there well into the argument," Zhaim said later, at the door to his father's quarters. "What did I miss?"

Lai waved him into the room. "Light-speed voice transmission, speaking R'il'nian," he replied. "Not quite the inflection I'm used to, but even an inherited language changes with time, and I'm guessing a couple of hundred thousand years separation. What we picked up was a warn-off—planet wide disease, with a very thorough description of the symptoms and course of the disease. We got a single point in time—they may have found a cure. But the symptoms and course sound almost exactly like Kharfun. I used conditional precognition the instant I heard the message. What I got was an overwhelming sense of urgency. I think I've been misinterpreting that. But if it is due to the disease, I wouldn't get that if they were all dead, or if they'd found a cure."

"Kharfun? Diseases don't just develop out of nothing. They spread. Now and then they mutate or jump from one species to another, as Kharfun apparently did. But how could Kharfun have jumped the gap between the Confederation and some isolated planet?"

"We know from Derry's discovery on the waterworld that the inhabitants of this planet were exploring toward the Confederation. And how many Human-crewed exploration ships have gone out this way and never reported back? All it would take is one contact of a carrier, and transport fast enough that an infected R'il'nian got back to his or her home planet. Besides, I checked the Kharfun idea out with CP. We're carrying immune serum and secondary treatments for Kharfun. Overkill, since we're the only two on board who'd get really sick, and we're both immune. I ran a CP on ditching them. They're going to be needed. Badly. If we can get there soon enough.

"Better get back to your room and get some sleep. I've already felt out the next jump—probably eight hours from now. And they're going to be rough, because I'm making them as long as possible, now that we're sure of the direction."

Marna

Marna was almost ready to trigger the avalanche when she knocked one hand against the control and flinched at the pain. What was wrong with her hands, anyway? Frostbite wasn't supposed to be possible with the thermal suits. Once again she sent her Healing sense into her own hands, this time checking her feet as well. The nerves were irritated, inflamed, but she could detect no indication of why.

Well, she wasn't going to let it interfere with the run she'd spent most of the morning setting up. Avalanche surfing had become somewhat of an obsession. It wasn't that dangerous with properly adjusted equipment and advance planning, but it was thrilling. Now she looked down slope, identifying her landmarks. She had preplanned emergency teleports from half a dozen places along her run, and she made sure they were all set firmly in her mind in case the avalanche she was ready to trigger grew beyond her control.

She made the final adjustments on her forcewebs, this time including levitation circuits that would make her effectively less dense than the snow she would be riding, and scowled again at the clumsiness of her hands. She triggered the slide, and then she was aware only of the thunder beneath her, the need for constant, tiny adjustments to stay upright in the chaos she rode, and her landmarks sliding past at dizzying speed.

The avalanche slowed as she passed her final landmark and moved into the runout zone—all too soon for Marna. For a brief moment she had been able to forget her plight. She stopped and reset her forcewebs to allow her to ski back to the lodge, then nearly fell as her foot cramped violently.

Good thing that hadn't happened during the run, she thought as she sent her mind into the foot, easing the cramp and searching for its cause. Neurological again—but why? Her symptoms were disturbingly similar to those of the plague. But she'd been back on Riya for two years, now. Not many bodies had survived the two centuries since the dying, but she'd sent others besides that first desert mummy to their final rest in the sun, touched them in love and pity. If the plague lingered, she should have felt its effects long since. But the symptoms she was feeling now …

There was so much they had never learned, and never would learn, about the plague. The majority view, and the one that explained Marna's continued good health, had been that contact with a living or recently dead victim was required for transmission—that the causative agent, whatever it was, could only replicate in living R'il'nian cells.

If she was in fact coming down with the plague, that fact needed to be added to the warnoff broadcast, for it indicated that the planet was still dangerous.

She had planned to ski back to the lodge, but the warnoff was more important. Although she increasingly avoided Windhome, finding the memories it held too painful to face, she knew it was where she wanted to die. Modify the warnoff first, she thought as she set up the teleport, and then she could allow herself to despair.

But when Marna relaxed her determination and allowed herself to feel again, what she felt was not despair, but an overpowering sense of relief. She grieved for the tinerals, but not for herself. She would continue to update the warnoff for as long as she was able, but then she would go to the meadow where she and Win had once made love, and leave her body there for the scavengers, letting it return to the life of the island. She had not realized, until it was lifted from her shoulders, how heavy a burden the continuing decision to live had been.

Lai

10/18/35

"Got it," Cinda said absently, even before gravity had returned to normal. "Lots stronger, of course—that star's only a couple of light years away, now. And I think ..."

"It's changed!" Lai said, fighting back his excitement. Up until now, the message had been the same every time they picked it up, obviously a recording broadcast over and over. Now he was listening to a woman's voice, weary to the point of exhaustion, explaining that the life support system had given out on something—an isolation satellite?—from which she had been monitoring the planet. She was returning to her planet to die, and she gave explanations of how to access visual broadcasts of the plague, with repeated and vehement warnings against trying to land on the doomed world. That part, he decided, he would not translate. But the visual broadcasts were certainly worth examining, assuming he could work out how to get the ship's equipment to display them.

That problem turned out to be minor—there were, after all, only so many ways to encode an image. It took only hours before they could look at the plague effects—and Lai was increasingly sure that they were looking at the effects of Kharfun. And in that case, he argued, there would be no danger in visiting the planet.

The crew, he found rapidly, had other ideas.

"It's not that we don't trust you," Elik said. "We trust you completely to keep us safe. It's just that we don't trust you to keep yourself safe."

"Elik's found three possible jump points in the fringes of the system—a couple of days from the inner planets on system drive," Captain Tova said. "I know that you are going to want to check for any survivors and examine the planet. But before we make the final jump, you agree to do it our way." The rest of the crew nodded in agreement. Zhaim looked outraged, and Lai sent his son a firm *Shut up and let me handle this*. He could take the situation over if he had to, but that was strictly a last resort.

Captain Tova continued: "Examine the planet from orbit first. If surface examination is needed, you teleport down one of the crew—Cinda's volunteered—in an isolation suit. If there's any question at all about the disease, you 'port the volunteer back directly and leave the suit on the planet. If the isolation's breached, if there's any chance that she could carry contagion, she stays on planet." Cinda was nodding in agreement. "You get the information you need via mind-link from Cinda."

"But mind-link's unethical ..." He was stretching that point. He wanted to get down to the surface himself!

"Bullshit," Cinda replied, startling everyone in the control room. "I'm alive today because the Lord Derik suggested a mind-link as a safety precaution when I had to do an antenna repair in really nasty conditions. It was a strong enough link he was able to take over completely and teleport me out of a situation I'd never have survived otherwise. Forced mind-link, or influencing another person without their permission—yes, I'd object to that. But letting you use my eyes and ears—to the extent they can be used in an isolation suit—there just isn't a problem. I'll be insulted if you refuse."

She meant it, and she was right. There were guidelines for the ethical use of esper abilities, and this situation was well within the guidelines, however much he personally disliked it. "But suppose there is no danger?" he asked. "Suppose I'm right, and it turns out to be Kharfun? We have supplies on board to fight a few cases of that, and that last message implied that we'll find at most a few of my people left alive."

"Convince me that it's Kharfun and we have the supplies to treat it, and I'll back down. But I will not risk you, I will not risk the Confederation, and I will not risk my ship."

All of which was quite correct, Lai thought, if not exactly what he wanted to hear. "Agreed," he said reluctantly.

Zhaim, predictably, was outraged. "The trouble with you," he said as they walked back to their cabins, "is that you always see all of the sides of every question, and it paralyzes you."

Except, Lai thought, the side that insisted that Zhaim was the greatest danger the Confederation had ever faced. He had argued, as much to himself as to others, that Zhaim was simply slow to mature. He had loved his son, still loved him. But three months of enforced intimacy had led to some unflattering comparisons. Derik had been slow to mature, yes—stories of the wild youth of Lai's older half-brother were still circulating. But Derik at his worst had been thoughtless and irresponsible, never deliberately cruel. By the time Lai had been born, Derik was beginning to develop some sense of responsibility, or Lai's parents would never have allowed him to handle Lai's own early esper training. Lyra had been right about that. And Zhaim …

Zhaim was older now than Derik had been in Lai's early memories. And while he was undeniably brilliant in his chosen field of bioengineering, he was seriously lacking in ability to understand the motivations of others.

"Seeing all of the sides of every question," he told Zhaim, "and the knowledge that I do, is precisely what makes me able to hold the Confederation together. Think about it. And while you're at it, you might consider that the crew was arguing for my safety—and yours."

10/19/35

The last jump put them into the outer fringes of the system, headed at an angle toward a blue inner planet and adjusting momentum at a rate that would have been impossible without artificial gravity, and difficult without Lai's ability to swap momentum between the ship and handy asteroids. For once Zhaim, as a powerful esper backup, was genuinely helpful, and Lai was unstinting in his praise. But the new change in the broadcast warning more than countered his relief that Zhaim was doing something right. After two years on the planet the single survivor—no question now that she was alone, or female—was showing symptoms of the disease.

He didn't know when the change in the broadcast had occurred. Less than two years ago, but before they had made the final jump. The message had included daily updates with detailed descriptions of the woman's symptoms for eight days, but did that mean she had died after eight days, or that another update would come soon, or that she had simply been too weak to continue the updates after eight days? Nineteen hours since they had picked up the message, now, and another twelve hours until they could begin the final deceleration into an orbit around the planet. He should break and get some sleep. Leaving the momentum changes entirely up to the ship's in-system drive would have been a possibility, but would have taken several days before an orbit was achieved. This way was faster, though it meant the last few hours would be exhausting for him and for Zhaim both.

He didn't think he could sleep until he knew whether the survivor was still alive. He leaned back and closed his eyes, trying to think if there was any way Kharfun infection could have survived so long on a planet empty of possible hosts. The message droned on in the background, unchanging. He had it memorized by now.

When the words changed, he jerked awake, momentarily confused by the cushions supporting his head and the light blanket over his body. But she was still alive! That was the important thing. He struggled upright, listening carefully to her voice. Hands and feet paralyzed, pain and muscle spasms throughout her body, esper talents very little affected. Still following the pattern of Kharfun in everything except the fact of her infection after all her people had died. He opened his mind, feeling for the echo of her words and trying to pinpoint them on the world ahead. They had a rough map, now, and he thought he could locate her in the subtropics, in one of the major ocean areas. A cloud band hid what he thought was the location, but there must be an island there.

Try to deepen the contact? No—she was again insisting that no ship should land and risk contagion, and he was afraid mind-touch would let her pick up his own ambivalence. He could not let her die alone—but neither could he abandon the Confederation. "Can we contact her?" he asked Cinda, in the seat beside him.

The young woman shrugged. "No telling what kind of receiving equipment she has with her, but I can send a voice transmission with the same characteristics as her outgoing light-speed message. Just remember we're still several light-minutes away. There'll be a noticeable delay."

Mental interfaces were available for Humans, but few non-R'il'noids could control their thoughts well enough to use them without feedback when accuracy was critical. Cinda used a combination of direct mental input and the switches and buttons on her control board, checking the results on her monitor before nodding to Lai. "That should be it," she told him. "Hold down this pad if you want your voice transmitted."

He was suddenly speechless, with no idea of what to say. Not adolescent shyness, exactly—though that probably had a part in it. He had not met a female of his own species since his last great aunt had died, five centuries ago, and never one who was not a relative. But his father, the last person who spoke the language he had been born knowing, had died a mere quarter of a century ago. This woman had been alone for eight times as long—and for him, there had been the company of both R'il'noids and Humans. For her, there had been no intelligent company.

He could not risk panicking her. Both her transmissions and his own knowledge of Kharfun told him that she must be in agony, held to life only by her own determination to serve some purpose in her death. He had to assume her esper abilities were at least the equal of his own, and while a survivable teleport took some time to set up correctly, a suicide teleport did not. He ran over her last transmissions in his head, and nodded. If he was reading her aright, she would not live for herself, especially if she thought her life to be a danger to others. Teleporting to her side, which was what he wanted to do, would more than likely provoke her suicide. But she would fight for life if she thought that her life would serve others. Not wholly sane—how could she be? But an admirable kind of insanity.

He touched the transmit pad and spoke aloud, a very brief message: "We need your help." Then he sat back and waited for the interminable minutes it took for his message to reach the planet. He still didn't quite dare mind-touch, but he did stay open wide on an empathic level. That left him open to emotions on the ship—some fear and worry from the Humans aboard, but not bothersome. Zhaim's disgust and lack of sympathy for the woman below, even in sleep, were far more jarring, and he found himself trying to tune his son out.

His message should be reaching her—now! He felt her shock and disbelief, then the slow growth of curiosity, and gasped with relief. He didn't dare try enough contact to get the sense of her reply, but at least he hadn't startled her into a suicidal state. He let out a sigh and saw Cinda smile in response, followed a moment later by emotions of relief and pleasure from the rest of the crew. He waited for the woman's verbal response, phrasing possible answers in his head.

"Who are you? What help can I give? This planet is contaminated—please, whatever you do, don't try to land here."

"I'm Lai Tarlian, R'il'nian. We've been monitoring your broadcasts as we moved in—we should be in orbit in another of your days, but nobody will go down without an isolation suit. Your symptoms seem to match a disease that just about wiped my people out ten millennia ago. We have immune serum and the necessary drugs on board. But we need to know how you were exposed. Kharfun normally spreads by person-to-person transmission. Can you tell me exactly what you were doing thirty to forty-five days ago?"

Again the long wait. This time he got to his feet and stretched, then teleported the cushions and blanket out of the crowded room. "She's alive," he reported to the crew in Galactica, "and her symptoms are still matching Kharfun. Except for how she was infected. I've asked her what she was doing during the critical period."

The recorded broadcast had cut out with the woman's first answer, and Lai jumped in spite of himself when the voice came through again. "Avalanche surfing, if you must know. Would an image help? Or—perhaps we could touch minds, and I could give you my memories? The delay isn't really necessary."

Lai settled himself back in the chair as he reached for her mind. *No, it isn't,* he thought. Her mind came into his, hesitant at first, then in a rush that told him how desperately alone she had been. And the texture of her mind . . . *Are you a Healer?* he asked, irresistibly reminded of Bera.

Yes, and with the affirmative came the memory of her years on the isolation satellite, thinking at first to protect her people from what had turned out to be a minor disease, but that isolation later becoming her own protection from a much more serious problem. Then, almost shyly: *My name is Marna.*

Marna. Avalanche surfing? Is it winter where you are? The spot where he thought she was located was in the subtropics of the summer hemisphere.

No, it's very near the summer solstice. And there are no good, snow-covered mountains in the winter hemisphere, so I was at an old resort area in this hemisphere, nearer the pole and at a high elevation. Her mind opened a memory to him, of snow and speed and the awesome power of the avalanche beneath her. His own mind, conditioned from birth to the importance of avoiding risk, flinched away from the danger of what was, to her, no more than an extreme sport. Then the significance of what she had said reached him.

You were in permafrost country? Where it's below freezing even in mid-summer? Is there any chance you touched a body that had been frozen since death?

Her mood flipped instantly from excitement to near-despair, and an image of a frozen body. *Very few bodies survived. When I find them, I give them the funeral rites they should have had.*

He shared her grief, and tried to send her that fact. *Of course. But Kharfun requires a living host to replicate. Dehydration at normal temperatures kills it. If tissue is frozen shortly after death, it can survive and remain infective.*

The others—they were all mummified, or only bones. He had a brief image of a desiccated corpse, buried in drifted sand, and blinked back tears triggered by her emotions. *Last month—she was frozen.*

How long was a month, here? *You couldn't know. But it sounds more and more like Kharfun. If I teleport you a vial with the proper reagents for the fast test, can you add a bit of your spinal fluid?*

Brief hesitation as she assessed his purpose. *Send me three. One for me, one for a mammal from R'il'n, one for a tineral.*

Good. Keep track of which is which. A positive test is green crystals forming in the reagent. Takes only a bit longer than the delay in our light-speed conversation. He looked around the control room, locating the medic, Kalar. "I need three Kharfun test vials, right away," he said. "When you've got them to me, hunt out the immune serum and Kharfun drugs. And the base sequence for the Kharfun virus. The standard test will be enough to convince me, but in deference to our Captain—" he bowed his head toward Captain Tova—"and to Marna, I think we probably ought to do the gene sequence to verify that the disease is Kharfun."

"Marna?" Cinda asked. "Is that her name? Well, I'd better go get the isolation suit. She's going to need nursing, though doing that in an isolation suit …" She rolled her eyes as she started for the door, and then hesitated.

"Lai, get her to give you the teleport coordinates where she is, will you? I don't want to spend time trying to find her in that blasted suit."

Kalar hurried back in as Cinda left, the two performing a dance of avoidance in the narrow door. "Here's the test vials," he said, then gulped audibly as Lai teleported the vials to Marna. Cinda might not know as much as Kalar about medicine, Lai thought wryly, but the medic almost certainly would not be able to accept teleportation without mental damage. He thought Cinda was looking forward to the experience.

Marna had teleported a sample of her own spinal fluid into the first vial, and repeated the operation with a scarlet-feathered, winged quadruped that she regarded as a pet. Now she was reaching out, searching for a R'il'n-derived animal Lai recognized at once. *Xira?* he sent. *I hoped I'd finally found a planet with neither Xira nor mice. So far, the only planets with R'il'nian or Human inhabitants where one isn't found, it's because it's been out-competed by the other.*

Mice?

The Terran equivalent of Xira. He watched as she located one of the ubiquitous opportunists and teleported a sample of its spinal fluid into the third vial. She glanced back at the first vial, and Lai relaxed a fraction more. Already a greenish tinge clouded the vial, and as they watched, the green sparkles grew more pronounced. Marna waited several minutes more to make her report.

Mine's green, all right. The other two aren't showing any trace of change. Lai, why?

Your immune system's based on detecting viruses by esper. But Kharfun's invisible to esper. We've evolved away from the old antigen-based system, probably because when it goes wrong, all kinds of autoimmune diseases result. But with Kharfun, the esper system doesn't work and the old system does. And Kharfun requires a highly evolved nervous system to replicate, so it doesn't affect animals— even R'il'n-derived animals. My people were lucky—we were already closely associated with Humans when Kharfun first hit us, and with their aid we found a cure, based on their ability to produce antigenic immunity to the disease. He glanced around and saw Cinda, bulky in the isolation suit, standing just outside the doorway, with Kalar bustling toward her.

Humans?

Very much like the R'il'nai, but less mature. Some R'il'nian genes, even. Cross breeding's possible. Marna, I'm alone, too. I've had the Humans and crossbreds for company, so I haven't been as much alone as you have, but—you understand why I had to find you, once I even suspected you might exist?

He felt her shock at the idea of the cross breeding, but full explanations could later come. *This ship,* he sent, *is crewed by Humans. At this point, I'm sure they're immune to your plague—but the Human volunteer I'm teleporting down is in an isolation suit, and she'll stay in it until we've confirmed the Kharfun by genetic sequencing of the virus. She has synthetic immune serum and the other drugs needed to start secondary treatment, and I'll stay in touch with you to block the pain. May have to break a little to help get the ship into orbit, and there's a lot I'll have to show you about reversing the effects. Can you give me coordinates to land Cinda?*

Lai reached for Cinda's mind and body, preparing for the teleport even as he waited for Marna's response. The image that came into his mind at first was fuzzy but beautiful: a pocket valley, floored with flower-spangled grassoids and watered by a spring-fed, pebble-bottomed stream he could have stepped across. Then the image faded. *No,* Marna said in his mind. *I came here to die. If I am to be nursed, it will be in my own bed.* He felt her gather her mind for a teleport, and the valley vanished, replaced by a sharply visualized room looking out on breakers and a beach of amethyst sand.

This is my workroom, she sent firmly. *I will be in my sleeping room, down the corridor from the inner door. And be quite sure that your Cinda understands the importance of staying in her isolation suit. I will not be responsible for any further spread of this disease.*

Marna

10/26/35

Marna's nose twitched. Some of the smells were familiar, as if she had programmed the "breakfast" option on the automated food dispenser—something she rarely did, preferring her own cooking to synthetics. Others … She sniffed again, hoping to identify the unfamiliar but tantalizing odors. Warmth spilled across her face—the sun must have risen from behind the mountain at the island's core. Footsteps …

Footsteps?

Startled, she turned her head toward the door and opened her eyes. An unfamiliar face looked in, copper-skinned, with dark, short hair in tight curls. Not quite R'il'nian, with a rather large face extending higher up the front of the head than it should, but similar enough she could read the expression. The large mouth widened in an open-mouthed smile. "Awake? Good. Would you like some breakfast?"

The language wasn't R'il'nian, but it was comprehensible—Galactica, that was it. The language Lai had put into her mind while he had held the pain at bay. Abruptly Marna's thoughts caught up with her body. "What are you doing out of the isolation suit?" she demanded. This *had* to be Cinda, the most junior member of the Human crew.

"Fixing your breakfast," Cinda replied. "It's all right. We got the viral DNA sequence late last night, and it's a known variant of Kharfun. I had it a few years back—mild case, but I'll still be immune. And that isolation suit was driving me crazy! Lai will be down later, but he's exhausted and sleeping it off. I'm afraid breakfast will be rather unimaginative—using your kitchen has been a case of pushing buttons and seeing what happens. I did fix some chocolate from the ship's stores, if you'd like that."

"If that's what I smell, I'd love some," Marna replied. Thoughtfully she tried wiggling her fingers and toes. They felt weak and twitched more than she liked, but the techniques Lai had led her through seemed to be working. She wished she could remember the last few days better. All she was sure of was that Lai had tried to support her through the worst of the illness, and that she had let him transfer a good deal of information directly into her mind. Her esper felt stronger than her body, so she teleported her bladder contents to the soil beneath one of the trees surrounding her house instead of trying to get out of bed and walk.

Cinda reappeared, carrying a tray with a typical bland, synthesized breakfast and a steaming mug. Not at all the fresh fruit and nuts she preferred, but Marna took a cautious sip from the mug. Bitter and sweet at once, with a creamy texture and a strange but pleasing flavor. She took a second, larger mouthful, and decided that she liked the strange beverage. "This is a Human food?" she asked. If Lai could eat it, she told herself, so could she.

"Chocolate? It comes from a plant that grows on most Human-occupied planets today. I think it came from our home planet. Now, Lai said to be sure you ate a good breakfast—your body needs it, even if you don't feel that hungry. Then you can get up if you want to."

Marna's eyes narrowed. "And who does Lai think he is, to be giving me orders?" she said.

Cinda looked at her. "You're a doctor, right? Haven't you ever told patients what to do? And Lai knows a lot more about Kharfun than you do, even though he's not really a doctor."

Marna looked down at the tray, considering Cinda's words. Logically, they made sense. Emotionally … "I will accept Lai's advice," she said, stressing the last word. "But neither he nor anyone else tells me what to do. Now, what are you having for breakfast?" She teleported the synthetics back into the recycling bin.

"Ship's food. Believe me, it's no better than your synthetics. But I've plenty, and I suppose it would be a change. And if you'll tell me how, I'll try to prepare what you want for the noon meal."

"That would be satisfactory," Marna said coolly, wondering why she was so prickly this morning. Certainly she had no reason to snap at Cinda, though she was still annoyed—for no logical reason—with Lai.

Part of the problem, she decided after she had eaten, was her physical condition. Not the plague-damaged nerves—Lai's instructions were letting her restore those with surprising speed. But her scalp itched, her body felt sticky, and she could smell her own stale sweat. There was a fresher in the personal care room, insisted on, like the food synthesizer, by the architectural program. She rarely used it, especially—she glanced out the window—on as beautiful a day as this. Not when a swim in the bathing pool was so much more refreshing.

And why not? She got to her feet, staggering a little, and wove her way onto the wide, covered porch. Cinda was in the herb garden, working her way along the rows with a frustrated expression on her face. She looked up at Marna's exit, and started toward the house.

"I'm just going to the bathing pool," Marna called out. "Those plants are all medicinal. The eating plants are this way, the other side of the hedge." She stepped off the porch, catching her balance with some difficulty, and began walking through the fragrance garden, picking a selection of scented leaves and petals as she went. She dropped her harvest into the steeping basin, and then slid gratefully into the warm pool.

The water felt wonderful against her skin. She was too languid to swim, but she alternated thorough scrubbing of body and hair with watching and advising Cinda. She could hardly bear to think of meeting Lai face to face, later that day. In some ways, thanks to several days of mind-to-mind contact, she knew him as well as she had ever known anyone before. In others, he was an interloper, an invader of what she had come to think of as her private planet. And so far as she knew, he was the only surviving male of her species. In a way, they were fated for each other. And Marna hated the idea of being fated for anything.

She could neither hasten the physical meeting nor postpone it, so she simply avoided thinking about it. "No," she called at one point, "those aren't ready to eat until they turn purple."

Cinda nodded and called back, "Anything you'd particularly like for lunch?"

"Kava pods, I think. Two rows to your left, and look for the ones that are fairly plump but haven't turned yellow yet. Steamed with some telana—that's the fine-leafed herb along the border ahead of you. And salad greens—those are just this side of the herbs—with some thinly sliced jagga root."

Cinda's pelvis and breasts were well developed—she must be close to ovulating. No, Marna caught herself, Lai had told her enough about Human biology that she should know better. The women of her own people, ovulating once a century at the most, changed visibly when ovulation was near. Sexual relationships were important as a part of bonding between the R'il'nai, and helped encourage the transition to fertility. But the physical changes needed to bear and care for a child occurred only rarely, and generally only after a substantial period of sexual activity. Humans, ovulating once a month, remained physically ready for childbirth and nursing for most of their short life spans.

What effect would living with such a species have had on Lai? Marna glanced down at her own narrow-hipped, breastless body, then looked cross-eyed at a strand of wet hair hanging in front of her eyes. Since that first visit to the city, she had simply lopped off strands of hair that got in her way. There was a mirror in the personal care room, but it had been a long time since she had used it for anything but checking for dirt smudges. If the only male of her species was coming to meet her that afternoon, perhaps she ought at least to even up her hair and find something to wear that was a little more flattering than her usual shorts and ragged tunic. She lay back in the scented water, trying not to think, until Cinda finished her gathering. Then she followed the young Human to the house, where she found herself telling the girl how to use her cooking equipment.

"What's he like?" she finally asked Cinda, over lunch.

Cinda chewed thoughtfully before answering. "It's a stupid word, but I'd have to say he's nice. When we heard we'd be transporting him out here, we all figured he'd be—well, aloof, at the very least. He's not. He's interested in us, in our work, in why we're in the exploration service—maybe even nosy, except he backs off if we're even a little hesitant about answering. I suppose he could read our minds if he wanted to, but I don't think he does, or wants to."

Marna bit into a crisp slice of jagga root, enjoying the sweet-sour, slightly nutty taste. It was not unusual for two space-going species to be friendly—an inherently unfriendly or warlike species rarely developed the technology for star travel without destroying itself. One species taking orders from another— that was unusual. And actual cross breeding—that, she would have said, was impossible both biologically and socially. But from what Lai had told her it had happened. "What is the relationship between the R'il'nai and your people?" she asked.

"Parent and child," she responded, "or maybe parent and teenager would be more like it. All Humans have a little R'il'nian ancestry. A long time ago—

over a hundred thousand years, Lai says—my ancestors were just starting to learn to talk. They could communicate, and they were pretty good group hunters, but they weren't really good at abstract ideas. It's gotten all mixed up in religion, and history and philosophy, but a R'il'nian got stranded on the Human home planet. My people thought he was a god, because he never got older. And he had children, and those children had children, until all of my people had a little bit of his line behind them. And he taught them, too. Eventually he taught them to build starships, and led some of them back to his people. Those he led were my ancestors. Those who didn't follow him are still on Earth—or rather, their descendants are."

That stranded R'il'nian must have been very lonely, Marna thought. Lonely enough that the local females began looking attractive after a few centuries. It didn't explain the biology that made cross breeding possible, but it made the first social step seem more reasonable. "So what happened to those that did follow this stranded R'il'nian?" she asked.

"The R'il'nai said there were certain rules of civilized behavior we had to follow. Like not trying to take over a planet with another intelligent species on it. And they showed us a couple of planetary systems they said we could use. What we did within our own systems was up to us. Our leaders at first were Jarn's close descendants, the ones who'd inherited his long life and other abilities. What we'd call R'il'noids today. And they were good leaders. I think all of the older planets in the Confederation today have stories about a golden age when everyone was safe and well fed and happy. There were a few problems—the Maungs, for instance. The R'il'noid leaders could handle them, and as we spread out and there weren't always R'il'noids to handle the problem, they asked the R'il'nai for help. The R'il'nai said they weren't going to waste their time defending a race that was destroying itself—we had a war going on between two systems without R'il'noid leaders—and they'd help only if we let them arbitrate disputes between systems." She paused to chew a mouthful of Kava pods. "These are really good."

"You aren't worried about problems with eating my food?"

Cinda shook her head. "As a general rule, Humans can eat anything R'il'nians can and vice versa. Now and then Humans are allergic to some R'il'nian foods, but it doesn't happen often."

So the R'il'nian would have no problem with survival on this "Earth," though it still didn't explain why the DNA was so similar. "How did they arbitrate disputes?" Marna asked.

"Took away the offensive weapons from both sides. Sometimes they could even take away the cause for the dispute, but not always. But no internal interference with either side. That actually worked fairly well. The types that wanted to conquer other planets got their noses out of joint pretty often, but the civilian populations were generally happy. Then the Kharfun epidemic hit."

Marna shuddered and was silent for a moment, remembering the day on the satellite when she'd first heard of the epidemic. She'd wanted to rush back, to help with trying to find a cure for the new disease, but the pathogen she was studying herself had not yet been proven harmless. "You said you couldn't get Kharfun."

"No," Cinda corrected her, "I said it didn't make us particularly sick. It doesn't. I've had it, which is why I'm immune now. But remember most of our leaders were R'il'noid, and it was deadly to them. Then it crossed over to the R'il'nai. They were spread out over a dozen systems when the epidemic hit. Three were like your planet—essentially no survivors—and most of the others lost an overwhelming majority of their populations. They did find a cure—tradition says that it was due to Humans and R'il'nians working together. But most of the R'il'nai died. And they had a very low reproductive rate, compared with Humans. Some of the Human planets couldn't function at all after they lost their leaders—they lost interstellar flight at the very least. Others attacked each other. But a few of the Human planets got together and sent a delegation to the surviving R'il'nai, asking that since there weren't enough of them left to continue guarding us against the Maungs, they try to impregnate a few Human volunteers so we'd have crossbreds to protect us against each other and the Maungs again."

"And?"

"It worked. Only three planets, at first, but those three stayed free of Maung infestation and thrived. And the R'il'nai, and later the new R'il'noids, protected those three against the other Human planets, too. Pretty soon other systems wanted to join the Confederation. Eventually, those that didn't join were either taken over by Maung infestations or knocked themselves right back to barbarism." Cinda finished her lunch, licking the last bits off her lips, and stood, collecting the dishes and carrying them over to the recycling slot. "Would you like some help with your hair?" she asked tentatively. "We have a couple of hours, but if you'd rather nap I'll certainly understand."

She'd ask about the Maungs and the biology of the cross breeding later, Marna decided. Right now ... She ran a hand through her hair, clean and silky after her swim, but from the feel of it a wide and fairly random assortment of lengths. She looked again at Cinda. Cinda's face wasn't pretty by her standards, but she had no doubt that the men she had known would be attracted by the rounded body. She'd better get herself looking halfway decent, but at the same time she felt ashamed of being so superficial. And doubly ashamed of feeling so flustered by this meeting!

She decided she did need some assistance, and there was only one source available. She ran her hands through her hair again. "I think it needs some trimming," she admitted. "I would appreciate your help." And what about clothing? She had slipped on a light tunic after her bath. But what would Lai be expecting? Ceremonial nudity, or elaborate draperies? She glanced at Cinda, who was wearing a tunic over a one-piece garment that covered most of her body. What did she have? She had a vague memory of shopping for clothing in the city, but had she brought those clothes here? Was the memory even of the short time since she had returned to Riya, or was it left over from the days before the epidemic?

"I think," she told Cinda as the young woman arranged her hair, "that I have some clothes behind that door to your left. But I have no idea of what's considered appropriate dress in your culture."

"Varies a lot from planet to planet," Cinda replied as she pinned up the last strand of Marna's hair, "though on Central I hear anything goes. Don't shake your head too much. Your hair's such a lovely color I didn't want to trim it short, but I'm not sure how stable this arrangement is. Let me see what you have … Oh, this is lovely! Just the color of your eyes!" She held up a deep blue robe, the color of the evening sky when the brightest stars were just starting to appear. The sheer overrobe was even darker, sprinkled with stars in various tones of gold, silver and red gold that brought out the coppery gold of Marna's hair and the silver veining in her eyes.

Marna had selected the outfit in part because the cut made it easy to move in, but she had never worn it. "You're sure it's not too much?" she asked Cinda.

The young woman's eyes were dancing with suppressed merriment. "My Lady," she said formally, "you're nervous, right? I certainly would be, after not seeing a man for twice as long as a long Human life span! Well, I suspect Lai's going to be even more nervous. It's been five centuries since he's seen a R'il'nian woman, and then it was a relative. I don't think it really matters what either of you wears. But dressing well and feeling beautiful will make you feel more confident. And this," she said as she held the robe up against Marna's body, "is beautiful."

And I am not just a girl being silly about a boy, she told herself as Cinda helped her into the gown. I am a hostess, welcoming a guest to my planet. A guest that I hope will stay, and with me repopulate my planet. She looked at herself in the neglected mirror. Riya's sun had darkened her skin a little, reddening the tone until it harmonized better with the lighter red gold of her hair. That hair was piled atop her head, the longer strands arranged in loops that looked planned, rather than the results of her haphazard trimming. As Cinda stepped back, Marna turned in front of the mirror, studying her reflection. She did feel more confident, she decided. But before she could say anything to Cinda, there was a hesitant tap on the door to the front room.

"That's Lai," Cinda said. "I'll be in the garden." She ducked out, leaving Marna alone in the house.

For an instant panic returned, but then Marna saw herself in the mirror again. She didn't look like a silly adolescent, she told herself, and she wouldn't act like one. She lifted her head and swept down the hall to the main door.

"Marna?" Lai said when she opened the door. His voice was hesitant, and he waited for her specific invitation before entering her home. He *is* nervous, she thought, and that gave her the courage to stand back and gesture him into the large front room. He was a little taller than she was (like Win, her mind insisted on saying) though with a far more sober expression than any she could remember on Win's face.

"Welcome to my home and to my planet," she said formally. "And my thanks for your cure. Our Healers tried, but ..." She had to stop speaking, surprised by the sudden outpouring of tears as she remembered the deaths of everyone she had known.

"Ours would have failed, if it hadn't been for their Human students," he replied.

The sound of his voice, speaking the language she had never hoped to hear again from a living person, triggered an even deeper storm of weeping. Lai moved closer, his arms coming tentatively around her shoulders. When she leaned into his embrace, his arms tightened around her. After a moment she felt moisture on her hairline, and realized that he, too, was crying. *We can't just go our separate ways*, she thought, still crying too hard to speak.

No, he responded, *whatever happens, we have to stay together.*

But could they?

Lai

10/26/35

Lai wasn't sure whether he was asleep and dreaming he was awake, or truly waking up. He didn't normally dream, in the Human sense. He slept, and while he slept his mind processed short-term memory into permanent storage, but the process was better controlled in the R'il'nai than in Humans, and rarely produced the side effects Humans called dreaming. When the need was great enough, he could stay awake and alert for several days at a stretch. He had done that to help Marna control the pain of her recovery from Kharfun, and when he finally let himself sleep, the sheer amount of short-term memory to be processed resulted in dreams—mostly of Marna and what she had been through.

She had never opened her mind to him completely, nor had he opened his to her. There were things too personal to share, and others, like the details of the cross breeding project, that he was afraid would repel her. His love for Cloudy, and the weaker but still deep relationship with Elyra, he had kept hidden for both reasons. But he and Marna had opened their minds to each other enough that he felt he knew her far better than he had ever known another woman.

She was not totally sane—how could she be, after two centuries of thinking herself the only survivor of their species? Neither was she actually insane, at least by Human or R'il'noid definitions. In R'il'nian terms, however …

There were her mood swings. Those he thought he could deal with, after a lifetime of living with Humans and R'il'noids. He thought he was seeing some leveling out already, though it was hard to be sure of anything, given Marna's physical condition.

Then she showed an irrational refusal even to consider changing her mind, once she had decided on something. That had showed up so far mostly in her attitude toward anyone attempting to land on Riya. So far as he was concerned, the first brief test had confirmed her plague was Kharfun. The fact that she had responded to Kharfun treatment had convinced even her planetary computer. Marna herself seemed doubtful even when the DNA sequence proved that her symptoms were due to Kharfun. But what if her rigidity affected other decisions, like whether to leave Riya?

Most frightening of all was her tendency to generalize her experience of one individual to an entire group. Cinda was kind, caring, and willing to accept some risk to her own life in order to help another. Marna had automatically extended that profile to all Humans. Lai recognized that individual Humans varied far more than individual R'il'nai, and while Marna's generalization might work for the Bounceabout's crew, it hardly applied to all the Humans in the Confederation.

He rolled over, decided he was really awake, and sat up. Was Marna awake? She ought to be—a quick check of the terminator on the planet below confirmed that he had slept close to twenty-four hours. When he touched Cinda's mind gently, she confirmed that Marna was awake and active, and expecting him down later that afternoon. He also got a hint of Cinda's attitude, and added, *Forget the matchmaking.* He didn't think Cinda paid any attention.

His conditional precognition still insisted that it was vital, for his own happiness as well as the future of the Confederation, that he bring Marna back with him. But CP didn't work very well when choices other than his own were involved, or if he failed to recognize a possible choice—as he had with Cloudy. It worked beautifully for weather or ecological forecasting. It could even be used to identify any points where future physical events could be changed by a small change in the present, such as certain types of weather modification. If his own actions could influence the choices of others, and he identified his own options properly, it could provide guidance even if the choices of others were critical. But it was as useless in forecasting Marna's actions as it had been in forecasting Zhaim's. It gave him probabilities, but probabilities that were very little changed by his own choices. He knew that getting Marna back to the Confederation was important, but he had no idea of how to get her to agree.

He detoured by the galley for a snack on his way to the ship's cramped fresher, and then pulled on clean leggings and his best tunic. Nothing like Zhaim's costumes, of course. Lai still wasn't sure whether to be amused or appalled by his son's preoccupation with clothing. But the overtones he had picked up from Cinda suggested he should at least make an effort to appear well dressed.

He teleported to the clearing in front of Marna's house, a little surprised by the emotions aroused by the thought of meeting the R'il'nian woman face to face. He didn't even know what she looked like, he realized suddenly—neither of them had ever thought of looking in a mirror. His mouth was dry as he raised his hand to tap at her door.

She didn't answer immediately, though he thought he saw Cinda ducking around a hedge from the back of the house. He had time to look around and see that while the front of the house was surrounded by vegetation that at least looked natural, there was a vegetable garden on the south side, and screens of shrubbery that looked planted farther back. Then an unfamiliar R'il'nian opened the door. "Marna?" he asked tentatively.

He had hoped for companionship, and perhaps one day for a child. He was not prepared for the poised, dark-skinned beauty who gestured him into her home, coppery gold hair piled atop a regal head, silver-veined blue eyes emphasized by the dark blue of her gown. "Welcome to my home and to my planet," she said formally as he entered the large, light room. She smelled faintly herbal, of leaves and flowers and sunshine, and he barely heard her thanks for his medical help. He saw the tears begin to form in her eyes and said something depreciating about his help, but she only began weeping harder, openly. Uncertainly he put his arms around her and opened the surface of his mind to her, and he felt her grief that everyone she knew was dead. His own tears began to flow in sympathy, and he tightened his physical hold.

They did not open totally to each other, any more than they had when their relationship had been of the mind only. They tasted each other's grief and loneliness, but their deepest thoughts remained private. Yet they soon sealed their union with a passion that astonished both of them, and after that evening there was never any doubt that they would stay together.

Exactly how they would manage it was a far more difficult problem. Both were aware of the problem, and both were determined not to let it escalate into more than a minor disagreement.

Marna recovered full use of her body rapidly, which delighted both of them. The Bounceabout was left in geostationary orbit, with Lai teleporting up occasionally to be sure everything was working properly, but the crew and Zhaim came down in the landing craft. The crew members were no problem. Marna welcomed them to her planet, and gave every sign of liking them.

Zhaim …

Zhaim appeared to destroy any interest Marna might have had in the Confederation and the crossbreeding project. She made her dislike for Lai's crossbred son quite clear, and worse, seemed to extend that dislike to the whole crossbreeding project. By the time they had been on Riya three fivedays, Lai was beginning to wonder if he had missed some third alternative that would have involved neither bringing Zhaim with him nor leaving him in effective charge of the Confederation. He still loved Zhaim, but he was feeling more and more that his son was not a suitable heir. He wished he had more of a choice in the matter.

Convincing Marna to come back with him, though, was still his main goal. Thus he found himself, far too early one morning, climbing the mountain at the island's core.

"Lai, come on. It's only about half an hour until sunrise."

Lai grimaced and checked his levitation struts before reaching up for another invisible handhold. If the rock crumbled under his hand, he would float rather than tumbling to the darkened valley below. He hoped Marna, above him and dancing with impatience, was taking similar precautions, but he was ready to grab her telekinetically if he had to.

Why was she so determined to climb the slope instead of levitating to the top? He pulled himself up far enough to feel for another toehold, and paused again to catch his breath. However much he deplored her thrill-seeking behavior, he had to admit that her physical condition was far better than his own, even though she was only half a month over Kharfun syndrome. And his was a lot better than it had been three fivedays ago. At least she had agreed they could teleport back to her house!

He considered cheating a little, using levitation to boost himself up the slope, then looked up at Marna, dim against the early morning sky, and decided not even to try. He didn't want to give her any excuse not to listen to him.

They still agreed on some things. They had both been alone for so long that even the thought of separating was impossible. Both wanted a child, though Lai was far more aware than Marna that it would be years, perhaps centuries, before that was possible—Kharfun had some long-term effects on fertility. Marna, however, thought in terms of repopulating her planet. Lai had grown up in a small, closely related population where inbreeding depression was a constant concern. They might manage seven or eight generations, but that would probably be it. CP confirmed his gloomy assessment. He didn't think Marna had even checked. But he still believed that even one or two more generations might make a difference in the future of the Human population—if they could avoid the birth of more like Colo. And like Zhaim, he was finally willing to admit.

And while she still thought in terms of her own depopulated planet, Lai could not simply abandon the Humans and crossbreds of the Confederation. Bringing Marna back with him was important—crucial!—to their future. And she seemed unable even to grasp the concept of leaving her home planet.

He pulled himself up the final slope to struggle to his feet on the relatively flat top of the mountain, walking the final few steps to rejoin Marna. She smiled up at him, patting a rock adjacent to hers, and he dropped onto it with a sigh of relief. Only then did he raise his eyes to the ocean surrounding the island.

Most of the rim of the old volcanic cone at the island's heart had eroded away over time, leaving this one, flat-topped spire. From here, most of the island was visible, as was the ocean beyond and two of the other islands in the archipelago. "Magnificent view," he commented once he was breathing normally again.

She grinned at him. "Wait until you see what sunrise is like up here," she said, and glanced at the eastern horizon. "It's still a quarter of an hour or so. Good time to ask questions?"

"Sure." He forbore to mention that she had claimed half an hour until sunrise while they were still struggling up the sides of the spire in near darkness.

"Cinda was telling me a little of the history of the Confederation. She mentioned a hostile species, the Maungs. I always thought ..."

"That overly aggressive species killed themselves off before achieving interstellar flight? That's one of the major reasons my people felt responsible for the Humans—one of ours gave them star travel. But the Maungs aren't hostile—incompatible would be more like it. They're a symbiotic species, with the body and the nervous system—to use R'il'nian terns—reproducing independently.

The eventual nervous system goes through a free-living, flying stage, from which it infects newborn bodies that would die without that infection.

"Trouble is, the free-living stage isn't intelligent at all. It'll infect anything warm blooded with a complex brain that doesn't give off a signal it interprets as already infected. R'il'nians give off that signal. Humans don't. And in Humans it's a genuine parasite. Parasites infecting a Human reproduce pretty inefficiently and parasitized Humans are sterile, so an infestation is theoretically self-limiting. But parasitized Humans tend to get delusions that they're better than Humans or Maungs, and they've actually been known to kidnap and kill Maungs to start the parasite reproductive cycle. The Maungs are just as unhappy with the situation as the Humans are."

Marna leaned back on her hands. "Sounds like the best solution is to keep the two species apart."

"Which is exactly what we try to do, with the full cooperation of the Maungs. It helps that a parasitized Human is very easy for a good esper to spot. I can spend a couple of fivedays in a stellar system and count and roughly locate every parasitized Human in it. They're unmistakable, though it takes a while to home in on the individuals. And if the parasitization is caught early enough, within half a year to a year, the parasite can be removed with no permanent damage. Crossbreds vary a lot in that particular ability, but enough have it, at least in a weak form, that it makes a real difference in the relationship between Humans and Maungs. Personally, I consider the Maungs to be an excellent excuse for our real role—keeping the Human planets from destroying each other or trying to take over planets used by other intelligent species."

"I like the crew. But this business of mixing species …" She shuddered, apparently unable to find words to express her disgust.

"They are likable." He remembered Cloudy. In many ways the two of them had been closer than he thought he would ever be to Marna, but at the same time there had always been the difference in potential life span between them. "But they vary a great deal. And they tend to copy each other, to develop a kind of follower mentality. If the leader is one of the bad ones—and there are some very nasty individuals—the whole society may be corrupted, and the individuals are rarely even aware that anything's wrong. The crossbreds vary a lot, too. There are some very good ones, individuals you'd like at least as well as the crew. There are also some bad ones—but I think I've found the reason for that." He didn't want to get into a discussion of Zhaim, so he looked toward the eastern horizon, where a growing brightness heralded the return of the sun.

No red sky this morning. The morning star, a planet so bright it was faintly visible in the daytime sky, blazed against a blue background that faded to apple green at the horizon. The green grew lighter as they watched, culminating in a brief flash of unbearably bright green as the sun first showed itself. They both stood and walked forward a few steps, watching the sunlight flow down the eastern face of the crag on which they stood. "Worth coming up here?" Marna asked as the sun finally painted a path of light on the ocean all the way to the amethyst beach.

"Worth coming up here," Lai replied. "I'm not so sure about *climbing* up here." He looked at her reproachfully as he bent and rubbed an aching calf, then spread his scratched and skinned hands for her appraisal.

"Poor Lai," she laughed. "Shall I Heal the nasty ouchies?" Her mind touched his, the wonderfully gentle touch of a Healer, and he laughed and nodded.

We do have green flashes on Central, he thought, *though not your amethyst beaches.*

That's one of the things that makes Windhome special, she thought back as she deftly Healed his pulled muscles and damaged skin. *Amethyst is just a form of quartz, and this particular suite of volcanic rock has lots of amethyst phenocrysts. See?* She picked up two of the rocks that crowned the spire and knocked them together, then turned the freshly broken surfaces up. Lai took one of the pieces, turning it in the sunlight. A lighter, translucent inclusion sparkled pale purple.

"So is that why you're so reluctant to leave?" he asked, knowing there was something more.

She turned away from him, lowering her head and eyes. "No," she said, almost inaudibly. Her mind touch was gone, cut off by the shields she had erected.

"Why, then?"

"You'll laugh at me."

He might have his doubts about her sanity, but that was a matter for pity, not amusement. "No, I won't."

There was a long silence as the sun rose higher in the sky. Finally she spoke. "You aren't the first man I loved."

"My parents," Lai said, "would have been shocked if I'd suggested more than one child by the same mate."

Marna's head turned a little, and Lai could see her smile. "So would mine. But Win and I were planning to have a child when I got back from the isolation satellite. Then the plague came … Lai, I know he's dead. I was in contact with his mind when he died. But there are times when I still hear him speak to me. I can't leave him!" Tears were running down her face.

And there have been times, Lai thought, when I have thought I heard R'il'nian voices. "What does he say to you?" he asked.

She looked at him in surprise, and then slowly and haltingly began to tell him about Win, interweaving a good deal of her own doubts and her memories of the lover two centuries dead. Lai listened intently, searching for patterns in the communications. Not bound to Windhome, he thought, or even to the planet. That argued against whatever she was hearing being some kind of psychic impression. And generally good advice. Sane advice. If Win was indeed her own subconscious, he represented the sanest part of her mind. "Have you asked him?" he said when she finally fell quiet.

"Ask him?" she repeated, obviously astounded by his acceptance.

He turned her to face him, taking her hands in his. "Marna," he said, "I don't know what lies beyond death. I don't know if you heard your own subconscious in Win's voice, or if something of him, whatever is beyond death, stayed to help you when you needed it most. What I don't believe is that whatever you heard was tied to this island, this planet, even this system. Whatever you've been hearing, it can follow you wherever you go. Ask."

She stood, unmoving, and Lai realized that he had meant every word he had said. There were a lot of things he did not understand. The cross breeding—he knew it was possible, thanks to initial tetraploidy followed by random gene loss or inactivation, and he even knew how to manipulate it. But how did the DNA compatibility come about? Why were some crossbreds fertile? For that matter, how had he managed to arrive at Riya just in time to save Marna? Who was he to say that a personality could not become a kind of guardian angel after death? Sometimes, he said to himself, you just have to admit that you don't know.

Marna freed her hands from his, and reached up behind his neck to pull his head down to hers. "Thank you," she whispered. "Thank you for believing me." She kissed him, and for a moment her mind was open to him—not completely, but more so than ever before. Then she vanished.

Lai walked to the west edge of the rock spire and looked down, toward her house. He couldn't see people at this distance. Even the house was little more than a clearing in the forest canopy, though the ship's landing craft was a brilliant spark of reflected sunlight on the beach. Would his words have any effect on Marna? He didn't know—but at least this bit of not-knowing had a fair chance of being resolved.

Marna

11/11/35

Marna had thought to spend the day in the garden, but Zhaim was in the front room, working at the computer interface. Her own fault; she had agreed that the planetary computer should have the information stored in the

Bounceabout's data banks, and Lai had Zhaim handling the transfer. She had taken the precaution of isolating the new data.

How Lai could accept, let alone love, Zhaim was totally beyond her understanding. She could not stand the crossbred near her, and when she found him in her home, and at her invitation, she decided at once to spend the day visiting some of her favorite places on the island.

Zhaim could not leave her alone. He must have heard her in the food preparation area, fixing a snack to take with her, and he bustled in, smirking and preening himself.

"Is there anything I can do for you, My Lady?" he inquired. Marna had hard work suppressing a visible reaction. Zhaim was speaking R'Gal, which to her sounded like very sloppily enunciated pidgin R'il'nian. Further, she was too good an empath not to catch the calculation in his manner.

"No," she replied in Galactica, choking down the bile at the back of her throat. "I will be out all day, and probably tonight as well. That should give you time to complete your data transfer." And I will take along a predator warnoff, she thought. Set to you. I may even set one in my sleeping room. I do not trust you at all, and I do not understand why Lai does.

He put a look of concern on his face. "Is that wise, Lady Marna? Perhaps I should accompany you."

Marna gritted her teeth and decided to put the warnoff on its highest setting. "Zhaim, this was a vacation island. It is tamed, safe. I have survived for two centuries alone; I am unlikely to have problems now. I have it on good authority from your father that I cannot be infected twice with this Kharfun syndrome, and that is the only thing I have run into in two centuries that I needed help with. What I do need is solitude. I am not used to so much company." She turned away from him, going into her sleeping room to collect the spare warnoff, walking clothes and her sleeping bag, putting them into a light pack with her lunch. Thank goodness she had made it clear as soon as she was well back on her feet that this room was to be entered only on her specific invitation, and if the warnoff in the room left Zhaim curled into a mewling ball, well, he had been warned.

Marna was agitated enough to teleport directly to her first destination, a secluded beach. Once there, she lost no time in stripping off her climbing clothes and wading into the surf. As she swam, she calmed enough to decide that she did not want Lai to hear of her expedition from Zhaim, and reached out to him mentally. *Lai?*

Warmth, caring, a very slight sense of relief.

Keep Zhaim off my back, will you? I need to be alone to think things over.

Amusement and exasperation. *I've tried to get across that his officiousness is not appreciated. When will you be back?*

She had already decided to spend the night in the meadow where she and Win had once made love, and she visualized the trail she would be coming down in the morning, and how to reach it from the house end. *The first fruit and nuts are ripe. Let's have breakfast on the trail.*

He gave her a brief mental hug before fading from her consciousness.

Marna walked out of the surf, teleported her used clothing back to the cleaner at the house, and carried her pack up the hill to a freshwater pool where she washed the salt from her body and hair. Exasperation, she thought, when she herself could barely stand Zhaim's presence. Not so surprising, perhaps, on reflection. She was a far stronger empath than Lai, an awareness that brought neither surprise nor pride. She had been unusually empathic even by the standards of her own people, and Lai freely admitted that the last survivors of his culture had totally lost the Healing tradition, which in part depended on high empathy. His esper talents, on the other hand, were far better than her own.

His use—or rather non-use—of those talents did bother Marna. He handled conditional precognition with an ease and versatility that astonished her, and he had no hesitation in his use of the physical talents—teleportation, levitation, and telekinesis. Telepathy … She frowned as she toweled her hair, now evenly cut, if short, and climbed into her coverall. She had been in mental contact with Lai enough to be sure that he could, if he wished, read every thought of every person on the ship, including his crossbred son. It would have been a fight with Zhaim, but the Humans would not even know their thoughts were being read.

Marna started along a trail that led gently uphill through open forest with occasional views of the ocean. She wasn't that far from her home, and she heard tinerals singing ahead. She walked into the next clearing, one that had a break in the foliage looking out over a little bay, and sat on one of the rock benches. Sapphire, she identified the blue-feathered tineral, and Onyx, and several others from the satellite as well as one or two of the island natives and a couple of the hybrid infants. They wouldn't come near the house while Zhaim was there, and she had missed their singing.

She relaxed slowly, listening to the tineral music and looking out at the breaking waves below her. The Humans on the ship had seemed to fear mind touch, regarding the reading of their thoughts and memories as a particularly heinous form of robbery. In their case, she supposed that use of conditional precognition in place of telepathy was justified, though it meant that her own Healing talent might not work on Humans. Healing required mind-touch, and it required trust. Even Cinda, by far the most willing of the Humans to accept mind-touch, and been a real problem to Heal when she had sustained a minor cut.

Lai needed the trust of the Humans to help them, and they would not trust him if he used his telepathic talent freely. She might prefer that he did not feel bound to help them, but she could not really wish he had less of a sense of responsibility. And she thought that the way he used conditional precognition would replace telepathy quite nicely, as far as the Humans were concerned

The crossbreds, however, were something else entirely. The R'il'nai had the ability to feel the emotions of others, what she called empathy. Humans had a different kind of empathy based on their ability to imagine the thought processes of others. Not nearly as accurate, and relying much more on early training, but good enough to allow them to live in social groupings.

Zhaim had neither. And according to Lai, he was the best of the crossbreds.

Marna sighed, got to her feet, and returned to the trail, accompanied by a chorus of tinerals. A few Riyans had been born lacking empathy, but such children had been considered severely handicapped, unable to live in normal Riyan society. The usual treatment was implantation of a kind of artificial conscience during the first year or two of the child's life. Zhaim had had no such treatment. Marna wasn't even sure that Lai recognized what was wrong with Zhaim, or that his son was not simply slow to mature.

As far as she was concerned, the whole crossbreeding project was an obscenity with which she wanted no contact.

She tipped her head back and looked overhead, where Riya's sun sent occasional blinding shafts through the leaves. It must be nearly noon, and the tinerals were stuffing themselves with the first juicy fruits of the kikia trees. She had planned to stop for lunch at a waterfall half an hour's walk ahead, but she was getting thirsty, and the fruit would be a welcome addition to her meal. She scanned the tree branches, locating a cluster of the triangular fruits, rosy with ripeness, on a branch too slender for even the smaller tinerals to navigate safely. She detached three of the fruits telekinetically and levitated them down to her hands. She carefully placed two atop the contents of the pack, and sucked on the third as she walked. Not much flavor—that would come with the later-ripening fruits—but she appreciated the kikia as a thirst quencher.

By sunset Marna had meandered through most of her favorite places on the island, and reached the little meadow that was her goal. She'd come here the first time with Win, two centuries ago. It was here they had pledged to give one another a child, and here, much more recently, that she had come to die. She couldn't actually see the sun set because of the trees surrounding the meadow, but she could and did look at the sky overhead, watching the red and gold fade from the scattered clouds and the first stars appear.

She hadn't really tried to contact Win before, aside from that one unplanned appeal for help after the avalanche. She felt rather silly, sitting on her sleeping bag and calling the name of a dead man into the dusk, but he was with her almost at once, arms around her and breath warm on her hair.

Win, what shall I do? I can't stand to be alone again. And I can't stand to leave you, either.

His laughter bubbled in the back of her mind. *Leave me? You can shut me out, love, but you can't leave me. Place—I'd almost forgotten that. You've done the job Tyr set you, and done it well. It's time to move on, love. Go with Lai. How else can I give you the child we promised each other?*

But the crossbreeding, Zhaim …

Part of your new task, love. His voice took on a touch of sadness. *Riya's not ours any more, Marna. Still, she deserves to be loved. That's part of your new job, too. But for now you need rest. Sleep, love, and then face your new life with courage.*

And she did sleep then, deep and dreamlessly. When she woke the meadow was still beautiful, but no longer a place it would break her heart to leave. She took a last look around as she gathered up her belongings, saying good-bye, and started down the trail.

Lai

11/12/35

The sun was just rising over the shoulder of the mountain when Lai opened the shuttle airlock. "Mountain climbing again?" Cinda asked, sticking her head out of the small food preparation area.

"Just hiking today," he replied, glancing down at his coverall. He could have done with less clothing in the warmth of the island, but Marna's visualization of the trail had included a good deal of underbrush. Zhaim had been more concerned with the fact that after half a year away from Central, Lai's wardrobe was getting scruffy. Perhaps Lai ought to take Marna up on her offer to have the planetary computer make him and the crew some fresh clothing, though he thought Zhaim's assertion that he needed a better wardrobe to make an impression on Marna was superficial. "I'm meeting Marna," he added.

"She likes chocolate," Cinda said firmly, as she poured two servings of the beverage into a stasis container and handed it to him.

Was everyone determined to treat his relationship with Marna as courtship? he wondered as he thanked Cinda and fastened the stasis container to his belt. It wasn't, really. He and Marna had no disagreements about their feelings for each other, only about whether they should go back to the Confederation, which he still considered essential.

He was rather touched by the crew's concern. Marna did like chocolate, and it had been thoughtful of Cinda to remember that. Zhaim … He sighed, checking the fork in the trail ahead against Marna's mental map, then turning left.

He hadn't been this way before. The feather trees with their finely divided foliage were familiar enough—they were common on Central, brought from R'il'n. So were the small mammals scurrying along their branches. Tinerals were relatively new to him, though he had seen enough of Marna's pets to recognize them and enjoy their singing. But where were the birds? He couldn't think of a Confederation planet without birds, but on Riya feathers seemed confined to the tinerals, which Marna had already told him came from some other planet. The fact that R'il'nian included a word for feather argued that there had been feathered creatures on R'il'n, but none seemed to be present on Riya.

On the other hand, what was the plant off to his right? Instead of branching upward from the roots, it gave the impression of branching downward into the ground. Another plant looked like the skeleton of a geodesic dome, with a huge, brightly colored structure in clashing shades of pink and orange—flower? Fruit?—growing inside the dome and protected by it. He moved closer, and found that the colored filaments were being visited by small, winged creatures covered with rainbow scales. A cautious mental probe of one confirmed that the creature had a backbone and six limbs, the middle two modified for flight.

Plant defenses tended to run more to physical protection such as thorns and sticky trunks than poisons. Lai picked his way around an unfamiliar but very hostile-looking bush that was trying to take over the trail, and was glad he'd elected to wear the tough coverall.

That brought his thoughts back to Zhaim. There were times he wondered not only about his son's motivations, but about his common sense. Surely Zhaim should have noticed by now that his sartorial elegance was not attracting Marna. It hadn't stopped Zhaim from suggesting that his father should take more care with his dress, or even from offering Lai the use of his own wardrobe, as they were very nearly the same size. Why? Lai tried to picture himself jumping the little brook that crossed the trail in one of Zhaim's costumes, and grinned. Marna might have been amused, but hardly impressed. On the other hand, Zhaim was just vain enough that he might have thought that his clothes would make his father more attractive to Marna, and there was no doubt that Zhaim wanted to get back home.

There had been other suggestions. Zhaim thought Lai should simply kidnap Marna if she refused to return to Central with them. "That's hardly the way to gain her cooperation, even if I could do it," he had chided his son, and then found himself wondering if Zhaim even understood the concept of cooperation. All Zhaim could see was that Marna was not totally rational. Lai was impressed with how well she still functioned after two centuries on her own.

As for his son's most recent suggestion, that Zhaim go back to Central with the Bounceabout while Lai stayed on Riya with Marna … Marna would probably have agreed. A year ago, before Zhaim had tried to cancel the referendum against slavery on Bomba, Lai would have accepted it as well—at least until he had checked it out with conditional precognition. Maybe even then, he thought, remembering the uncertain result he'd obtained from attempting to use CP on leaving Zhaim in charge before this trip.

He paused as the trail entered a grove of haro trees, looking up to confirm that the triangularly braced branches—another example of the upside-down vegetation of Riya—were heavy with ripe nuts. It was an odd arrangement, with each cluster of nuts hanging in the center of a triangle of limbs. Lai used telekinesis to pick several ripe clusters, packing them into the string bag he had tied to his belt before leaving the shuttle. Haro nuts and chocolate—he was bringing his share of their breakfast.

He wasn't sure at first what Marna had brought. The spiny gray globes she lifted out of her backpack did not look at all inviting. Once they had settled side by side on a log, she showed him how to strip off the spiny husks, revealing a smooth, green-gold fruit into which she bit with obvious pleasure. Lai followed her example, finding the taste sweet with just a hint of tartness, and a spiciness that reminded him of cinnamon or cloves while being distinct from either. "Good," he said, taking another bite.

"And it goes well with the chocolate," she agreed. "Pala fruit, it's called. I'll miss it."

It was the first intimation that she was even considering leaving Riya. "You managed to contact Win, then?" he asked cautiously.

"Yes. He said to go with you. But he said Riya needed someone to love her, too."

Lai shelled a couple of the haro nuts, thinking. "Won't take us nearly as long to get back to Central, with the flagged jump points, as it did to get here. And coming back to Riya, in a straighter line than through Murphy, should be faster yet once we find and flag the jump points. Do you think Riya could be loved by Humans?"

Marna looked thoughtful. "Maybe. I'd have to think about it, after I meet more Humans. But Lai, there is one thing you must promise me if I go back to your Confederation with you. I want nothing to do with the crossbreds or the crossbreeding program. I may be stuck with Zhaim on the way back, but that's got to be the end of my involvement."

He knew she disliked Zhaim, but he hadn't realized the extent to which her distaste extended to the whole crossbreeding program. "Zhaim's not typical of all crossbreds," he protested. "You'd like Nik and Kaia. And I have to work with the crossbreds, to keep the Confederation running."

"You do as you wish and as you feel you must. Just leave me out of it." There was no room at all for compromise, the light mental contact between them told Lai.

Nik had been Bera's last student, Lai remembered. His brother would have been delighted to interact with another Healer. He hadn't realized until Marna spoke how much he had looked forward to her meeting his closest friends. His youngest children, too—Zhaim was obviously a lost cause as far as Marna was concerned, and had Lai questioning his own competence as a father even more strongly. But surely she would like Wif, Ania, even Cloudy's child, though he didn't know Roi well enough yet to have any idea how the boy would react to Marna. And given the way Zhaim had turned out, Roi might be better off left at Tyndall.

"I wish you would consider meeting those I count as friends," he said, but he felt her resolve harden even as he spoke. Better simply to accept her feelings, and hope that the attitude of the Humans she would meet would teach her that all R'il'noids were not alike. "I won't pressure you to have anything to do with the crossbreds, but keep your options open."

He glanced around for a distraction, not wanting to let her talk herself into an even harder position. Their log was on the bank of a small stream, and upslope, looking into the sun …

"Look," he said. "There, just below the little waterfall. Are those more of the tika berries you were showing me a couple of days ago?" The bushes had distinctive, star-shaped leaves, backlit against gray rock.

"Oh, yes," she exclaimed with one of those mercurial shifts of mood that left him dizzy. "And those look ripe—first this year."

"Want some?" he grinned, walking upstream toward the waterfall. The berries were black, with a purple sheen, and the size of his thumb. He reached for one, and then jerked his hand back as he felt how thorny the bushes were.

"Told you they had thorns," Marna chuckled as he sucked his scratched finger. "Pick them with TK."

The berries were every bit as good as Marna had promised, with a stronger and quite different flavor than the pala fruit. Lai ate a couple of handfuls of the berries, teleporting a similar number into Marna's cupped hands, then found a stick and began poking under the bush, studying the root system. "Wonder how they'd do on Central," he said aloud.

"They don't transplant well," Marna answered, "but they come up far too easily from seed, and they're hard to get rid of. That's why I don't have any in the garden. That and the thorns. I don't know anything about the Central ecology. Do you think some of the plants from here would be safe to introduce?"

"Central ecology's mixed—about forty percent each from R'il'n and the Human home planet, Earth, with the remaining twenty percent from all over. Tell you what. We've got loads of high-quality stasis space on the Bounceabout—used it for food storage on the way out, plus XP ships always have a medical stasis area. Pick the plants you'd miss most, and I'll use CP to determine if they'd be compatible with the Central ecology. CP's really good at that—no sentient choices involved. Those that aren't a potential problem we can take with us—seeds, cuttings, even small plants. And don't forget the tinerals. Not just your particular pets, but enough breeding stock to provide some genetic diversity. I ran the CP on them a couple of fivedays ago—knew you wouldn't want to leave them behind."

She looked up at him, face glowing with pleasure, then came into his arms in a happy rush. After a moment she pulled back to look up at his face. "They won't travel quietly," she warned. "And my special pets are not going to travel in stasis."

"So we go back with a traveling orchestra," he grinned down at her, turning her a little so they could walk back down the trail, side by side. "Which reminds me—how do they manage to stay in tune with each other so well?"

"Something on the order of a hundred millennia of selective breeding," Marna smiled up at him. "Actually, they'll harmonize with anything, even my singing. And I'm a terrible singer."

Too bad, Lai thought, that he probably would not be able to hear how the tinerals responded to Derik's clear tenor.

Marna

12/6/35

It took Marna the better part of a month to select all of the plants and tinerals she wanted to take with her, and Lai was kept busy checking the compatibility of each species with the Central ecosystem. Tinerals had died out within a generation or two on the mainland, unable to defend themselves against large predators, but Marna had found, and now went back to, a number of populations on isolated islands. She brought back young stock of three different types: jewels like her own, with single-colored, usually brilliant, feathers; skies, with feathers shaded white at the base to shades of blue or gray at the tips, and natures, with laced, relatively dull feathers but the best singing voices of all. Marna had a hard time keeping a straight face when Lai was claimed by a young azure sky he named Spring, and every member of the crew had his or her special favorites. Zhaim was outraged, but Marna suspected that was jealousy—he was the only person on the island that the tinerals refused to go near. She hoped the tinerals wouldn't be bothered by having him on the ship.

The plants ...

Marna had started out thinking of pala fruit and tika berries, and perhaps the frostberries that grew near snow line in the mountains. Then the haro trees, and of course all of the favorites from her garden, including scented herbs and healing plants like the raindrop plant she had never quite succeeded in growing in the moist climate of the island, and that led to all of the other medicinal plants still growing in the Healers' robot-tended greenhouses, and the propagules at the Healers' center ...

Lai finally dug in his heels the day she took him to the main Healers' center and suggested he run CP on every plant in the database. "Marna," he said through gritted teeth, "the Bounceabout is a *small* ship. The stasis area is considerable for the size of the ship, but it is not infinite. It certainly cannot hold propagules for the entire ecology of Riya! There is no possible way we can take everything you want on this trip. Once we are back on Central and a direct route has been flagged, we can send a stasis freighter or two and you can bring in what you want. As far as this trip is concerned, we're simply out of stasis volume.

"In fact, we're out of volume period. You and I will be traveling together with four tinerals in the Captain's cabin—it's the only one large enough for two people. The two empty specialist cabins and the crew's recreation area are already packed with non-living material you want to take. Each of the crew members has volunteered to share his or her cabin with a tineral, and the rest of the tinerals will take up the medical stasis space.

"Some of the R'il'n-derived plants may even grow on Central already—I'm no botanist. The botanists and herbalists I know—like my half-brother Nik, who'd give his right arm to see this place—are all crossbreds, but they'd know Humans you could work with. We'll put this file in the Bounceabout's data banks, and you can go over it with botanists on Central. For right now, we just don't have room for anything more. I'm not sure we have room for everything you've picked out already."

For a moment Marna was indignant. After all, she was giving up her whole planet. And he'd promised that she need not have anything to do with the crossbreds! She felt Win sigh in exasperation at the back of her mind, and realized that Lai was simply stating facts. He and the Human crew alike had made it plain that the Bounceabout was a small ship, and the Human crew members had suggested repeatedly that they were running out of stowage space. As for the crossbreds, Lai had not even suggested she work with them, only that they could help him identify Human botanists and herbalists. She felt a very brief sense of curiosity about this herbalist half-brother of his, but thrust it down ruthlessly. She was not going to have anything to do with Zhaim's kind!

The Bounceabout was in a geostationary orbit at the island's longitude, and Lai finally teleported her up to see just how little space was left. "How long did you say you were confined to the ship?" she asked, as she looked around the cramped space.

"Seven months from Murphy," he replied. "We'll need only about a tenth of that, going back. And if you'll let my crossbred relatives anchor, we can teleport back to Central from Murphy."

Marna looked around and shook her head. No wonder the crew, and even Zhaim, had been so happy to spread out on Riya, and so doubtful about the amount of stuff she wanted to take back with her. "All right," she sighed. "I'll start paring things down. But you'd better be right about the freighter."

Four days later she sat on the widened bunk in the Captain's quarters, with Lai's arm around her, and watched Riya shrink in the view screen. The cloud-streaked blue crescent shrank noticeably as the in-system drive kicked in, and then blurred. She blinked a time or two, and realized that she was crying.

It's never easy, saying good-bye, Lai's mind whispered into hers, and there was a deep sadness mingled with the thought.

You've had your losses and your good-byes, too, she thought.

Yes. But it's better saying good-bye then never having the opportunity.

She leaned against him, taking comfort from his nearness even as she wondered at his sorrow.

Zhaim

12/20/35

"Zhaim, I do not have time for this right now. Go away and bother somebody else." Cinda had not even bothered to look at Zhaim; her attention remained fixed on the screen before her.

As a general rule, Zhaim had excellent control over his temper, especially when his father was around, or someone who might report to his father. A good part of that control, however, was achieved by the fact that he could and did let himself do exactly as he pleased when his father was not aware of his actions. After three months in close contact with his father, followed by almost two under the unfriendly scrutiny of the insane female that had bewitched the old R'il'nian, his control was wearing thin. A mere Human's refusal to give him his proper title, or even to look at him, snapped the last remnants of that control. He swung his arm back and slapped the com expert, hard.

The sting of his hand hitting its face was deeply satisfying, as was the crack of its head hitting the wall of its cubicle. Stupid Human, he thought scornfully. Not even sense enough to web into the isolated workstation. He nudged the limp body with his foot, shrugged, and turned away. Next time she'd know that he was not to be ignored.

The chime that warned of a coming jump sounded as he was about to enter his room, half an hour later, but he thought nothing of it. Now that they were using flagged jump points, the jumps were no more than mildly annoying. He continued into his quarters, having time for no more than a brief moment of surprise as the wall jumped and slammed into his body.

*   *   *   *

The first thing Zhaim was aware of after that was the blare of the emergency siren. He opened his eyes and winced at the brightness of the room lights, then realized that he was lying on the floor at the base of a wall, with his feet in a corner well over his head. He closed his eyes again and assessed his sensations. His whole left side was aching, probably badly bruised, and he had the beginnings of a ferocious headache. When he tried to move, his right ankle gave a warning twinge. How had he gotten into this position? Flagged jumps were supposed to be smooth!

He opened his eyes again, wishing the siren would cut out, but then he remembered that everyone was supposed to check in at the emergency alert. His check-in button was on the opposite side of the room, above his bunk, and his head ached too much to let him use telekinesis. Snarling, he managed to roll over and crawl to his bunk, discovering that while he hurt all over, everything seemed to work. He gritted his teeth and climbed onto his bunk, then slapped the check-in button.

The siren cut out completely rather than simply reducing its volume, which should mean that he was the last to check in. He must have been the worst hurt, he thought, and spared a moment to feel sorry for himself. But what had happened? Sore as he was, it seemed he'd have to go to the control room to find out.

Everyone else was there. His father and the Riyan woman were in the captain's cabin, bent over a figure stretched on their bed; the rest of the crew were reporting to the captain in the adjoining control room. Zhaim's father looked up as his son entered, and his face hardened. Then he looked over at the Riyan.

Marna shook her head. "She'll be all right," she said aloud. "But she'll never remember what happened. That concussion destroyed any short-term memories. The last thing she remembers is balancing the chips."

"The computer says she finished the job," the captain said. "But the spare chips were still in the circuit when we jumped. She should have removed them before she keyed in that the job was finished."

Uh uh. "Is that why the jump was so rough?" Zhaim asked ingenuously. "Threw me right against the wall and knocked me out." There. That would give them a reason for the girl's unconscious state. She hadn't webbed herself in, she'd been derelict in her duty by keying in that she had completed the balancing when she hadn't, and she'd been thrown into the wall.

Marna simply looked down at the girl's face, where a bruise was becoming visible. "I don't think she did key it in," Marna said. "From the way we found her, she recovered consciousness briefly, and tried to claw her way back up to the computer. The task-complete button is set apart from the others, and I think she hit it by accident. Bad design. And I think she was knocked into the wall by a hand. Left cheek bruised; the concussion's from a blow on the right rear of her head. And everyone else was accounted for." She looked directly at Zhaim.

"I've got us located," the navigator broke in abruptly. "Not too far off our aim point. And there's a planet within in-system drive range. Auroral emissions indicate free oxygen and nitrogen, so it might even be possible to breathe the air."

Marna closed her eyes, apparently reaching for the feel of the distant planet. "Life," she said. "No sentience, I think, but just possibly food."

Food? They were worried about food? "We can replace the chips?" Zhaim asked, suddenly realizing just how severe the problem might be. He still couldn't believe they'd left such an important task to a Human, the lowest ranked member of the crew, without a crosscheck from the captain.

His father stared at him, his face set. "No," he said. "The spares as well as the main chips were damaged by that jump. And it appears the synthesizer wasn't properly secured for that rough a jump, and it's not working. We needed the space, so we're carrying minimal food reserves. As for pulling Jarn's trick, forget it. Jarn was a starship designer. And it took him several millennia on a hospitable planet with a broad genetic base to pull it off. None of us knows enough about a jump-drive to build one from scratch."

"While we may be able to live on that planet," Marna added, "it is probably not going to be easy."

"What we are going to do," Lai said, "and I know it's a long shot, is try to contact the Confederation via telepathy. We're not that much farther out than my last contact with Kaia and Derry. Once we're on the ground and have a start at locating food, you are going to go into a tight link with me and we are going to try to use the power plant, which is *not* damaged, to reach someone in the Confederation. If we can't do that within a couple of fivedays, we may have to stay on the planet for a while. Eventually, I expect a strong telepath will be listening for us from Murphy, or even following the jump points we flagged, looking for us. But that may take several years."

Zhaim had always thought his father's green and gold eyes were too warm in their expression, especially toward Humans. At the moment, they made his own ice and silver look steamy. He glanced back and forth between Lai and Marna, confirming that both were looking at him with expressions close to loathing. They might not be able to prove he was responsible for their plight, but neither of them showed the slightest doubt as to what had happened. Marna had obviously gotten all she would be able to from the Human's mind—lucky for him that the blow had destroyed her short-term memory. And there was really nothing his father could do without proof—it was the Humans and R'il'noids, not his father, who controlled who would be Lai's heir.

All right, Zhaim thought. I will be very, very good, and I will not open my mind to either of you. I can wait, for years if need be, and as long as you have no proof, you will come to trust me again, in time. "Of course," he said aloud.

But reach Central telepathically? From here? The female wouldn't even try, of course—that would involve mind-touch with the other crossbreds, something she seemed determined to avoid. So it was up to him. Could he do it? Would his father use him up, kill him in the attempt? He'd cooperate, he decided, but he'd protect himself as he did so. Getting back to the Confederation was important, but it wasn't worth getting back dead.

Marna

1/2/36

Atoms, Marna thought, were their own mirror images. So were diatomic and triatomic molecules. They might bend and jiggle a bit, but at any given instant, you could not tell the original molecule from its mirror image.

Put four atoms together, and you couldn't count on that any more.

Consider something as complex as an amino acid, and you could virtually guarantee that the molecule and its mirror image would no longer be identical.

It wasn't just a topological oddity, either. An organism that used a particular type of amino acid as a building block could not use the mirror image of that amino acid. Biological processes on any particular planet tended to use and produce a single suite of amino acids, apparently depending on which coiling direction of DNA won out in the earliest stages of evolution on that world. Marna could no more survive on food from a planet where life used amino acids that were mirror images of those in her own body than her right hand would fit smoothly into a left-hand glove.

On average, R'il'nians (and Humans) could use amino acids produced by life forms on about half of the planets with DNA-based life—so-called left-handed amino acids. Marna's first concern, once she was sure that the planet on which they were marooned had DNA-based life but that intelligence had not yet evolved, had been whether the life was left-handed or right-handed. If it was left-handed, they could extract the amino acids and use them directly. If it was right-handed, they would have to try to grow some of the plant material brought from Riya—they could use right-handed amino acids as energy sources, but not as building blocks to repair their own bodies.

She had not expected that both types of life could survive and evolve side by side, but on this planet, which they had named Mirror, that was exactly what had happened.

Marna rotated her shoulders and stretched, looking along the beach. Life was only just invading the land, and they would have to depend on the ocean surrounding the island on which the landing craft rested. What life there was on land depended on moisture from the sea. Red, green and purple slimes coated the wave zone, constantly blowing small bubbles. Further inland, but still wet by the spray, irregular towers of calcium carbonate sheltered organisms that apparently secreted the towers—land corals, Lai called them. Near-microscopic but mobile creatures fed on both, but so far as Marna could determine, right-handed organisms fed only on other right-handed organisms and left-handed organisms fed only on left-handed food sources. She still hadn't worked out how creatures far too small for a nervous system determined the difference. Even she could hardly tell without her Healing sense.

The planet was not and, if Marna and Lai had their way, never would be comfortable for R'il'nians or Humans. The partial pressure of oxygen was high enough, especially right along the coast—the slimes were excellent photosynthesizers, and the bubbles they blew were greatly enriched in oxygen. But it was hot, even here in the temperate zone, and the total pressure of the atmosphere was far too high, as was the partial pressure of carbon dioxide. They had breathing masks, though they were awkward and no one could eat while wearing them. Still, they could at least work outdoors without full suits.

The weather …

Marna studied the sky, which was still a very pale yellow, and the gently heaving sea. No sign of the storm yet, but she could now feel it coming, as Lai had even before they landed here. But Lai had also insisted on unfaulted bedrock, and Marna, on an island where both isolation and food from the sea were possible. This island had been the only choice outside of the sweltering tropics.

Since the Bounceabout was a working exploration ship, the shuttle was designed to allow exploration without contamination. The island was enclosed in an invisible bubble that allowed no living matter to leave. Whatever they did to keep themselves alive, it would not contaminate this truly unique twinned ecosystem. If they could get the chips they needed to repair the ship, now in orbit, the two R'il'nians planned to do their best to get this planet recognized as a research site, to be studied but not contaminated.

If they could get the chips. The best chance for that lay in Lai's being able to contact his friends in the Confederation, something he and Zhaim were working on from the ship even as she studied the planetary ecology and tried to work out how to keep them all alive until they could get the chips. She could only hope it would not take years, and that they could survive the storms until the chips arrived.

A sound from the left attracted her attention, and she looked up from her improvised worktable to see the shuttle's little exploration boat come around the point and make for her beach. "Got some big ones," Cinda called as soon as the boat was in shouting range of the beach. "Still all soft-bodied, though. Got a couple I hope are right-handed, 'cause I don't even want to think about eating them."

"Just wait until you get hungry enough," Marna called back as she walked down to the shoreline. She TK'd the boat to above the swash line, and moved forward eagerly to scan the contents of the various containers in the bottom of the little craft.

Healing senses identified four of the captives as right-handed almost at once—fascinating from a scientific point of view, but nearly useless as food sources. Two others were just as definitely left-handed, and those she lifted out of the boat, planning to take them up to her work area and check their amino acid profiles. That left one bucket with another bucket firmly wired on as a lid. "What's in that one?" Marna asked.

"The one I'm really hoping is right-handed," Cinda replied. "I was afraid it wouldn't stay in the uncovered bucket." Cautiously she unfastened the wires.

Marna's first impression was of a mass of writhing tentacles. She reached into it with her Healing senses, and realized it was a single organism, massing perhaps as much as her head. Left handed. The thing had threefold symmetry of a sort, with three main tentacles, each of which was divided into three sub-tentacles. No eyes, indeed little or no nervous system. But it did have one hard-wired behavior—it would swim up gradient toward a particular chemical, and attempt to ingest the source with a "mouth" where the three tentacles met. She probed deeper, trying to estimate the amino acid profile, and grinned.

"Sorry, Cinda," she said, "but I think this one's the best bet yet. Big enough to provide a meal for several people, left handed, and at first glance the proteins look right. And I think we'll be able to catch it with a baited line. Would you prefer it roasted, fried, or pan-broiled? Or perhaps cooked in a stew? Are they common?"

"We saw several. You're joking, aren't you? I mean, you're really talking about extracting the amino acids?"

"For now. Long term—well, we'd better hope Lai gets through. Otherwise we may be devising recipes for this thing. I think I can rig some baited lines. Once I do, see if you can catch some more, but don't go far from land. That storm is getting closer."

In all honesty, she thought, I am no more interested in eating it than you are. I hope Lai succeeds. And I hope we are both wrong about how severe this storm is going to be.

Roi

1/2/36, early morning

Roi frowned into the darkness, bewildered. Four squares—two green and two black—were arranged in a larger square with a gold edge. An inverted triangle, black with a silver edging, floated in front of it. A musical phrase suggested a dance to Roi, and left him wanting to hear more. He felt water running over his hands, and taste, smell and mouth-feel suggested some dish he did not recognize and could not put into words, but wished he could experience some day. Over all was the smell of lemon blossoms. All were very clear, if faint, and none of it made any sense at all.

Derik might be able to help him identify the food, Roi thought sleepily. He levered himself up in bed, remembering not to use telekinesis, and saw that there was a faint lightening along the eastern horizon—not enough to dim the stars yet, but it must be after midnight for Derik. The vision? Dream? Whatever it was cut out just as he asked the computer for a time check, confirming that it was far too late to com Derik, even if he were able to describe the sensation in words.

Why had he even thought of Derik? The R'il'noid was a noted gourmet who could probably identify the smell and taste by mind-share, but Roi couldn't do that over a com link. And Derik was far too busy to have time for a face-to-face meeting with Roi, now that vacation was over.

"Nightmares again?" came Davy's voice, and Roi suppressed a groan of exasperation. He'd had nightmares ever since he could remember, and as far as he was concerned, they were simply a part of life. Granted, they were more rather than less frequent lately, but Davy's concern was still more annoying than comforting. And the wash of light from the pressure-sensitive floor around the man's feet prevented Roi from seeing the stars.

"No," he replied, "not a nightmare. A dream, maybe." Or rather, it had started as a dream. No, he remembered staring into the dark, trying to remember a dream, when the strange sensations had started. And why was he even thinking of comming Derik? "Crazy idea," he muttered.

"What's a crazy idea?"

"Comming Derik, this time of night."

"Definitely a crazy idea. What made you think of it?"

"I don't know. But the idea won't go away." In fact, it was getting stronger.

"This isn't one of your hunches, is it?"

Hunches? He'd survived slavery in part because he followed his hunches. When he'd mentioned that fact to Derik, at the very end of vacation, the R'il'noid had seemed unsurprised. "Untrained conditional precognition," he'd said. "Not as potentially dangerous as the things I've been teaching you to control. Just go ahead and follow your hunches, or if that seems really crazy, contact me."

"I'm afraid that's what it feels like," Roi told Davy.

But contact Derik, at this hour of the morning? As he wavered, the quartered square, the triangle, the whole gestalt came back into his awareness. "Oh, hells," he swore. "Davy, would you mind getting me the computer interface?" Nik had made it very clear that he was not to use his esper abilities to get around this half term, and he did his best to comply. He could voice-com Derik from his bed, but he still felt uneasy doing it at this time of night.

Derik's initial response did nothing to reassure him. The R'il'noid was obviously still half asleep as Roi started to describe the suite of sensory impressions, but there was nothing sleepy about the way he interrupted Roi as soon as the boy had described the quartered square. "Anything in front of the square?" he asked eagerly.

"It's just stopped again, but there was an inverted triangle, about twice as high as wide, black with a silver edge. And …"

"Don't bother with the rest of the sigil now. We need to meet face to face, away from that damned suppresser field, as soon as possible. You said again. Did you experience it earlier? Did you get the time?"

"Five minutes ago." What was a sigil?

"Not much chance of getting the next attempt, but try to be down in the visitors' lounge within eight minutes. I'll meet you there. Get moving!"

Roi shook his head, pulled off the interface circlet, and stared at it. "I'm supposed to be in the visitors' lounge in eight minutes," he repeated, bewildered. "He seems to think it's important."

"Then you'd better get some clothes on, and I think you'd better use esper," Davy said as he tossed a pair of shorts at Roi and grabbed the float chair. He himself slept in a loose robe, and was decent by his own standards.

Roi was more concerned with temperature—they'd be going outdoors, and it was still early enough in spring to be cold. The shorts might satisfy Davy's ideas of decency, which his old friend seemed to regard as the main function of clothing, but they were not warm. He grabbed one of his bedcovers and his personal shield as Davy dumped him into the float chair.

Once outside the room door, Roi took over the chair controls, no longer hampered by the speed governor he'd had to deal with first half-term. He zipped down the corridor to the outside door so fast that Davy was hard pressed to keep up. Roi didn't often have this good an excuse to defy both school rules and Nik's prohibition against using esper, and he intended to take full advantage of the situation. When a proctor tried to stop him between buildings, he took the chair off the path and accelerated, with the man pounding after him and yelling at him to stop. A quick look over his shoulder confirmed that while the proctor was running after his chair, Davy had slowed to a walk. Roi was on his own.

He turned the corner around the student center, and suddenly realized that the administration building would be locked tight this time of night. How was he supposed to reach the visitors' lounge? He halted the chair at the door, confirming that it was locked, and looked back. The proctor was saving his breath to run, now, but Roi was cornered.

He tried to perceive the structure of the lock, but he had to flinch back in dismay. This was a school where a generous fraction of the students were espers, and the school in general and locks in particular were built with that in mind. The proctor stopped, purple faced in the light at the door, and proceeded with a gasping tirade against students in general and Roi in particular, though Roi couldn't remember even trying to break the rules before.

"That'll do," said Kim's voice behind Roi, and the boy turned to find Kim holding the door open. "Roi, your guardian's waiting in the visitors' lounge. It's all right," the assistant head added to the proctor. "I just couldn't reach you fast enough. Let his attendant in when he catches up, will you?" He moved back, letting Roi through the door, then followed as the boy moved his chair on down the hall to the visitors' lounge, which was outside the suppresser field.

Roi felt Derik's agitation at once, and was startled by the R'il'noid's generally disheveled appearance. He couldn't recall ever seeing his usually immaculate uncle with a pullover jerked on backwards, slippers on the wrong feet, and his hair covering one eye. Derik rushed over to his chair, grabbed his hands, and asked, "Can you give me what you felt, mind to mind?"

When Roi complied, Derik gave a long sigh and Roi could almost see him relaxing. "Come on over here where we can both sit down. Keep up the link with me—Kim, do you have some honey? Feed him while we're working, he's not used to this. Roi, the sigil should start again in about forty seconds. If—when—it does, try to send this back." His mind showed Roi a different pattern, again involving all five physical senses: three concentric circles, shading from brown outside to pale gold at the center, a horn fanfare, fur on a living body, the taste and aroma of freshly baked crusty bread, and the smell of carnations. Once Roi had absorbed the pattern a chevron appeared, floating in front of the circles. *You can take it directly from my memory when you need it*, Derik's mind said.

Roi started to agree, then froze as the square came back into his mind. He glanced at Derik, who nodded and pushed the other pattern at him. Push it back, Derik had said, and he tried awkwardly to send the new pattern toward the old one in his head. For a moment nothing happened, then the inverted triangle suddenly melted into a sphere, and he caught a faint echo of relief as the pattern vanished. Derik was grinning from ear to ear.

"What happened?" Roi demanded.

"Your father's trying to contact us," Derik replied. "You picked up his sigil—kind of an esper signature. More empathic than esper, really—the range is better and the distortion's less. That's why you were able to pick it up through the suppresser field. The message was the inverted triangle. That's code for 'is anybody listening?' Usual unplanned contact schedule is one minute on and four off, so that's why I assumed the five minute interval would repeat. The stuff I gave you to send back was my sigil, and the chevron's 'try again in an hour.' The sphere's an acknowledgment. We need to get to the Enclave and hook into the power plant there for boosting."

"We?" Roi asked. He wasn't sure whether to be flattered or terrified. Derik had mentioned boosting, but he hadn't really taught Roi anything about it.

"We," Derik confirmed. "You picked up that sigil; I didn't. Roi, esper and empathic talents are rather unpredictably correlated with each other. We know you're a good empath, and range and sensitivity tend to go with that. You're probably going to be very good at long-range communications, as well as Healing. Right now I need your sensitivity to help me set up a link with your father. Once the link is set up, I want you to drop out—I'll show you how, and we'll get Nik to monitor and make sure you're not overdoing it. But I do need you, an hour from now certainly, and probably for the next several days. Kim, can you get together what he'll need to keep up with his studies for several days—possibly as much as a fiveday—at the Enclave? And Davy, get his personal stuff together." He looked Roi up and down, and sighed. "Never mind clothes, he's still growing. I'll send someone back for you, Davy."

Kim was shaking his head. "Good thing I'm in charge while Nebol's away. He would not be happy about this."

Derik rolled his eyes up. "Roi won't be staying with me, he'll be at the Enclave, under the supervision of the medical staff, and probably Nik's supervision as well. We'll see that he keeps up with his studies. Roi, you're going to have to be completely passive for this teleport. The inner Enclave shields are way stronger than Lyra's. They're keyed to Inner Council members only. I can take you in, but only if I am totally in control. Understand? All right, let's go."

The next half hour was a bewildering array of new impressions. The teleport itself was no problem, though their destination was strange. Floor, walls, ceiling and the lounges scattered across the room were all the same shade of deep blue, giving Roi the impression he was floating underwater. The light when they popped into the room was shadowless, but a sharply directional source came on, defining the furnishings, as two strangers in gray hurried in.

"Get him on an interface lounge with a glucose drip," Derik ordered. "I'll show him how to hook into the power plant when I get back." With no more warning than that, he vanished.

Roi stared at the approaching strangers. Was he supposed to obey them? While he tried to make up his mind, they lifted him out of the float chair and laid him on one of the lounges, barely giving him time to grab the bedcover draped over his legs. The room was cold! When the woman who seemed to be in charge approached him with a needle in her hand, he decided enough was enough. He might be a raw beginner, but he did understand telekinesis well enough to stop her a couple of armlengths away from his body. When Derik reappeared, with Nik at his side, Roi and the medic were glaring at each other, neither sure of the other's intentions.

"I'll take care of it, Geri," Nik said. "It's just a glucose drip, Roi. You've had them before when Derik was working you hard. Did Derry think to introduce you? No? Well, this is Geri, the head of the Enclave medical staff. Geri, this is Roi Laian, Cloudy's kid." His hands were busy as he spoke, sliding a needle into Roi's neck and taping it in place.

Laian? He didn't have a last name in the school computer. Cory was Coryn K'Derik Tarlian, and Xazhar was Xazhar K'Zhaim Laian, but he was just Roi. "It's not Roi Laian at school," he told Nik.

Derik, shoving a couch next to Roi's, snorted. "Nebol's being bloody-minded, that's all," he said. "He wants a Çeren index. Officially you're R'il'noid, and hence Laian, since Jelarik's tests. I won't probe Nebol's mind without permission, but I really think Zhaim did, and left him with a negative attitude toward you. Now, you've been using a light-duty mental interface on the school computer. This one's heavy duty—designed to let you draw power from the Enclave generator. It looks like the light-duty models designed for weak espers, but it won't feel like one. Wait and let me show you how to use it." He moved what looked like a ball of light from the upper end of the lounge down over Roi's head, then climbed onto the lounge next to Roi's and pulled a similar ball of light over his own head.

Roi bit his lip uneasily. The interface felt wrong, as if his old fears of the computer reading his mind, even taking him over, might be possible with this kind of connection. He felt Derik clasp his hand physically as well as mentally. *Relax and copy what I do,* Derik's mind told him. *This is the power plant. You draw power like this.*

Sunshine in the desert was his first impression. Light that made his eyes water, and heat increasing until he felt his skin was crisping and his blood boiling. He jerked back, trying to avoid the heat, and found himself back on the lounge, shaking with reaction, his whole body covered with sweat.

"Mmph," Derik said. "That's not going to work. Try it this way."

By ten minutes before the planned contact time, Roi was no closer to mastering the power plant. "It's like trying to hold the sun in my hands," he told Derik. "Why do you want me with you, anyway? I don't understand this stuff."

Derik took a deep breath. "Roi, remember when I told you about having to do things because they needed to be done and no one else could do them? There are seven people on this planet who I hoped would pick up anything your father tried to send. I contacted three of them before I went out to Tyndall. Gave them your times, even. Then I contacted the others from Nik's. None of them got anything.

"I don't like this any more than you do, Roi. But your father would not be trying to make contact at this distance unless it was important, and you are my only chance of reaching him."

"Derik, I don't understand how to do this. I'm scared." He was ashamed to admit that, but he just didn't see how he could go through with the power plant contact. He was terrified that he'd let Derik down, and yet from what the man said, refusing to cooperate would let him down, too. Surely there was some other way!

"Scared is all right. It helps keep you from making stupid mistakes. Panic isn't; it stops you from thinking. We've got eight minutes left. Let's try something different. Instead of trying to copy what I do, let me do all the power-draw and feed power to you. It's not as efficient as letting you contact the power plant directly, but your sensitivity seems to be getting in the way of that. Remember all I want you to do is to help me find your father. Once I link with him, he can sustain the link. You drop out then. Nik, monitor and give him a lifeline back."

This time the heat was bearable. Roi leaned into Derik's mind, aware of Nik's support as well, but mostly exploring the feel of this new linkage. The square came back into his mind, much stronger this time. He reached toward it, pulling Derik with him, and felt an almost audible snap as the two minds connected. Derik's relief and the command to drop out came almost together.

Roi broke the connection with Derik, carefully, and pulled harder on Nik's lifeline. He opened his eyes to find himself back on the lounge, and turned his head to look at Derik. His uncle was breathing deeply, mouth open as if he were struggling for air, and as Roi watched Derik's head began whipping back and forth. "Nik?" he asked uncertainly. "Is that right?"

Nik was already scrambling around the head of Roi's lounge to reach Derik, with the medical team moving out of his way. As he touched the gasping man, Derik's body arched in a violent spasm that almost threw him off the lounge. "Derry, break, dammit, you're killing yourself!" Nik screamed. His face had gone bone-white, and the freckles stood out like spots of dried blood.

Roi gulped. "Is there anything I can do?"

Nik stared at him for a second, and then reached over to grab his hand and lay it on Derik's. "I can't reach him," he said. "I'll give you a lifeline, the way I did before. If you can contact him, tell him to break. His body can't support this. But if I tell you to come back, you do it. Immediately!"

The sigil was gone, and the only way he could think of contacting Derik was through the power plant. He dived back into the searing heat, and found a ghost of Derik's mind, still trying to draw power. He followed it, whimpering inwardly at the intensity of the pain, until he found Derik's wildly oscillating personality. He clung to Nik's support on one side and pulled at Derik on the other, until he realized that Derik's mind was still anchored, somewhere out there. In contact with his father? Whatever, the dizzy swoops through nothingness were slowing. He caught a faint message from Nik: *Whatever you're doing, it's helping. The convulsions have stopped, and his color's better. But he still needs to break.*

He tried to open, in spite of the pain, and found he could hear a little of what his father was trying to say. Some kind of accident, and parts needed— the numbers and letters that followed made no sense to him, but he memorized them even as he reached back to Nik. *What's the code for try again in—uh—a day and a half?* That would put it in daytime for him and Derik both. He was increasingly aware that they were both short of sleep.

Derik was repeating back the codes Roi had already memorized. He must have the essentials by now, and Roi tried to make his uncle hear him. *Nik says come back right now, your body's in trouble.* He picked up Nik's answer to his query—two chevrons, with a triangle beneath, and shoved it between the two minds. An instant of surprise, a gentle shove, and he was back on the lounge, this time with one of the medics holding a loose mask over his face. He twisted his head away to look at Derik. His uncle was no longer convulsing, but shivering violently and his face looked green. Geri was hurrying toward the R'il'noid with a basin, and reached his side just in time for Nik to lift and steady Derik's head as he used it.

"Hot packs and heated blankets," Nik ordered. "And some hot soup, once he settles enough to keep it down. Roi? You all right?"

"No hot packs," Roi replied, shuddering at the thought. "I just feel scorched all over. I think I'd like some soup, though. I don't think I can face any more honey."

"Scorched?" Nik asked as he tucked hot packs along Derik's torso, leaving Geri to wrap heated blankets around the shivering body as he went to Roi. "Let's see—you do look like a bad case of sunburn."

"Psychosomatic," Derik managed to get out between chattering teeth. "We have to do something in the next thirty-six hours to let him pull power without that happening. Everybody's all right, but they had a freak accident and burned out the jump chips. Get hold of Kaia, will you? She'll know how to get hold of the replacement chips. How we go about getting them out there is still a problem, but that can wait until we can contact Lai again."

While Nik was doing that, one of the medics brought over a tray with two mugs. Geri propped Roi up and held one to his mouth. "Drink," she ordered, and after one taste Roi gulped down the rich soup.

Nik returned with firm orders. "You both eat, spend a few minutes passing your information on to Kaia, and then get some sleep. Derry, don't you dare try contact again without proper backup. You're damned lucky Roi was able to find you and get you back. And if you won't listen to me, you will to Kaia. I made sure she knew what happened."

Derik managed a shaky smile. "Thanks, Roi." *I think you saved my life,* his mind added, and his gratitude soaked into Roi's mind like gentle sunshine. "I still don't know exactly what happened. The link felt solid enough at first." He looked over at the mug Roi had almost finished. "I think I could keep some of that soup down now, Nik."

Roi was half asleep by the time Kaia arrived, arousing just enough to check the codes Derik gave her against those he had memorized. He was hardly aware of being carried to an unfamiliar bed.

Lai

1/2/36

"Zhaim, why?" Lai could not remember being so angry with his son. Not even the time he had found Zhaim using Humans as raw material for his so-called art. Lai was radiating fury, but Zhaim showed no sign that he was even aware of just how outraged his father was. Could Marna be right in insisting that Zhaim was totally incapable of understanding the emotions of others?

It made sense, not only in terms of Zhaim, but for so many of the lab-bred R'il'noids.

"You were killing me," Zhaim snapped back.

"Zhaim, I was monitoring you. You were working at close to capacity, yes, but you were nowhere near overload. And I was ready to back off—smoothly—if you did approach overload. As it was your jerking out of the link the way you did almost killed Derry. I still don't understand how he managed to recover. He must have had some kind of lifeline back to his body on Central." Lai stopped, looking sharply at Zhaim. His son's head was in his hands, his whole body expressing utter exhaustion. He had, he decided, underestimated Zhaim again. As an actor. "When you've quite recovered, I'll see you on the surface," he said, and teleported himself to the shuttle.

The crew members were spread out, exploring, but he could see where Marna had set up a sketchy laboratory near the shore. He was tired himself, and still shaky from reaction to Derry's near-death, and he wanted company he could trust. He grabbed a breathing mask and cycled through the airlock, yawning repeatedly and finally teleporting in a bit of shuttle air to equalize the pressure in his ears, and then set off down the beach.

He wasn't sure, as he came up behind Marna, whether she was dissecting a slimy mass of tentacles or cooking it. "Supper?" he asked dubiously, and she tipped her head back to look up at him, upside down.

"Not unless you want to test directly for possible allergens," she grinned at him. "They're plentiful, easy to catch, and have a pretty good amino acid balance. Nobody's had the nerve to see how they taste, yet, and they don't have all the vitamins and minerals we need. I thought you were going to spend most of the day up on the ship, using its power to try to contact your Confederation."

"Got through to them."

She jumped to her feet and spun to face him. "Got through? You mean you contacted someone? But—Lai, is something wrong? You feel upset."

"Zhaim," he replied grimly. "I thought I could rely on him for this—after all, he doesn't want to be stranded out here, either. But he managed to convince himself I was asking for more than he was able to give, and pulled out of the link—no warning at all. I was afraid for a minute or so that the disrupted linkage had killed Derik. I did manage to give Derik the information that we needed the chips to do repairs, and I hope he got the chip codes. We've got another mind-link scheduled in thirty-six hours, and Derik was so exhausted I didn't have much choice but to agree and give him a nudge back to his body."

"Derik," Marna said coldly. "Another of those crossbreds."

"You think I should be trying to link with a Human at that distance, with no warning? Derik is my half brother, and one of the best all-around espers in the Confederation—the best, when it comes to xenotelepathy. I'm not saying that you'd like him, or that you need to have anything to do with him. But I've known him ever since I can remember. He gave me my first lessons in using my esper talents—Father thought he was a better teacher than any of the pure R'il'nai still alive when I was born. Yes, I am upset, at not being able to trust Zhaim to give me the backing I need to communicate with Derry without risking his life."

Marna lowered her head, looking down at the tentacled monstrosity she was dissecting. "I'm not exactly enthusiastic about this as a meal, myself," she admitted slowly. "Why do you need further communication, Lai? If they know that we need the chips, and which ones …"

"Delivery," he responded promptly. "They'll get them to us, eventually. If they need to, they'll put a sensitive esper on another exploration ship with the chips and follow every jump point we've flagged until they pick me up. But that could take months. With a second good contact, I can tell them exactly where we are. With a really solid contact, we might even be able to teleport the chips out here, and be on our way in a matter of days, or even hours. But I can't do it by myself, and I won't trust Zhaim again."

Marna turned and walked away, giving him a brief empathic invitation to follow. "So you want me to take Zhaim's place," she said slowly. "Lai, you promised I wouldn't have to be in contact with any of the crossbreds. Being on the same ship with Zhaim is bad enough."

"Zhaim won't be in the link. Not after today. And you needn't be in contact with anyone but me. I can shield you from Derik's mind entirely, if that's what you prefer." Considering her reaction to Zhaim, he wasn't sure how she'd respond to Derik, anyway.

She paused, looking out at the growing waves and then turning to look along the beach. "I would like to see this world studied properly, some day," she said. "We don't have the equipment. And I'm getting more and more worried about the weather. I'm not sure the shuttle will provide adequate shelter in a really bad storm. Quite aside from the food situation, we ought to leave as soon as possible."

Lai reached forward in time, focusing specifically on the planet's atmosphere. "That storm's still getting worse," he said, "and I can't find a thing in the way of trigger points that would let me defuse it. I'm not even sure we have that thirty-six hours until next contact. Certainly not much longer. We'll need to move inland if we can't get the chips teleported here and head back to the Bounceabout."

Marna turned back to face him. "All right," she said. "We don't have enough fuel to be running the shuttle back and forth all the time, and we need to stay near the shore for food if we're going to stay here for any length of time.

I'll work with you on the contact. But only if you promise that once we get back to your Confederation I need have *nothing* to do with the crossbreds."

I've already promised that, Lai thought. I didn't like it then and I don't like it now, especially for the youngsters. But if Zhaim's an example, I'm not very good at being a father. Cinda thinks Marna's like a human being who likes monkeys, but can't face the idea of human-monkey hybrids. I'd hoped maybe actually meeting the crossbreds—those like Nik, and Elyra, and the children—might break that down. But the important thing for right now is to get home.

"I've already promised that," Lai said aloud. "But I don't see any other way of getting home quickly."

Marna sighed and walked back to her improvised lab, looking down at the creature she had been dissecting and then glancing back at the sky. "All right," she said finally. "But you don't even try to get me to have anything to do with the crossbreds or the crossbreeding program."

"Agreed," Lai said sadly. But he didn't like it, as much for her sake as for his own.

Roi

1/2/36, afternoon

Roi didn't recognize the room at first. Last night it had been shadowless blue—walls, ceiling, carpet, and furniture all the same shade. This afternoon the furniture and carpet were gray, the ceiling glowed white, and the walls, now with windows showing seashore and mountains, shaded from the white of the ceiling at the top to the soft gray of the carpet at their bases. And the room seemed filled with strangers. Roi sent a wordless plea for help to Davy, and the man squeezed his shoulder in reassurance.

Well, not all strangers. Nik was in one corner talking with a cluster of the now yellow-clad medics, and Elyra was gesturing to another woman, one who looked strikingly like her, but half again her height. Several people were stretched out on the lounges, their heads hidden by the glow of the interfaces. Roi wasn't sure, but the hands on the nearest looked rather like Derik's.

Roi didn't know what he was supposed to do, but Elyra raised her head, saw him, and dragged her companion over to his chair. "Get your homework done?" she asked, and then, without waiting for an answer, "Roi, this is Kaia, your other guardian. She's my mother's sister, so it's not too surprising we look alike. She's been getting together the chips your father needs."

Cory was gradually teaching Roi the proper etiquette for a R'il'noid. Roi knew Derik preferred a much more relaxed interaction, but he wasn't so sure about this woman, who as nearly as he understood was as high-ranking as Derik. So he bowed his head politely and murmured, "I am most pleased to meet you, Milady."

Kaia laughed and ruffled his hair. "It's not that I don't appreciate good manners," she said, "but I like being called 'Milady' about as much as I suspect you enjoy having your hair messed up. Though you're very good at not showing it. 'Kaia' will do quite nicely between ward and guardian, thank you. *Have* you done your homework?"

"Davy brought me over here, didn't he?" Davy had earlier made it clear that he wasn't taking Roi anywhere until the boy had done his homework.

"I don't have to remind him very often," Davy said. "But he was a little excited today."

"Would you rather have had Lukon?" Kaia asked amusedly.

There are times, Roi thought, when it seems everyone knows more about me than I do. He might not have met this guardian before, but she obviously had been keeping an eye on him.

"Lukon was never more than Nik's first idea when we realized how badly the Kharfun had affected Roi," Derik's voice broke in, and Roi looked up to see his uncle on his way to join their group. "We had Davy within a few hours of the time Roi mentioned him, and from then on the only real problem was prying him away from Nik. Caught up on your sleep, Roi?" There were dark circles under Derik's eyes, but otherwise the R'il'noid looked alert and cheerful.

"I didn't lose that much sleep," Roi replied. "But I'm awfully hungry."

"Midafternoon here," Kaia said, "but it's after suppertime at Tyndall. You'd better eat before we start." She glanced at the wall, and a tray exited a hitherto invisible slot and floated over to Roi's lap. The food it carried looked more nourishing than interesting, but Roi found he was too hungry to care.

"Over here," Derik said, and guided the float chair to a spot surrounded by lounges. Most of the occupants were sitting up by now, and the majority were eating. All looked up and nodded welcome as Roi and Derik approached.

"This is Roi Laian," Derik announced. "He picked up his father last night as well as stabilizing me, and I want to include him for sensitivity. He may be helpful on precision, too, and that's what we want to test right now. Roi, the actual contact will be tomorrow afternoon, and we're going to try to get the chips out to your father, or at least out to Murphy. We're going to be working in a meld, which is new to you, with you, Mako and me as the foci." He nodded toward a tall, thin man with russet hair and darker russet skin.

Mako swallowed the pastry he was chewing and nodded solemnly at Roi. "I'm the best at teleporting," he explained.

Derik studied Roi's face. "You Healed that sunburn, didn't you? No more Healing for a while, I want you to save your esper energy. Well, that's why I have Lunia here." This time, the person who responded was a plump woman with purple-black hair and eyes and very white skin. "She's the best of us at drawing power and feeding it to whoever needs it. I want you to practice linking with her and let her handle the interface with the power plant. Nik will monitor you, since you're used to him, and Elyra will do the same for Lunia, as well as providing you with additional support if you need it. Korol and Tavia will be monitoring Mako and me."

Roi nodded. When Lunia extended her hand he accepted both physical and mental touch, but cautiously. Her mind felt a little harsh, but he was getting used to that. What surprised him was the way she pulled back and looked at him in astonishment. "Derik," she said sharply, "you had this child pulling power directly?"

"Not on purpose, once I realized how much trouble he was having. I—got myself into trouble, and he dived in to help me."

"Next time remember that sensitivity can be a liability as well as an asset. He feels like Bera—same soft touch, same sensitivity. And Bera never could stand full contact with the computer. Said it felt like it was trying to take her over. Roi, there are some techniques you can use to make the contact easier. If Derik doesn't know them, I'll teach you. But for right now, let me handle all the power plant contact."

Lunia's mind might not be comfortable, but it was far better than the power plant. Roi learned to accept and use the power Lunia channeled to him, first directly, then through the computer interface. By the time he had been working for half an hour he felt able to work with the new arrangement, and was once again ravenously hungry.

Derik grinned when he asked for more food. "Controlling that much power takes energy," he commented. "You'll be eating all you can hold for the next couple of days, and you'll probably lose weight even so. One of the things you need to learn is to eat while you're working. A glucose drip helps, but it's limited. Right now you break and eat."

Roi obediently swallowed more of the thick, sweet beverage Elyra pressed on him. He was hungry enough to swallow it eagerly, but he still wondered about the taste he'd gotten in the contact last night—no, early this morning. They didn't seem to be doing anything right now, so when Derik came over to check how he was doing, he asked the question that had first brought Derik to mind. "What was the food Father was thinking about last night?"

"You mean the stuff in his sigil? The fruit and sweet cream and nut pastry combination? One of his favorites. It takes a little preparation, but I can ask the kitchen to fix some tomorrow. You've earned it."

Roi blinked in surprise. He'd intended only to ask what the food was, and he hadn't really expected a chance to try it. He still had major doubts about being a crossbred—the responsibilities seemed awesome, and the privileges had mostly repelled him. But at least this particular privilege seemed harmless.

"What we're doing," Derik went on, "is practicing teleporting as a meld. It should be easier with your father at the other end, but for the moment we're doing exchange teleports with Murphy. If we could exchange the chip package with another of exactly the same mass, that would take care of energy and momentum. Problem is, we can't get the masses exactly the same, so with high relative velocities, we still have to deal with the differences in energy and momentum."

"So far," Mako added, "we've smeared three test boxes over the inside of the receiving vault, and triggered one small earthquake on Murphy. When we helped jump Zhaim out, we could transfer any excess momentum to the ship. Besides, Zhaim's a good teleport in his own right, if a little careless, and he was able to make his own fine adjustments. But we don't dare do that with the ship in orbit, and a box of chips can't make its own adjustments."

"I don't want you trying to do much with the teleport itself," Derik broke in. "You'll have to be part of the meld tomorrow to help us find your father. What I want to check today is whether you can improve our ability to sense if the masses we're trying to exchange are the same. Go ahead and link to your support group, through the interface. Good. Now link with me."

It felt crowded at first. Roi had linked with Derik and Nik at the same time, but adding Lunia and Elyra made him feel as if he were being crowded out of his own mind. Then Elyra came into his consciousness. *We're your support group. Lean into us whenever you need us, but you don't need to be aware of us. Concentrate on the link with Derik—he's the one who's coordinating the whole meld.*

Gradually Roi managed to adjust the links so that he felt poised between Derik and the others. When he felt stable enough to open his eyes, he found that the windows had faded away, and the room was blue again. So were his hands, which he hadn't noticed when he was first in the room—the change must be in the lighting. He closed his eyes again, and felt Derik reach out in the other direction. He was hardly aware of Mako, only of reaching, with Lunia's power feed propelling him outward with the others. As part of the linkage he felt the test box in the vault far below the room, and the other box, far away and moving far too rapidly, and then Mako's perception stabilized the second box. He felt the others set up the exchange teleport, but it didn't feel right—like some of the tiles in Coryn's pattern chess set, he thought. Exchanging some pairs was harder than others. At the last moment, he dug in his mental heels.

Problem?

They don't match.

Can you feel the difference between packing material and chips in our test box?

Yes.

Kaia's going to put a graduated-density slab of the packing material under your hand. See if you can adjust the packing material in our box so the box as a whole feels the same as the one on Murphy. Let us do the teleporting, you just concentrate on what changes are needed so the boxes feel the same.

It seemed to take forever before the two boxes felt the same, but finally the planned teleport felt almost right, and he nodded mentally to Derik. *That's as close as I can get.*

He wasn't actually involved in the teleport, but he was tightly linked with the others, and he felt the jar as the two boxes slammed into the shock foam in their respective receiving vaults. *I'm sorry,* he 'pathed to Derik. *I did the best I could. Honest.*

You want a demonstration of how we were doing without *your help?* Derik sent back, with a trace of amusement.

Don't even think about it, Mako sent, and Elyra chuckled in Roi's ear.

"That's the first teleport today that's left the boxes intact," she said. "My guess is that they'll want to try it again with you balancing the masses, but with the real chips this time. That way, if the direct teleport tomorrow doesn't come off, they can start tracing the XP-13's route from Murphy."

Derik nodded. "Break and eat, first," he said, rubbing his temples. The room changed again to gray and white.

Roi looked around at the others. His own headache barely reached the level of conscious pain, but if the others had been involved in even more unbalanced teleports than this one … "Headaches aren't hard to Heal," he volunteered.

Derik hesitated. "How much would it take out of you?" he asked.

"Not much. It's a lot easier than repairing tissue damage."

Derik thought for a moment, and then nodded. "We need to be at peak efficiency for the teleport, get a good night's sleep, and be in really good shape tomorrow. We double the rest break before the next 'port, and Roi, you eat all you can during that break. And don't wear yourself out Healing us!"

Roi nodded as he reached for Derik's mind, and then winced as he caught the intensity of the pounding in the R'il'noid's head. Headaches with no actual physical damage *were* easy to Heal, and after the amount of practice he'd had on Ander's migraines, it took less than a minute to stop the pain in Derik's head. He turned to Lunia next, feeling her throbbing skull through the link he hadn't completely dropped, then looked inquiringly at Mako.

"It's like having Bera back," Lunia said wonderingly, and Mako seemed to make up his mind.

"Go ahead and try," he said.

Roi was getting used to people being surprised the first time they linked with his mind at the depth needed for Healing, so Mako's reaction to his initial contact didn't bother him. The expression on the R'il'noid's face after the headache stopped made him want to laugh until he remembered how he'd learned to Heal. "Is Flame all right without me being around to stop her headaches?" he asked Derik.

"Is that where you first found you could Heal someone else? She hasn't complained, but then she wouldn't. Same kind as Ander's?"

Roi nodded, wishing he were allowed at least to visit with his old friends.

"I won't go into her mind, so I can't know for sure when she's having problems. But if Nik'll give me some of the same medicine he gave Ander, I'll try to spot when she's having trouble and see if it helps. I'm sorry, Roi—I know you'd rather have them with you. But it just wouldn't work right now. Better eat. We want to try a live 'port out to Murphy still this afternoon."

Roi sighed and joined the others in stuffing himself. He was beginning to make friends at Tyndall, especially since Coryn had dragged him to a meeting of the pattern chess club. Xazhar was still an enemy, but he was finding that not all of his own age group looked up to Xazhar. Still, he missed his old friends more all the time. Being free wasn't as—well—free as he had once thought. It seemed to involve a frightening amount of responsibility, and a lot of learning. He wasn't sure Flame would enjoy that, but Timi and Amber would never be happy as slaves and he wanted them to share his freedom, uneasy though that freedom had turned out to be.

It wasn't that he didn't trust Derik's intentions, or that his friends wouldn't be even more lost at Tyndall than Roi was, and far less able to protect themselves. But Derik could be woefully blind to the way his actions sometimes countered his intentions. And Roi didn't trust Brak, Derik's overseer, a bit more than he had when Davy first refused to name the man. Unfortunately Derik did trust the man, and nothing Roi had tried to get rid of Brak had worked. About all that was left was a full-scale tantrum, and Roi had studied Coryn's attempts to manipulate his father enough to be pretty sure that wouldn't work.

He sighed and looked down at his tray. The adults were still eating, but for the moment he was satiated. He raised his eyes and looked out the window at the mountains, their peaks beginning to glow pink in the light of the setting sun. Must be close to lights-out at Tyndall, and he'd been up awfully early this morning. No wonder he felt so tired, in spite of his nap. But the mountains were beautiful. He'd missed Derik's mountains while he was at Tyndall, but these were even more impressive. Maybe he could live where he could see mountains, someday. But just now, he had to do what he could to get his father home. This time, he thought, he would know enough to welcome the R'il'nian's attention.

Derik

"All right, Roi. Go ahead and link up with your support group, and then come in." The linkage this time was almost immediate, with none of the hesitation that had marked the boy's first attempt. Derik tested the connection, then reached out to Mako. The meld snapped together so easily it was hard to believe the group was working together for only the second time. Even the power flow seemed smoother—ah, Lunia, her headache gone, was able to feed power to Derik and Mako as well as Roi. *Make sure he gets power first,* he warned her.

He didn't use half of what I was channeling him before, she responded.

Long as he doesn't have to go into the power plant himself. He pulled the meld together until the individuals became part of a single personality and reached, first for the package in the vault beneath them, and then for the much more distant one on Murphy. Through Roi he felt the difference in mass and the small, finicky adjustments until the two masses were balanced. At the same time, he activated the sublight communication with Murphy, warning the staff there that another package was incoming. Both vaults were spring-mounted to bedrock and filled with heavy-duty shock foam formed around the packages, but he suspected that the staff was diving for cover anyway. Given the roughness of the earlier transfers, he didn't blame them.

Roi hadn't quite caught on yet to the fact that the meld acted as a single mind, and signaled *ready* when he was satisfied with the mass adjustment. Derik/Mako switched the two packages, then teleported the Murphy package from the Central vault to Kaia's hands.

"Looks good," she reported a moment later. "How about the other end?"

"They're saying 'hurry up and get it over with'," Derik reported. "Told 'em we'd done the transfer and would they please look and check the acceleration record." He released the meld, pulled off the interface and stretched. "Not even a headache this time. Beautiful work, Roi."

Nik pulled off the boy's interface, catching Roi in the middle of a yawn. "Sorry," Roi said sheepishly. "I think I'm still on Tyndall time."

"And I'm on Seabird Island's," Nik replied, yawning in sympathy. "Three in the morning. Anything from Murphy yet?"

In response Derik activated the speakers, letting the others hear the excited babble on Murphy, where the staff had confirmed the markings on the Central box and were checking the built-in accelerometer. Kaia grinned when she heard the acceleration. "Those chips will take well over ten times that without damage," she said, "and I put triple the number needed in that box. If tomorrow's direct teleport doesn't work, they can take those and start following the XP-13's trail."

Roi was trying to suppress another yawn. "Get him and yourself to bed, Davy," Derik advised. "Let him sleep a little late tomorrow, but try to get him through his homework before lunch local time. The rest of you—see you for lunch. We need to start listening about two in the afternoon, though actual contact'll likely be a bit later."

The others began teleporting away, leaving only Nik, Derik and the medical staff in the interface room. "Why don't you bed down at the Enclave tonight, Nik?" Derik suggested. "Shift toward local time, so you won't be trying to go to sleep during tomorrow's contact." He took Nik's arm, guiding his exhausted brother out the door and down the hall.

"And save you from the effort of 'porting me back and forth," Nik yawned. "Nothing I absolutely have to do at home." He stumbled on for a few strides, and then asked, "Does Roi know why you're keeping him separated from his old friends?"

Derik shook his head. "He and his father got off to a rocky enough start—partly our fault, for not realizing he simply didn't believe anything he was being told. And Lai meant well. He thought Roi wouldn't want to be reminded of his slavery, and the boy *is* going to have to work with other R'il'noids. A lot more than Lai realized at the time. Roi needs to make friends at Tyndall. But I'm not going to risk driving another wedge between Roi and Lai by telling the boy that keeping him isolated from his slave past was his father's idea. I think he suspects, but I'm not going to tell him outright. And Lai was pretty specific on that. We're going to have to work to get Lai to accept Davy, though I think we can justify that on the grounds that Davy's slavery was a political accident."

"It's hard on Roi, though. I hope he and his father can work it out."

"So do I."

Lai

1/3/36

Wind whipped Lai's rain-wet hair into his face, and salt and sand stung his eyes. He ignored the sensations, focusing on the bedrock beneath his bare feet. He and Marna were making a cavern twice his height in the rock while replacing the rock with shock foam made in place from the ship's supplies, with a chip box foamed into place in the center. They completed the final check and broke apart. "Think those'll do?" Marna asked.

He shrugged. "One of the three ought to," he replied. "I'm just hoping we can manage a good enough contact to try a teleport. Otherwise it'll be the better part of a month, even if we can give them a good location."

A gust of wind almost blew them into each other as they struggled up the crude path to the shuttle, now firmly tied down against the approaching storm. Captain Tova was watching through the darkening gloom, and unlatched the outer door to the airlock as they reached it. Hastily they piled in, struggling to close the outer door against the force of the wind. The shuttle air pressure was being kept only slightly above ship's normal, nowhere near that of the planet's surface, and their ears popped repeatedly as the pressure in the lock was pumped down. The crew was waiting with towels, dry clothing and chocolate.

"I don't see why you couldn't do that from inside the shuttle," Captain Tova said.

"Would have, it we'd known it was going to get that bad that fast," Lai replied. "But standing right on the rock reduced the energy we had to use, and we wanted to save all we could for the contact. It's going to take enough to get up to the Bounceabout so we can use the power plant, even counterweighting. Ready to go?" He held out his hand to Marna.

Once they had teleported to the orbiting ship, they ate and then lay down side by side on the Captain's bed. Lai handled most of the power draw—Marna found the ship's power plant uncomfortable—and wondered if Derry would have recovered enough in a day and a half to make the contact. Marna provided considerably more support than Zhaim had, along with precision beyond Lai's own ability, but Lai himself would be responsible for the contact. He located the island and the three caverns beneath it with his mind before reaching out with his sigil.

Derik's answer came almost at once, considerably stronger than he had expected. *Got the chips,* Lai's brother sent, *and we're prepared for an exchange teleport, but give us your exact location first, just in case.* A pause on Derik's end, as Lai added their position to his mind-send. *Got it,* Derik replied. No, not just Derik; his sigil was slightly fuzzy, with that golden glow behind it that indicated a tight meld centered on Derik.

We've foamed in three standard sensory chip boxes, Lai sent, showing Derik exactly where the caverns and their contents were. *The chips are duplicates of our records, and if you can get them there intact, you'll be able to read them.*

Our minds work similarly, Derik sent back, with a trace of smugness. *That's what we've been using for practice. Got three sets of the chips you need out to Murphy yesterday, without anyone on the other end capable of a teleport.*

Intact? If the meld could handle a one-ended teleport to Murphy, the two-ended teleport to Mirror should be easy.

On our last try the Murphy staff didn't believe we'd really exchanged boxes 'til they looked. His mind showed Lai the chip boxes ready for exchange with the ones Lai and Marna had foamed in place. No, not quite ready, the masses were shifting slightly even as Lai watched. When they stabilized, the match with the Mirror boxes was uncannily close. He tightened his connection with Derik on one side and Marna on the other, and they exchanged the first set of boxes. He checked briefly with Zhaim, outside the meld with Marna but monitoring the seismograph on the shuttle. No shock measurable above the background of the storm, and when he teleported the first Central box up to the Bounceabout, the enclosed chips looked fine.

He reached for Cinda's mind on the shuttle below, and felt the floor rocking under her feet. *Want to come up here and check if the chips arrived undamaged?* he sent, and teleported her up when she signaled an enthusiastic *Yes!* She didn't want to be on the shuttle with Zhaim, he realized as he handed her the box.

Derry had indicated that they had three boxes ready to exchange. *The Mirror boxes have three different sets of sensory chips,* Lai sent. *Are you tiring, or do you want to try the other two?*

Tiring? With this meld? I'm not sure what happened before, but it won't happen again. Sure, let's go ahead with the other two. Can we publicize your travelogue? The population's getting worried about you.

Lai grinned a little. *Sure, there's a commentary on the first chip in each box.* He wondered just who was involved in the meld, back on Central. Derik certainly—his sigil was the base of the meld signal. Mako—his touch was unmistakable on the teleport itself. He couldn't think of anyone back on Central with the control and sensitivity needed to adjust the masses that accurately. Even Marna could find very little room for additional adjustment.

By the third teleport, Cinda had the chips installed and was almost through her test procedure. But by then the Central meld was fading. *No serious problems,* Derry sent. *But the kid hasn't learned to eat and work at the same time, yet. We'll be listening in a fiveday.*

The kid? Lai wondered even as he sent the sign-off signal. Well, there were always youngsters growing up whose talents developed slowly. Probably Derik had found a young sensitive with exceptional ability at mass-matching and added him or her to the meld. Whatever, contacting that particular meld felt almost like contacting another R'il'nian.

Marna disagreed, vehemently—but then, she hadn't been in direct contact with the meld.

Lai sighed and sat up. His chip commentary had included the fact that the other R'il'nai had been wiped out by Kharfun syndrome, leaving only a single survivor who was returning with him. He'd added for Derik the fact that Marna, while friendly toward Humans, wanted nothing to do with the crossbreds after meeting Zhaim. One of Derry's strong points when he wasn't playing jokes was tact; he'd get the word out that a welcoming ceremony with large numbers of R'il'noids was not a good idea.

"We're back in business," Cinda said happily. "We can head for home any time. Well," she added as she looked at the swirl of the storm hiding the island in the view screen, "any time we can get the shuttle up here."

That, Lai thought as he probed the storm with his mind, would probably take another day. Two days ago, they'd been thinking months to years, and worrying about finding the food they'd need to survive. Just now, a day seemed intolerably long. He activated the com and advised Captain Tova of the restored status of the Bounceabout. "Bring the shuttle up when you can," he told her, "but don't push it. I'd say late tomorrow afternoon. And Marna says to remind you to be sure the isolating field is properly collapsed before you leave. We still want to preserve the planet as a scientific site."

"And I can practically guarantee that my xenobiologist back on Murphy would mutiny if I messed it up," the captain replied. "I'm not sure we can stay here for another day, though. I think we've lost two of the tiedowns in the last hour, and the shuttle's rocking badly. Is there any chance you could teleport us up?"

Teleporting another esper even marginally capable of teleportation, like Nik, was generally far easier than an inanimate teleport. Non-espers like Cinda who were willing to accept mind-touch were harder, but not impossible. Teleporting non-espers who had problems with opening their minds to others was likely to result in permanent mental damage to the teleportee. Lai didn't want to do that to the crew, and he thought the Captain was the only crew member other than Cinda he might be able to teleport safely. Teleporting the shuttle with its occupants? Maybe. Mechanical teleports of that kind were used on Central. But they were invariably set up in such a way that non-espers were unaware of the actual teleport, and he didn't have the equipment to manage a teleport without mental contact. Keep it in mind as a last resort, but the crew would probably have to be drugged.

That left flying the shuttle up to the Bounceabout. Lai probed the storm again with his mind even as he gulped down the nutrient drink Marna handed him. The storm wasn't homogeneous. In fact, there was a break approaching from the west—not a large one, but if the shuttle could be steered up between the more violent spiral arms of the storm ...

"Could you collapse the isolation field and take off in half an hour?" he asked Captain Tova. "I can take care of the tiedowns at the last minute, and use telekinesis to help the ship recover from buffeting."

"Better teleport Zhaim up directly," the captain said dryly. "He's not feeling well, and I'd just as soon not have to deal with him on a rough flight. Can you give me the exact time I need to take off?"

She's got more faith in me than I do, Lai thought as he disengaged from Marna and reached for Zhaim's mind. Seasick, he thought, and teleported Zhaim to his cabin in the Bounceabout with orders to stay there. He wished more than ever that Zhaim were not his heir. All he could do was hope that a child would be born with a higher Çeren index and without Zhaim's lack of empathy.

He didn't think Marna would approve of the natural crossbreeding he now thought was essential to avoid another like Zhaim.

"You have twenty minutes to prepare," he told the captain. "We should get a launch window in the seven minutes following that. Marna and I will link again and I'll talk you up through the tropopause, above the storm. It'll be rough—make sure everyone is solidly webbed in. Go ahead and start pulling in the isolation field now."

He and Marna ate and felt out the control system of the shuttle while they waited. The captain would be doing the flying—Lai did not consider himself to be even a decent pilot. But Lai had to know the delay between the time he gave a command—up, down, left, right, or speed changes—and the actual response of the ship. The storm was too chaotic for him to pick out individual gusts half an hour in advance, though he could detect relatively large calm areas on that time scale. But he could feel where the gusts would be a few seconds in advance. The best chance of success lay in matching his precognitive sense of where and when gusts and electrical discharges would occur with the total response time of the captain and the ship itself, and for that a few seconds was adequate.

"Go ahead and start your engines," he told the captain as the window approached. "Takeoff in about five minutes. You'll be flying a general course about seventy degrees above horizontal, initial heading thirty degrees east of magnetic south, turning slowly right as you climb until you're heading ten degrees west of south at the tropopause. Get up to about half the speed of sound at maximum acceleration and then hold speed steady unless I tell you otherwise. Once you're above the tropopause you can go supersonic and I'll release you to fly your own course. Bring the isolation field in to just outside the tiedowns—oops, feels like you just lost another one."

"Feels that way to me, too." Tension harshened the captain's voice. "Can you keep us from blowing away until takeoff time?"

That would take telekinesis, not teleportation. No problem for a few minutes, but he and Marna both had better gulp down a little more food. "Yes. Matter of fact I'll have you run up the engines to maximum about thirty seconds before liftoff time, and we'll hold the shuttle down until things feel just right for launch. You'd better plan to rotate to the right orientation about sixty seconds before liftoff—we'll unhook the final tiedowns then. Three minutes on my mark—now!"

That's a lot of mass, Marna thought

But we're holding it still. You're used to precise movements on very small masses, and I'm going to need that precision when the shuttle goes through wind shears, or maybe to bleed off a buildup of electrical charge. We can do it, Lady mine. He hugged her mentally, and felt her response. *Funny—I never thought of helping a ship through a storm as sexy.*

It's the degree of mind sharing involved. But right now we'd better concentrate on getting that shuttle docked. Oops. They both laughed at her mental image. They were tired from the teleport, but Lai found himself hoping they wouldn't be all that tired after they had the shuttle out of danger.

We could drop communication once they're above the tropopause and out of the storm. We'd have an hour or so until they dock. And Cinda won't disturb us, if we shut the door.

After we get the shuttle through the tropopause, Marna thought.

After.

1/8/36

The Bounceabout rapidly reached a part of space where long jumps were possible, with relatively short periods of maneuvering between jumps. They were closer to Central by the time the next contact was due than they had been when Zhaim was teleported out to the ship, and Lai felt no need to link with Marna for the contact. Derik must feel the same, because his sigil was sharp, with no indication of a meld.

Your sensory chips, Derik sent, *are the entertainment hit of the season. I think I've managed to convince most of the R'il'noids to give you and your lady some space when you arrive, but I'm not so sure about the Humans and the crossbreds that don't qualify as R'il'noids. Both Councils are frantic to have you back—Kaia and I have done our best, but there are some things we just don't have the clout to handle.*

That I can deal with, Lai replied. *It's the social interactions that are going to be tricky. Marna's been so turned off by Zhaim that she wants nothing to do with crossbreds.*

Just her? Not you?

At the moment I would not be distraught if something happened to Zhaim, but I don't consider him a model for all crossbreds. Of course I'll continue to work with the Councils. Given time, I think Marna will realize R'il'noids are not all like Zhaim. But she does need to be protected from them socially until that happens.

Lai thought he felt frustration in Derry's mental tone. *Going to create problems. But look, Lai, how were you planning to return to Central?*

On the Bounceabout. The crew deserves a hero's welcome.

And your lady doesn't want one. How about this? You should reach Murphy in a few days, and we know that's within comfortable assisted teleport range. Mako and I'll link at this end, and give you an anchor to teleport back directly to the Enclave. You can anchor for your lady, and she needn't have any contact at all with us unwashed R'il'noids. We'll put your return on a need-to-know basis, so the Inner Council and those you can trust to keep their mouths shut know you're back, but the general population doesn't. Central system to Murphy's what by ship—eight, ten days? Give the Bounceabout crew their heroes' welcome when they get here—you can even be waiting to greet them and Zhaim. Your lady's exhausted and after two hundred years of isolation I think most people will understand if she's not ready for crowds. There'll be some leakage, but nobody but the Inner Council ever needs to know you came back straight from Murphy.

Lai shared the idea with Marna, who reluctantly approved. *But don't inflict Zhaim on the crew,* she added.

Lai felt Derik's mental grin when he passed Marna's comment on to his half brother. *Nobody wants Zhaim,* Derry commented, *except the other twisted crossbreds and a lot of Humans who have no real idea what they're backing. He's actually popular. A lot of people think that Kaia and I are upstarts and wish we hadn't replaced Zhaim. Even I have to give him credit for superb public relations.*

If he ever steps over the line … But the line, for R'il'noids, was nonexistent as far as protecting Humans went. That hadn't been a serious problem, back before Çeren's technique became widely used. Today … *Let's schedule daily contact, Derry. We may elaborate a little on your plan, but I think it's a good idea.*

Captain Tova did not. She didn't object to sending Zhaim back to Central as fast as possible, and she understood Lai's anxiety to return. "But if you all are going to teleport back from Murphy," she said, "why take the XP-13 back to Central at all?"

The crew, who had been looking forward to their proposed visit to Central, did not appear to agree with their captain. Lai looked at them and said, "As a distraction. I've been gone almost nine months. I'm popular—for all the wrong reasons, perhaps, but people are going to be celebrating the fact that I'm back. If it were just me, I'd grit my teeth and try to pretend I liked it—but I don't think Marna's ready for that. If you return about the time people realize I'm back, you'll absorb a lot of the energy of that celebration. I'll make sure you all have private codes to contact me if things get out of hand, but letting yourselves be made heroes for a few days—that's about as long as people will stay really worked up—would be a real help to me and a great favor for Marna."

It all went so smoothly that he wondered, afterward, that he hadn't been more worried at the time. Zhaim, unnaturally subdued since his double disgrace over Mirror, followed Lai's orders to return to his own estate and stay out of sight without question. Marna spent most of her waking hours either hooked in to the Enclave computer, learning the history and background of her new planet, or exploring the largely undeveloped Enclave and its near-ruins and stasis-preserved buildings. Mechanical teleports, including the Enclave corridor system, were new to her, and being able to walk out the entryway from Lai's suite, proceed along the corridor for a few tens of steps, open another door and step into a winter sports lodge high in the mountains, all with no more fuss than a good deal of ear-popping, fascinated her.

Lai, too busy catching up on Council business to accompany her, was glad she was able to amuse herself so easily. He still had not opened his entire mind to her, and he thought that she also was holding back certain aspects of her past. If anything, he thought fleetingly, they were growing farther apart as she learned more about his planet. And certainly she showed no sign of relenting toward the crossbreds. But that was no more than a fleeting thought. For the most part, he was merely happy she had adjusted so well.

Marna

2/5/36

If there was one thing she loved about Central, Marna thought, it was the food. She'd had a choice only between synthesized food and her own cooking for so long that even the robot cooking of fresh ingredients at the Enclave made her mouth water just to think of it. The dinner Lai had held to introduce her to some of the Human physicians, herbalists and botanists had reminded her of her graduation visit to one of the best restaurants on Riya. That had been when food was cooked by R'il'nai whose passion for creating fine food equaled her own passion for Healing.

She hadn't cared for the formality of the dinner, though, and she'd asked Lai if there was any such thing as a restaurant on Central. He'd looked puzzled. "Why?"

"The Bounceabout's leaving in a few days. I wanted to have a last meeting with the crew members I know, and I don't think they'd be comfortable with the formality here."

"Ah," he said, nodding. "I'm not into that sort of thing myself—more Derry's line. But I think he left me a list of restaurants I should try, once." He paused a moment, reaching for the computer. "Here. There are several marked as unpretentious, but with excellent food. That what you want?"

"Yes!" So now she sat at an elaborately set table in a private room with her five friends from the crew, wondering what a pretentious restaurant looked like. Lai had given her Derik's recommendations for the dishes the restaurant prepared best, and the meal itself had been everything she had hoped for. Oh, some of the flavors and seasoning were strange, and she had added several culinary herbs to her mental list of plants to import from Riya. But the new seasonings appealed to her, too. Perhaps she should find out more about the herbs used for flavoring here?

"I wonder how this trout would taste with that herb you use with fish," Cinda said.

"Cyla? I have seedlings started, but they're not up yet," Marna replied, taking a final bite of the fish. The servers removed her plate almost at once, replacing it with another. Some kind of salad this time, with a dressing new to her. "Are Human servers normal?" she asked when the servers had left the room for a moment. "It doesn't seem a very fulfilling thing to do."

"Slaves," Captain Tova said, with a pinched look to her mouth. "You can feel emotions, can't you? When you're not shielding? Open your shields a little when they come back. But I can tell you right now they don't have much choice about what they do."

Marna stared at her. "Slaves?"

"Central's one of the planets that allow people to own other people," Cinda said. "That's one of the reasons I wouldn't want to live here."

The very idea of owning something still felt strange to Marna. She supposed she'd be indignant if someone had walked into her home on Riya and destroyed something precious to her, like the hair clasp she still treasured, but if Ruby had chosen someone else, of her own will, she'd have let her go. You didn't own an animal; you were responsible for it. Owning another sentient being was simply beyond her imagination. "You mean the R'il'noids are *that* perverted?" she gulped.

"Some own slaves, and I don't doubt Zhaim is among them," Kalar growled. "But most of the slave owners are Human. Humans and R'il'noids both vary. A lot."

Lai had tried several times to tell her that, Marna realized. The server returned with beverages for the next course, and Marna cautiously lowered her shields against the girl's emotions. Back aching, feet sore, but at least this owner allowed his slaves some comfort in their rest area, and would not put up with his guests abusing the servers. The girl felt lucky in her owner, and even luckier tonight with such an undemanding group to serve. Certainly she'd have preferred more choice, but the visualizations of what her lot could have been shocked Marna.

"You can't do anything?" she asked Lai that night.

"Slavery's a planetary matter, a Human choice. Neither R'il'nians nor R'il'noids have any voice in planetary laws. It's not the only thing I dislike on Central, but all I can do is make my disapproval plain. Marna," he added, his voice taking on a pleading note, "can't you see why it's so important I stay here? To try and counter that kind of thinking? Because I don't believe any more that Zhaim will."

Zhaim, Marna thought, would more likely throw his considerable influence the other way. But she'd been wrong about all Humans being like Cinda, she thought on the edge of sleep. Was it just possible she was wrong about all the R'il'noids being like Zhaim, much as the idea of the cross breeding still sickened her?

Roi

2/13/36

"Hurry up, Roi. You're going to be late for supper."

"I'm not hungry, Cory."

"I'll get him there," Davy said. "You go on, Coryn. I've had about enough of this sulking, Roi. Your father has other things to do than hold your hand, especially after all the months he's spent away."

Davy knew him too well, Roi thought. But he was getting to know himself, too, and he knew what was wrong. He was beginning to trust people. And of course once he trusted them, they let him down. Derik had acted as if he really cared about Roi, and convinced the boy that his father would care even more, especially after he had been such a help to the R'il'nian in getting home. Huh! His father and the woman he'd brought with him had been back on Central for almost a month, and as far as Roi knew Lai hadn't even asked about his son. He hadn't seen Derik since the teleports, either.

Well, Davy might haul him down to the dining hall, but he couldn't make Roi eat. Not when Roi had no appetite at all. He let Davy push his chair down the corridor, out the door, and along the weather-shielded path to the central building. Davy didn't leave until Roi was in the dining room and on his way to the three green tables.

In some ways it would have been easier if Davy had let him choke down something in his room. His classes were still with younger students, and most of his social contacts were with Coryn's age group. His only friends his own age were a handful he had met through the pattern chess club. But he had to eat with his own age group, and any friends he made through pattern chess in that group were promptly shuttled to another table in the dining hall. He ate under Xazhar's unfriendly eye, surrounded by Xazhar's admirers.

And Xazhar was not being ignored by *his* father. Zhaim had made a point of appearing at the school to collect Xazhar for a day at home every firstday since the XP-13's return. Xazhar had been bad enough fresh from a day with his father yesterday, but today he'd be worse—peevish at the restrictions of the school, and taking it out on Roi. Roi glanced at the table with room for his float chair, confirming that Xazhar, glorying in his status as Zhaim's son, was already seated.

But where were Malar and Sheeran? It wasn't like those two to be late for meals, and their absence gave him a sudden pang of unease. A hunch? Trust your hunches, Derik had said, and while he wasn't sure he trusted Derik any more, his hunches had gotten him out of trouble long before he'd ever met the R'il'noid.

He stopped his chair, looking around unsuccessfully for Malar and Sheeran and weighing his growing hunch against the certainty of a tongue-lashing from Davy. Malar and Sheeran were up to something, he was sure. Their attack on him last half term had worked because he had been too annoyed to pay attention to the vague feeling that something was wrong. He wouldn't make that mistake again. He turned his chair and headed back out of the room.

Nebol half rose, his face darkening. Getting angry, was he? Well, let him. Roi was in no mood to placate anyone, and Nebol had no more reason to be mad at Roi than he had to be mad at Malar and Sheeran. Roi guided his float chair out of the door and down the corridor to the path he'd just come in on.

Davy wasn't visible, but the path joined another halfway to the dorm and the intersection was cloaked by shrubbery. Where were Malar and Sheeran? Roi reached out for their mental signatures, and found Malar, easily. Hiding in the shrubbery? Why? He hesitated. Was he justified in even a slight reading of Malar's thoughts? Then the other boy's visualization fairly leaped into his mind, and he gasped in shock. Malar and Sheeran were both hiding in the shrubbery, on opposite sides of the path, and even as Roi caught their intention they leaped out of the shrubbery onto a totally unsuspecting Davy.

Malar was carrying a groundball mallet, and Sheeran a knife, and Roi cried out as the mallet smashed into Davy's skull. *Cory!* he screamed mentally, as he tried to block the next blow telekinetically. The chair was too slow to get him to Davy in time to help, and Derry had told him not even to try patterning a teleport for himself—but he knew the principles, and he had no doubt that Malar and Sheeran would kill Davy if he couldn't use skin contact to block them. He couldn't teleport with the shield on. He snapped it off, gritting his teeth against the buzzing in his brain, and reached for Davy. There—a large enough space for him to teleport into, and with Davy as a target he managed the jump, rolling as he landed to grab Davy. Sheeran's knife licked out, aimed at Davy but scoring Roi's cheek and continuing to leave a deep slash to the side of Davy's neck.

How much could he do at once? He had to block anything from coming within a fingerwidth or two of his body or Davy's, and Davy had been hurt, badly, by the initial attack. Only Roi's mind was keeping the torn artery in his neck from spurting blood. At the same time he was sharply aware of broken bones and the fact that Davy's brain was injured and swelling—how could he stop that? And he had to do it all through the buzzing in his head from the suppresser field.

Where was Coryn? He needed help!

Derik

2/13/36

Derik glanced out the window, noting with some surprise that the sun was well up in the eastern sky. For once, it seemed that his internal clock was synchronized with the local time after an interplanetary trip.

He couldn't blame the last month's travel on any desire on Lai's part to keep him away from Roi. He'd spent the time between teleporting the chips and Lai's physical return in summarizing the trouble spots that had developed during Lai's absence and suggesting who was best suited to clearing them up. Most of his suggestions were people he had not felt able to do without during Lai's absence, but he had not hesitated to put down his own name when he felt he was the best person for the job. Lai had gone over the summary, checked with the computer, and essentially accepted the list unchanged.

And Derik's assessments had been correct, he saw as he asked the computer for a rundown on recent Confederation events. He'd known his own missions were successful; it was a relief to see that the others he'd suggested had done equally well. Three additional high-priority messages he'd better check out before the Inner Council meeting, and then …

The third message was from Coryn. Dammit, if there was one thing Derik and Vara had agreed on with Coryn, it was that their son be taught from infancy that he was not, under any circumstances, to use his relationship with Derik for any special privileges. Cory had never sent Derik a high-priority message; he *knew* that high priority was reserved for situations that involved the welfare of the Confederation.

So why was he doing it now?

Unless …

Hells, it was less trouble to read the message than speculate about it. And if Coryn didn't have a damn good reason for using high priority …

The message was short, direct, and at first glance rude. "Tell Lai he'd better make time for Roi."

Make time for Roi? Wasn't Lai seeing the boy? Derik had consoled himself during his troubleshooting with the knowledge that his absence would allow Lai and Roi time to get properly acquainted. Marna might not want anything to do with the crossbreds herself, but surely she would not try to separate Lai from his son. Surely Lai had absorbed the report Derik had left, and was aware that Roi's lack of response earlier had been due to the boy's belief that he was being lied to. Well, Derik would certainly tell Lai of his concerns before the Council meeting. Meanwhile, he had just enough time to use the fresher and change clothes.

But when Derik arrived, half an hour before the Council meeting was due to start, there was no sign of Lai. Food—that was automatic, in a group of powerful espers who might be using at least their precognitive talents heavily. Only a few other members of the Inner Council were present. Derik joined Lunia.

"Lai not here yet? I'd hoped to have a word with him."

"You'll have to grab him the minute the session's over, then. He's only here for the meeting itself, these days."

Derik sent her a sense of surprise as he selected a rich pastry and bit down on it. *I'd hoped to talk to him about Roi.*

Good luck. He's not even speaking with Zhaim.

Derik swallowed the pastry and switched back to vocal speech, worried about the emotions he might send by mind touch. "I'm not sure that's a reason for concern." Considering the mischief Zhaim had done at Tyndall before leaving, Derik was more relieved than upset by a rift between Lai and that particular son.

"It's not just Zhaim. That woman he brought back considers the whole crossbreeding program as an abomination. And she's influencing Lai. It's slow, but he's pulling away from social contacts with R'il'noids. Limiting himself more and more to her and to Humans. You'll probably see the difference even more than we do, Derry."

Derik selected another pastry, sobered. A rift between Lai and Zhaim was overdue. A rift between Lai and R'il'noids in general was a matter of far more concern—especially if it extended to Roi, who really needed to feel that his father approved of him. He was beginning to think that Coryn had used the high priority correctly.

Whatever was going on, it had not been that bad for Lai himself. The R'il'nian looked fit and happy when he teleported into the room, more so than Derik could remember seeing him in centuries, and if he'd developed any general dislike of the R'il'noids, Derik was unable to detect it. "That woman," as Lunia had referred to Marna, was clearly good for Lai on a personal level.

The meeting went quickly, with Derik's report being the final and principal business of the day. By that time it was obvious that Lai was keeping the meeting strictly to business, and might well leave as precipitously as he had entered once he considered the business finished. So Derik finished off his report with, "I need to speak with you after the meeting, Lai."

Lai hesitated. "All right," he said finally, "but keep it short. Anything else? The meeting's closed." The others teleported out quickly, leaving Derik alone with Lai.

"What is it, Derry?"

"Roi. You have seen him since you've been back, haven't you?"

"No." Then, before Derik had time to do more than draw in his breath, "I'd like to, but the school thinks it would upset the adjustment he's made."

The school? Derik almost choked as he tried to speak and gasp at the same time. Then he remembered Nebol's attitude and his own conclusion as to its cause. "I'm going to kill Zhaim one of these days," he muttered.

Lai grinned. "I sympathize, but don't. I'd have to do something about it, and I can't get along without you."

The relationship between Lai and Zhaim must really have broken down, Derik thought. Too bad the Human population of the Confederation had made Çeren index so important. But Lai should have known not to trust the school's assessment of Roi, and for that matter, realized that the boy needed him. Unless ...

"You did absorb my report on Roi, didn't you?"

"Report?"

"In your personal section of the computer. Zhaim would have had access in the official section, so …" He stopped as he saw the expression on Lai's face.

"Derik, I haven't even checked the index on my personal stuff. Have you any idea how full that section of the computer is? Is there something I need to know right away?" There was a trace of hope in his face, and Derik realized that if he had not gotten the report, he might still think Roi wanted nothing to do with him.

"Number one: when you last saw Roi, he did not believe you were his father, or even that you were who Nik said you were.

"Number two: Zhaim managed to convince the school head that Roi was still a slave and my catamite, rather than your son. I thought I got that straightened out, but Nebol seemed awfully resistant to the truth. I can't prove it, but I suspect Zhaim used illegal mind control.

"Number three: who'd you think you contacted from Mirror?"

"You, from the sigil, but …"

Derik was shaking his head. "Roi doesn't have a sigil of his own yet, so I had him use mine. He picked you up initially, through a suppresser field, when no other sensitive on planet got anything. He's also responsible for that very pretty job of mass-matching that let us get the chips out to you so easily—not to mention saving me when I went into convulsions on that first contact. Lai, most of us can live with your refusing to have much to do with us socially. We don't like it, at least I don't, but we're adults; we can accept it. Roi can't. He's not even sixteen yet, and Nik and I had him thinking you'd really be proud of him. Instead you've ignored him, and I don't think he can take that."

"I would not harm a child," came an unfamiliar, troubled voice, speaking Galactica.

Startled, Derik looked toward the voice. He saw a woman with short, copper-gold hair, skin only a shade lighter than Lai's, and the relatively delicate features of the R'il'nai. Marna? He bowed formally, sensing that she would not accept the more usual greeting of outstretched hands. "Nor would I, intentionally," he said. "But is very easy to do harm without intention."

"Derik!" Lai's voice was as close as it ever got to anger.

"And who would know better than I do?" Derik replied bitterly. "Lai, check out that report. Better yet, go out to Tyndall—now—and let the boy know you care about him. I don't think Coryn would have contacted me the way he did if Roi wasn't pretty depressed. I know he was really looking forward to meeting you."

"Go," Marna said firmly, and then switched to a quick torrent of R'il'nian. Lai looked startled, then took three quick steps to hug and kiss her before vanishing.

And what, Derik thought, am I supposed to do now?

Marna

2/13/36

So this was Derik? Marna studied him thoughtfully. He didn't feel at all like Zhaim. There were undercurrents in him that bothered her, but there was also an overlying decency that fought to keep those undercurrents in control. Humans varied a lot, she had discovered over the past month. Lai had tried to tell her that, and that crossbreds varied just as much. Could she have been wrong, in lumping all the crossbreds together as monsters?

She had been listening long enough, unobserved, to know that this Derik was no friend of Zhaim. And at the moment, he looked as if he would rather be anywhere else. She had better speak, though she was not quite ready yet to tell him that she had in fact asked Lai to let him stay so she could observe him. "I have been foolish," she said aloud. "It never occurred to me that some of the crossbreds would be only children."

Derik relaxed a little, and smiled tentatively. "We all start out as children," he said. "Roi—Roi's special, and very vulnerable. He was raised a slave, partly in my ownership, and I don't think he's really accepted the R'il'nian part of his background yet. He needs his father."

"And what of his mother?"

Derik looked briefly panicked. "You'd better ask Lai. But no one's been able to find her. And we've been looking ever since we knew Roi existed."

She certainly would ask Lai. "And you—you *owned* this child?" That was to her still the strangest and most horrifying part of Central—that Humans, and crossbreds as well, considered they owned certain Humans.

"Yes. And thought at the time I was an enlightened and considerate owner. Now, knowing Roi better … I think Lai's right. Slavery has heavy costs, not only for the slave but for the owner as well. At the same time—I can't just turn slaves loose to starve, can I? And I won't sell them."

Marna turned and walked over to the food, gesturing to Derik to follow her. "Why don't you end slavery?"

"On Central? I would, now—but that's local affairs by Confederation law, and neither R'il'nians nor R'il'noids have any voice in local affairs. Only in the relationships between systems. Local affairs are run by Humans and those crossbreds with less than half R'il'nian genes. The best I can do is see that any slaves I own are educated for eventual freedom."

Marna poured herself a glass of wine, and for a moment they were both silent, reassessing their ideas of each other. Their silence was interrupted by

Lai's mind-touch, and from the way Derik jumped, the same message was sent to both of them. *Get medical help!* A second later Lai appeared, arms wrapped around two limp bodies.

Marna took one look and dropped to her knees at their side, reaching her hands out for physical contact. The man was half conscious from a blow to the head, with several broken bones and a couple of cuts that must have reached arteries and should have been bleeding much more than they were. The boy, a gangling adolescent with striking pure white hair, had only minor bruises and cuts, but he was totally focused on the man, controlling bleeding and neural swelling, which was fine, but trying at the same time to Heal broken bones and superficial damage. Hadn't anyone taught this child about prioritizing injuries?

Then she remembered what Lai had told her, that the Healing tradition had been lost on Central. The tradition, perhaps, but obviously not the genes. She tried to move in, only to find that the Human shied violently away from her mind-touch, even though he accepted the boy's. She felt the boy's frustration and fear, and reached wordlessly for his mind, nudging him toward the injuries that could kill the man and away from those that could wait for later Healing. She might not be able to Heal the man herself, but she could show the boy what to do.

Derik had vanished, but he suddenly reappeared on the other side of her patient, carrying a bag of fluid and tubing. "Roi, turn your head a bit to the left," he ordered, and when the boy obeyed, he slid a needle into the jugular vein. "Glucose," he explained. "Lai's bringing the rest of the medical staff."

Marna nodded, assessing the injured man through Roi's contact. One artery almost severed—that was a fast repair, and one the boy seemed able to handle on his own. The neural problems … *I don't know how it should go,* the young mind wailed in hers.

Like this, her mind showed him, and she guided him through the process of easing the man into a deep coma to reduce neural activity. Then the two of them together traced and restored the damaged circulatory system of the brain, finally removing dead and hopelessly damaged nerve cells and restoring neural links. Roi seemed particularly interested in the technique she used to determine where the links had been. Only when the man was stabilized and the medical staff had arrived and were swarming around them did she realize that Roi was partially paralyzed. And that he was one of the hated crossbreds.

"I had Kharfun when they found me," he explained.

"But he was almost over that by the time I left," Lai protested.

Derik, carefully removing the needle from Roi's neck, sighed. "Lai, pull up that report. He was shielding for a good eight months after the Kharfun, so Nik tried to explain the recovery process to him verbally. Roi got it wrong, and we didn't realize until solstice break. He's very good at faking normal motion with telekinesis and levitation, which is what you saw, but the nerve fibers and muscles were pretty well atrophied by the time we realized what he was doing."

"I'm not supposed to do it any more," Roi said. "I did teleport today, though. I'm sorry, Uncle Derry, but I couldn't think of any other way to get to Davy in time."

Derik stood up. "Under the circumstances, you're forgiven." He walked over to the wall slot, and came back with two mugs on a tray. "Better eat this. My Lady Marna, would you like something to eat?" He knelt by Roi, carefully pulling the boy into a half-seated position against his shoulder before holding one of the mugs to his lips.

Marna took the other mug, tasted the rich soup it contained, and began to think about what had just happened. The Healing had been an automatic response. That Roi was a crossbred … She hadn't reacted to that, during the Healing. She had only been relieved to have an assistant, however poorly trained, that her patient could accept. As she sipped, she studied Roi and Derik. Crossbreds. Like Zhaim, but she couldn't imagine anyone farther from Zhaim than Roi. At his age empathy shouldn't even be fully developed, but his was already so strong it would destroy him if he didn't learn to control it. Not to mention being extremely uncomfortable to any other empath around him—he broadcast his own pain far too freely. And there had been so much pain in his life. She'd better teach him that control, first thing. And prioritizing injuries, rather than trying to Heal everything at once! "What happened?" she asked finally.

"Sheeran and Malar," Roi replied angrily. "They weren't at the supper table. I got worried and went back to see what they were up to, and got there just in time to see them ambush Davy. I could keep Davy alive and stop them from hurting him worse once I had physical contact, but there was just too much to do all at once."

Lai nodded. "I was trying to locate Roi when I got a mental scream for help—I think aimed at your son, Derry."

"Coryn's the best friend I've got, there," Roi confirmed.

"Sheeran and Malar," Derik said. "Isn't that the pair Cory said ambushed and raped you?"

"What?" Lai gasped.

"I think we had both better check out that report," Marna said. "Meanwhile—Roi, do you want to go back to that place?"

Roi hesitated. "Some things I like. Classes are okay, even if I do have to be in with younger kids. Coryn's really helping me learn things, and I'd miss some of the others, too, like Ander and some of the others in the pattern chess club. But I hate having to eat with Xazhar and his clique, and always having to watch out for trouble outside class hours, and the suppresser field, even if I do have a shield this half-term."

Lai's mind touched hers. *Do you think you could accept having him here, at least occasionally?*

Just try and stop me. And abruptly, faintly, another mind was in hers, laughing. Win?

Thought I had it backward, didn't you. Backward? She thought back, trying to remember all the times Win had spoken to her, and suddenly remembered a spring morning when she had held Ruby's infant in her hands and grieved that she herself would never have a child. A child to rear and a child to bear, he had said, and she had thought the order of the phrases odd. But he had said something else, too: mine in spirit, if not by blood. And Roi was in many ways more like Win than he was like Lai. Oh, he was Lai's son in blood, no doubt about that. But he could so easily have been the child she had planned with Win. He needed his father, yes. But he needed a mother, too. Not to mention a good deal of training!

Roi was looking up at Lai, a little hesitant. "Are you really my father?" he asked.

"Yes. And proud of you. I didn't mean to neglect you, Roi. I honestly thought it would upset you to see me."

"Do you think I could visit now and then? Xazhar gets to go home with his father every firstday." Tentative as yet; feeling his way.

Lai smiled and caught his son's hands in his. "I think we can manage that, at least," he said. "But I'd better clear up a few things with the school. Anything else I should know first, Derry?"

Derik grinned, and Marna decided he was quite capable of malice toward those he considered had earned it. "Pull up the report and do a keyword search on Nebol," he suggested.

"He stays here tonight, regardless," Marna said firmly. "He needs to learn some control of that empathy of his, and he does have some injuries." *And don't you try to Heal them yourself,* she told Roi. *You've had more than enough of that for one day.*

Lai knelt beside them, taking Roi from Derik into his own arms. His mind touched Marna's with an image of one of the few empty rooms in their suite: a guest bedroom looking out on the mountains behind the Enclave complex. She thought approval and turned back to Derik.

There was a little sadness in his expression. "I don't think you need me any more," he said, and reached out to touch Roi's hand. "Stay friends, Roi. But for right now you need a family of your own, and I think you finally have one." He teleported away, leaving only the last of the medical attendants in the room with the new family.

Lai's mind reached out, gathering Marna and Roi into its embrace. "Let's go home," he said softly.

HOME

CORYN

2/13/36

"I don't care who you are," Coryn shouted. "Part of your job—a big part—is to keep us safe. Roi is not safe! He asked me for help; he screamed for it. Now you don't even know where he is—or Davy, either. Well, you'd damned well better find out!" Part of him was horrified at his own audacity in defying Nebol, but a much larger part was simply too angry to care.

He thought Nebol was just as angry, but the man was making a point of not shouting. "I am deeply disappointed in you, Coryn," he said quietly. "You are one of our brightest students, and your lack of loyalty to the school …"

"Loyalty to the school has nothing to do with the incompetent job you're doing!" Cory blazed back. Oh, oh, his internal monitor said. You've really gone too far over the line this time. Well? If he'd already gone too far, he might as well tell Nebol exactly what he thought of him. "Roi's probably the brightest student you've got, and you treat him like he's the slave that rumor had him the first half-term. I thought Father had straightened you out on that! Sheeran and Malar have been bad news since they were first year, but they're Xazhar's cronies, so they can get away with anything. Now they've done something to Roi and Davy both, and all you can say is I'm out of line for getting upset about it. I've never taken advantage of being Derik's son, but I'm going to on this one!"

"Never?" came a third voice. "I rather thought you were behind Derry's concern today. It's all right, Coryn. Roi's fine, and Davy will recover. I picked up the same mental scream for help that you did. Well, Nebol? What are you

225

going to do about those two troublemakers? And whatever made you try to convince me that Roi would be better off if I didn't contact him?"

Coryn recognized Lai—he'd been formally introduced to the R'il'nian on his sixteenth birthday, when he passed from childhood to adolescence. He had not expected to see Lai here, or feel the anger that oozed from the R'il'nian. And if Nebol had been responsible for Lai's apparently ignoring Roi … Part of him looked forward to seeing Lai take Nebol down a notch, but the more cautious part of his mind warned that while he had less than two months left at Tyndall, Nebol could make that time very difficult if he knew that Coryn had witnessed his humiliation.

Lai ended that internal debate by saying "Coryn, stay here. This may involve you, too. Well, Nebol?"

The school head drew himself up in his chair. "Sheeran and Malar have been in trouble in the past," he admitted. "But your suggestion that they have been targeting Roi is totally without proof. As for the disappearance today, I knew that you were on the grounds and assumed you had taken him—without notifying me." The implication that Lai was to blame was unspoken, but obvious.

Coryn felt a slight sense of questioning, and sent back, *He never said anything about your being here to me.* Aloud, he added, "Getting Roi to admit he's having trouble isn't easy. And there's no objective proof they were the ones who trashed his room and raped him last half term. He teleported the evidence away, but I met them coming out of his building, and they'd been up to something. Malar still had potting soil on his shoes."

Nebol snorted. "An untrained fifteen-year-old, who can't even learn R'Gal? Manage that kind of a teleport? Preposterous!"

"If he could teleport food into his stomach, which he was doing the first couple of months, he could certainly handle that. And he beats me all the time at pattern chess," Coryn responded.

I shall definitely have to check out your father's report, Lai's mind said dryly, and again Coryn was almost frightened by the controlled anger behind the thought. Aloud, the R'il'nian said, "Malar and Sheeran were on top of Roi and Davy—and trying to kill Davy—when I got there. Nebol, will you give me permission to examine your mind for evidence that Zhaim has been tampering with your attitudes?"

The expressions that flitted across Nebol's face were a fascinating study in mixed emotions, but the final winners were pride and indignation. "No," he said shortly.

"Then Roi will not be returning to the dorms this half-term. He may be back as a day student next year, but I suspect you will not be back as school head. We'll need to connect the Big'Un to the school computer with a two-way hookup so he can attend lectures and do his assignments for the rest of the half term. And the boys responsible are to be expelled. If they were older, I would insist that they be charged with attempted murder. Cory, I hate to ask you for the extra work this close to graduation, but could you get Roi's and Davy's things together and help your father get them to the Enclave? And can you manage a patterned teleport? I think we'd like you to continue tutoring Roi, if you can arrange it."

Coryn gulped. He hadn't expected this. "Uh—Father had me sharing Roi's esper lessons last break. But Roi's way ahead of me on that. He's pattern teleporting, but I'm not sure I'm ready."

Lai's face took on a brief faraway expression, then he looked at Coryn and smiled. "Your father says you're ready, even if you don't think you are. He'll be by for you in a couple of hours, so get going on packing at least what Roi will need right away. And Nebol—don't interfere and don't try to take anything out on Coryn."

As Coryn backed out of Nebol's office and ran for his dorm, his emotions were as mixed as Nebol's had been a few minutes before. Relief, certainly. Shock. Excitement that he was actually going to see the inner parts of the Enclave, coupled with apprehension that he wouldn't measure up. Disappointment that Roi would not be finishing the year at Tyndall—though that might be best for Roi.

Ander was waiting in Cory's room. "Well? Did you find anything out?"

"Uh—yes. Roi's at the Enclave. His father's not sending him back as a boarding student, and I'm supposed to pack up his stuff for him. Give me a hand on that? And I think they want me to keep on tutoring him, but I'll have to learn a patterned teleport for that." He carefully kept from mentioning Nebol's probable firing, or the order to expel Malar and Sheeran. The first wouldn't be Lai's doing directly, but once the governing board heard that Lai had taken his son out because he didn't feel Roi was safe at Tyndall, it would be only a matter of time. Probably not much time, given Derik's position on the board, though it might be hard to find another R'il'noid to replace Nebol at short notice.

Ander sighed melodramatically. "Back to Nik's medicine. Well, I'm glad for Roi, and for you, but I'm going to miss him. What do we need to pack?"

Marna

2/13/36, late night

Marna finished the report and looked over at Lai. She had expected to be surprised—everything about Central surprised her—but Lai looked stunned.

Evidently he hadn't expected most of Derik's revelations about Roi, now sound asleep in the guest bedroom. "He stays here," she told him, knowing him well enough to be sure he would agree. "Maybe not in the guest room—he needs room for friends and hobbies. But he stays with us. He needs a family. And you needn't comment about my change of heart. I must have been crazy to think all of the crossbreds would be alike. Even R'il'nians differed."

He grinned ruefully. "And as R'il'nians go, I'm a pretty poor father," he said. "But you weren't really crazy. Just very lonely, and off balance. I'm glad you're willing to accept Roi. I couldn't have left him at Tyndall, once I found out what was going on there."

"I'm not sure anyone could have civilized Zhaim," she said. "Certainly you were not the kind of father he needed. But what Roi needs is quite different. Love. And someone with the patience to help him build his confidence in himself." She felt his mind touch hers, wordless and loving, and leaned into it. *Lai, Derik said I'd have to ask you about Roi's mother.*

He hesitated a moment, and then for the first time opened his mind to her completely, so that she shared his love for Cloudy, always tinged with the sadness of knowing that she would grow old and die while he lived on, unchanging. He had wished she could bear him a child, but the genetics board had refused to allow it, insisting that even one chance in four of an insane esper was too much of a risk. Then the pain and bewilderment when she left him, begging him not to try to find her, and the much more recent discovery of why she had left him, and the even deeper pain when Roi had refused to acknowledge any attempt at contact. No wonder he had said that while saying good-bye forever was hard, it was harder yet not to have the chance. He was still trying to find Cloudy, but he was painfully aware that she had probably died, horribly, long before he even understood her danger.

His love for Elyra was less compelling, but still very much present, as was his feeling for their child and for his grandson, Roi's child.

In response Marna opened her own mind, sharing her memories of Win and their time together. She even included the strange episode that afternoon, when she had felt that Roi was, in a very real sense, the child that she and Win had planned together.

It never occurred to her to feel diminished in any way by the fact that he had loved and still loved others. If anything, she was a little surprised to find that fear at the back of his mind, and relieved to find that at least some of the crossbreds were conceived in love, and not merely as the results of a laboratory process. She felt him respond to the idea, giving her his own conclusions on the possible effect of the laboratory procedure, and examined them from her own training as a Healer.

Implantation, she thought. Getting a viable crossbred blastocyst was a matter of tetraploidy followed by good luck in the random chromosome loss that followed. It might be possible to influence the randomness of the chromosome loss, too. But natural pregnancies involved another step. Many apparently viable blastocysts never implanted, never rooted in the comforting home of a uterus, and the artificial process was designed to force implantation. Those like Zhaim, they now both suspected, came from those blastocysts that would not have implanted naturally. But what if the R'il'nian father used conditional precognition to determine if the little ball of cells had the potential to become a R'il'noid who would have the traits really needed to keep the Confederation going, and only allowed those who passed that test to implant? As a Healer, she could certainly do that. Could a R'il'noid? Lai knew what had happened; she had the training to assess it. Together they could work it out, and in far more detail than Lai and Elyra had managed—but for now the joyous intimacy of sharing mind and soul pulled them both away from the problem.

This was what she had missed, and so had Lai—this blending of heart and mind, so much closer than mere physical intimacy could ever be. Physical lovemaking was part of it, and an essential part, if the two of them were to have children. But how small a part! Her last individual thought was pity that the Humans could never know this sharing.

2/14/36

They were awakened early the next morning by the tinerals. Ruby, Emerald and Citrine were gathered at the door, heads cocked and singing short, experimental phrases, while Spring clung to the fabric draped across the window, her attention fixed on the three at the door. Lai and Marna looked at each other, sharing minds in a brief morning caress that also became a sharing of their curiosity. Marna opened the door with a thought, and the three younger tinerals flew out, with Ruby bounding behind. The two R'il'nians followed, curiosity aroused.

The enclosed courtyard with its swimming pool was still dusky, though the stars were no longer visible in the lightening sky. There were no tinerals in sight there, though it was where most of the unattached animals lived. The walls of the courtyard were transparent, and Marna could see Ruby scampering along the hallway to the guest room where they had left Roi. Tineral music filled the air, and as they turned the corner, they saw tinerals clustered outside Roi's room. A warm, immature and rather shaky baritone voice was almost lost in the tineral chorus. Abruptly it stopped, and Roi's voice said, "No! That's not the right harmony." Marna and Lai looked at each other and then stepped forward, somewhat hampered by the clustered tinerals, until they could look into the room.

Roi was sitting in front of the monitor they'd rigged the night before, the interface circlet half hidden by his hair. Tinerals were watching him from every surface in the room, and two of the usually independent nature variety were perched on his shoulders, while a third looked up from his lap. "I know we don't have the full two-way setup yet," Lai said mildly, "but aren't you supposed to be at least listening to lectures?"

The boy cringed, cowering as if he half expected a blow. He recovered quickly, forcing himself to look up at Lai. "I have fine arts this hour, sir. We're supposed to be doing variations on a musical theme, but ..." He looked at the tinerals. "What are they?"

"Tinerals," Marna answered. "They do their own variations, but try thinking the harmonies you want at them. And you'd better start thinking of names for the three that are on you. They seem to have chosen you for their person."

Roi looked unbelievingly down at the green, gold and bronze animal in his lap, and the tineral responded by reaching up to pat the boy's face. "Really?" Roi gulped.

"Unless I've totally lost my ability to spot a bond forming, I'd have to pry them away from you. Now try the song again, but this time think the harmonies you want at the tinerals."

He tried again, obviously delighted when the tinerals this time picked up his choice of harmonies, instead of inventing their own. Lai was smiling, enjoying the music, but Marna was analyzing the shakiness in the boy's voice. Due to the partial paralysis, she thought. He could not control all of the muscles needed for vocal production. *Lai,* she thought as Roi began coding the music into the computer, *I need to talk with those who know Roi—especially anyone involved in treating his paralysis.*

Later this morning? Then, a bit ashamed, *Derik or Nik would know better than I would.*

You've been away. Yes. And give me access to those early statistics you were thinking about last night, too.

Marna had met Derik, and while he and Roi had been enough to discredit her old idea that all of the R'il'noids would be like Zhaim, the variety of people in the room still surprised her. Some, such as Elyra and the two toddlers, she knew a little from the previous night's mind sharing. Nik—well, no wonder Lai had wished his half brother could go over the list of healing herbs in the Riyan computer! Jelarik had turned out to be a veritable mountain of a man, wider than tall, needing a special chair even to sit in the interface room where they were meeting, while Vara, who barely qualified as R'il'noid, was as fascinated by the tinerals as was Roi. Feline and Davy represented the Humans, and both seemed quite willing to fade into the background though Feline was obviously apprehensive of the speed with which Wif had found his way onto Marna's lap.

"That's one question answered," Marna remarked, smiling down at the child. "Roi's obviously capable of passing on the Healing genes." She looked over at Feline. "Better let me handle his training when he's old enough, but right now what he needs most is a stable, loving home." She'd have to be content as grandmother, she decided, hoping Feline's possessiveness would not trouble the child. "Now, Lai and I have both absorbed Derik's report, and I need to know exactly what you've done about the Kharfun paralysis, Nik. But first, is there anything else I need to know about Roi, if I'm to act as his mother?"

"He likes animals, and he's good with them," Vara said. "The month Coryn brought him home for vacation, he spent most of his free time in the stable, making friends with the horses and the barn cats."

Derik nodded. "Not sure I put it in the report, but he is—or was, before the Kharfun got him—a very good rider. He beat Coryn when I set up an obstacle race between them, and with a lot less experience. And a very athletic dancer, as well as being artistic."

Jelarik tapped the tips of his fingers together. "I'd say High R'il'noid on the basis of his esper abilities, though scoring him was quite difficult. A Çeren index of a hundred, which is what I gave him, is certainly too low. Especially considering his performance as part of Derik's meld."

"Weak points?" Marna asked.

"No self-confidence," Derik replied. "That hurts, because it's partly my fault. I think I see a little improvement, though not as much as I'd like. He may have problems dealing with frustration—the impression I got was that his mother taught him to use physical activity to burn off frustration, and with the partial paralysis—well, he can't do that any more. And the sound discrimination problem."

Jelarik nodded ponderously. "Both Derik and I thought at first the school had made a mistake. But we repeated the tests ourselves, with the same results. He gets so frustrated that we decided to stop the tests. He has so much else to learn that it is simply not important right now."

"So we'll just ignore that for the moment," Lai said. "Marna doesn't like R'Gal anyway. But we really have to see if there's anything we can do about that paralysis."

"Reverse precognition as a first try, I think," Marna replied. "Roi was fascinated when I used it as a guide to Heal the damage to Davy's brain. Nik, you say you've never heard of it? We'll tackle that after Roi's done his schoolwork. But for now—Elyra, Jelarik, Nik, you're all on the Genetics Board, right? And familiar with Lai's suggestion that Çeren's laboratory technique was a factor in producing crossbreds like Zhaim?"

Elyra looked eager, Nik unhappy, and Jelarik combative. Jelarik was the one who spoke. "We had to do something. There just weren't enough good espers being born."

"Did Çeren himself consider his work to be a permanent solution? Did he or anyone else ever examine possible long-term effects precognitively?"

"Bera did," Nik replied. "She could be very good at long-range stuff, but she was sometimes erratic. And she never liked the lab techniques, or the Çeren index. I know Çeren himself took her seriously, and was pretty upset his last century or so that people were treating his work as some kind of final solution. I don't think he ever considered it more than a stopgap. But it was needed at the time."

"At the time," Marna repeated. "But you agree he would not have objected to an extension and modification of his work?"

This time Jelarik looked a little less pugnacious. "Extension, yes. Perhaps modification. But we can't abandon it!"

"I've taken the data Lai had, including Ania's conception, and analyzed it using my Riyan medical training. What Lai did—and probably what Jarn did—has some parallels with the laboratory technique. But it went further. I don't think Lai was aware of it himself, but he used conditional probability on the fertilized eggs. Only the ones that felt right ever had any chance of implantation."

Derik and Vara were looking at each other in surprise. "I wouldn't have agreed to a natural pregnancy," Vara said slowly. "But I did agree that Derik could use CP on the fertilized eggs to determine if any would be implanted. So Coryn had the safeguard you are suggesting."

"Closest you'd let me come to a natural pregnancy," Derik remarked impishly. "Seriously, I've been doing it for centuries. Course I'm so nearly sterile there aren't that many fertilized eggs to check."

"I think the father in a natural pregnancy may also be influencing which chromosomes are lost and even which sperm fertilizes the ovum," Marna added, "though I'm less sure about that. And R'il'noid mothers could be playing a role as well."

"Actually, using CP on the blastocysts is not that uncommon," Jelarik commented.

"Jelarik, would you know which lab pregnancies were from scanned blastocysts?" Lai asked, his voice excited. "Because if you do, we might have a check. Nik alone has fostered—how many, now, Nik? Must be close to fifty kids who couldn't be socialized by their parents. Check if any of them were CP'd before implantation. And what fraction of the overall total were."

Jelarik was looking more positive now. "Of course," he exclaimed. "I'll see to it at once!" He could not rise without assistance, but he could and did still teleport.

It wasn't what she really wanted, which was more love in the process. But if it prevented the births of more like Zhaim, it was still worthwhile. She hoped she could convince Lai that it was not his parenting that had made Zhaim what he was.

Roi

2/14/36

Roi started to pull the interface circlet off his head, and then hesitated. Did this computer have a logoff sequence? If so, what was it? He tried the same sequence he used at school, and discovered that the computer was evidently programmed to drop its connection to the one at Tyndall on that sequence. The wall monitor continued to glow gently, but when Roi finished removing the circlet, it changed to an alien but beautiful landscape.

In some ways the room was rather like this half-term's room at Tyndall—a corner room, with a bed and a door to the hallway on one of the inside walls, and two doors on the other, with the monitor between them. He'd done and stored most of his homework during class, so he had some time free. Was he supposed to stay in the room, or could he explore? He had already determined that one of the doors concealed a personal care room—much more luxurious than the one at school—while the other opened into a smaller room. Bigger than Davy's room at Tyndall, he thought, and it had a window.

He felt a stirring, and looked wonderingly down at the feathered creature sleeping in his lap. Was it really to be his?

So many things he didn't know, and he had seen no one to ask since the two R'il'nians had looked in on him. The food that had arrived shortly afterward had been as much better than lunch at school as school food was than the slave chow he had been used to, even allowing for the fact that he didn't have to sit opposite Xazhar to eat it. But had he been moved here permanently? Would Davy be allowed to rejoin him?

Roi had enough of an empathic link with Davy to be sure his old friend was safe and well. But why was Roi himself here? He'd teleported from his chair to Davy's side when the man was stricken down; he remembered that clearly. And he remembered his terror and frustration when he'd realized that he could not keep Davy alive and Heal him at the same time, and the order to keep his mind firmly wrapped around Davy's during a teleport. He relived the wonder of the woman's mind—Marna's—against his own, showing him how to let some of the injuries go while she guided him in Healing the others. Someone who could show him how to *use* his gifts—and Healing was one ability he thought of as a gift, rather than a curse.

He looked out the window—no, a door, like the one at Nik's—at the mountains he'd missed at Tyndall. He could guide his float chair out the door and smell the forests that cloaked the lower slopes—but was he allowed to? He even thought, though he wasn't quite sure, that some of the clouds floating above the peaks were really more peaks, covered with snow. If this was really the Enclave it would be close to winter here, and while he hadn't actually seen mountains with snow on them, he'd seen lots of pictures.

He looked down again at the tineral in his lap, marveling at the intricate pattern on each feather—bronze along the shaft, shading out to a complex pattern of copper, green and gold. He tried to touch the folded wings, but his control of his arms was still only marginal, and his hand fell much more heavily than he had intended on the delicate creature. It awoke, startled, then looked up at him with adoring eyes and sang an inquiring trill as it butted its head against his hand. The other two, curled together on his bed, lifted their heads and fluttered to his shoulders, adding their voices to the song of the first. Their feathers were patterned also, but the colors were different—one in tones of green, and the other in a complex mixture of gold, tawny, beige and brown. He stroked the one in his lap in apology for his accidental roughness.

Marna's voice came in at the door. "I hope you like pets other than horses and cats, because it certainly looks as if those three tinerals have chosen you. How did the computer hookup work?"

Roi looked up to see Marna standing in the doorway. She was followed by Nik, with a box in his arms, and Davy, with his left arm firmly strapped to his body. "Fine, My Lady," he said shyly, and Marna snorted.

"I may be stuck with 'my lady' on formal occasions, but I don't have to like it. My name is Marna. Now, let me ask that question again. What worked well, what worked poorly, and what didn't work at all with that computer hookup? Because for the rest of the term, at least, you'll be living here and using that hookup to attend classes. Next term we'll see—but this is home for you, now. That doesn't mean your father and I will give you everything you want, but it does mean we will try to do what's best for you."

What she implied was mostly good, he decided, if he could believe it. He'd wished for a family like Coryn's. But the "best for you" worried him. He'd heard his father talking with Nik, back before he had believed Lai was really Lai, or even his father. And one of the things Lai had said several times was that Nik was to keep Roi away from other slaves. Would he ever be able to see his old friends?

Argument would not change someone's mind—rather, it tended to make their original opinion stronger. He'd learned that very early, as a slave. Logic might work, as it had changed Derik's mind about teaching Roi the patterned teleport—but he'd had both Nik and Coryn behind him on that one. He wanted to see his old friends, but he didn't have a good logical argument for his desire, and he decided it was better not to risk turning his father against the idea until he knew the R'il'nian well enough to craft a reason that might sway his father.

Better stick with the computer and the tinerals for right now. "It worked fine for the discussions and lectures," he said. "Only—well, it didn't work quite as well on the classes where we do something besides talk. Like fine arts, and a science class where we're going outdoors and studying a little stream near the school. And it's kind of lonely here. I'm really going to miss the pattern chess club." He was a little surprised at how much he was already missing the other students, even some of his own age.

"Coryn will be over to tutor you most afternoons about this time and staying for supper sometimes, but today I want to see exactly how you're handling the Kharfun paralysis. That disease killed everyone I knew and loved. I'm not letting it destroy you."

That knocked everything else out of his head for the moment. Nik had given up on him—he knew that, even if the physician had acted as if Roi only needed to try harder. Certainly the techniques Nik had shown him had helped, but those techniques had been focused on regenerating nerves he could still find. The ones he couldn't find were the problems. "Like you did with Davy yesterday?" he asked hopefully. He'd given up on riding or dancing or even walking again. But if Marna could really show him how to restore those nerves …

"I'm going to start with that, yes. How much do you know about conditional precognition?"

"Not much. Derik said to follow my hunches, that I couldn't get in as much trouble with that as a lot of other things, but he concentrated on what he thought I had to know right away. We only had a month."

"But you do know how to Heal broken bones?"

"Sort of. But that's one of the things I had to figure out for myself. Derik and Nik say they can't teach me how because they don't really know what I'm doing."

"Had to?"

"My early owners were pretty rough. But they expected me to perform, no matter how much it hurt. I learned to Heal my own injuries just so I could stay alive. Later on I found I could help my friends, too—but only if we were really close. I have to get inside their heads to Heal them."

"Trust," Marna said, "and acceptance of mental contact. That's why you could Heal Davy yesterday, when all I could do was guide you. And why I brought him along this afternoon. He still needs those breaks in his arm Healed, as well as a couple of cracked ribs. I want you to Heal those breaks, but I want you to learn the first steps toward reverse precognition in the process."

Roi swallowed. He had no problems with Healing Davy, if the man was willing, but he was less sure about using the Healing process as a learning tool. "Is that all right?" he asked.

Marna gave him a quick hug in response. "Bless you for asking, but yes, in this case the only question is whether Davy's willing."

"And I'm just anxious to get the broken bones back in order," Davy said. "I gather from what the Lady told me that you're going to need more massage and general physical therapy than ever."

"Davy, sit down, and the two of you link up. Roi, link with me on the other side of your mind—that's it. Nik, if you want to follow what I'm trying to teach him, link with me but stay out of Roi's consciousness. Good, that's it. Roi, show me what you'd normally do to Heal a fracture ..." A pause, while Marna's brows drew together. "Yes, that's what I suspected you were doing. You're using your own body as a model. That's why you were having so much trouble Healing Davy's brain. It's actually fine most of the time for bones, but this time I want you to Heal the bone as if it were nerve tissue. That means you go back a bit in time—twenty-four hours ought to be fine for this—and use the bone as it was then as a model. Follow what I'm trying to show you."

Go back in time? Even with Marna guiding him it seemed to take forever before Roi thought he understood what she was trying to show him, and it seemed to take three times the time and effort to do the actual Healing. She finally made him stop and eat, saying that he had done enough for one session.

"You're doing fine," she told him as he swallowed a cup of fruit juice. "Now, the next step is to go back that way in your own body. You'll have to go back a lot farther—to before you were sick. That means you'll have to allow for the fact that you've grown since then. Try to pick a time when you were moving, and very aware of your movements. This is one time I'll need to have full access to your thoughts and memories, so I'll be able to tell what you're doing and give you the guidance you need."

"Dancing?" he suggested. He even knew the dance he wanted, the first he had choreographed after Derik had bought the group. He understood now, as he had not understood at the time, just what Derik was doing that day he had first led the group outdoors. He tried to go back to that day in memory, and suddenly he was swept away, with the memory almost more real than Marna's presence.

Outdoors! They had all been house slaves and Roi, at least, had never seen the sky. If Derik had led them to an open area, like the fields around Tyndall, Roi suspected he would have hit the ground, made dizzy by the sheer space around him, as quickly as Timi had. But their first sight of the sky had been through tree branches bright with autumn color, dancing restlessly in the breeze that never reached the ground. Amber had taken two steps and stopped, her head tipped back, staring with hungry eyes at the sky. Flame, as usual, had turned to Roi, ready to accept his assessment of the situation. And Roi?

His mother had told him about the sky, but he had never expected it to be this far away. Around him and in between himself and the sky, though, were the dancing leaves. I can make a dance for us out of this, he thought, and somehow fear evaporated, lost in the intensity of creation.

They had never performed the dance as he'd visualized it, with the living trees as a backdrop. The leaves had fallen by the time they were ready, and by the time the season had repeated he had been unable to move and had no hope of ever dancing again. But some of the early practice sessions, when he'd been working out the moves in the forest …

"Yes," Marna said. "That's a good time to go back to. But what you need is not memory. You have to go back in time, as you did with Davy, and get the pattern of how the nerves controlled the muscles. Then bring that pattern back to the present and use it as a guide to force the nerves to regrow. The memory is only a help in finding the right time to go back to. I'll nudge you in the right direction, but you have to do the work yourself."

All right. He had to go back, as he had with Davy (though he still wasn't quite sure how he'd done that) and study the way his nerves and muscles had worked two years ago. First he tried to start with the memory, but Marna kept pushing him away from that. Look back in time. He hadn't been trained yet to look forward, but he knew his hunches were a weaker version of the same thing. Could he get a hunch backward?

Twice he had to break for food, but the possible reward—being able to walk and maybe even ride again—kept him trying. He finally fell into the right mindset from sheer exhaustion.

Hand and arm fluttering, like the leaves above his head, and suddenly he felt the way the muscles had to work, and the impulses firing along the nerves to make the muscles contract in exactly the right pattern. Feverishly he memorized the pattern, and brought it back to the present. His arms were longer now, and he had to stretch the pattern to make it fit. But he could feel the uninjured spinal cord, and force the nerve fibers to grow out from it, following the pattern from the past. Muscles—the ones he had working were easy enough, but those already had nerves. The ones he was after, the inactive ones, were almost impossible to find—little more than strings. At Marna's urging he connected the nerves anyway, and finally collapsed back into the float chair, exhausted.

Marna was holding a cup to his lips, and he gulped down the contents without even tasting them. Only after he had finished the cup did he try to move his hand as he had in the memory.

Nothing happened, at least nothing he had not been able to do before.

He looked up at Marna, feeling betrayed, to find her smiling at him. "It's all right, Roi," she said. "You've got the nerves back. But it's been a year and a half since you've used the muscles, and the only way to grow muscles is to use them."

Roi was beginning to see what Davy had meant when he said Roi would need more physical therapy than ever. Marna was digging through the box Nik had carried in, muttering to herself, and finally came up with a furry yellow ball, just the right size to fit Roi's hand. "Thought I'd stuck these in," she commented as she wrapped Roi's fingers around the object. "Squeeze it."

More modeling material? But instead of giving unevenly beneath his fingers, the ball gave off a discord that made Roi wince.

"You've been compensating," Marna told him, "using the muscles you can control to make up for those you can't. In order to exercise the atrophied muscles properly, you have to stop doing that. This ball will help, at least with the hand. If you use all the muscles equally, the sounds will be harmonious."

He looked doubtfully at the ball and tried again, this time concentrating on closing the fingers that had been limp before. The sound was still somewhat discordant, but considerably better than the first time. Marna nodded approvingly. "The important thing right now is feedback," she said. "The balls should work for your hands. We need to work out something similar for the other major muscle groups."

Nik picked up a blue ball, turning it in his hands. "Why not bring Kaia in on this?" he suggested. "She's a genius at electronics, and I can see lots of potential rehab uses for this technology."

"Technology?" Marna asked in surprise. "Why, I suppose it is—but I brought them from Riya as children's toys."

Toys. Like the modeling material Nik had given him. Roi tried squeezing the ball again, and this time succeeded in producing something that sounded a little like a chord. With practice, he might even be able to play a tune on the ball. Or stroke the tineral in his lap without fear of harming it. He tried squeezing with each finger in sequence, and managed a rather poor modulation of the chords. The tinerals joined in, a little hesitant.

"Decided on names for them yet?" Marna asked.

"Do I really get to choose names for them?" he asked. "Can they stay with me?"

"Yes. They're all what we used to call the Nature type, and it was traditional to name them after natural objects. Not that you have to. They're all young—only about a year old. They'll keep growing, and by the time they reach breeding age, they'll be too large to fly."

He visualized the two on his shoulder moving away so he could see them, and they fluttered back to the bed. He thought of an image he'd seen in class, of Central as seen from space. "Forest," he said, looking at the green tineral, "and Desert," shifting his eyes to the tawny one. "And you …" He looked down at the animal snuggled in his lap. Grassland? Prairie? "Meadow," he decided finally.

Coryn

2/14/36

"Come on, Cory. You're the only one who's been in Lai's home. What's it like?"

Coryn finished putting his report into the computer and turned to Ander. His friend had already been in bed when he had returned the night before. Mornings were always busy—there hadn't been time for much talk until now, when Ander had completed his own tutorial assignment. "All I saw was the room where they had Roi," he said. "Father's been telling me for years that Lai's just busy. The Lady Marna—well, she's not the ogress rumor claims. Took one look at Roi and decided he needed a mother, Father says. Mom could have told her that."

"What's your father think of that?"

"Happy, on the whole, I think. No question *I'm* happy. Roi as a cousin is rather fun. But if he's got his own family, I can have mine back. I think I'll be able to stay ahead of him for the rest of the term. Maybe another half-term in most subjects, but he's starting to ask questions I can't answer, and I'm just as glad I'll be gone by next term. Want to walk down to the visitors' lounge with me? Father's picking me up there, for another lesson in patterned teleporting." He shuddered melodramatically as he opened the door.

"You really think Roi would get ahead of you, with the late start he's got?" Ander finally spoke again.

Coryn's lips pulled back in a savage grin. "The one I *almost* feel sorry for is Xazhar," he said. "Roi's better than he is, even if he doesn't believe it. I don't think he'll challenge Xazhar in plasmaball—he thinks it's a stupid sport. But I saw him dance, Ander, before the Kharfun. If the Lady Marna manages to reverse that paralysis—and I think she's going to try—he's going to be good enough to challenge Xazhar even on a physical level, as well as being smarter. And Xazhar's not stupid. Up until now I'm the one he's had to contend with for top student, and since I'm two years older he can put it down to age difference. He won't be able to do that with Roi."

"Now if you could just convince Roi of that ..."

"Roi," Coryn sighed as he opened the door to the visitors' lounge, "is a born victim. Bright as they come, but he doesn't have a clue how to stand up for himself."

Derik, deep in conversation with Kim, turned as the two boys entered the room. "Not born, made. Oh, the high empathy's innate, and probably led to his reluctance to hurt anyone else—he feels any pain he inflicts. But slaves who try to stand up for themselves don't survive long. And he survived for close to fourteen years before I got him." Then, turning away from the boys, "Kim, if Nebol won't make the announcement, you're going to have to. I can't speak officially for the board before they've met, but as far as the rest of this term goes, you're really the only choice."

Coryn and Ander looked at each other and then at Derik and Kim, ears wide open. Would they learn more by trying to be invisible and hoping the two adults forgot they were there, or by asking questions?

"The students have to know," Kim said, seeming to reach some kind of decision. "Since you two walked in on this, you might as well know, but this is confidential until I tell you otherwise. Probably no more than a few hours before the word is out. Nebol has resigned, effective at midnight tonight. Someone has to keep the school going, and it looks like I'm the only one who knows enough of what's going on. Coryn, you're the top student of the oldest group. What do you think would be the most effective way of breaking it to the students?"

"Go through the year leaders," Coryn responded promptly. "They'll be flattered, and most of them have quite a lot of influence. Seventh year will be a problem—they don't have a clear leader. So will tenth—Xazhar's furious about Sheeran and Malar getting expelled. Call the leaders in individually, tell them what's going on, then have a mass computer announcement between final study and bedtime. That'll give time for the spread of controlled rumors." He stopped, suddenly aware that he was not planning to be at the school that evening. Should he cancel the meeting with Roi? He looked at his father in sudden indecision.

His father was ahead of him. "That's about what Kim and I thought. Ander, am I right in assuming you'd normally be the actual rumor spreader for twelfth year? Could you handle that? I'll let Kim suggest what he thinks would be most effective. And you might alert the rest of the year leaders that they need to see Kim before or immediately after supper. Leave Xazhar to last—I think his grandfather is going to have to talk to him. Cory, that's part of your job—if Lai's not there, tell Roi you need to tell him about the problem of how Xazhar is going to react to Nebol's resignation. I'll be busy rounding up the rest of the board for an emergency meeting before the official announcement. All right? Come on, Cory."

Roi was in his float chair, eyes half closed as he stroked a feathered creature in his lap. He lifted his head as his friend entered. "Coryn, look!" He managed to turn his right hand over in his lap, and carefully, one at a time, moved his fingers.

Coryn had watched Roi struggle for control of those fingers often enough to appreciate what he was seeing. "Roi, that's wonderful!"

Roi nodded happily. "I can't do much with them yet, and I've got an awful lot of nerves to hook up again. But I know how to do it now! Marna said she'd help me with that, and then it's just a matter of exercising the muscles. It's going to take time, but she said in a couple of years I should be able to do everything I used to do. Why didn't your father stay for a few minutes? I'd like to show him, too."

That reminded Cory of the haste with which Derik had teleported him here—less of a lesson than getting Coryn where he needed to be as fast as possible. "He's trying to get the Tyndall board together. Roi, I need to give your father a message from him."

Roi looked thoughtful. "I only really met him last night," he said, "but Marna said I should explore and get used to the place. She said this is my home now, like the farm is yours, and I need to learn my way around. We could go look." His eyes had a trace of the sparkle they hadn't shown since the day of the race, and Coryn grinned in response.

"Lead the way," he replied.

Roi's door opened onto the intersection of two hallways, one straight ahead and one running off to the right. "I think this is the way Father and Marna came this morning," Roi said as he turned his float chair to the right. The wall they moved along looked very ordinary, with the mother-of-pearl sheen typical of an idle projection system. On their left, plantings at first concealed their view, though when Coryn tried to touch the leaves he found an invisible barrier. They had moved half the length of the corridor when Roi stopped his chair where a path ran through the plantings.

"Door?" he wondered aloud, and turned toward the path. The transparency melted away, allowing a light breeze to caress their faces. They entered a weather-shielded atrium, surrounded by transparent walls, with Roi's father swimming around a very ordinary looking pool. The R'il'nian looked up as they approached, and waved them on to the pool. Split-braining, Coryn thought. He'd seen his father often enough with most of his brain engaged with the computer while a small fraction stayed with his body. Coryn would probably be able to do it himself someday, but that was one of the last R'il'nian abilities to develop in crossbreds.

"Join me?" Lai invited as they approached the spot where he now had his elbows hooked over the edge of the pool. "I need to get back in shape to keep up with Marna."

"Cory's father wanted him to tell you something," Roi said, leaving Cory to wonder if Lai had caught the flash of terror on Roi's face at the suggestion of swimming.

What Coryn said aloud was, "Father's trying to round up the rest of the Tyndall board. He said Nebol's resigned, and the only possible replacement for the rest of the term is Kim. *I* think that's great. But I don't think Xazhar will, after Malar and Sheeran got expelled. Father said you'd have to talk to him."

Lai levitated himself out of the pool, emerging perfectly dry—I'll have to learn that trick, Coryn thought—and waved the boys to a cluster of chairs alongside the pool. "Roi," he said, "would you mind sharing some of your memories of Xazhar? Derry said the two of you didn't get along very well."

Roi hesitated, then forced himself to lift his head and meet his father's gaze directly. Cory, watching, saw shock and unhappiness cross the R'il'nian's face. He's finding out some things he doesn't like, he thought. I hope Roi's including the time Xazhar tried to drown him, back when they were insisting he take physical education with his age group. Good thing the infirmary and Kim managed to put a stop to that. The instructor didn't see it, and Nebol never believed Roi's word against Xazhar's.

Lai sighed. "Roi, Coryn, when you learn to use CP properly, don't let that stop you from paying attention to your hunches. It's a mistake most of us make, and sooner or later it gets us killed. CP is good at answering questions, but it doesn't tell you what questions to ask. Hunches are sloppy, but sometimes they can tell you when you need to ask questions. I shouldn't have let Zhaim raise Xazhar, but at the time I was just so happy he seemed to be showing some responsibility …

"I'll certainly have a talk with Xazhar. If nothing else, it sounds like he needs to be straightened out on just who you are. Better go ahead and have supper, both of you. And Roi, ask Marna to teach you to get oxygen directly from the atmosphere to your lungs while you're swimming. It really would be good exercise for you." He touched Roi's shoulder, lightly, and vanished.

Both boys were hungry, and while Coryn would have loved to stay and see more of the courtyard, Roi was already heading back toward his room. Food first, Cory decided. He wondered how long it would take for Roi to be able to face swimming again.

Roi

4/15/36

It wasn't that Roi objected in principle to the idea of a birthday party. A small, family party like Coryn's would have been fun, a validation of the idea that he was indeed a person in his own right and not just a piece of property. Even a larger party involving most of the adults he had met over the last year would have been acceptable, given Coryn's repeated emphasis that sixteen was an "important" birthday, the occasion of his official change in status from child to adolescent. He wouldn't have another such birthday until he was thirty-two and became a young adult rather than an adolescent.

His father wasn't content with that. Lai wanted to use the occasion of Roi's sixteenth birthday to validate his son's High R'il'noid status, claiming that Jelarik's preliminary test of "over a hundred," combined with the fact that Jelarik's testing had not even covered Roi's Healing ability or fully explored his sensitivity, virtually guaranteed that Roi's true Çeren index would be well over the critical hundred and eight. That meant a "birthday party" that was practically a command performance for the entire Inner Council and the Genetics Board, and an open house for all of the other High R'il'noids who were on planet and interested in coming.

"Most of them won't show up," Coryn assured him. "They didn't for mine. Just the Inner Council and the Genetics Board, and they didn't stay long. Lots of neat presents, though. And they can always congratulate you on how well you're doing in school. Eighth year next term, when you started this term with no formal schooling at all."

"They'll show up for mine," Roi predicted gloomily. He had tried everything he could think of to get out of the huge birthday celebration, up to and including the tantrum he had not dared try on Derik. It hadn't worked on Lai, either. "Father insists on its being a big celebration, and he's leaning on people. And a lot of them own slaves. Some of them have owned me. I don't want to meet them socially. I particularly don't want to meet Zhaim socially."

"That, at least, I have managed to talk your father out of, at least as far as your birthday is concerned," Marna said as she entered the room. "Luckily there's a planet way out back of nowhere that needs some genetic engineering done. Zhaim apparently is good at that, so Lai sent him off to do it. And I'm keeping an eye on him while he's doing it. He won't be here tomorrow. Neither will the others who thought they owned you but who are not actually on the Genetics Board or the Inner Council. Lai's made it quite clear that they are not welcome, though he says he can't do that with the Inner Council. Been practicing the emotional shielding techniques I taught you?"

"Intensely," Roi replied.

"I know," Marna said. "It's not going to be easy. I'm gritting my teeth and coming, and that should take some of the pressure off you. Lai's convinced me I have to, sooner or later, and this way we can share the impact. I see they've finished your new clothes," she added as she nodded toward the clothing stand Roi was trying to ignore.

Roi glared at the tunic and trousers, white velvet embellished with gold, topazes and pearls. "I'll never get them on. I may have all the nerves hooked back up, but I still don't have any strength in my muscles."

"For this I'll drop the prohibition on Davy helping you or even using esper. I'm not sure I could get into that creation without help, or at least telekinesis. Just as well I'll be wearing the gown I brought from Riya, the one your father first saw me in. And you'll be able to use the float chair. I have to stand for two hours."

"Be glad it's only two hours," Coryn advised. "Mine was most of the day. You've only got to be on display for a couple of hours tomorrow morning, and then in the afternoon it'll just be friends dropping by. How are you doing physically? Hold your arms out."

"He'd do a lot better if he'd just spend some time in that pool," Marna said as Roi lifted both shaking arms in front of him. "Well, that can wait. Let's get through the birthday first."

Lai walked in, cocked his head at the formal clothing, and nodded. "Good," he commented. "I think that gives the impression we want."

"Impression," Roi said bitterly.

"Roi, haven't you understood yet why I'm doing this? I know you don't like it. Neither does Marna. Neither do I. But you are my son, and one I am very proud of, quite aside from the fact that you are all I have left of Cloudy. If we did not have this reception for you it would be taken as proof that either I did not care for you or you were not High R'il'noid. I've managed to keep it short, on the excuse that you are not yet fully recovered from Kharfun syndrome. But Roi, if there is one thing you must have learned in order to survive as long as you did in slavery, it is how to pretend. Use that knowledge. You don't have to *be* a young aristocrat if you don't want to, but you can act like one."

"Derik and Nik both kept telling me not to pretend." Not that he'd paid much attention to that.

"Not to people who are trying to help you," Marna said. "But I'm certainly going to be pretending tomorrow, and so can you. Be polite. Hauling off and hitting someone isn't going to help you. But there are ways of being quite devastatingly polite."

Lai looked amused. "As you were to Zhaim? Just remember, both of you, that not all of these people are bad. Roi, you don't have to be more than formally polite to former owners, or those who you know abuse slaves. Marna can give you some ideas of how to deal with them. But don't take it for granted they're all bad, either. Most of the older ones are people I think you'll enjoy knowing. You can adjust the hover height on that chair, can't you?"

"You mean with the controls? No."

"We'll have to fix that before the reception. There's no reason for you to deal with the psychological disadvantage of having people looming over you. Run the chair hover height up until your eyes are level with those of whomever you're talking to."

"And if you don't want to meet their eyes," Marna added, "look through them or over their heads, not down."

The way the other students had first treated him? With Marna's coaching, Roi thought, maybe this wouldn't be as bad as he'd expected.

*   *   *   *

Roi had explored Lai's suite and the surrounding grounds, and he was familiar with some of the other parts of the Enclave complex. The reception room was new to him. It was huge, with a high ceiling and polished floor, both of inlaid wood that glowed golden in the sunlight. It was high up, too—something he'd suspected from the way his ears popped as they moved along the corridors, and verified as soon as he was able to look out the windows. To the east, looking into the morning sun, was range after range of mountains, the highest well covered with snow. To the west, the mountains fell away until at the edge of sight he could see the ocean, and the ground under the windows was dusted with fresh snow.

Inside the room, trays loaded with beverages and finger foods eddied through the air, and Roi hastily lifted his float chair enough to assure that the trays wouldn't clip him on the head. Much better than having slaves doing the serving, he decided. Those trays were heavy!

The first five guests were just arriving, coming through a wide door set between two of the windows. Jump-gate, Roi decided. He could see a handsomely appointed anteroom through the door, but the windows on either side of the door showed nothing but mountains. The first group included two strangers and three he knew—Lunia, Jelarik in a float chair considerably larger than Roi's, and Kaia. They crossed the room to deposit the packages they carried on the table there, then greeted Roi with a formality he found somewhat daunting, at least until Kaia winked at him. Kaia and Jelarik stayed near him and introduced him to the Inner Council members and the Genetics Board. The other High R'il'noids—far more than Coryn had led him to expect—introduced themselves. Most were strangers. Lai and Marna drifted away, for which Roi was briefly grateful—Marna was attracting more attention than he was, and her absence reduced the crush around him.

He was frantically memorizing names and faces rather than watching who was next, so it was a total surprise when Kaia announced, "Inner Councilor Colo Kenarian." He swung his eyes sideways while lengthening his focus, so he was looking through the R'il'noid, head up and trying to remember everything Marna had told him. "I believe we have met before," he said icily, keeping his voice low and much steadier than he had thought possible.

"What? Nonsense." Roi was shielding, but he still picked up the R'il'noid's puzzlement. The slave owner must know Roi had once been a slave, but he was so sure that once a slave came into his hands, it never left alive …

"Five years ago," Roi said, even more softly, and suddenly he was aware of two figures moving in to flank him. Then Marna's mind touched his, questioning, and he felt the R'il'nian's anger as Roi shared his memories of the desperate effort to maneuver his own sale and of others, friends, he had seen die at their owner's hands.

"Out," Marna said, her hand resting reassuringly on Roi's shoulder. "Go now, quietly, or I'll throw you out."

Lai snagged a glass off of a passing tray, and held it to Roi's lips. "Drink," he ordered. "It's fruit juice and peacemint tea, with lots of honey. You need the sugar. Can you stand another half hour?"

He was shaking, Roi realized. Anxiously he looked around the room. *Roi,* his father said in his mind, *any other former owners here? Colo's on the Inner Council—I couldn't exclude him. But I told the others who'd owned you to stay away.*

No. Except Derry, of course. Isn't he coming? He hadn't seen Derik for close to a month, and he didn't understand why.

Marna's mind-touch was faintly amused. *He's been off planet, running an errand for me. He'll be by as soon as he can, probably this afternoon.*

Roi relaxed a little. Half an hour to go, Lai had said, and the whole thing was supposed to last two hours. Could an hour and a half be over already? Probably at least that, given the number of names and faces stored in his head. *I think I can handle another half hour,* he thought.

That half hour passed in a daze. He was aware of Marna moving away again, taking a large part of the curious crowd with her, and Lai's unobtrusive presence nearby, his black outfit, conspicuous in the jewel-toned assembly, a mirror of Roi's white one. As the crush lessened, Elyra came by for a second time, trailing a man with green eyes, chocolate skin, and rather startlingly yellow hair, "Roi, this is my half brother Loki. He's a dancer, too."

Loki Faranian? For the first time that day Roi felt like showing his respect, but all he could think of was to gulp, "I hope I can see you dance, some day."

Loki grinned. "Get that body of yours working again. Y'know, I had Kharfun myself once—not as bad a case as you've had, but tough enough so that I took up dancing as physical therapy. You're actually ahead of me there—Derry says you were good enough to improvise a dance to Fisan's music even before he got you. Get a bit more control of your body, and maybe I can work with you a little." Loki's grin flashed again.

"Even before he got you …" Yes, he'd said that, acknowledged Roi's harsh past without being blinded by it. To Loki, Roi thought, even having been a slave didn't count next to the promise of talent. He made a firm promise to himself to work harder on rebuilding his nerves and muscles.

Then the last of the guests were drifting away, leaving him alone except for a few people he knew. He looked around, confirming that only friends were near, and collapsed back into his chair.

"I'm sorry," Roi said, seeing his father's black out of the corner of his eye.

"Sorry? What for? I've been looking for an excuse to tell Colo Kenarian off for years, and I'm glad Marna did it. You handled the situation just fine."

"Excuse ?"

"Roi, what power I have is because I am perceived, by R'il'noids and Humans alike, as being impartial. If I start taking sides—and slavery is a very contentious issue right now in the Confederation—I'll lose a lot of the influence I need. If I come down on those who abuse slaves, it'll be seen as taking sides against the pro-slavery faction. But a father protecting his son—that everybody understands."

"I'll never think slavery's right."

"Good. We need more of that point of view, and with your background, nobody's going to put it down to politics. But work at seeing the complications. It's not a simple issue."

"Like Freedom Now, at school? They're anti-slavery, but they kidnap slaves and abandon them in places they've never been before. The ones that don't get caught and resold right away mostly starve—you can't live on this planet without skills. They'd be better than an owner like Colo Kenarian, but I'd have been pretty upset if they'd kidnapped me from Derik."

"Good—you're seeing some of the complications. But this event was not supposed to be about lessons in planetary sociology. I think it's time you had some food and took a look at your presents."

Roi looked over at the gift tables (and it was tables, now; several had been added) in disbelief. He wasn't quite used to the idea that nobody owned him; owning things himself still seemed strange. And this pile … "I don't even know what half of the stuff is," he exclaimed. "And how can I ever figure out who it's from? Or where to put it?"

"Oh, the Enclave staff'll inventory it and help you with appropriate thank-you's. We did separate out the gifts from people who really know you—thought we'd take those down to the courtyard along with some of the refreshments. You didn't get time to eat much. Ready to go? And get out of that elegant creation?" He grinned, obviously as eager to get out of formal wear as Roi was.

Two hours later Roi was alternating between examining presents and eating. His own favorite was an old and very beautiful pattern chess set from his father, the tiles superbly balanced and feeling almost alive in his mind. "It was Bera's once," Lai said. "I think she'd have wanted you to have it. It's the kind Healers liked, with natural tiles." Roi wasn't sure what to do about his gift from Vara and Marna, who had given him Flight. Whatever was he going to do with a horse? For that matter, where was there space for the herb garden that Davy and Nik had promised him when the weather allowed? He supposed Marna's injunction that she expected him to be riding the horse by his next birthday would be helped by Kaia's gift, a skintight suit made on the same principle as the balls from Marna's toy box—if he used all his muscles in balance to move, he could make music. If he tried to use the stronger muscles to compensate for the weak ones, the discords set his teeth on edge.

Lai had teleported in and out of the courtyard several times, and was looking pleased with himself. What about? Roi wondered. Then Davy walked around the edge of the pool toward them, an anxious expression on his face. "A hundred and forty-seven," Lai told him.

Davy's face split into a wide smile, and Roi looked back and forth between Davy and his father, puzzled. "A hundred and forty-seven what?" he finally inquired.

"Jibeth survivors," Marna replied. "Faculty members. That's the errand Derry's been running for me."

"I don't know how much you know about the GoodNews cluster," Lai said, "but they don't welcome outsiders. The information we got here was that the Jibeth school had been destroyed and everyone connected with it had been killed. Then Davy showed up and Nik started investigating. Turned out that with a few exceptions, which included all of our contacts in the school, most of the faculty and students survived, but were enslaved. The students were sold on a number of planets, and Nik managed to trace and rescue several hundred before I got back. They all said the surviving faculty had been enslaved as personal physicians by the leaders of the various factions that had combined against the school. Seems their blasphemy in using those of Bera's Healing techniques that they could was outweighed by their successes as far as the leaders' personal well-being was concerned."

"My home world needs people," Marna said, "and after I talked to Davy, I thought that perhaps we could reestablish the Jibeth school on Riya. Derik volunteered to go to the GoodNews cluster and rescue as many of the faculty as he could find. From the sound of it, he got most of those who were still alive."

"A hundred forty-seven," Davy repeated. "There weren't more than two hundred to begin with, and a lot of them were old. Some would have died of age, and with the stress of eight years of slavery ... How did he do it?"

"Not easily, was the impression I got," Lai said. "He'd hoped to be back for Roi's birthday celebration, but at the end he didn't dare teleport away from the transport until they'd made their first jump out of GoodNews space. I anchored for him to teleport back today. Anyway, they'll all be here in a couple of fivedays. Needing physical and mental healing, I suspect, as well as baths.

Derry had some rather harsh comments about the limited water supply on the transport."

"You mean he had to go without a bath for a whole day?" Roi grinned.

"More like a whole fiveday. The last cult he was negotiating with apparently considered cleanliness sinful. But the transport's not really equipped to handle that many people. They can manage oxygen, food and drinking water—just—but that's about it, and they weren't equipped with cold sleep drugs. I've sent another to meet them halfway, with medical staff as well as water. And don't you laugh at him when he shows up, Roi."

"I won't. But you should have seen him when he showed up in the middle of the night after I got your sigil. I don't think I'd ever seen him look so disheveled before."

"I have, when he's working hard."

Roi blinked in surprise. He had known Derik first as an owner and later as a surprisingly patient teacher, and aside from the R'il'noid's role in contacting his father, he had never really seen him working for the Confederation. He knew that at least half of his father's attention was always tied up in the computer, monitoring the interactions among the widely diverse planetary systems that made up the Confederation. Had Derik been doing the same, behind the foppish facade? Was Roi himself expected to do this? He flinched away from the thought, concentrating instead on the silky feel of the wooden box that held Bera's pattern chess set. Could he talk his father into a game? All in all, he decided, birthdays weren't that bad. But he was just as glad they came only once a year.

Amber

4/15/36

Amber was close to despair. She was the youngest of the four—no, three, now. It was still hard to believe that Snowy, who had in many ways been the most alive of their little group, was dead. The others … Flame, who had known Snowy the longest, still refused to believe in his death, though she must have seen how ill he was when Master Derik had forced them to leave. She really believes what Master Derik has been telling us, Amber thought. That Snowy is still alive, but needs special help. Not for a slave. She didn't know why their owner persisted in lying to them, but to her it was obvious. A sick slave might be allowed to die or be killed, but the end was the same.

Nobody bothered with a seriously ill slave, and she had seen enough to know that Snowy's illness had been serious.

She glanced around the time-out room and sighed in exasperation. She liked Timi, and she would back him up with her last breath, but he did not have and never would have Snowy's finesse. Their current plight was proof of that. Snowy had certainly provoked Brak in the past, but he had always done so when Brak's retaliation would be obvious to their owner. Defying the overseer when their owner wasn't even on planet was downright stupid. Amber didn't see how Timi had expected anything but what had happened, which was a beating for Timi and close to a day in the time-out room for all of them. And it was cold! It wasn't supposed to be anything worse than boring (which was a great improvement on how their previous owners had enforced discipline) but with Brak in charge it was often too hot or too cold, the lights were either too bright or off entirely, and there was no food or water.

Timi had taken over leadership of the group when it became apparent that Snowy wasn't returning. Amber had backed him—Flame refused to believe that Snowy was really gone, and Amber knew better than to think Timi would have followed her—she was still the baby of the group, in his eyes. But they were in the time-out room far too often these days. Derik had been patient so far, but Amber lived in fear that Timi would go too far and get them all sold. She wasn't sure she could face another owner like Kuril, or being separated from the other two. But if Timi continued to act as he had, she might not have any choice.

She glanced over at Timi. There was just enough light that she could see him, curled up with his arms holding his sides after the beating he'd provoked out of Brak. If Master Derik had been present to witness that beating, Brak would have been out of there. That had been what Snowy had been working toward. Timi just didn't have that much patience.

Amber jumped as the lights came up, and a grinning Brak appeared in the door. "You're all sold," he said, "and I won't have to put up with you any more. You've got half an hour to clean up."

Brak can't sell us, Amber thought as she gave her hair a quick brushing. Master Derik must be back. If I can get a chance to talk with him ... But there was a cold knot in her stomach as she tied her hair back and slid into a clean tunic. Timi was moving stiffly, obviously in pain. How could they dance for a new owner, if Timi was hurt? And without the dancing, they were just attractive flesh, to be used up at their new owner's pleasure. Would they even have a chance to see Master Derik?

The habit of obedience and fear of Brak kept them together as they walked to the underground parking area. And Derik was there, damp-haired, grinning, and looking thoroughly pleased with himself. Not at all the attitude she'd expect if he'd just ridded himself of them, and he waved them into the jump-van and then climbed into the pilot's seat himself. Taking them to their new owner? Or might Brak have been lying?

She pressed her forehead against the right side window, now transparent. The ceiling opened and the slab under the van lifted out into the afternoon sunshine. The vehicle took off, and then turned to follow the coast northward. She looked back as long as she could, watching Derik's estate shrink and disappear. She had spent more than two years there, with the sky over her head and the wind in her hair. It had been easily the best two years of her life since the almost forgotten day of the slavers' raid on her home city. Now … She gulped a bit as her last view of the estate was cut off by the window frame.

"Problem, Amber?" Derik asked, surprising her by the use of her real name. Usually he called her Sunrise.

"Brak said you'd sold us," she replied, trying to keep the tremor out of her voice.

He grinned broadly. "Not exactly. I am giving the three of you to my nephew. I'll still be keeping track of you. Amber, Timi, Flame, wait until you meet your new owner before you start getting upset."

Nephew? And he knew all of their names? "I knew you had a son," Timi said dubiously.

"Right. Cory and Roi have gotten to be good friends, though Roi's closer to your age. Jump coming up." The windows turned milky, blocking vision.

I'd like to see what goes on during a jump, Amber thought. As usual, she saw only that they were in a different place when the windows cleared. Still flying up the coast, but now they were over a wide bay, sheltered by a row of islands, and turning toward the land. The beach was broad and the land sloped up from the water, rather than being edged by cliffs. Higher still were mountains, more rugged than Amber had seen near Derik's, with the most distant showing white against the blue horizon. Snow, she remembered vaguely. If only this new owner would let her go outdoors sometimes!

"That's the core of the Enclave," Derik said as he piloted the jump-van down toward what looked like a stone outcropping. Buildings were all around, she saw as they descended—not a single monolithic structure, but separate, apparently unconnected buildings nestled into the landscape as if they had grown there. They touched down on the stone slab, which immediately began sinking until they were in another underground storage area. Derik waved them out of the jump-van and herded them into a lift-shaft and then along a corridor. He paused at the second door, which faced a window looking out over the bay.

Davy opened the door. Not the tense, worried man that Amber remembered from Kuril's, but a relaxed, confident Davy with a broad grin on his face. "Thank you, milord," he said as soon as he recognized Derik.

"Thank Marna," the R'il'noid replied. "She's the one who thought it up. How'd Roi manage the day?"

"Better than I'd thought he would. I didn't see it, but I gather Colo Kenarian showed up. Roi recognized him; he did not recognize Roi, and Marna just about threw Colo out. I don't think Lai made any objections to that, either. Right now Roi's tired, but almost as happy about the Jibeth situation as I am. Go on in."

Lai and Marna. The R'il'nian, and the survivor he had brought back from a distant planet, also settled by the R'il'nai. And this was the Enclave, the hereditary home of the R'il'nai? With Davy here? What was going on?

Then Derik herded them through a garden entrance into a hallway, and down the hallway to an enclosed courtyard with even more extensive if less formal plantings and a swimming pool with three people sitting beside it. Two were facing them, and their resemblance to the tridees she had seen was obvious. Their informal dress surprised her—both wore shorts and loosely fitting tunics. The third figure was in an invalid chair with his back to them, and turned at their entrance. White hair cut to a short cap, the same deep bronze skin as Lai, and as he turned she saw the eyes, golden as honey. Snowy? But Snowy was dead, wasn't he? His expression at first was simple pleasure at seeing Derik; then he saw the three of them and his face mirrored the shock that Amber felt on her own face. Derik was saying something about a birthday present, and the boy's face was modulating from astonishment to a blazing joy that totally erased her doubts.

"Snowy," she whispered in disbelief, and was passed by Flame, screaming Snowy's name and almost knocking him out of the float chair. Amber followed more slowly, trying to assess Snowy's condition as she came. Taller than he had been a year and a half ago, she thought, but thin, and when he threw his arms around her they felt pitifully weak. "Snowy," she said again, hugging him back. "What happened? We thought you were dead."

"Derik said you weren't," Timi said from beside her, and Snowy reached out toward him with one arm, keeping the other around the two girls. He can barely lift his arm, Amber thought as Timi grabbed the outstretched hand with both of his own. "Only we didn't exactly believe him," Timi continued.

"He kept telling me you three were all right, but he wouldn't let me see you," Snowy gulped. "I don't blame you for not believing him; it took me nine months to take in what they were telling me. Sometimes I still have trouble with it. Derik, can they really stay with me?"

Derik had said he was giving them to his nephew, Roi. "You're Roi, then?" she asked. "Derik's nephew?"

Lai spoke. "He is Roi, he is my son—which makes him Derik's nephew—and Derik transferred all three of you to Roi effective as of his sixteenth birthday, which is today. That was in case he didn't get back from GoodNews in time. Roi, remember what we were talking about earlier today. But for right now, why don't you show your friends around and explain things, since I gather Derik didn't?"

"They want to talk about me behind my back," Roi commented after they had followed a path between flowering shrubs to another corridor. "Derik and his surprises! My room's here." He led them into a room easily twice the size of the one the group had occupied at Derik's, but crowded with furniture. Bed, chairs, a desk of sorts, what looked like exercise equipment, and three four-legged animals with wings flying around the room, singing. "Tinerals," Roi said. In the wall opposite the door was a transparent area, with mountains beyond. Amber moved to it, mesmerized by the scenery.

"I've always been able to do some odd things," Roi was saying, "but my mother told me to hide those abilities—that I'd be killed if anyone found out. She never told me anything about my father, but when I got sick, it was a disease that's minor for Humans but deadly for R'il'nians and some R'il'noids. When I got over it enough to notice anything, I couldn't move at all, and they said Lai was my father. I didn't believe a word of it. And they wouldn't let Derik see me at all. Then they sent me to a school, after I learned to fake moving again."

Amber listened, still looking out the door, as Roi told them of the frustrations and triumphs of his last year and a half. School. She remembered school, from the dim and wonderful time before slavery. They'd had a lot of opportunities to learn for the last six months, she realized. They'd had to hide their activities from Brak, but she'd wondered a time or two at how oblivious Derik had seemed to their interest in the computer. Could he actually have wanted them to do as they had?

"What are you going to do with us?" Timi asked bluntly when Roi was finished, and Amber heard the edge of defiance in his voice.

"You'd rather be sold to someone like Kuril, or even worse?" Amber snapped at him. "Sno—uh, Roi, don't mind him, he didn't mean it the way it sounds. We're all still pretty shook up."

"He meant it," Roi replied, "and it's a perfectly reasonable question. Unfortunately I don't know the answer. This is a total surprise to me, and I'm not sure yet what I *can* do. I'm not even sure what the difference is between my being an adolescent instead of a child. There has to be some way you can wind up free. Davy's on what's called conditional manumission, for instance—he helps me through school, and in return he goes free in a couple of years. But slave law is one subject I've carefully avoided learning anything about. Too depressing. I'm not going to free you to starve, though, or to be kidnapped and sold back into slavery. That's what they think happened to my mother. Timi, are you all right? You're moving like something hurts."

"Brak," Flame said. "He beat Timi up and threw us all in the time-out cell."

"Maybe I ought to try just telling Derik what he's like instead of hinting."

"Roi," Amber said, "a slave has to work by hints. But if I understand things right, you're not a slave any longer. Try asserting yourself. They may get mad, but they can't sell you."

Roi looked startled, then thoughtful. "Old habits," he said. "But sometimes I need to have that pointed out. I will tell him. Though right now I'm just feeling grateful to see you all again. Timi, want me to check you out? Turns out Healing is one of my esper talents."

"Esper?" Timi snapped, his voice hostile. "Have you turned into one of those damned mind rapists, like Kuril? Or your uncle?"

"Derik's not," Roi replied, obviously trying to control his temper. "If he'd read your minds, or Brak's, he'd know what that louse was up to. And I'm exactly what I always was. What Derik and Marna have taught me is two things. First is control. You think I like having people scream their thoughts and emotions into my head? Especially the kind of thoughts and emotions I was getting as a slave? I learned to turn it off, but it was a panic reaction, and then I couldn't get anything, even when they were trying to explain how to make my body work again. That's why I'm still more than half paralyzed.

"The other thing they're teaching me is ethics. Like never go into another sentient mind uninvited. Marna says there are exceptions, but they all have to do with saving lives. Right now I'm not even supposed to judge that—just contact her. And I'm not going to risk getting her mad at me, even if I wanted to read anybody's mind. Which I don't."

"Kuril did."

"Kuril's unethical. Not just my opinion; every decent esper I've met feels that way. There's ethical people and unethical people and every shade in between, and it doesn't have much to do with esper abilities. I'm not going to force my way into your mind, Timi, or any of the rest of you. I just wanted to let you know that if you're hurting I can probably do something about it."

Amber looked down, remembering the time she had taken a bad fall during a dance. She had been sure her leg was broken. She could still recall the panic that had overcome her as she wondered whether she would be raped to death or simply sold for spare parts, now that she was useless as a dancer. Snowy had been beside her almost at once, she remembered now, his hands cradling the leg. "Be careful," he had warned when he released the leg, and he had been staggering worse than she was as Timi helped her to her feet. Now she could only look at him, remembering. "My leg *was* broken," she said. "You healed it, didn't you."

He nodded. "I couldn't have asked you. Kuril could read anything you knew, and I thought I'd be killed out of hand if anyone knew I could do stuff like that. And you trusted me enough I could do it. I probably couldn't have if you'd *known* the leg was broken, but I got to you fast enough you didn't have time to realize."

"You've healed all of us at one time or another, haven't you," Flame asked, and hugged him when he nodded.

Timi looked at the two girls, both now obviously on Roi's side, and gave in. "I'll accept that you did your best when we were all slaves together," he said. "But I do not want you in my mind. For healing or anything else."

"Could we go outdoors?" Amber asked, feeling a distraction was in order. Timi had clearly gone as far as he would go, and she wanted to break this confrontation before things got worse again.

"Just open the door," Roi grinned. "Why don't we start the tour by walking around the outside of the building? No tinerals, though—Meadow, Desert, Forest, get back on the bed."

Roi

4/16/36

Roi sighed and snuggled deeper into a familiar pair of arms. Other bodies shifted to accommodate him, and he jerked his eyes open in response to a quickly suppressed yelp. Timi on one side, Amber on the other ... "Flame?" he asked anxiously, realizing he was in his room at the Enclave, where Davy had insisted that for that night, at least, Roi sleep in his bed while the other three slept on the inflated mats he had arranged on the floor.

"Just bruises," Flame assured him as she picked herself up off the floor. The window was becoming transparent in response to the movement in the room and the light outside, and the rising sun waked them all. "I don't suppose you can heal bruises."

"Sure, if you want. Like to see what I'm doing?"

Timi looked wary and Amber curious as Roi stretched out his hand to Flame. He had to go through her mind to reach the bruised hip, so it was easy enough to set up a link that allowed her to share his perceptions. The injury was fresh, so his first concern was to repair the oozing capillaries and remove the leaked blood. Then search out the inflammatory chemicals—not much, this soon after the blow. He'd have to remember that bruising was easier to Heal if he could get to the bruise immediately. When he released her hand and mind, Flame looked at him in open astonishment.

"I don't think you read my mind at all. I know the feel of that. But I think if there was any mind reading it went the other way."

Privately, Roi didn't know if he could read her mind without any awareness on her part or not, but he had no desire to try. "I don't need to read your mind to Heal," he said. "Just the body memory, so I know how things were before the injury. Oh, those headaches you get? I can stop those the same way."

"I'm not sure we're supposed to be up here," Timi commented as he and Amber slid off the bed. "But you were upset about something. We tried to hold you to stop it, and I guess we all dropped off to sleep holding you."

"Nightmare," Roi responded. He didn't even remember now what it was about, but he must have been broadcasting empathically in his sleep. He made a mental note to ask Marna if there was a way he could block against doing that. But it had felt *so* good to have the others close against him in sleep.

He lifted his head and looked around for his float chair. Marna, like Nik, insisted that he not use esper to augment his weak muscles, and he had gotten in the habit of leaving the chair where he could grab it from the bed—but he hadn't locked it in place last night, and it was now floating against the wall. Amber saw the direction of his gaze and started over to the chair, but Davy opened his door and saw her. "No," he said. "He needs to get his body working again, and he can get that far. Let him do it."

Roi gave Davy a hurt look, knowing already that argument would do no good—Davy was probably following orders from Marna. When Marna made up her mind about something, even his father thought twice about challenging her, and on something like this, he would be more likely to agree with her. So, he had to get to the chair on his own, without using his esper abilities. Neither his balance nor the strength of his legs was up to the distance, so he'd have to lower himself off of the bed—hopefully without landing as hard as Flame had—and crawl.

It was humiliating, especially in front of his friends, but arguing would only delay the inevitable. He worked his legs off the side of the bed and let himself slide down, controlling his fall by clinging to the top and then the side until he was half sitting on the floor and leaning against the bed. Then he lowered himself the rest of the way and began dragging himself across the floor to the support chair. To his surprise, the other three took up positions to his sides and behind him, forming a kind of honor guard as they matched his slow progress across the floor. He could control the hover height, now, and he brought the chair as low as he could before locking it in place and dragging his reluctant body into it. When he raised it to its normal height, his old friends hugged and cheered him.

He'd made new friends, but he doubted that any of them would have thought of such a show of support. Even Timi, who had been acting more like a rival last night, now seemed solidly behind Roi.

"Thought you could do it," Davy said with a grin. "Marna said to tell you that your father's away for a few days, but she's expecting the four of you to join her in the courtyard for breakfast in half an hour."

Breakfast was an uneasy meal. Roi wasn't quite sure of his own feelings toward Marna. He adored her, and treasured what she could teach him about the use of his abilities. But was his growing love for her a betrayal of his love for his dimly remembered mother? Was he in some way competing with the father he was beginning to love, and whose love for him he was beginning to recognize, for Marna's love? "Loving someone," Marna had told him, "isn't a matter of possessing that person. You can love lots of people at once, and accept that you are not the only person they love." But he was half Human, and he suspected that Human and R'il'nian views on love might differ. Mostly he avoided thinking about it.

For his friends, Marna was a frightening unknown, as powerful and threatening as any new owner. It would take them a while to feel secure enough to ask questions, so Roi tried to guess what they wanted to know, and asked the questions himself.

"Of course you can all use the swimming pool," she replied to Roi's question as to whether his friends could swim. "Including you. I can't think of a better exercise for you right now. Much better than crawling across the floor. Have fun—you're on vacation. I have work to do."

Roi found himself wondering if Davy's conversation with Marna—and he must have had one, to tell them she was expecting them for breakfast—had been before or after Davy had insisted that he get to his float chair without help.

Roi had used swimming to condition his body for dancing ever since he could remember, and he agreed with Marna intellectually. The swimming pool simply was not dangerous, especially since Marna had taught him to exchange the stale air in his lungs with fresh air from outside. Nor would anyone try to drown him here.

Emotionally …

He still could not look at the pool without remembering Xazhar's attack. Not just hands holding him down, but crude telekinesis as well. Another minute, and he suspected he would have tried a panic teleport, suppresser field or not, and from what he had learned since, he almost certainly would not have survived such an attempt. Only the fact that Xazhar had posted lookouts, and those lookouts had warned of the instructor's return, had released Roi while he was still rational enough not to risk revealing himself. He'd been close enough to drowning that the instructor had excused him from the class for the rest of the half term—to his considerable relief—but nobody but Coryn had ever taken his version of what had happened seriously. At least not until he had shared his memories with his father.

Now he lay on the massage table that Davy had moved to the courtyard and watched the others swim to the music of the tinerals. The two girls were racing each other back and forth along the pool, while Timi, still stiff, swam lazy circles. Davy finished his massage and swung Roi down to the exercise mat at the edge of the pool. "Get your floor exercises done," he said, "while I see if the Lady Marna needs my help. She's making a new home for the Jibeth school; the least I can do is see if she needs any help in working with my friends."

The arm exercises weren't too difficult, now, nor was lifting his head. Getting his shoulders clear of the mat took all his strength, and he could manage it only for a fraction of a second. Lifting his legs, even one at a time, was just about impossible, and while he could roll onto his side, he couldn't seem to brace himself there.

"Wouldn't it be easier to do those in the pool?" Flame asked.

"They're not supposed to be easy," Roi temporized.

Amber wrinkled her hose thoughtfully. "Underwater can be as easy or hard as you make it. And the Lady Marna said swimming would be good for you."

"Come on," Timi urged. "She did say you were on vacation. You can paddle around, even if you can't swim like you used to. You aren't afraid of her, are you?"

Afraid of Marna? Not in this context! But such a fear would at least make some kind of rational sense. His real reason—the totally irrational fear stemming from Xazhar's attack—would be interpreted by Timi as rank cowardice. And sooner or later, if he kept out of the pool, Timi would find out why. Before he could change his mind, he took a deep breath and rolled into the pool.

His first reaction on hitting the water was close to panic. But the girls caught him almost at once, easing him into the water so smoothly that his head never went completely under. "Hang on to the side and do your leg exercises," Amber suggested. He obeyed, clinging to the side and realizing that Marna's exercises had indeed restored his hand function enough that he had no problem gripping the edge. And the water gave him far more range of motion for his legs than he could manage fighting gravity. He began to relax as he experimented, finding that the water supported him as smoothly and forgivingly as ever. He could even release his death grip on the edge of the pool, first one hand at a time, and then moving along the edge of the pool in an awkward side stroke.

His friends moved with him, and after a while he rolled to his other side so he could see their faces. Flame and Amber were beside him, forming a living wall with their bodies, while Timi was a stroke or two ahead of Roi. He struggled on, aware that he was tiring, and noticed that Amber was missing. He lifted his head to look for her, and suddenly realized that he was in the middle of the pool. His feet began to drop, and he clawed at the water, close to panic.

"I'm right here," Amber said from behind him, and her arms and Flame's reached out to steady him. "Rest a little and catch your breath."

"Put your hands on my shoulders if you're tired," Timi said from in front of him, and there was no trace of last night's rivalry in his empathic broadcast, much less the active hostility Roi had sensed from Xazhar. They'd be rivals again, and increasingly, but under pressure these friends would come together. He could trust them. He wished Timi would trust him.

He stretched out again on the water, rolling back to his other side to ease aching muscles, and stroked grimly toward the poolside, suddenly aware of just how tired he was. Luckily it wasn't far—he must have come most of the way across the pool without even realizing that he had left the comfort of the poolside.

Marna, followed by Derik and Davy, came back into the courtyard just as Roi finally grabbed the edge of the pool. "It's about time," Marna commented as she approached. "I've been ready to throw him in."

Derik grinned and went down on one knee at poolside. "Here," he said, "give me your hands. Up we go—hey, your lips are blue. Davy?"

Davy had already grabbed a towel, and wrapped it around Roi as the two girls exited the pool. Timi tried to follow them, but missed and slid back into the water with a grimace.

Derik rose and cast a practiced eye around the pool. "Built for levitation," he commented. "Better put in a ladder if the kids are going to be swimming here. Meanwhile, Timi, grab my hands." He hoisted the young slave to the edge of the pool, eliciting a yelp of pain as Timi's weight came onto his lifted arms.

"Timi," Roi said, "if you won't let me check that, then the Enclave medical staff had better take a look at it. Brak beat him up," he added in explanation to Derik. "Day before yesterday, I think." He looked questioningly at Amber, who nodded in confirmation.

"Brak?" Derik said. "I don't know what you've got against him, Roi, aside from the fact that he's an overseer. And you get along all right with Davy."

Roi looked at Derik, inviting mental contact, and for the first time deliberately opened his memories of the time Derik had owned him. The shock on the R'il'noid's face caught Marna's attention. "Roi!" she said sharply.

"Need to know," Derik said at once. "The only thing he did wrong was wait this long. I'd—forgotten how hard it is for him to complain about anything. And I thought I'd picked up the worst of it on that contact after the poltergeist reaction. I didn't."

Part of his reason for dumping his memories on Derik had been sheer annoyance, Roi thought, and he knew Marna would have more to say about that. But he really should have tried harder to make the R'il'noid understand just how nasty Brak could be. Meanwhile … "Timi," he said, "can you at least tell me exactly what hurts, and what sets it off?"

"Left side. Bending to either side hurts. So does reaching over my head. I've been hurt worse."

"How about breathing deeply? Coughing? Laughing?" Marna broke in.

Timi backed up a step. "Look, I'm fine. So I'll be sore for a day or two. It's happened before."

"Don't back into the pool, Timi," Roi warned. "But with the Lady Marna taking an interest, you've got three choices. Let her Heal it, let me Heal it with her looking over my shoulder, or let the Enclave medical staff deal with it. Doing nothing is not an option. Believe me, I know." He snuggled into the towel and sipped at the hot chocolate Davy had brought him.

Timi swallowed visibly, and Roi didn't need to read his mind to know what he was thinking. "The Enclave medical staff is all right," Roi said. "Not like the slave medics we used to have to deal with."

"They're good," Derik stated. "Roi's better. He Healed a couple of headaches for me, and a broken collarbone for Nik, with no training at all. With the Lady Marna coaching him, I expect he's even better now."

Quit pushing him! Roi sent to both Derik and Marna. His face was hot with embarrassment, but his mental message could not stop more endorsements from both Davy and Flame. He dropped his head, and managed to get his hands up to hide his face. "I'm sorry, Timi," he said. "I'll help if you want me to. But we really do have to make sure Brak didn't hurt you badly. I don't like your still being sore today."

"You really healed Derik?" Timi asked doubtfully.

"Yes. Though the first time I gave him the headache too."

Timi looked over at Amber. "What do you think?"

The girl shrugged. "Up to you. I'd trust Roi, myself."

Timi gritted his teeth. "All right. But I'd just as soon not know what you're doing inside me."

Just as well, Roi thought within seconds of contacting Timi. He'd expected broken ribs, but he had not expected to find a jagged end within a hair's breadth of puncturing a lung. *Marna?* he called, and outlined what he thought he could do. Accelerate Healing, then put a kind of smooth mental wrap around the splintered ends of the worst fragment so it wouldn't do more damage moving. Finally ease it back into place, and then start knitting the bones and surrounding soft tissues together.

Marna changed the order—steady and pad the bone fragment, tell Timi to lie down on the exercise mat, realign the bones, and only then start accelerated healing just before he began tack-healing—but basically let him do the Healing. Roi didn't hear her say anything to Davy, but the man was holding a cup to his lips when he collapsed back into the float chair.

"You all right?" Flame asked anxiously. "You didn't look nearly that tired after you fixed my bruises."

"Fresh bruises aren't much harder than headaches," Roi mumbled. "Bones are harder. Bones that were broken two days ago and the pieces shifted around and messed up the area around them are miserable. Timi, stay flat on that mat for another half hour, and take it easy for at least four days. Even with accelerated Healing it's going to be that long until your ribs are anywhere close to normal strength. I've got things lined up and kind of tacked in place, but your own body has to do most of the real healing."

"Broken bones?" Derik inquired sharply. "Brak beat him that badly?"

"The only reason he didn't break a few of my bones was that I'd learned by the time you got us that it's a lot easier to keep bones from being broken than it is to Heal them. Dammit, Derik, I've been trying to tell you he's no good."

"And I keep forgetting how you understate things." Derik was quiet for a moment. He finally shook himself and looked over at Roi. "I need to do some thinking. But Brak's out. Today. If you'll excuse me, my Lady?" When she nodded, he simply teleported himself away.

Amber gulped. "Is that one of the things you can do?"

"Teleport myself? Yes, but I'm not supposed to without permission and somebody checking that I'm doing it right."

"Come up with some legitimate destinations, and your father or I will pattern some for you," Marna said as she stood. "You know how to use the computer and the food delivery system from here, don't you? Get your friends signed on and have lunch out here after Timi's had enough rest. And Timi, Roi did know what he was doing when he told you to take it easy. If he doesn't sit on you if needed, I will." She left the courtyard more conventionally than Derik, but with no less authority.

"'Doing nothing is not an option,' you said," Timi commented. "I see what you meant. Does that mean I shouldn't do things that hurt? Like raising my arms? Going to make it kind of hard to keep my hair combed." He looked pointedly at Roi's short cap of hair.

Roi looked back, suppressing a grin. Timi's hair was almost as long as his had once been, but it grew in loose ringlets that tangled far worse than Roi's hair ever had. "Far as I'm concerned, you can do as you please with it," he said. "Forget about staying pretty and salable. Just remember if you whack it off you're stuck with the results—I can't put it back, and I know I felt bereft at first when I found they'd cut mine while I was sick. Davy, can you help him, whatever he decides? He really shouldn't be raising his arms for a few days."

Timi's eyes widened, and a grin spread across his face. "You were born a slave," he said. "I grew up on a spaceship. Can you imagine this mess in free fall? Cut it off, Davy. I can't wait to get rid of it. How long before I can swim again, Roi?"

Derik

4/16/36

How did Humans ever get anything done? Derik wondered. He was tied into the computer, combining his own knowledge of the personalities and prejudices of the rescued Jibeth faculty and students and the members of the Inner Council, Marna's information on Riya, and the computer's information on the locations, crews and operations of Confederation ships and the various legal hurdles to be overcome in establishing the Jibeth school on Riya. From this information he was working out the best next moves toward reestablishing Jibeth, and then using his conditional precognition to evaluate the possible alternatives. He'd handled far more difficult and less congenial problems in the past. But how Humans managed without the ability to split their attention completely left him wondering.

His own mind was split between the part working on the Jibeth problem and his personal life. Not that Jibeth was really a problem—more a matter of optimizing opportunity. But concentrating on Jibeth and Riya while trying to deal with his personal life would have been impossible without his ability to split-brain.

"Why do you need an overseer?" Marna had asked him mentally. "Why do you even own slaves?"

Things had seemed so simple two years ago. He owned slaves because it was expected of a person of his social status on Central, and because he was lonely without them. He had an overseer because he never knew when he'd have to be away, sometimes for long periods, on Confederation business. High sex drives were not uncommon among R'il'noids, who often inherited hormones from one side of their heritage and receptors from the other. Neither was low fertility. An emotional need for long-term relationships was rarer, and he had all three. Most R'il'noid women were socialized to maximize their production of children, which meant that few were willing to spend time with a partner known to be almost sterile—much less the amount of time he wanted.

He'd tried for his first couple of centuries to deny the part of him that wanted a lasting relationship—and he was still trying to live down the reputation that had earned him. Later he had tried gentler relationships with Human slaves—but Humans grew old and died. His life cycled among looking for someone he could relate to, decades of happiness with his beloved, and bleak depression as he tried to adjust to the inevitable death of his lover. Male or female mattered far less than the person within, and he had begun to think he had found his next partner in Roi.

Then had come the discovery that Roi was not Human, but as R'il'noid as he was himself. That had been a shock, but no greater shock than the futility of Lai's search for Roi's mother. Derik had sold slaves at times—usually in response to badgering by the buyer, and only to what he thought would be good homes. When he saw Lai's problems in searching for Cloudy, he tried to check on several slaves he had sold over the last decade.

Tried.

After that he had not sold any more slaves.

But Roi had accepted, even encouraged Derik's interest. Lai understandably didn't want the boy harassed, or even reminded of his years as a slave. That didn't mean he wouldn't let Roi make his own decisions when he was older, and there was even a chance—a very good chance, Derik thought now—that Roi would not age and die in such a pitifully short time.

That hope had vanished with Derik's first, accidental linkage with Roi, when he'd realized that Roi's encouragement of his advances had been based solely on the boy's determination to survive and keep his friends alive. And how many of his previous loves had felt the same way? He had always felt that not invading the minds of non-espers, except when needed for his own safety or the safety of the Confederation, was a moral absolute. CP, which was far less invasive, was adequate to warn him when actual telepathy was needed. But how often had his refusal to read the minds of others produced harm to the very individuals he was trying to spare?

He knew that Roi, as a potential Healer, was being taught a slightly different moral code. Perhaps he should talk to Marna about her views on the morality of mind-touch.

The final blow had been Roi's memories, far more complete than the earlier accidental mind linkage, of what it had really been like to be Derik's slave. He'd always thought of himself as a considerate owner, accepted and even beloved by his slaves. Roi had hinted that things weren't that simple, but the boy had been unable to come out and tell him that while he might have meant well, the actual situation from a slave's point of view was something quite different.

As if on cue, the computer reported that someone without authorization was trying to contact it from the slave quarters. Brak? Derik had pulled Brak's computer permissions when he'd fired the man. He was still angry at his ex-overseer's response to being fired—no remorse, no apologies, just a scornful "I'll get a job I like better a lot easier than you'll be able to replace me." Derik activated the visual pickup and looked at the face on his screen. Chip, he identified the youthful countenance. He had bought Chip as a boy soprano—when? Ten, twelve years ago? He'd kept him when the young soprano's voice had broken, hoping that the adult tones would still allow the boy to sing. By the time he realized that wasn't going to happen, he'd quit selling slaves.

"What is it, Chip?" he asked, trying to access Roi's memories of Chip. Well liked among the other slaves, intelligent, and at least from Roi's point of view, he'd been doing a lot of what should have been Brak's jobs. Interesting.

"Sir, Brak's not here, and it's several hours past suppertime." Chip looked and sounded apprehensive.

"I fired Brak," Derik said, and heard gasps from the other slaves, out of the line of sight of the visual pickup. "Can you distribute the food tonight? Then come up here—don't bother to eat first yourself. I want to talk with you."

Derik was still coding dinner into the computer when Chip arrived. "Sit down, eat, and don't look so worried," he said as he placed his first selection on the table. "You're not in trouble. Remember Noon? At least that's what I called him. He turned out to be Lai's son. R'il'noid. Lai's named him Roi, partly after the boy's mother. I gave Roi the other three dancers yesterday, and found out today what Brak has been up to. Roi has a hard time remembering he's not a slave any more." From the stunned expression on Chip's face, he'd handed the young man a bombshell. "Eat," he urged, "and try to relax."

Chip took small, careful bites, savoring every mouthful. After a moment he looked over at Derik. Clearly, Derik saw, he was putting the disparate pieces together. Finally, Chip nodded, as if agreeing with himself in some silent discussion. "Timi doesn't show bruises," he said. "It wasn't the first time Brak's gone after him."

"He won't again. I don't want to get another like him, which means I need to take my time finding another overseer. Roi said you were doing a lot of the routine things, like getting the others fed tonight. Would you be willing to keep that up?"

Chip almost choked on a mouthful, then thought for a moment before answering, a reaction that pleased Derik. "I can distribute food," he said, "and watch for injuries. I can't do anything about them except tell you, and I can't keep records. Do—do you think we could have something that tastes better now and then? Not this good," and he nodded toward what to Derik was a very plain meal, "but maybe a little change from that brown mush we get."

Brown mush? He *had* been leaving too much responsibility to Brak, though now that he thought about it, he remembered that Brak had requested a change in diet for the slaves, suggesting that the food from the estate kitchens was not well balanced nutritionally. He was pretty sure his assent had been given with an "if they like it," but he doubted now that Brak would have paid much attention to that. And Roi's memories simply were not focused on food, though Derik did recall Coryn's amazement that Roi seemed to find school food palatable.

What Roi's memories did tell him was how much courage and initiative it had taken for Chip even to mention the problem. Too bad the boy was a slave who couldn't keep records, or take care of simple ailments, or even recognize when more expert medical treatment was needed.

Wait a minute. Davy was a slave. And Roi's memories did indicate that Chip was fairly bright. Bright enough to learn what he'd need to see that the other slaves were properly cared for? He had the attitude Derik was looking for, and he wasn't too old to learn—about Cory's age, in fact. He needed to consult with Roi and Davy both about this, he decided. Too bad Lai hadn't gotten around to developing a sigil for Roi, and teaching the boy how to use it through the Enclave shields, but Derik had to see Marna tomorrow about the Jibeth plans. He could talk to Roi and Davy then, and if they agreed, set up an appointment for Chip to talk with both. Meanwhile, Chip was looking more and more apprehensive.

"I don't see any problem with having the kitchen fix your meals," he said. "Brak claimed the stuff he was giving you had better nutrition, but I'm starting to think it was just easier for him. You go talk to the food programmer about breakfast tomorrow—I'll alert him you're coming. It'll have to be balanced, but it doesn't have to be boring. Finish your supper first," he added, as Chip seemed ready to jump up and leave immediately.

Some kind of apprenticeship, he thought, if Davy just knew of an older overseer who felt the way he did about his charges, and who wouldn't mind training a slave as his successor. Maybe even consider the possibility of a conditional manumission for Chip. Yes, he definitely had to talk with Roi tomorrow.

Roi

4/20/36

"This is never going to do."

Roi jerked into wakefulness, at first startled by the words, then recognizing his father's voice. He was too hemmed in by his friends to do more than turn his head, but the words went relentlessly on. "Roi, we need to talk. See me in my office after breakfast, would you?" With that, Lai turned away, closing the door behind him.

It was his first contact with his father since Derry had given his old friends to him, and Roi wished he had been better prepared. His father had not wanted him associating with slaves, and now he had found the four of them snuggled together in Roi's bed. Roi gulped down breakfast without even noticing what Amber had chosen. What could he do about this? One of the things he had done over the last three days was search the computer for information about the differences between adolescence and childhood. As an adolescent he could own slaves in his own right, and Derik had given the three to him, not to his father. In theory, what happened to his friends was up to him.

In practice, he didn't know if he could defy an order from his father. He could try, he decided as he choked down the last bites of breakfast. But his stomach twisted at the thought. He'd gotten around owners' intentions before, but the closest he'd ever come to defying a direct order was that time at school, ignoring the proctor's order to stop—and then he had simply been obeying Derik's order to meet him. This time, it would be his own choice. By the time he guided his float chair through the door of his father's office, all he could think about was protecting his friends.

"I'm not getting rid of them," he blurted out before his father could even say anything.

Lai looked startled, then grinned. "Good for you," he said, "but I wasn't even going to suggest you get rid of them. Where did you get that idea?"

Roi stared at his father, feeling as though he'd thrown his whole weight against something that had turned out to be only an illusion. "What you said this morning," he said. "And you told Nik to keep me away from slaves. I think Derry too."

"Roi, I didn't know you. You wouldn't let me know you. I thought seeing other slaves would just remind you of your own slavery, and I didn't want to do that. Derry finally convinced me I was wrong—he's been planning to give those kids to you eventually for a year and a half, but he had to talk me into it first. And from what Marna said, they've done more to get you back on your feet in less than a fiveday than she and I have managed in a month. All I meant this morning was that the bed looked a little crowded. Doesn't anyone ever fall off?"

"That's why we moved the mats next to the bed," Roi replied sheepishly. "But there isn't room for a bigger bed, with all the exercise equipment and everything."

"That's the second reason I wanted to talk with you. The first—Roi, what are you going to do with your friends?"

"I'm not sure what I *can* do."

"Forget 'can' right now. What do you *want* to do?"

"I want them to be free, and to learn enough that they can do what they choose when they're free. But I'm not sure how to go about it."

"Any idea of what they want to do?"

"Timi was raised on a starship—he wants to go back to space. Amber's more interested in medicine. Flame—well, I can't get her to be interested in anything except staying with me. But I want her to be able to do something else if she wants to. Could they use the education programs on the computer?" They already were, but this seemed to be a good time to ask.

"Of course. That's the way Marna set it up. But they've missed a lot of education, Roi. They may have trouble catching up enough for those particular careers."

"Timi and Amber know how to read and write and do basic math. They taught me, before I ever met Nik—or Derik, for that matter. Of course none of us could admit it."

"Talk to Nik about what Amber would need to learn, and I'll introduce you to a couple of people from the Space Academy who can advise you on what Timi would need. Probably lots of science and math for both of them would be the best, though it's no guarantee. Have you done any thinking about school next year? You have a lot to catch up on, too. And you really need to socialize with other R'il'noids, though neither Marna nor I want to send you back to living at Tyndall. There are other schools, though we'd be hard put to find something as good as Tyndall academically."

Roi started to chew at his lip, then hastily stopped. He'd thought that old habit was broken, but now that he could start using his face more normally it seemed to have returned. "The last few fivedays of the term, with the computer hookup, worked pretty well," he said. "Most of the problems were with courses where we were doing something instead of just being lectured to. And I do have some friends who'll be there next year—in the pattern chess club, for instance. I missed that."

"What about going as a day student next year? Derry says you'd have no problem with a patterned teleport between here and the visitor's lounge at Tyndall, and your friends are going to need a lot of study time on the computer. They could work on the education programs while you're at Tyndall."

"And I could help them out when I get home?" Home. It was still a strange concept for him, but it was starting to feel natural.

"At your age at Tyndall, you'd normally be tutoring younger students. Kim thinks you'd have problems, because the students you'd normally be tutoring are the same ones you started in classes with last year. It might be worth checking if you could get tutoring credit for working with your friends."

"Yes! Uh—if I could teleport from here to Tyndall, maybe I could teleport to Derry's too and add another student. Derry wants to train one of his older slaves to take over Brak's job and then free him. I think Chip'd be good at it, and Davy's found an older overseer who'll take him on as a sort of apprentice while he fills in 'til Chip's ready to handle the job by himself. Chip needs to know some medicine, too, and I bet he'd learn it faster if I help."

"Better add a schoolroom," Lai said, looking amused. "Which gets us to the second reason I wanted to talk to you. You and Marna and I, we're a family now, and we want to keep it that way. But you need more room, and we just don't have it in this building. You know how the corridor system works?"

Roi was briefly puzzled. "Sure. It's a bunch of little rooms with jump-gates between them. For a non-esper, I guess it just looks like a corridor, except for the ears popping. I can feel the jumps, and I think I saw how you adjusted them when we were going to my birthday party."

"Don't actually try making the readjustments on your own until I check you out and you have a map. The point is, we can adjust the default jumps to make any building in the inner Enclave as close to the front door as your room is now. How'd you like to take your friends and go looking for new quarters? You'll need room and computer hookups for the five of you, some kind of exercise area, preferably a swimming pool, a place for horses—Marna says it will be a long time before you can ride by yourself, and we can put in a stable if there's enough room for pasture space—room for the tinerals … What else?"

Roi grinned. "A place for the herb garden Nik and Davy promised me," he said. "Are you serious? I can really look for a place with more room, and still be close to you and Marna?"

"I'm serious. I suppose you could say it's your real birthday present from me. Marna and I are expecting all four of you for dinner, by the way. Tie into the computer with me, and I'll show you how to access the map. I've had the computer flag some of the places that might fit your needs."

The map was no problem, nor was using it as a guide to readjusting the jump-gates. Lai nodded in approval within a few minutes. "You have it," he said. "Keep the light-duty computer interface on—you're close to being able to do without it, but I'd rather you had a little more practice first. Contact me through the computer if you need to. And Roi …"

"Yes?"

"Don't take any chances on getting either of those girls pregnant."

Roi stared at his father, outraged. "You think any of us *likes* that kind of stuff? After what we've been through? Besides, Nik took me to meet some people who had Coven syndrome. There's no *way* I'd take a chance on putting a child through that."

"Attitudes change around your age. Just be careful, and don't hesitate to come to Marna or me if you change your mind. And one other thing. You are responsible for those kids. I do not have the time to referee arguments or keep them out of the hair of people who are busy on Confederation business. That's up to you. Understand?"

Keep Timi out of everyone's way? Well, he'd done it at Derik's, though he suspected it might be harder now. "I understand," he said.

✳   ✳   ✳   ✳

"You're getting a whole building for a birthday present?" Timi asked, sounding both awed and jealous.

"The use of one," Roi replied. "Room for a bigger bed, at least. And enough computer terminals for all of us. Timi, Amber, if you want to go into space and medicine, you're going to have to really study science and math. I'll help all I can, but you've got to do the learning."

"You'll really free us?" Timi gulped.

"Told you I would if I could, and it seems I can. But I can't make promises on the space and medicine stuff—Father says you may have gotten too far behind to catch up on the things you'll need to know. You'll have the teaching programs on the Enclave computer, and advice from people who know the fields, and I'll help all I can. I have to go back to school myself for classes in a couple of fivedays, and you'll need to study while I'm not here. I'll help all I can evenings, but it'll really be up to you."

"Will we have room enough so that we can study separately?" Amber asked.

"One of the things we'll look for is rooms of your own, though I hope we can still sleep together."

"That's cut down on your nightmares, I think," Davy remarked. "Did you ever sleep alone before, except as punishment?"

Roi and Flame both shook their heads. Amber said, "Before I was a slave," and Timi nodded.

"I wouldn't mind trying to sleep alone again," Timi said, but he didn't sound very sure of himself. Not too surprising, considering he'd probably had more isolation time than the other three put together.

"Separate rooms for everybody, so you'll have a place to keep your own stuff and sleep alone if you want to," Roi said. "We'll see if we can find a place everybody likes."

"Make sure there's a place Nik and I can plant that herb garden," Davy said, "and I'd like a bedroom with a window. Facing the sunrise, for preference."

"Aren't you coming along?" Roi asked.

"No. Remember to look for an automated stable and pasture for the horse. And space for the tinerals, though I'd better take them to the atrium right now."

"A horse?" Flame inquired eagerly, while Timi closed his eyes briefly in resignation.

"Horses," Roi replied. "Father says I won't be able to ride alone for a while, so I need to look for mounts for you, too. But he said not to worry about the stable, as long as there's room enough for one." He had been shedding the relatively formal clothes he had donned for the meeting with his father as he spoke, and was struggling into loose trousers and shirt. He grabbed a jacket in case they went outdoors, tossing it into the carrier on the back of his float chair. "Let's go."

The Enclave, Roi quickly realized, was a ghost settlement. Some of the older sections—though not the buildings his father had flagged—were in ruins. Others had been placed in stasis—but the buildings had either been stripped and then abandoned for years before stasis had stopped further decay, or they had been frozen in time at their occupants' deaths, sometimes still with clothing and even food intact. Two of the first seven looked possible, though Roi was doubtful about the suitability of the second for the horses, and Timi took a violent dislike to the fifth.

The eighth set Roi's teeth on edge, although he could not say why. It was not dilapidated, nor did it look as if the owner would be back any moment. It looked more as if it had been carefully cleaned and repaired before being put into stasis, and the floor plan indicated a basement area with a pool and free space for exercise equipment, as well as plenty of room for all five of them. The view was beautiful, with the mountains to the east clearly visible, though the building itself was not so high that the difference in air pressure from Lai's building could not be bridged with three or four jumps. There was an outbuilding that looked as if it could be converted to a stable with little trouble, and a meadow area that could be fenced for a pasture.

Timi loved it at first sight, and the girls, while preferring the above-ground rooms, also thought it was by far the best place they'd seen. Roi was unable to express a reason, but he was increasingly uneasy. "Let's look at that basement area," he suggested, hoping to find a reason to reject the building.

The lift shaft was working normally, but the bloodthirsty murals on the basement walls gave them all a shock. "They'd be easy enough to change," Timi insisted. "Let's look at the recreation area and the pool." He pulled the door aside.

Roi's eyes insisted the room was empty, just a large, brilliantly lit space tiled in white and silver. His esper senses screamed of suffering, blood, and death. Gasping with horror, he spun the float chair and bolted, careening out the first door he saw at the top of the lift shaft. Not until the others had caught up with him did he realize that he was outdoors, not in the corridor system.

"What was that all about?" Timi demanded. "It was just a room, and a good one for all that exercise equipment of yours."

"It was a torture chamber," Roi gulped. "I've got senses you don't, Timi. There is no way I'd go back into that building, let alone that room."

"Afraid of a building?" Timi asked scornfully.

"Shut up, Timi," Amber broke in. "Be fair. You didn't like that place the rest of us did, and he didn't even try to talk you out of your feelings. Give him the same courtesy he gave you, at least. Roi, I do have one question. How do we get back without going in the building?"

Roi hadn't intended to contact his father, but this must be exactly the kind of situation Lai had in mind when he told Roi to keep the interface on. He reached for the computer and through it, uncertainly, for his father's mind. *Is there an alternate way back into the corridor system from where we are?*

Where—Oh! Of course the computer picked that one up from the parameters I gave it, but that's Zhaim's old home. I don't think you'd want to live there. Yes, there's a corridor entry point in the garden. It's a small building in the heart of a maze. Look for an evergreen hedge enclosing a rose garden—yes, that's it. Fairly simple maze, really. Turn left just inside the gate, then right, then left twice in succession, then two rights, three lefts, three rights and you should be there. Keep a light contact until you're sure you're back in the system.

Simple, Roi decided. And a rose maze sounded innocent enough. He led the others to the gate, and hesitated. Even the maze gate felt malignant—but they had to get back to the corridor system.

Once they passed the gate, he found his problem was to keep the girls moving. The roses, he had to admit, were magnificent. Amber and Flame were both enthralled by the huge, fragrant blooms on head-high bushes. Still, there was something subtly wrong about the flowers, a hint of decay in their perfume. The stems were unnaturally thorny, and interlaced in a way that made the maze walls all but impenetrable. And why were they blooming a few days after the winter solstice?

They were perhaps a third of the way into the maze when Roi took a closer look at what he first thought was a half-open flower, and realized that he was looking at a living hand, bleeding where thorns had scratched it. Horrified, he reached out mentally. Nothing. The thorny stems were pumping blood, not sap, and the ground beneath the bushes was rich with human bones, but there was no mind to feel the pain of the bleeding hand. "Move it," he ordered, dry-mouthed.

Timi, who had been showing some impatience with the girls, was happy to take on the job of speeding their movements, and they were within one turn of their goal when Amber suddenly gasped, staring at another hand.

"Go on," Roi said sharply, and again reached out mentally—but this time he reached a mind. Not a sane mind, or one that felt the pain of the bleeding hand, but this bush was taking its sustenance from a living body. This time he didn't even think twice about contacting his father, nor was he surprised when Lai brought Marna into the link almost at once.

Get your friends out of there, Marna told him. *I'll take care of it.* Roi felt her horror and his father's anger, and bolted for the building at the heart of the maze. He was ashamed of his own cowardice, but a last glance backward caught Marna flicking into view. *You do not know enough yet to handle this,* she told him. *Concentrate on protecting your friends.*

Roi found his friends huddled just inside the door, obviously confused by finding themselves in a corridor when they had entered a small, isolated building. "It's all right," he assured them. "All the corridors are like this. It's just not as obvious when you enter from another building. Let's see ..." He accessed the computer map again, blinking in surprise as he encountered a message from his father. *Try this one. I've already reset the corridors. It'll need some work, but it's structurally sound and you and Faran would have liked each other.*

Faran? One of Elyra and Loki Faranian's R'il'nian ancestors, perhaps? One of the corridor directions clearly led back to the entryway to the building they had just left, so he sent his float chair in the other direction.

Three jumps and a good deal of ear popping down the corridor—perhaps thirty steps from the point of view of the others—they came to a clear sliding door opening onto a rolling, stone-fenced pasture with foothills rising behind it. An outbuilding that could have been a stable was visible off to their left, and there was another door on the other side of the corridor. It took Timi two tries to open it.

In some ways, it was the most dilapidated of the buildings they had seriously examined. Wall and window coverings hung in shreds, and most of the furniture was unusable. Too large, was Roi's first impression as he looked at the floor plan. The U-shaped building was huge—but most of what they needed was in the eastern leg of the U, looking toward the mountains. There were ten comfortable bedrooms, with separate bathing and storage facilities opening off each. A small greenhouse, its panes fallen in, occupied the northernmost end of the wing, and the open end of the U faced north, where the winter sun to the north drenched the grass and the empty swimming pool. Against the sunlit south wing would be a good place for an herb garden, Roi thought. Turning back to the south, they found a huge, bare room that could serve as general living and study quarters, and beyond that another large room. "Bedroom," Flame pronounced. "See that depression in the floor? Looks to me like a levitation bed. My second owner had one—he was so fat he'd have crushed us otherwise. But they're really comfortable, and that one looks big enough we'd all have to work to fall off. What's beyond those doors?"

What was beyond those doors turned out to be a bathing room with most of its fixtures inoperative, and a room Roi thought had been intended as a wardrobe—though most of its racks and drawers would need replacement. The bathing room had another door at the far end, and when Timi opened it Roi looked in bewilderment at the large, high-ceilinged room beyond. Floor, walls and ceiling were all padded, and recessed handholds were scattered around with a fine disregard for gravity. "It would make an exercise room," he said doubtfully. "The floor plan calls it a C-G gym."

"C-G—controlled gravity!" Timi exclaimed, moving out into the room. "Roi, see if it works!"

"Computer says yes," Roi replied. "But what is it?"

Timi grinned. "Come out here a ways—that's fine. Now tell the computer to reduce the gravity—slowly—to about a tenth of normal."

Roi felt his weight come off his seat bones, and the girls backed up into the bathing room.

"Now get up and walk over here," Timi said, eyes dancing.

"Timi, I can't …" Roi started to say—but was that true? His legs certainly wouldn't support his normal weight, but from the feel of the chair, he didn't weigh much right now. Carefully he pushed down with hands and legs, and found that he did indeed have the strength to lift his body. He took a shaky step, then another. "I can walk," he whispered. His vision blurred, and he realized with surprise that he was crying. Timi caught his hands and steadied him as he almost fell, but the near-fall was from lack of balance in the low gravity.

"A little practice, and you'll be dancing again," Timi said smugly. "And I'll have a chance to get back my free fall skills. This one?"

Roi glanced back at the girls, who were nodding enthusiastically. "This one," he agreed.

Marna

2/20/36

Roi, Marna thought, would certainly not have been able to handle this. She wasn't sure she was up to handling it herself. Her training had been in Healing fellow R'il'nians, who would recognize her Healing touch for what it was and either cooperate fully or refuse Healing, and in Healing animals, who generally did not make any clear distinction between their own minds and another mind contacting them. Humans did make that distinction, but were often unwilling to accept the contact of another mind.

She had succeeded with the girl who had been buried beneath Zhaim's roses only because the mind had already been insane. Enslavement had been such a shock that the girl had been totally unable to bridge the gap between the first twelve years of her life and the years of slavery since, making it easy to separate the two. Marna sank into a chair and looked down at the sleeping body. Physically seventeen, she estimated, but when the mind awoke it would be only twelve, with no memory at all of the years of slavery.

She still was not sure of the morality of what she had done. But what other options were there? She could not have Healed the girl with the memories intact; the mind was too aware of what had been done to the body. She wasn't ready to expose Roi to such a moral quandary yet, though on this planet he'd have to face similar problems eventually.

The former Jibeth student who had been helping her and Nik came to her side with a mug of soup, and Marna smiled her thanks. Nik looked up from checking monitors across the room. "Lai said to remind you he invited all the kids for supper," he said, yawning, and grinned at her quick check of the stars outside the window. "You have time. Sometimes I wish Seabird Island weren't so far east of the Enclave, or that I weren't so addicted to rising with the sun."

Marna finished her soup and stood. She had time, but not that much if she was to bathe and change out of her bloodstained working clothes. "Thanks for your help," she told Nik as she walked out of the room. In theory, the rescued students all knew about teleports. In practice, seeing someone disappear before their eyes bothered them, so Marna made a point of getting out of their sight before teleporting.

Roi, when he arrived with his friends, was fairly bubbling with excitement. "I can walk!" he crowed as he moved his float chair up to the table. "We found a place where there's a gravity shaper and I can walk with the gravity set low. Course my balance is off, but Timi says that's practice, not muscle. It's that last place you suggested, father, but I think just the east wing is more than big enough. It'd take a lot of fixing up, though." He looked anxiously at his father.

At the same time, his mind reached for Marna's and Lai's. *Were you able to do anything? Did you find out how she got there?*

Split-braining, Marna thought, and not very good at it yet. He wanted to know what had happened, but he didn't want to upset his friends any further. "I've been telling you that you'd be able to walk again," she said aloud, hearing Lai assure the youngsters that there would be no problem repairing the old building.

"I didn't go deep enough to pick up the C-G gym," Lai said. "Faran was an artist in many fields. That's one thing that's far more common in Humans than R'il'nians—you take after your mother that way. But Faran was one of the exceptions. He lived too long ago for me to have known him, but he designed the reception room we used for your birthday. I think he'd have liked you, and you him."

The girl will be all right, though she'll never remember the last five years, Marna told Roi mentally. *I think she'll join the Jibeth colony on Riya. Lai, what did you do about Zhaim?*

"It felt welcoming," Roi said, "even before we found the gym. Not at all like the one with the roses."

"They were beautiful roses," Flame said wistfully. Amber looked questioningly at Roi, who shook his head slightly.

They don't know about the skeletons, Roi sent to Marna, *and I'm not going to tell them.*

Zhaim wasn't admitting anything, Lai put in, *and I certainly can't prove he did anything illegal. I did reset the shields on the Enclave. He can't teleport in* now, and he'll need to ask specific permission any time he needs to fly in for an Inner Council meeting.

The definition of 'illegal' on this planet needs to be changed, Marna sent angrily.

Roi was biting his lip and looking troubled. He'd left the discussion of the renovations needed for the building to his father and the three slaves. *Elyra did say I should share a memory,* he thought, *but I'm still not sure I did the right thing.*

He felt very guilty to Marna. No matter what he had done, he was better off facing it. *Go ahead and tell us,* she thought.

He hesitated, visibly gritting his teeth (and so much for the split-braining, Marna thought), then opened a memory to them.

Marna had seen Zhaim as a rather odious person who had not received the treatment he needed for a moral condition with which she wanted no contact. Seeing him from the viewpoint of one of his slaves was far worse. What he had done to Flick …

I'm not sure *it wasn't just a nightmare,* Roi thought soberly. *And there didn't seem to be any right way to help him.*

And she had been trying to shield him from her own moral ambiguity? *Sometimes,* she thought back, *there is no right way. But you tried to do what was best for Flick, not what was easiest, or best for you. Given the choices you had, I'm not sure I would have done any better. Roi, you are a Healer and an empath, and that means you feel guilt easily. One of the first things I had to learn in my training was to recognize when guilt was appropriate. Honest mistakes, when you have thought through your options and put the well-being of your patient first, should help you learn rather than destroy you, but even then, the kind of guilt you are feeling would be excessive. I don't think you even made a mistake. Save the guilt for when you have been careless or hasty, or had your priorities wrong.*

Roi's mental tone brightened. *Do you think Flick could still be alive?*

Unlikely, came Lai's response. *I know now what I strongly suspected before, that Zhaim's been lying to me about giving up his 'hobbies.' Lyra was right in telling you to pass that memory to me. What you gave me won't hold up legally, but it's enough so that I can check out his eyrie personally. I don't really expect to find any victims from before the Riyan expedition …most of them probably died while he was gone.* Aloud, he remarked, "General repairs are straightforward enough. I'll instruct the computer to get a robotic maintenance crew in immediately. I'd suggest we focus right now on habitability …plumbing, lighting, control systems, computer hookups, cleaning, and minimal furniture. We can strip the surfaces and put on a white coating for the moment, and you can decide later what you want in the way of decoration. Did you look at the west and south wings at all?"

The four looked at each other with sheepish expressions. "No," Roi admitted. "I was too excited about walking, and then we looked at the courtyard. Davy, there's a perfect place for the herb garden, against the north wall of the south wing, where it'll be sheltered and still get sun all day. And a huge swimming pool, if the crack can be fixed, and an old orchard … I think it has the equipment for a force field around it. Do you think the tinerals would like it, Marna?"

Marna smiled. "They'd probably love it," she replied. "But don't expect them to leave you any fruit."

"It's located about like this place," Lai said, "and the west wing overlooks the beach. Similar elevations and air pressure, so we can adjust the corridor system defaults to put it right next door. I'll take care of that when I get the repairs started, and you should be able to move in before the next school term starts. Get Vara to look over the stable and see what's needed there. And ask her advice on additional mounts for your friends. You should not be riding alone, even when you're physically able to. Especially not on that horse Vara picked for you."

Two more R'il'nian abilities, Marna thought. Object reading, or he would not have felt so haunted at Zhaim's old home, or so welcome at Faran's. And split-braining…actually at a younger age than it would have appeared in a R'il'nian. Why did the Confederation place so much emphasis on the Çeren index, which at most measured the number of R'il'nian-derived active genes, and so little on the specific abilities needed to hold the Confederation together?

Because in Çeren's day there was a pretty strong correlation, and a real need for an objective ranking system. Çeren himself devised the lab breeding system that I now think decoupled his index from the specific abilities needed. Both his innovations were adopted too quickly, but their adoption was demanded by the Humans who make up most of the population of the Confederation. And Humans are so short-lived they have no good feel for the law of unintended consequences.

Roi? she asked, raising her shields slightly to keep her exchange with Lai private.

He's better than he thinks. But Derry says there's a genuine problem with his sound discrimination…that's a pretty basic R'il'noid ability. And he doesn't really want to test high. Have patience for another six months and we'll find out. But I'm stuck with Zhaim as an heir, and there's nothing I can do about it as long as he's careful not to break any laws that apply to him. And there aren't many that do.

Marna grimaced. There were times she was tempted to go back to Riya, with the transplanted Jibeth school for company. But she didn't want to leave Lai, and she had known him long enough now to realize that his sense of responsibility for the Confederation would never let him abandon it. And that loyalty, she thought, is exactly why I love him. She glanced back at Roi, as excited and happy as she had ever seen him. He would be better off on Riya if anything ever happened to Lai and to her, she decided. She'd have to tell him that.

Zhaim

6/26/36

It was all the bastard's fault, Zhaim decided. He'd been opposed from the start to his father's highly unsuitable liaison with a Human female not even approved by the Genetics Board. The resulting brat should have been killed at birth, or, failing that, as soon as it had been recognized for what it was.

Lai had not seen it that way. Instead, he had gone into what Zhaim considered a panic mode, acting as if the brat needed protection from Derik, of all people. That had led to a number of off-planet assignments for Derik, in the course of which the old R'il'noid had deduced the existence of Riya.

Riya! Zhaim ground his teeth at the thought of the female Lai had brought back with him. Never mind the fact that a purebred child for his father would threaten his own status, though that was bad enough. And the Riyan had hated all R'il'noids. He could have accepted that, perhaps even used it to pry his father away from her. But from the instant she had met Lai's bastard, her attitude had changed. Now she hated only a few of the R'il'noids, most notably Zhaim and his allies. And that personal slight was unbearable.

He'd amused himself with the brat in the past, using his son and that ass Nebol to make its time at Tyndall as unpleasant as possible. If it had been killed, so much the better, though he would not risk his father's wrath over a direct attempt to destroy it. Now, however, it had gone into Zhaim's home in the Enclave, alerting Lai to Zhaim's embellishments there. That, together with the wedge Lai had driven between Zhaim and Xazhar, was too much. The bastard must be punished.

Not killed, or even injured—until it was properly tested, its legal status would be that of its high R'il'noid son, a future Inner Council member. Zhaim had no intention of risking the legal reprisals that would follow any attempt to harm anyone close to his own status. And there would be legal reprisals, and more. His father might be elderly and overly sentimental, but only that sentiment had saved Zhaim on Mirror.

Xazhar was still, in a limited way, loyal to his father. Zhaim's son wouldn't attack the bastard directly again, but he had no hesitation in passing on information about its school performance and even gossip. Zhaim knew the brat was close to catching up with its age group academically, and had been approved for the pattern chess team. Through Xazhar's conversations with some of the pattern chess players, Zhaim had a third-hand report of its hosting a meeting of the pattern chess club at the Enclave—a report that had included its obvious emotional involvement with the three slaves that Derik had given it. So far as Zhaim himself has concerned, he could not imagine being hurt by anything done to anyone else—but he had seen the effectiveness of the technique too often not to recognize that it worked. And given the right situation, he could attack the brat's slaves quite legally.

The right situation—that would depend on what Xazhar could tell him. The critical question was whether the bastard ever took its slaves out of the Enclave. And—he checked the time—Xazhar would be waiting for him in the visitors' lounge at Tyndall. He made a point of being sure the teleport was smooth, with no implosion to give away the fact that his power outweighed his control.

"When are you going to teach me a pattern teleport?" was Xazhar's first remark on reaching Zhaim's home. "Roi does it, so it can't be too hard. And linking so you can 'port me gives me a headache."

"By himself?" Zhaim smiled. "Most unlikely. Perhaps with Lai's assistance, or Derik's. He may even think he's doing it alone. Trust me, he's not. And in the long run, they're doing him no favors. Wait until you're truly ready." The brat was teleporting itself? At sixteen? That was unwelcome, but Zhaim was careful not to let his reaction show. "So what's the news this week?"

"Roi," Zhaim spat out. "Looks like he'll head up the pattern chess team next year. Damn him, he's taking away some of *my* followers. And I'm really having to work at academics—he's not in the same classes I'm in yet, but he may be by vacation." Xazhar didn't come out and say Roi was a rival for his position of class academic leader, but the implication was there.

"Why don't you defeat him on his own ground? Challenge him at pattern chess?"

Xazhar looked at him with a mixture of contempt and—yes—fear. "In the first place, pattern chess is a sissy game. Why should I want to play it? In the second place, didn't you teach me to challenge only when I was sure I could win? I haven't played that much, and he's good. He was beating Coryn K'Derik regularly last year, and the only reason he took so long to get on the team was that stupid age-for-grade requirement. Grandfather and Great-Uncle Derik may have let him win—he thinks they did—but you can bet Coryn didn't. And Coryn was one of the best pattern chess players Tyndall's produced in years. Roi's better. He handicaps himself playing other students—limits how many tiles he moves at once. But there's no way he'd do that with me."

"And your own chosen sport?"

"Father, I'm not going to impress anybody by beating a cripple in a physical sport like plasmaball. Besides, he's not exactly a novice in free fall. The plasmaball team was called in to help out when the school had a seminar on free fall maneuvering last fiveday. Roi's barely able to manage a walking frame in normal gravity—he still uses that float chair a lot. But he handles himself as well as some of my team members in zero-gee. Seems one of his slaves grew up on a starship, and it's been giving Roi lessons. That one's interested in plasmaball, even if Roi thinks it's stupid. Roi's even taking it to see the planetary tournament."

Did Zhaim detect some reluctant admiration in Xazhar's comments? Never mind, the information was worth it. He didn't trust Xazhar enough to ask for the information he really wanted, but he was able to pick up most of it without asking. Xazhar was an avid fan of professional plasmaball as well as the captain of the Tyndall team, and ready to talk for hours about his favorite sport.

So Zhaim encouraged his son's interests as they walked together into the small dining room. The food preparation and service were automated—Zhaim would not trust slaves with his food—but still far better than Tyndall, and Zhaim had made a point of ordering dishes he thought would appeal to Xazhar.

"There's a group from the school going," Xazhar said over the delicately seasoned Whitefire sour-root salad. "This is good. One of yours?"

Zhaim nodded. "One of the Whitefire cultivars. Too bad they won't grow without the excessive UV that caused their home planet its problems in the first place."

Xazhar shrugged. "So they've got an export product, at least according to my economics instructor." He finished the last bite as the next course appeared on the table—this time meat from a new animal Zhaim had engineered, with a choice of sauces on the side. Xazhar tried several of the sauces, settling on the most familiar one. After a short time busily eating, he added, "Roi's not going with the school, though. Probably just as well. He spoils that slave rotten."

Zhaim made a noncommittal noise, though he was burning with impatience for Xazhar's information. He had to wait, getting information on the brat—as opposed to plasmaball—a bit at a time, perhaps one sentence during each course through a long dinner.

By the time he returned Xazhar to school a day later, he was heartily sick of plasmaball—but he had the information he'd wanted. The bastard had succeeded in convincing its father—*their* father, Zhaim reluctantly admitted to himself—to let it attend the game anonymously. The old R'il'nian had undoubtedly used conditional precognition to insure that the brat would be safe, but Zhaim had been careful not even to think of actually harming the Human woman's child. He might not be able to use CP on a long time scale, but he thought that he might even be ahead of his father in understanding how CP worked. As long as Lai kept his use of CP narrowly focused, Zhaim thought he could get around it. Given time, he might even be able to block it.

7/6/36

By the day of the game, Zhaim had recovered sufficiently from his overdose of plasmaball to enjoy the sport.

Plasmaball as played at schools level was a safe, if highly physical, game. School players were required to wear gear that protected them from the plasmoid—tamed ball lightning—that they attempted to control. For professionals, there was no such requirement. Each player had the choice of wearing full protective equipment, which interfered with speed and mobility, or taking the risk of lesser protection with greater mobility. Deaths were not unusual during professional games, and Zhaim looked forward to the sport.

This, however, looked like a disappointing game. Both teams pushed out into the null-gee playing volume heavily armored, which meant the game would be one of strategy rather than nerve and electrocution. The rules prevented players from crossing the neutral zone between teams, so even the clash of protective body armor would be absent. Zhaim looked around and quickly identified the pair of spectators he was after, white head and black. Good seats, as he had expected, but not conspicuous ones. They were close enough to his own seat that they would leave at nearly the same time, as he had hoped. He settled back to enjoy the game, keeping a corner of his attention on his quarry.

They were talking together, even arguing, and Zhaim sniffed in disdain. Any slave that talked back to him would rapidly become raw material for his art. Had this brat no concept of the responsibility of a slave owner to maintain discipline? Hastily Zhaim controlled himself. He could be angry at the black slave, but if he was to succeed, he must control his hatred of his—the term galled him—half- brother. He forced his primary attention back to the increasingly boring game.

Roi

The only plasmaball games Roi had ever seen were at Tyndall, so he took the heavy armor for granted. The sheer size of the professional arena did startle him. School games were played in zero gee, but in a much smaller and more rectangular volume and with little room for spectators. Here he found himself looking around at thousands, even tens of thousands of spectators, many of the faces barely visible from where he was sitting. Even the fourteen players seemed more like insects—beetles, perhaps—than people.

The plasmoid appeared and grew to playing size on the plane separating the players, and the referee's whistle signaled the start of the game. A yellow and a green player flung themselves at the plasmoid. It rocketed into the half ellipsoid defended by the greens, who promptly took control. Timi was bouncing in his seat with excitement as the plasmoid streaked toward them. "Wow, look at that," he gasped as sparks flew when the ball bounced off the boundary just in front of them. A green player suddenly loomed up, redirecting the ball toward the goal basket at the other end of the arena. The plasmoid was moving too fast for the yellow players to block, and the arena erupted with cheers as the first goal of the game was scored.

"How do they do that?" Roi wondered aloud. "The armor's got to be slowing them down, and it does seem to affect how they're using the controllers, but they're stopping and spinning in midair with nothing to push against."

"They're using something to give them reaction force," Timi replied. "Probably air jets, like we used on the ship. I think they're mounted on those belts and wrist and ankle bands they all wear. What I don't see is how they control them and how they avoid hitting each other with the air blast."

Roi frowned, studying the players. The action had moved to the far side of the arena and the players were insect-sized again, but aspects of the strategy were actually clearer from this distance. The players, unlike those at school, seemed to have no feeling of up or down, but were truly maneuvering as if the orientation of the spectators did not exist. And the plasmoid had bounced off the walls of the playing volume enough to show that the null-gee volume was an ellipsoid, not a box. Those players had to be thinking in three-dimensional geometry. "There's more to it than I thought," Roi admitted.

The yellows had the plasmoid now, and tried a bounce shot off the boys' side of the volume, but a green player was there, well over their heads, to send it to one of his teammates. This time Roi managed to get a good look at the head inside the protective helmet, and glimpsed a metal mesh cap hiding the player's hairline. "Brain-wave pickup?" he wondered. "Something that picks up wanting to go a particular direction and speed and fires the air jets or whatever accordingly? Damn. I don't talk to Xazhar if I can help it, but I know some other members of the school team. They'd know. I just never bothered to ask. I think you're right about the air jets. But it's complex—probably multiple jets, computer-controlled. Otherwise they wouldn't be able to move directly away from each other." He paused, thinking, then grinned at Timi.

"Think you could modify our C-G Gym so it'd have a curved wall we could bounce balls off of?"

Timi nodded. "Hey," he said, punctuating his statement with a punch to Roi's upper arm, "maybe we could get some of whatever they use to move. They'd sure help maneuvering in free fall."

Roi punched him back, grinning. The walking frame had really helped his upper body strength, and while he still wasn't nearly as strong as Timi, he could hold his own in the shoving matches they got into occasionally. "I'm supposed to use low-gee to help develop my muscles, remember? I might consider seeing if I can get one for you to try once you get through that physics module on the computer." Not that Timi needed that much inducement to study, now that the head of the Space Academy had agreed that he was catching up on his science and math fast enough that he might be able to enter the Academy in three years or so.

Roi leaned back in his seat, watching his old friend more than the game—which he still thought was silly, though some of the three-dimensional maneuvering interested him. At the moment, he and Timi were getting along fairly well. Roi had always wanted his friends to be free, but Timi had seemed unable to believe that until Roi actually began the first legal steps toward conditional manumission. Roi doubted they'd ever have the easy relationship they'd had as fellow slaves, but at least Timi was no longer trying constantly to prove himself better than Roi.

They were in no rush to leave. Roi in the walking frame found it difficult to maneuver in crowds, so he'd told the Enclave pilot to pick them up half an hour after the game was over. By the time they left their seats, the halls were nearly deserted. "Maybe we *ought* to see if we could get some of those maneuvering units," Roi commented as they walked side by side down an empty corridor. "They had us using reaction guns during that seminar a couple of fivedays ago. I knew enough to point it directly away from my center of mass if I wanted to go somewhere, but a lot of the others seemed to forget everything they'd learned in physics." He grinned at the memory of one of the students who'd made his life miserable that first year green-faced and spinning out of control. "Good thing they had the plasmaball team there to chase down the ones who couldn't control their motion—or their stomachs."

"Going to go out for plasmaball when you get your strength back?" Timi asked.

"Hardly! But if those things work the way I think they do, they'd let me dance in free fall. I saw some moves today that could be adapted into a dance, I think." From the moment he'd realized he would be able to move normally again, he'd wanted to get back to dancing. That was still a long way off in normal gravity, but in free fall skill and precision were more important than strength.

Timi, who had never regarded dance as more than a way of staying alive, rolled his eyes. "You dance," he said. "I'll practice space maneuvers."

It was amazing how fast the arena emptied. Roi had been hard put to stay upright on his way in through the crowd, but now the halls stretched out before them, deserted except for a few cleaning robots. The sound of their own footsteps and the rhythmic thump of the walking frame echoed from the bare walls. Roi thought he heard other footsteps, but only faintly. Then a figure suddenly appeared at an intersection ahead, arm raised. Zhaim!

Roi had never met his half brother face to face, but he had seen him through Flick's eyes, and he knew that Derik and his father both considered Zhaim responsible for most of what had happened to Roi during his first school term. Instinctively he tried to step back, reverting to his slave background.

And Timi moved between them, arm up to block the blow Zhaim appeared about to deliver.

All Roi could think of was the forced sale laws. "Timi, no!" he said, knowing that if Timi attacked Zhaim, Zhaim could force Roi to sell Timi— to Zhaim. And Timi's conditional manumission wasn't far enough along to protect him, if anything could protect him against Zhaim.

"Out of my way, slave," Zhaim ordered, and Roi wasn't sure which of them he meant. Certainly Timi made no move to obey either of them, remaining stubbornly between them. Zhaim swung his arm at Timi, who blocked the blow, grabbing at Zhaim's arm in an attempt to stop another blow. Roi, frightened more for Timi's sake than his own, saw that Zhaim was badly off balance and reached for the frictional forces between Zhaim's foot and the floor, hoping to distract the R'il'noid.

The distraction turned out to be more than he had expected, as Zhaim fell heavily. Furious, the R'il'noid scrambled back to his feet. "That slave attacked me," he snarled, and I'll have it."

Technically, Roi was not a slave any more, and he *could* talk back to Zhaim. "He was defending me," he replied, a little more shakily than he would have chosen, "and you're not getting him for that." Had there been a flicker of uncertainty in Zhaim's eyes, just for an instant? If so, it was gone at once.

"You'll get the official notification tonight," Zhaim sneered, "and if you've got any brains at all you won't fight it." Abruptly he was gone, leaving behind a sound like a thunderclap.

Timi gulped and looked at Roi. "What are you going to do?" he asked.

"Fight him," Roi said grimly. "I wish Marna were here, instead of being away trying to stop that epidemic. Or Derry. But Father was pretty clear that you guys are my responsibility. I think there's something we can use in your defending me—he looked uncertain, just for an instant, when I brought that up. Come on. I never wanted to hear about the forced sale laws again, but all I know is what I learned as a slave. Now I've got to find a hole in them. Class work can wait."

Zhaim's notification was indeed waiting when they returned home. Roi had twenty-four hours to comply—but if he filed for adjudication, which was the first thing he checked on, the compliance deadline would automatically be extended until the adjudication was complete. He had eighteen hours to file. He spent most of the night studying the adjudication procedure, while Timi and the girls pored over the text of the forced sale laws. He'd go over those himself, too, but his first priority was to make sure the adjudication filing was set up to give Timi the best possible chance.

As the person requesting adjudication, he had the right to specify three possible adjudicators, with Zhaim making the final choice. Since both Roi and Zhaim were R'il'noid it would be a Confederation adjudicator who would hear the dispute, even though planetary law was being invoked. Zhaim could challenge all of Roi's selections as biased, but he would need objective cause to succeed. Roi wanted an adjudicator who was not afraid to rule against prominent people and was willing to consider a slave's motivation, but also an adjudicator who had a reputation for integrity so that Zhaim would find it difficult to challenge Roi's selection successfully. The Enclave computer, the Big'Un, held that kind of information, and Lai had taught Roi how to ferret it out.

By early the next morning he had a list of six possible adjudicators, all on planet, all fitting the requirements he had coded into the computer. Two in particular appealed to him, with a third close behind. Follow your hunches, Derik had said, and these two people felt right. He put them down as his first and second choices, with the one he was almost sure of as third.

He thought about skipping school for the next few days, but finally decided that since he had to get some sleep, in class was the place to do it. He could get away with being inattentive for a few days a lot more easily than he could get away with not showing up at school. He filed his challenge before leaving the others asleep, and when he got back home Zhaim's response awaited him.

Two days! He had less than forty-eight hours to put Timi's defense together, and if he failed, Timi's fate might well be the same as Flick's. So far he'd been numb, reacting almost automatically to Zhaim's threats. Now, awakened to the very real threat to Timi's life, he was almost paralyzed with fear. He wasn't even sure how to get to the adjudication.

No! If he let fear take over, he would not be able to help Timi. Let fear motivate him, yes. What he had to do was important, vitally important. Too important to let fear rule him. He'd known that, as a slave. Maybe some of his slave background could even be useful in this new life.

He managed to build a wall between his fear and his consciousness, concentrating on the forced sale laws as if they were a school assignment. And they were exactly as he remembered, but rendered into legal language. If a slave attacked a free person, that person had the right to buy that slave. There were all sorts of provisions for setting the price of the slave, and how the owner and the person attacked could come to some agreement, with the owner paying recompense instead of turning the slave over, but all of the provisions depended on the agreement of the injured party. Roi had no credit to pay Zhaim off, and he doubted Zhaim would accept such recompense, anyway. The R'il'noid was after revenge, not credit.

Maybe he should talk to his father? His hunches felt very positive about Kyrie Talganian, the arbitrator whom Zhaim had accepted, but he didn't get any strong feelings about his father. Roi was Lai's son, but so was Zhaim. Further, his father's attraction to him was basically emotional, based on his love for Roi's mother. Zhaim was his father's heir. Surely his father would side with Zhaim, handing Timi over without question. If only Marna or Derik were available!

There had to be more to the forced sale laws than that. People used slaves as bodyguards, didn't they? How could that be possible if someone like Zhaim could buy any slave who tried to defend his owner? And Timi had been defending him, and that was the claim that had brought that brief flash of uncertainty to Zhaim's expression.

He rubbed his eyes and looked out the window. Close to midnight, and while he intended to stay away from school the day of the adjudication, he had to show up again tomorrow, even if it was only to sleep through classes again. Even the tinerals were asleep. "Anybody find anything?" he asked.

"Maybe," Amber replied doubtfully, "but it's way out of the time range you were searching. It seems to be aimed at modifying the forced sale laws, though."

"Passed later? Shoot it over here—that's it, Amber! Fifty years it took them to figure out that the forced sale laws made slave bodyguards impossible, and then they chose a completely different name. The exclusion clauses." He fought his way through the legalese, mentally translating its meaning, and suddenly realized the implications of what he—not Timi—had done. What the exclusion clauses said, in plain language, was that an owner could elect to take the blame if a slave attacked on orders from the owner. For a bodyguard, protection was considered an implicit order. So far, Timi was covered if he could just qualify as a bodyguard.

But Roi had countermanded that implicit order, and Timi had ignored his order not to try to protect him from Zhaim. "Oh, hells," he muttered, dropping his head into his hands."

"Won't it help?" Timi asked.

"It would if I'd had the sense to keep my mouth shut. Might still, but I've got to find out how it's been used in the past. And how Kyrie Talganian has adjudicated. You guys get to bed. I need to do this myself."

He was so tired by the time he teleported to Tyndall that he slept through almost all of his classes, deeply enough that several of his instructors caught him. Kim was waiting when he returned to the visitors' lounge to go home.

"You know," he said, "there are three hundred students here. I'd have thought at least two hundred ninety of them were more likely than you to sleep through class, but you're the one who's been doing it, for two days straight now. Are you going to tell me why, or shall I ask your father to find out?"

Roi gulped. He still didn't trust his father to take his side against Zhaim, but he had to get away from the school during at least his first two classes of the afternoon tomorrow to attend the adjudication hearing. He'd thought he had each of those two instructors sufficiently confused they wouldn't realize he was missing from the school entirely, but if they'd spotted his sleeping in class, they'd be suspicious to start with—and he still hadn't worked out how to get to the adjudication. Lying to Kim wouldn't work; the man had almost as good a truth-sense as his research indicated for Kyrie Talganian. Maybe he could get away with telling part of the truth?

"I've been studying some laws, sir," he replied. "There's an interesting case being adjudicated tomorrow. Local laws, but in a Confederation court."

"Which you were no doubt intending to attend, instead of school? It has the advantage of being original, at least. And how were you planning to get there? *Not* an unpatterned teleport, I hope."

"I, I haven't got that quite worked out yet, sir," he said, and only then realized that in his exhaustion he had implicitly admitted to planning to avoid classes tomorrow. He tried to keep his face impassive, but once again fear threatened to overwhelm him. What would happen to Timi if they couldn't get to the adjudication?

"The adjudication process," Kim said after enough of a pause to tie Roi into knots, "is something you should know about. So I will arrange that you attend a session, accompanied by a school proctor, and it might as well be the one you are so interested in. You will, of course, give a full written and oral report on what you learn. What time? And would it be better to depart from school or directly from the Enclave?"

Roi almost went limp with relief. Getting himself to the adjudication had been problem enough. But he'd studied Kyrie Talganian's adjudication style enough to be reasonably sure that Timi had to be there to speak for himself—and getting himself and Timi to the adjudication was the problem he had planned to tackle that afternoon. "I'd planned to take one of the friends I'm tutoring with me," he said, too relieved to question Kim's motives. "It would probably be easier to leave from the Enclave. It's about an hour after school noon."

"That would be what—nine in the morning, Enclave time? Eight at the Adjudication Building. I'll have a proctor with a jump-van take you back to the Enclave to pick up your tutee after your morning classes tomorrow. I'll have him take you home now, too—you shouldn't be trying even a patterned teleport if you're falling asleep in class."

Roi got more time to sleep that night than he had expected, thanks to Kim's taking over the transportation problem. But he spent what seemed an appalling part of the night lying awake in the big levitation bed, his friends piled around him. Tomorrow frightened him. That was nothing new, he told himself. Every new owner had frightened him. The difference was that what *he* did could make so much difference in Timi's life.

What would he do if the adjudication went against him, and Timi was taken from him? His lip was bleeding by the time he decided that however uncertain the ethics, he would make sure that Timi did not suffer what Flick had. Marna, aware of his continued distress over what he had done to Flick, had both confirmed Flick's death and shown him how to modify what he had done so that it could be reversed at a later date. If Kyrie Talganian ruled against him, he would go to his father, and to Marna too, once she returned. But he would also go into Timi's mind if he had to, to make sure Timi was never aware of what Zhaim might do to him. Timi might never forgive him, but he knew enough about Healing now to know that he had a lot better chance of repairing whatever physical damage Zhaim might do if Timi was never aware of it.

7/9/36

The adjudication building, unlike the Enclave, was designed to impress rather than to be comfortable. The proctor had left them at the entrance, and the towering doors and high-ceilinged halls left Roi feeling very small and even more unimportant than usual. He remembered his father's advice at his birthday party: No matter how frightened he was inside, he could pretend confidence. He lifted his head and gripped the walking frame, thumping down the long corridor as if the people staring at him did not exist.

Timi walked beside Roi, eyes flicking from side to side as he took in the walls towering over them. He knew the risks, but he also trusted Roi's belief that this was his best chance. There was no place to hide but the Enclave, and Zhaim knew that far better than did either of the boys. Maybe he should have gone to his father, Roi thought as they reached the end of the entry hall and were directed along a side corridor. But this felt right. He still was not sure his father wouldn't side with Zhaim.

Kyrie Talganian. He located the name over a door that looked just like all the others. When he turned toward it the door opened, revealing a desk with a woman seated behind it and three chairs arranged facing the desk. The Enclave computer had displayed no image of Kyrie, but in person she looked rather as Amber might in a decade or so—blond, blue-eyed, and perhaps a bit too rounded. She looked up and gestured toward the chairs, frowning a little as she saw Roi, her eyes on the walking frame.

"You are?" she asked briskly.

"Roi Laian, Milady, and this is Timi." Roi tried to keep his voice firm.

"Sit down. At least you have the courtesy to be on time," she said with a frosty smile. "During the adjudication process I am Adjudicator. As you are challenging Zhaim's claim, he has the right to go first—when he gets here. Can you manage a normal chair?" She looked annoyed, but her shields were so good that Roi had no idea what her annoyance was about.

Nor did she give any further indication of her emotions in the ten minutes or so until Zhaim arrived, sitting quietly and expressionlessly at her desk. When Zhaim walked in, his expression arrogant, she had him identify himself, exactly as Roi had done. "You are late," she said tonelessly. "Let the adjudication begin." She nodded at Zhaim.

"That slave," Zhaim said, pointing at Timi, "attacked me, in direct defiance of its Master's orders. Knocked me down. I am bruised and shocked. I demand that it be turned over to me for proper disposal." He shifted in his seat and winced, obviously inviting the adjudicator to inspect his injuries.

Roi had difficulty controlling himself, but a warning glance from Kyrie restrained him from speaking until Zhaim's testimony was complete, with the adjudicator showing no interest in examining Zhaim's bruises. Then the adjudicator nodded. "That is your view of what happened," she said, and then turned to Roi. "Now yours."

Roi swallowed and licked his lips. "In the first place," he said, "Timi did not knock Zhaim down. Zhaim fell when I cut the friction between his foot and the floor."

Kyrie spread her hand on the desk and looked at Roi. "Oh? Cut the friction between my hand and the desk."

Roi reached for the interface between her hand and the desk, felt out the intermolecular bonds, and snapped them. The adjudicator's hand slid abruptly sidewise, and she drew her breath sharply. "Impressive," she said, showing no other evidence of surprise. "And in the second place?"

"Timi was trying to protect me. We both knew about the forced sale laws, but until I started studying them for this adjudication, neither of us was aware of the exclusion clauses. Zhaim came at me with his arm raised as if he were going to hit me, and Timi got between us. I told Timi not to, because I was afraid of exactly this—that Zhaim would try to use the forced sale laws to punish Timi."

Kyrie nodded sharply and shifted her gaze to Timi. "And why did you disobey a direct order from your owner?"

For Roi, Timi's resentment of the question was obvious. He could see Timi struggling to control his temper and give a reasonable answer. "I thought Zhaim was threatening Roi, and the Lady Marna said she thought Zhaim might be a danger to him. And I knew the only reason he was telling me not to protect him was to protect me."

"Preposterous," Zhaim snapped. "Why are you going through all this nonsense?"

Kyrie did not shift her gaze from Timi. "Out of order," she said. "Have you ever disobeyed your owner before?"

Timi's eyes had a trapped look, but Roi had repeatedly emphasized how important it was that he tell the truth as he saw it. "Well, yes," he said reluctantly. "Mostly when he thinks he can't do something and I think he can. The Lady Marna told me once to do what was best for him, not what he told me to do."

Kyrie nodded again and turned back to Roi. "How old are you?" she asked.

"Sixteen and a few months."

"And you use a walking frame. Why?"

"Kharfun. I only started using the frame about a month ago—I was in a float chair 'til then. The frame was one of the things Timi thought I could do and I didn't."

Kyrie sat quietly for a moment, and then turned to Zhaim. "Have you anything more to say on the facts of the matter?"

"The fact is that I was assaulted in a public place by that." He pointed at Timi. "I demand that it be turned over to me!"

"Your request is denied, Zhaim Laian, with prejudice."

Denied? They had won! Roi started to turn to Timi, relief flooding through him, and then saw Zhaim's face, the normal bronze deepened almost to purple. "With prejudice?" Zhaim snarled. "Are you implying *I* am at fault in this?"

"You have attempted to mislead this adjudication into believing that a legitimate defense of his crippled owner by a slave was an aggressive attack. Protection has always been considered an implied order, though there was a time between the enactment of the forced sale laws and the exclusion clauses when protective behavior could be and was challenged.

"Protection in defiance of an explicit order is one of the oldest adjudicatory problems in slave law, and there are at least four guidelines. Age of the owner—protection overrides obedience if the owner is a child; obedience normally overrides protection if the owner is a young adult or an adult. Roi is technically an adolescent, neither child nor young adult, but barely out of childhood. Physical and mental competence of the owner—no insult to you, Roi, but both your physical condition and your ignorance of the exclusion clauses made you incompetent to give the order you did. The extent to which the slave had been trained in intelligent disobedience—no formal training in this case, but Timi has clearly been encouraged to use his own judgment in doing what is best for his owner. And finally the slave's own reasons for disobeying an order, which in this case were based on his perception of you as a threat.

"On the basis of your demeanor and the statements made during this hearing, I am inclined to agree with that perception. Therefore," she began, but Zhaim reacted before she could complete her statement.

"You'll pay for this insult, Kyrie Talganian," he snarled as he jumped to his feet and jerked open the door.

"You started this process, Zhaim," a familiar voice came from outside the door. "You will accept the legal consequences. A good many laws may not apply to you, but this does." Roi turned his head, shocked, as Lai stepped through the door, gestured Zhaim back inside, and closed it behind them. "Proceed, Adjudicator."

The woman nodded her head to Lai in acknowledgment, and then looked back at Zhaim. "You are barred from approaching Roi Laian except in the presence and with the permission of your father or the Lady Marna until he is fully adult—forty-eight years from now. Further, any attempt on your part to harm the slaves of Roi Laian will be counted as an attempt to harm Roi Laian himself—that is, as an attempt to harm another High R'il'noid. You are dismissed."

Zhaim looked back and forth between Kyrie and his father in apparent disbelief. Slowly his shoulders slumped. He gave Roi a last, bitter look and vanished with a thunderclap that made Roi and Timi jump. Lai shook his head. "I apologize for my older son's manners," he said. "But he does respect the law, once he cools off."

Roi had been watching his father in disbelief. "You took my side?" he asked. "Against Zhaim?"

"I took the side of justice," Lai replied, "and so did you. I knew about this—the computer alerts me any time a Council member gets involved in any legal proceeding. If you had come to me, I'd have told Zhaim he didn't have a legal leg to stand on. But by the time I found out what was going on, you'd already challenged Zhaim's claim and were finding what you needed in the computer. I almost shoved the exclusion clauses under your nose—I've changed the linkage in the computer now, so they come up automatically when the forced sale laws are accessed—and when Kim contacted me about your sleeping in class I told him to arrange transportation for you. But I thought that letting you challenge Zhaim would be good for both of you."

"You might," Kyrie said dryly, "have contacted me about this. I did not even realize that Roi was so young or crippled until he entered my chambers."

"I didn't have to," Lai grinned. "Unlike Zhaim, who has a lamentable tendency to confuse just with legal, and an even more lamentable one to assume that anything he does is legal, I know the law—and I knew that in this case Zhaim was wrong. I also knew that he would accept a legal ruling far better in the long run than an order from me—he thinks I'm an old fuddy-duddy. Your ruling keeping him away from Roi was a pure bonus."

Roi thought he understood why his father had left him to fight Zhaim by himself, but he couldn't help resenting the fear he had lived with for the last few days. From the expression on Timi's face, he was even angrier than Roi. But Kyrie's order barring Zhaim from harming Roi's slaves just might be worth the suspense of preparing for and enduring the adjudication—if Zhaim complied with it.

Roi had done a good deal of thinking about—and dreading—his father's reaction to his defiance of Zhaim. The one possible reaction that had never occurred to him was approval. He was still too dazed to react very much as his father urged him and Timi to their feet and out a back entrance to a waiting jump-van. Lai couldn't teleport Timi, of course, but Roi was still awed that his father would care enough about his feelings to fly them back to the Enclave himself.

They were halfway back before he recovered enough to ask, "Why?"

"Why what, Roi? Telepathic manners go both ways, you know. If you want me to read the question from your mind you have to push it at me a little."

Roi hadn't really thought about what question he wanted to ask, he'd simply felt confused. But there was a problem that had confused him for a long time. Maybe this was the time to ask about it. "Why are Timi and Amber—yes, and Davy, too, slaves? I was born a slave, and so was Flame. Nik, and Derik too, said I wasn't, partly because my mother wasn't legally a slave. They said because she was kidnapped. But Timi and Amber and Davy were all born free and kidnapped into slavery. Why are they slaves?" Sitting beside Roi, Timi was nodding eagerly.

Roi felt his father's unhappiness, but there was no resentment of the question. "Not everything that happens is legal, Roi. Your mother's kidnapping should never have happened—would not, if she had not been trying to hide her true identity. Her kidnappers have been caught and punished—and while I do not approve of slavery as a legal punishment in general, in their case it was appropriate. Davy—has he ever told you anything about the GoodNews cluster, Roi?"

"Not by name, but wasn't that where you said Derik found the Jibeth faculty? Davy did say that the people on his home planet weren't very tolerant."

Lai smiled a little. "That," he said, "is a true masterpiece of both understatement and forbearance. The GoodNews cluster was settled—long before I was born—by a number of groups that wanted to practice their own beliefs without interference from outsiders. They joined the Confederation as a group, so the Confederation has no right to interfere in their internal affairs. Jibeth was originally a philosophical group with a strong emphasis on bodily health, and the group was one of the original colonizers of the GoodNews cluster. There are three suns circled by five planets that are at least marginally habitable, with several continents on each, and until a few centuries ago everything seemed as if it would work.

"Roi, I am not against religion. I have my own, and Marna and I share a great many of our beliefs. But 'I believe' shades into 'I know,' and there is a very fine line between 'I know' and 'anyone who does not acknowledge what I know to be true is either a demon or an idiot, or inspired by one.' That's happened in the GoodNews cluster, and since it's technically internal affairs, I can't do a thing about it. Ironically it was Jibeth, probably the most open philosophy in the cluster, that was proscribed—but the enslavement of Davy and the rest of the Jibeth school was legal under GoodNews laws. All we can do is what we're doing—tracing and buying as many of the people from the Jibeth community as we can find. And advising the GoodNews leaders that they are headed down a path that will probably end in destroying their civilization. That 'we' is not the Confederation, by the way. It's Marna, and

Derik, and Nik and I and quite a few other R'il'noids who think the Jibeth tradition is worth preserving.

"Timi and Amber—what do your remember about your enslavement, Timi?"

Timi shook his head and swallowed. "I was on a spaceship," he said. "I think they killed all the grownups. I'm sorry. I remember the ship, but the attack's awfully blurred. And I don't think I want to unblur it."

Lai nodded. "Sounds like piracy, and that is very illegal under Confederation law. Roi, you and Timi work out what you can about the details—Timi's home planet is important. Same with Amber. The Confederation can and will go after pirates. But keep up that conditional manumission you started. Not only will it give them a better start in freedom, it will probably be a good deal faster than proving they were never legally slaves in the first place. Any other questions?"

Nothing else as serious, but Zhaim's abrupt departure had raised one question in Roi's mind. "Why was Zhaim's teleport so noisy?" he inquired. "He knows how to swap air, doesn't he?"

"He knows," Lai replied. "But he's careless, and he has more power than control. Ready to learn yourself? I think you're ready to start patterning your own teleports, and you do have good control."

"Yes!" Roi exclaimed, almost forgetting his resentment.

"We'll start this evening, then," Lai grinned.

Lai

7/12/36

Marna was predictably furious when she returned. Lai was prepared to defend himself against any loose object in the room, but Marna seemed to have decided that such a display of temper would be childish, and confined herself to a verbal tirade, coupled with a complete blockage of mental contact. When she ran out of breath temporarily, Lai managed to interject, "Do you think it really hurt him?"

Marna stopped short and glared at him. "Lai, you know how much he cares about those friends of his."

"And how much pain it's going to cause him when they grow old and die and he doesn't. Yes, it was uncomfortable for him. But do you think it really harmed him, to find out that he can stand up to Zhaim and win? It certainly didn't hurt him at Tyndall. Kim says that more and more of the students in his age group are copying his short hair and generally beginning to model themselves after him rather than Xazhar."

"Is that what you want for him? To be a leader? That's not what *he* wants."

"No. But he's not a follower by nature, either. And he *is* R'il'noid. He's not going to have much choice. Marna, if you'd been on planet, or Derry, he'd probably have asked for help. I told him the kids were his responsibility, never thinking he'd run into a conflict with Zhaim over them, and by the time I found out about the situation, he had picked his three possible adjudicators, and I knew that any of them would have judged in favor of a slave who was trying to defend an owner Roi's age, quite aside from Roi's physical condition. Zhaim accepted Kyrie because she's been on wide circuit for most of his lifetime, and he wasn't familiar with her adjudications. Roi got that information from the computer—as Zhaim could have, if he'd bothered— and I knew from the instant Zhaim accepted Kyrie that the only real danger to Timi was if Zhaim lost his temper and tried to defy the adjudicator's ruling. Which is why I showed up at the end of the adjudication. Zhaim does obey the law when his temper's under control. And we now have a legal ruling that Roi's slaves are out of bounds for him."

Marna sniffed. "Zhaim needs a lot more laws applying to him," she said. "He doesn't seem to do anything—or refrain from anything—unless he's forced to."

Lai sighed. He couldn't argue with her, but he did understand the origin of the block against applying planetary law to R'il'noids. It should have been applied only to R'il'noids doing their duty as R'il'noids, rather than as Zhaim and several others now used it—but who could have predicted the rise in the number of R'il'noids with no sense of responsibility for their actions? Bera hadn't been the only R'il'nian to be uneasy at Çeren's techniques, but none of them had thought to apply conditional precognition to that particular problem. Lai wasn't even sure CP at the time would have shown the problem—it might well be that the increase in the number of R'il'noids had produced more positive effects over the centuries than the negative impact of those R'il'noids like Zhaim.

"Talk to Roi and Timi," he suggested. "Don't just ask them what they think; observe them. I know it's steadied Timi—he's beginning to believe that Roi really does want what's best for him. And Roi—*I* think I see a lot more self-confidence. Derry agreed, once he finished telling me what a terrible father I was and actually talked to Roi."

"I will," Marna said grimly. "And you had better be right."

She never actually apologized to Lai, nor did he expect her to. But her mind-touch made it clear that she had found no real harm to either Roi or Timi.

9/28/36

By the end of the half-term Roi was producing problems of quite a different sort at Tyndall. "We're running out of what we can teach him without R'Gal," Kim told Lai at the pre-vacation conference. "History and arts—the subjects in which we normally keep the kids together by age—are no problem. He's caught up with his age group, and we teach the framework material in Galactica anyway. The breadth stuff is at least accessible in Galactica. But the linear subjects—math and science, where we let kids go through at their own pace—well, he's starting to need concepts that just can't be expressed in Galactica. We've never had a kid with anything like his intelligence who can't hear the sound distinctions needed for R'Gal."

"And the problem's real." Derik was sitting in on the meeting, as one of the people who knew Roi's history best. "Jik and I both verified it. In fact, we verified it so often that he's starting to get hysterical at the mere suggestion that we repeat the test again."

Marna shifted in her chair. *Go ahead and say what's on your mind,* Lai thought at her.

"You're treating this as a mental problem," she said. "Is it possible that there is physical damage to his hearing? I've never actually checked on that."

Derik straightened up, his expression eager. "Some of his early owners were very rough. It's certainly possible. Could you check? If that's the problem, he could probably learn to read and write R'Gal, even if he has problems speaking it or understanding the spoken language."

"It won't be easy," Kim said thoughtfully, "but it's worth trying."

"Put if off until after vacation," Lai said. "This will be his first holiday since he's recovered enough to walk. Let him enjoy it. Vara's already arranged to come out and give all of them riding lessons until they know their horses and the trails, and Roi's even found a horse Timi is comfortable on. The kids have a good swimming beach as well as the pool, Davy and Nik are more than halfway through planting that herb garden and I suspect Roi's eager to join in, and between Marna and Derry they'll have as much instruction in other sports as they can handle. I think a few fivedays of just doing what he wants to do will be good for Roi. He's had little enough chance in his life so far."

They were all capable of some degree of conditional precognition, but none of them thought to apply it to the problem of Roi's hearing. After all, what could they expect to learn?

Roi

9/14/36

Roi had invited Feline and Wif to join the group when he moved into his new quarters, but Feline had been reluctant, and Elyra had declined to push her during school term. When Roi repeated the invitation over the school holidays, Elyra must have pushed much harder, as Feline accepted. She was wary and hostile at first, but a pony for Wif, the shallow, protected beach, and the friendship of the two girls, both of whom she had known at Kuril's, won her over to the point that she was willing to consider staying with them when school started. "As long as you don't start considering me your property," she told Roi.

Wif's second birthday was celebrated in free fall in the C-G gym, to the delight of Ania and the other children present, and to the consternation of most of their parents. Roi and Timi were kept busy herding the children, and Roi simply ignored the parents. Derik, who'd volunteered to help the boys in what he insisted on calling kiddie roundup, made no secret of his amusement at their parents' worries. Elyra, who'd been stuck with reassuring the other parents, agreed. "It's not as if they were in danger, with all that padding and the nets," she said scornfully, when the party was over. "I do confess to being a little surprised that none of them got sick, especially with all the sweets they ate."

"The younger they are, the easier they take to free fall," Derik said as he helped Roi fold the nets telekinetically. "Don't let the parents bother you, Roi. The kids loved it."

"Ania's already wanting to come back," Elyra chuckled.

"Wif would probably like that," Roi replied. "Timi's giving him and me both free fall lessons almost every day. Amber too, sometimes, but she's not as far along." Was it just his imagination, he wondered, or was there an element of courtship in the interaction between Derik and Elyra? He hoped so.

"Want to work on your self-monitoring?" Derik asked Roi after Elyra had left with Ania. "I've got an emergency meeting in the interface room, but there'll be plenty of unoccupied lounges. I can set one up to warn you if your blood sugar starts dropping, and you try something that normally causes blood sugar problems and try to spot it dropping before the sensor does."

"We'll take care of the rest of the cleanup," Amber assured him. "Not that the robots leave us much to do."

Derik's meeting, Roi saw at once, involved his father, Marna, Zhaim, and Kaia as well as Derik—the strongest members of the Inner Council. *Don't worry,* Derik's voice came into his mind. *Zhaim's not going to try anything with your father and me here.*

He wasn't worried, really—but he was too aware of Zhaim not to listen to the verbal part of the conversation, especially when he caught the name of a familiar planet. Palinor. Flick's planet. He knew already that Flick's rebel friends had won their struggle, and the Confederation was negotiating with the new planetary government. And from the sound of the discussion, a problem had arisen. The group in the room were trying to work out why the new government had suddenly turned hostile to the diplomat who had previously done so well.

Roi still felt he owed Flick, and once he had learned to follow the Palinorian situation on the Big'Un, he had done so—but this turn of events was new. He went back into the computer, and realized almost at once what the diplomat had done. But why? He had to find the background information on Ambassador Crowling before he understood. But why wasn't the problem obvious to the Inner Council members? Not until he searched the computer again did he realize that he had a piece of information, from an almost forgotten conversation with Flick, that he could not find in the computer.

And he wasn't supposed to be listening. But now that he thought about it, he couldn't remember anyone telling him that he wasn't supposed to listen to open conversations. He just knew he wasn't, just as he knew he wasn't supposed to listen to conversations between his father and Marna. But why? And did the prohibition hold even when he had information the others lacked?

They ought to know, he decided. Before he could change his mind again, he took advantage of a break in the discussion to blurt out, "Could I make a suggestion?"

Every head turned toward him, and he wanted to sink through the lounge. Zhaim's expression was openly scornful; his father and Derik looked stunned, an expression that rapidly spread to Marna and Kaia. Not really angry, he realized after a moment. Just totally surprised, as if they had forgotten he was there. He licked his lips nervously, and fought back a desire to chew on his lower lip.

Derik and Lai exchanged glances, and Lai spoke. "Of course. Any new ideas are welcome."

He'd thought to lay out what he thought was the missing data, but in his nervousness he just blurted out what he thought was the solution. "Maybe if Ambassador Crowling brought his family to Palinor..." His voice trailed off as he saw the scorn on Zhaim's face.

"Ridiculous," Zhaim sniffed.

"Shut up, Zhaim," Kaia said absently. "Or at least run a CP first. It's good. I get—mm—over half? Check me, Derry. That's a lot better than anything else we've thought of. Why, Roi? Why would having Ambassador Crowling's family on Palinor make that much difference?"

Roi gulped. "It's the speech he made," he said. "When he mentioned the carleys."

Lai nodded. "His daughter is paralyzed. She has a trained carley that acts as her hands. They're very useful, and almost impossible to breed."

Useful? "They're a major crop pest on Palinor. Flick considered them vermin, to be wiped out in any way possible."

"And if that's the way the Palinorians understood the reference ..." Kaia said.

"Are captured adults trainable?" Marna asked.

"From pest to export product?" Derry grinned. "It's a possibility. And I like Roi's idea of letting Ambassador Crowling's daughter show the Palinorians what her father meant when he referred to carleys."

"Kaia, Zhaim, you two get to work on the possible permutations," Lai ordered. "The rest of us—Roi, how did you know we were discussing Palinor?"

He'd known he wasn't supposed to be listening! "I'm sorry," Roi said contritely. "I heard the name and I knew it was Flick's planet and I just felt that I still owed him. So I listened. And then I realized he'd told me something that wasn't in the computer, about the carleys being pests, and I thought you ought to know ..." He wanted to sink through the floor.

The three adults exchanged glances. "Roi," Lai said, "you're supposed to be listening and learning all you can. There is nothing wrong at all with your listening to us. But you understood what we were saying?"

"Yes," Roi replied, now totally bewildered.

"Derik, you say you checked the phoneme problem?"

"Exhaustively."

"Do it again. Now. I want to hear exactly how you're giving the test."

"No! Please? I can't do it. I've tried and tried and I always get it wrong." Roi didn't know why he hated the test so, but he felt he'd be sick if he had to take it again.

Lai stood and walked over to Roi's lounge, leaning down to put his hand on Roi's shoulder. "It's not you we're testing this time, Roi. It's the test itself. According to the test, you can't learn R'Gal. But we've been speaking R'Gal—I'm speaking it right now. You're not, but you obviously understand it. There has to be something wrong with the test. Come on, Derry."

Three sounds following each other, and he had to pick the one that was different. The first three triads were easy. So was the fourth, but on that one Derik's emotions suggested he'd made a mistake. The seventh he couldn't call at all, and at that point his father broke into his frustrated silence. "Roi, how many different sounds did you hear?"

"Three."

"So did I," Marna said, and Lai nodded.

"There's nothing wrong with your sound perception," Lai said. "It's better than your testers', that's all. Try it with me, only we'll make a little change in the procedure. If you can't hear one sound as different from the other two, tell me whether you hear three different sounds or all three alike."

"As anyone else would have done anyway," Derik groaned. "Sometimes you follow instructions too well, Roi. Did I really give him two different sounds on the fourth one?"

"You did," Lai said as he sat on the edge of Roi's lounge. "R'Gal doesn't distinguish between them; R'il'nian does."

He should have felt relieved, Roi thought as he closed his eyes and concentrated on hearing his father's voice. Instead, everything felt increasingly wrong. He shouldn't have listened to the conversation. He shouldn't be taking this test. He felt more and more as if he were walking into a deadly trap.

"Third," his voice said, a long way off. "Second. All three the same. All three different." His stomach was increasingly knotted with nausea, and he shivered as sweat poured off his body.

Then the triads topped, replaced by a sentence. "Roi, do you understand what I'm saying?"

Of course he understood. But whatever was causing the nausea and feeling of being trapped resisted his whispered "yes."

"Can you answer me in the same language?"

Yes. No. The white-haired woman who bent over him was huge, slapping frantically at him and screaming that never, never, *never* should he use that language again, or even admit he understood it. The slaps hurt, a little, but her terrible fear flayed his soul. And the fear was for him.

"Cloudy," came an anguished voice from somewhere else, and arms were around him, and his hair was wet from his father's tears.

"She didn't understand," came another voice. Marna. And her arms were around him, too, her mind-touch gentle as she soothed him back to the present, to the interface room. Not to forget, but to understand and accept that his mother, in her deep love for him, had done her best to protect him—but she herself had never realized he could be accepted as a crossbred. *It wasn't that she didn't want you speaking or understanding R'il'nian,* Marna's mind-voice told him, *but that she feared it would lead to your discovery. And you've* been *discovered, for almost two years now.*

Roi opened his eyes, to see Zhaim looking puzzled and both Derry and Kaia with tears in their eyes. "Did I broadcast that?" he asked Marna, and she smiled at him.

"You broadcast the emotions," she said, "but you'd better switch back to R'Gal for now. Your father and I are the only other people who understand R'il'nian."

Understanding R'Gal and R'il'nian wasn't hard. He'd been doing it all his life. In fact, Marna and Lai decided that Cloudy's reaction had probably been to his babbling R'il'nian as soon as he had developed the coordination. Remembering that he was allowed to understand both languages now, and answering in the same language he was addressed in, were harder. He still had enough of his earlier conditioning that he found it difficult to speak either language freely, and he was still too shaken to pay much attention to the adults.

He didn't really react when Kaia said, "It's been close to two years since the Kharfun, hasn't it? Not enough time for a really precise Çeren index, but we can't get that at his age, anyway. And we should be able to get it within a few points."

"Hasn't he had enough for one day?" Marna said sharply, and then looked at the others. Communicating mentally, Roi thought. They know now they can't talk in front of me without my understanding them. He struggled back to alertness as Marna said "Oh," and stood up, leaving his father to support him.

"It's just a cheek swab test, Roi," Lai said as she returned. "We've been guessing at your Çeren index for two years, and having problems because of your apparent failure of the phoneme test. It's about time we ran the Çeren test. It'll take about half an hour."

It was a long half hour. Roi wasn't sure what he wanted his Çeren index to be. If he were Human, he might have a chance of influencing the laws that allowed slavery on Central. Derik and his father would be disappointed, but his friends would be happy. Of course Jelarik seemed very certain that he was R'il'noid. Roi hoped he wouldn't actually qualify as high R'il'noid. He had problems enough making decisions for himself. He wanted no part of making decisions for the whole Confederation.

But all of these thoughts were fleeting. He had trouble concentrating on anything for more than a few seconds at a time. The adults in the room were watching the computer readout as if the intensity of their gaze could somehow make the test progress faster. Most of their faces, and their broadcast emotions, betrayed a kind of wild hope. Zhaim alone radiated apprehension, his eyes flicking back and forth between Roi and the readout. Roi closed his eyes and burrowed into Marna's arms, deliberately refusing to look at the wall screen.

"Thirty-nine," he thought he heard her say, and felt as if a great weight had been lifted from him. Human! His life was his own, to live as he wished. He was sorry to disappoint Derry and his father …

Derry didn't look disappointed. In fact, he'd grabbed Kaia's hands and the two of them were dancing around the room. Zhaim was screaming, "No! It can't be!" and blundering toward the door. Had everyone gone crazy? Bewildered, Roi pulled back until he could look up at Marna's face.

"One hundred thirty-nine, Roi," she said, and gently pushed his head around so he was facing the monitor.

A *hundred* thirty-nine? His mind felt sluggish, and for a moment he couldn't think what the number meant. But Derik was a hundred thirty-two, and Zhaim one-thirty-five …

"Oh, no!" he gasped in sudden horrified comprehension. He *wasn't* Zhaim. Growing up to be like Zhaim had been his greatest fear from the moment he realized that Zhaim was his half brother. And now they wanted him to take Zhaim's place? Through the panic that was threatening to tear his mind apart he reached for safe darkness.

"Roi, no!" he heard Marna's startled exclamation, but he would not, *could* not face this. Darkness surrounded him.

Flame

9/18/36

Nobody ever tells us anything, Flame thought.

She didn't resent it, exactly. It was just the way things were. But she did worry about Roi. It wasn't like him, just to disappear without any warning. And after four days, with all the adults acting upset and worried, she couldn't help but worry herself. Even Davy was acting concerned, though he wouldn't tell them anything.

She got off the bed and walked over to the window, squinting against the low sun. The horses were grazing in the cool of early morning. One of the cats was picking her way toward the main building, shaking dew off her paws with every step. Everything looked normal—except Roi wasn't there.

Flame climbed back onto her bed and sat, cross-legged, looking out the door of her room toward the closed door across the hall. She was pretty sure Derik was still behind that door. The Lady Marna had guided him down the hall to the room the evening before, and ordered him to get some sleep. From the looks of him—disheveled, distraught and staggering—he'd needed sleep. And he'd want to clean up when he awoke. Flame glanced smugly down at the clean towels and clothing beside her on the bed. He might, of course, simply teleport himself out of the room, but if he used the fresher, she'd hear it. And she thought he was the most likely of the adults to tell her what had happened to Roi.

She heard Timi urging Amber to take an early morning swim with him, and Amber suggesting they wait a couple of hours until it was warmer. Then Feline's voice, and Amber offering to saddle Wif's pony and lead him around for a bit after breakfast. Flame did her best to ignore them—she'd eaten breakfast in her room—and concentrated on hearing any sound from across the hall.

The others had all been quiet for close to an hour when she heard the sound she'd been waiting for. She uncrossed her legs and picked up the towels and clean clothes, then walked across the hallway and tapped at the door. "It's me, Flame," she called. "Would you like some clean clothes?"

She felt the light touch of his mind, no more than verifying her identity. "Flame? Yes, of course. Come on in."

She heard the latch on the door release, and slid it aside. Derik was just coming out of the fresher, his hair still wet. She handed him a towel, and then the clean clothes. "Would you like breakfast?" she asked brightly.

"Already ordered it from the computer." He was polite, but he still looked worried.

Flame hesitated, but it sounded as if she'd have to ask outright if he knew anything. "Please, sir—do you know where Roi is? It's not like him to just go off without saying anything."

Derik was silent as he pulled on a light shirt, his face taking on that half-there look that meant he was in mental communication with someone else. Then he turned to her. "How long have you known Roi, Flame?"

Flame blinked in surprise. "Since before we started dancing. Before I learned to count. A long time, anyway."

Derik nodded once, quickly. "All right. This is privileged information, Flame. If Roi wants to share it with the others, fine, but you don't on your own. Understand?"

Flame's first reaction was relief. Derik was speaking as if Roi would be coming back—but then why was he so worried? But she had no problems waiting for Roi's permission to share information. "I understand," she said.

"We finally ran a Çeren test on Roi. He panicked at the result and teleported away. Marna was in enough contact that we're reasonably sure he survived the teleport, but all we know is that he went somewhere dark and that he felt safe there. But feeling safe doesn't mean that he is safe. We need to protect him, but we have no idea where he is."

"Inner Council level?" Flame asked, and had to grin at the shock on Derik's face.

"How ..."

"He never really believed Jelarik's evaluation as high R'il'noid, but he wouldn't have been surprised by it. And I don't think he would have panicked at being lower. More likely relieved. So it had to be higher."

Derik nodded. "I expected him to be Inner Council level. It's more than that. He's four points above Zhaim. And Zhaim's not happy about it."

"Oh, my." Flame said, thinking how inadequate that response was. Roi— her Snowy—as Lai's heir? And forced to compare himself with Zhaim? He wouldn't even think about Zhaim if he could help it. "I bet Roi's even unhappier," she said.

Derik just stared at her for a moment, then nodded. "You know him better than his father does," he said. "Flame, will you help us find him? Not to coerce him. Not even to get him to come back, if he doesn't want to. Just to be sure he's safe. Especially safe from Zhaim."

"Safe from Zhaim?"

Derik was walking up and down the room now, with quick, choppy strides. "R'il'noids are immune from most planetary laws. That goes back to an incident when a borderline R'il'noid working on Maung sweep was executed for traveling at the time of a new moon, a capital offense in that culture, and several million people died because the Maung infestation wasn't caught until it was too late for treatment. But there is a Confederation law, with death in its teeth. A R'il'noid who kills another R'il'noid who tests higher, or less than thirty-six points lower, must be executed. Execution's not mandatory for an attempt that fails, but it's certainly an option. That's why we all agreed that Roi had to be tested as soon as we realized that the language problem wasn't real. Once Zhaim knew that Roi was a serious rival, we had to establish Roi's Çeren index to give him legal protection from Zhaim. Extrapolating Wif's index wouldn't have held up in a death penalty case. But if we don't know where Roi is, and if Zhaim thinks he can kill him without our being able to prove it, especially before he cools down enough to think ..." He spread his hands in a gesture of futility as he turned to face her.

Dark and safe. She could think of one place, but was it the right one? And if Derik searched it, wouldn't Roi just teleport away again? Perhaps to a less safe place? Her face must have given her away, because his lit up with sudden hope. "You have an idea?"

"Maybe. But he'd hide from you. He might accept me." She paused and looked directly at her former owner. "You really won't make him come back?" She had no problem helping Roi, in any way she could. But she would not be a party to forcing him into anything. Had she already gone too far?

"Being a part of the Inner Council—not to mention the possibility of leading it someday—is far too much responsibility to be anything but voluntary. Even the choice has to wait until he's a lot older than he is now. At least another sixteen years, and full members have to be at least sixty-four, though my guess is that his father will want him to start sitting in and just listening much earlier. He needs to learn enough so that he can make a reasonable choice whether to participate, and he needs protection from Zhaim. The Inner Council and the Genetics Board, and now you, are the only ones who know. If Roi prefers, we'll keep it that way, so he can grow up with as little pressure as possible. But we do need to know that he's all right."

Flame tugged at a loose strand of hair, then found herself chewing on it. Sheepishly she spat it out. "On that I'll help all I can."

Derik nodded eagerly. "Tell me what you need and where you need to go. Will you take a finder with you? Not to force him back—that has to be his decision. But if you let us know he's all right, we can make sure Zhaim can't get at him."

Flame glanced down at herself. She was wearing a light shirt and shorts, all she needed against the temperature of the building. But she'd need warmer clothing if Roi was where she thought he might be, and her hiking boots. "A sleeping bag and hot food in stasis," she said. "Basic medical supplies—Roi's taught us a little about how to use them. A light. And I'll need to change clothes. We'll try your place first." She grinned at Derik, and then hurried back to her own room. Giving orders to her former owner felt strange, but surprisingly satisfying.

Trying to find the right cove was less satisfying. She could see it in her mind, but going from that image to how it would look from the air was harder than she expected. And she hadn't realized that Derik's estate would have such a long coastline, or so many coves.

"Look," he said, as they took off from the third beach, "are you trying to find the beach entrance to the caves?"

Flame stared at him. "You know about them?"

He grinned at her. "Take a good look at the path and the stepping stones. None of my overseers have known, though I suppose Chip will. If Roi's there he's safe from Zhaim—my shields are set to allow Roi in, but not Zhaim. But it's a little cool. If he's too cold to shiver, call for help. You remember how?"

She nodded. "One push on the button if I find him and he's all right. Three if he's hurt or I need help."

Derik nodded as he angled the jump-van down to a new beach. Flame squinted at the headlands framing the cove. Not quite what her memory held—but then she saw the fresh scar on the cliff, and the unfamiliar tumble of rocks in the surf just below the scar. She looked at the back wall of the cove, and saw the bushes that concealed the low arch of the cave mouth.

"I'll have to check several places," she said as Derik handed her the light and her pack. "Don't help me put the pack on. I'd just have to take it off again to get through the opening." She walked up the rise, the sand sliding under her feet, and stopped at the cave opening. She was barely able to push the pack through, and she had to wiggle under the arch on her stomach. Sand cushioned the crawl, but she was still glad she had changed into the tough coverall.

Once inside she stood, waiting for her eyes to adjust before flashing her light around her. She'd never been in here with such a bright light before, and the entry cavern was far taller than she had expected. On the other hand the pool to the left of the entrance, huge as it had seemed, was now revealed as hardly three strides across. None of the obvious side caves were of any size, but she dutifully flashed her light in each before returning to the only real exit, an unpromising vertical crack in the back wall. She had to find and follow the thin trickle of water flowing into the pool to be sure it was the right crack.

Again she was barely able to negotiate the entrance, even holding her breath, and she had to take the sleeping bag out of the pack before she could squeeze it through the opening. But that should be the last tight spot. The trail beside the stream was narrow in spots, but the rock walls themselves no longer scraped her shoulders. She repacked the sleeping bag and slipped into the pack straps, then started along the trail.

She sang as she walked, the old, sad slave songs that she and Roi had once sung together in childish treble voices. His voice had deepened now, to a warm baritone, but hers was still a silvery soprano. He might not recognize her voice, especially the way it echoed in the cave, but the old songs would be familiar and comforting.

The trail crossed the stream, and Flame knelt to examine the stepping stones. The rock of the cave was smooth, wet, rounded, and somewhat slippery under her hands. The stepping stones were flat-topped, angular and gritty. She shook her head, annoyed with herself for never noticing the difference. But would it have meant anything to her, before Roi had insisted on telling her how caves were made? Probably not.

If they'd known more about caves, she reflected as she checked the shallow side chambers off the trail, they would never have dared explore as they had, with only borrowed glow sticks for light. Realizing that Derik had known about the cave, she could see where he had blocked off side routes that might have been dangerous. Roi had always insisted that Derik meant well, she recalled.

A side stream tumbled down a slope to join the main stream, and she hesitated. The combination of "safe" and "dark" had reminded her at once of the small cavern in which the side stream originated, as a spring welling up in a small pool. The dancing group had hidden out there more than once when Brak was being unusually harsh. She wondered now that she had never questioned Brak's acceptance of their absence. Had Derik been covering for them, while letting them think they were defying him? At any rate, this was where she had the greatest hope of finding Roi.

She finished the final bars of her song, then called out, "Roi, it's me, Flame. Can I come up?"

The only answer was the echoes of her own voice, bouncing repeatedly from the cave walls.

She pulled a strand of hair into her mouth and began to chew on it. Roi might not be there. Or he might not want her, though that thought hurt. Or he might be there, but injured or unconscious. One way or another, she had to find out.

She thought she could still get through the narrow tunnel to the spring cave, but not wearing the pack. She shrugged out of the straps and began climbing toward the darkness, still singing breathlessly, pushing pack and light before her.

Roi

Roi tried at first to stay in the safe darkness inside his head. But he kept finding himself in Zhaim's pleasure chambers, looking through Zhaim's eyes as he remolded Timi's screaming body into a monster from his nightmares. Again and again he fought his way to darkness and cold, and every time he fell back into the horror of another R'il'noid's pleasures. Not always Zhaim, either. He was Colo Kenarian, using mind-touch to force his slaves to beg for the indignities he heaped on them. He was owners whose names he had forgotten, and birthday well-wishers whose emotions had barely impinged on his shields.

Gradually he became aware of thirst, and hunger, and bone-chilling cold. When he was most nearly sane he welcomed them. If he died, the nightmares would go away. Wouldn't they?

He was yet again seeing through Zhaim's eyes when he heard singing—an old song, one his mother had once sung. Then a voice—Flame's voice?—asking to join him. No! He would *not* call her into Zhaim's power.

Scraping sounds, and a stab of light that struck at his eyes like a knife. He tried to raise an arm to block the light, and discovered that he was unable to move. Paralyzed again?

"Roi! You're cold as ice! And your clothes are soaked. Out of them and into the sleeping bag, right now!" Hands stripping off his sweat-soaked clothing—or was he ripping the clothes from a potential victim? Maybe he ought to call for medical help … No!

Flame's body, hot as fire, against his own—his own body, like ice against her breasts.

"Honestly," came Flame's voice, echoing oddly in his ears, "sometimes I think you don't have as much sense as Wif. I ought to call for help—I told Derry I would, and you're not even shivering …"

Her words triggered an almost convulsive shudder, and suddenly he could not stop shivering, his teeth chattering so hard he could not have spoken even if he had been able to control his muscles. Flame held him tightly, crooning anxiously, and Roi burrowed closer, his body demanding her warmth. Derry, she'd said. He hadn't looked through Derik's eyes, or Kaia's, or those of any of the other R'il'noids he liked. "You don't have to *be* Zhaim, you know," she said softly. "You can still be you."

He could still be himself. He was too cold and shivering too hard to think very clearly, but that was a thought to hold on to. He could choose not to be another Zhaim.

He must have held that thought into sleep. When he awoke it was with a raging thirst, but sharply aware of Flame's body against his own in the warmth of the sleeping bag, and of his against her. She had left the light on low, turned against the wall to give shape to their surroundings, and when he opened his eyes, it was to look directly into hers—or into his own? Horrified, he realized that his shields were completely down, and he was sharing her mind. Had been, ever since she had found him. "Sorry," he stammered, as he rebuilt the barrier between their minds.

"What for?" she replied. "You were sharing, not invading. I don't mind that. Of course it was a little confusing. And those awful nightmares! But it was—well—nice, too. Let's get a drink. You made me thirsty. And then we'd better eat something."

Flame might not have Amber's intelligence, but at the moment her simple practicality was welcome. Roi slid out of the sleeping bag and buried his face in the cool water of the spring pool. The cave wasn't really cold, but by the time he had satisfied his immediate thirst and washed the half-dried sweat from his face and hair, he was shivering again. No sense even trying to put on his clothes—a quick feel had told him they were mostly still wet, and stiff in the few dry areas. They weren't really warm enough for the cave, anyway. He crawled back into the sleeping bag, exhausted by even that slight effort.

"Drink this," Flame said as she handed him a warm cup. The aroma of the soup made him realize how hungry he was, and he swallowed the rich broth eagerly, pressing his hands around the heat of the cup between swallows. He was barely aware of Flame taking the cup from his hands as he fell back into sleep.

"What's wrong with me?" he demanded the third or fourth time he awoke. "All I do is sleep."

Flame turned the light up and sat cross-legged next to the sleeping bag. "Making up for the nightmares?" she suggested. "It was four days from the time you disappeared until I found you here. And if you were having nightmares like the ones you shared with me all that time ... Well, maybe your body knows what it needs better than you do."

"Four days? Flame, how long have you been here?"

She shrugged. "Don't know. Didn't bring a timekeeper. We're almost out of stasis food, but I don't know how much Derik packed. Plenty of trail food left, but no more hot stuff unless we can build a fire. Do you know how to build a fire?"

"I know we need something that will burn and a place for the smoke to get out. I don't think we have either here. Derry packed food for you? He—Flame, I will not let them turn me into another Zhaim!"

"Why should they *want* to? They've got Zhaim. And from what Derik said while we were looking for the right cove, they're not very happy with him. That's why they were so excited about you, and want to protect you from him. Roi, Derik said it has to be your choice, after you're old enough to understand all the responsibilities involved. Right now all they want is that you study and be safe. He said that nobody even has to know except the Inner Council and the Genetics Board."

"I understand the responsibilities," Roi growled. "And I want no part of them. I don't want to make decisions for other people."

"You'd do a better job of it than Zhaim would," Flame responded. "You kept us alive and together. Timi tried, after you were gone. But the only thing that really saved us was that you'd gotten Derik to buy us."

"You trust me too much," Roi told her. But even as he complained, he knew Flame had an annoying habit of seeing the obvious things that he sometimes overlooked.

By the time they had eaten half of the trail food, soaking the stuff in cool water to get it to chewable consistency, Roi was ready to consider at least moving down to the entry cave. "We're both filthy," he told Flame. "So's the sleeping bag, and nothing will dry in here. We could wash stuff out in the pool in the entry cave, and then put it outside the cave to dry. Maybe even find something to burn, so we can have some hot food." He looked hopefully at Flame.

"You don't have to convince me," she laughed, and squeezed her eyes shut for a moment. "There's lots of dry branches on the beach. Would they burn?"

If Flame's visual memory said there were dry branches on the beach, there were. And he could speed up the molecules to light a fire. "Let's go," he said, picking up the sleeping bag and Flame's pack.

They reached the entry cave early in the morning, when the stars were just winking out. There was barely enough light that Flame could see to gather an armload of driftwood while Roi made a determined assault on his clothes and the sleeping bag in the little pool. By the time she returned, the light outside the cave entrance had brightened. Flame crawled back into the cave and stood blinking for several minutes while she pulled off her coverall and added it to the clothes Roi was working on in the pool.

Light through the leaves hiding the entrance, together with the reflected artificial light from the pool, created a fascinating pattern on her bare body. Roi traced it with his eyes while he continued to scrub at the sweat-soaked fabric, and then looked away as he suddenly realized what he was doing. But why? They were all familiar with each other's bodies. Why had Flame's body suddenly become something different and enticing? He examined his memories of the period they had shared minds, and she had been disturbingly aware of his body.

What had his father said? "Attitudes change, about your age." Well, he didn't need them changing right now! He had more than enough changing in his life at the moment, thank you!

"Give that to me; you're scrubbing so hard you'll tear it apart," Flame scolded. "See if you can get a fire started. One of the trail food cans is empty; try to heat some water in it. From upstream."

Starting a fire was easier than he had expected. Keeping the smoke from choking them both was harder, but he eventually found a place where the natural air flow in the entry cavern took the smoke to a crevice high in the wall, and they had their first hot food in several meals. To his surprise, Roi found himself enjoying it. The cavern pool was too shallow to swim in, but he did manage to wash the worst of the grime from his body. He even helped Flame retrieve the rough-dried clothes and sleeping bag from the rocks outside their shelter, though he couldn't help ducking every time he heard an unidentified sound. Flame rolled her eyes in exasperation but said nothing.

"Why shouldn't I worry about being found?" he finally snapped, after an hour of brooding.

"Roi, Derik knows where you are, and I'm sure he's told your father and Marna. They were worried sick about you. Derik dropped me off on the beach, out there, with a finder. I was supposed to hit the button once if I found you and didn't want help; three times if I needed help. I should have hit it three times, but I couldn't. But if I hadn't signaled at all, Derik would have come after me and found you that way. And he knows the cave, probably better than we do. Think about the stepping stones."

She looked angry. She had reason to be, he thought. Her decision not to call for help had probably been his. But when he thought about it, he had to admit that the cave had indeed been modified to make it a safe playground for Derik's younger slaves. So Derik, and probably Lai and Marna as well, knew where he was, and Derik knew the cave well enough to teleport to any place in it.

He was being silly about hiding, he finally decided. He wasn't quite ready to return to the Enclave yet—if he did that, he'd have to face what his Çeren index meant. And he had to work that out for himself before he went back, without pressure from anyone else. But he would take a swim in the ocean tomorrow.

The weather did not cooperate. A storm blew in from the ocean overnight, and by morning rain and wisps of fog almost hid the shoreline. "Why didn't you make me get out and swim yesterday?" Roi snapped at Flame.

To his surprise, she snapped, "I'm trying to let you make up your own mind!" turned, and stalked across the cave. She turned back only to add, "You told Timi often enough that he needed to learn to work around the things he couldn't change, like being a slave. Maybe you need to take your own advice. You can't change being Lai's son, or your Çeren index."

Roi bit back an angry retort, and for several hours they both simply tried to ignore each other, trapped in the cave by the rain, without even a fire for comfort. How dare she talk back to him like that!

But his ability to feel the emotions of others told him how miserable she was. As the hours went by, some traitorous part of his mind kept whispering that he was making Zhaim's error, not caring about her feelings as a person because he did not perceive her as a person in her own right. That, he realized, was the difference between Zhaim and the R'il'noids he respected. He thought he had chosen not to be like Zhaim—but it seemed that was not a decision that needed to be made only once. He had to choose at every turn—and this time, he had chosen wrongly.

"Flame," he said softly, and saw her head turn, her expression wary. "I'm sorry. I shouldn't have snapped at you like that. I guess the weather's got me in a bad mood."

She looked at him for a minute, and then tried a tentative smile. "Me, too. Roi, do you think you could dry out some wood the same way you started the fire yesterday? I'm hungry, and I don't think I can face any more of the cold-soaked trail food. I'll bring wood in if you can dry it."

Of course he could dry it out—why hadn't he thought of that? More, he could drag wood into the cave telekinetically, if he just knew where to "look" for it. "Can you share your memories of where the wood is?" he asked. "If you can, I think I can use my mind to drag it in."

Hot food put them both in a better temper. It was still raining by the time the weak daylight faded, but surely it wouldn't last long, this time of year. Roi hadn't learned how to forecast the weather yet, but his perception indicated the storm didn't extend too much farther to the west. Maybe they could swim tomorrow.

It did clear by noon the next day, but Flame almost provoked another burst of anger by refusing to accompany Roi. "Why?" he managed to control himself enough to ask. "You like swimming."

"No sunscreen," she replied promptly. "You don't sunburn; I do."

He looked at her milky skin, then down at his own deep bronze. She'd given him a perfectly valid reason. But he knew what her sunscreen container looked like, and where it was kept. The shields on his building at the Enclave were set to allow him access. Could he bring her sunscreen here?

He closed his eyes and felt for the container, back in her room at the Enclave. There. He used sand to balance energy and momentum, and teleported the sunscreen to an air pocket in Flame's pack. "Take a good look in your pack," he suggested.

She gave him a thoughtful look and began digging in her pack, eventually coming up with the sunscreen. "Derry didn't remember this," she said. "Thank you, Roi." She leaned over and kissed him.

Again, he was startled by just how charged the contact was, and jerked back. "I'm going to have to talk with my father when I get back," he muttered. "What are you looking so smug about?"

"You said 'when,' not 'if,'" she replied as she rubbed sunscreen onto her body. "Get my back, will you? I can't quite reach it." Had he made up his mind, without even realizing it? He hastily smeared the sunscreen on Flame's back, trying to ignore what he was doing, then challenged, "Beat you to the shore," and wiggled through the entrance side by side with Flame.

It was an even race. Roi's legs were longer, but he was still a long way from recovering full strength, and the sand, even moistened by the rain, did not give the best of footing. Still, Flame reached the surf only a stride or two ahead of him. They plunged into the waves together, and alternated swimming and lying on the beach for the rest of the afternoon. For the first time since he had left the Enclave he felt clean. How long? It seemed just yesterday and forever.

"This is the last of the trail food," Flame said that evening. "Do you know how to catch fish?"

Roi shook his head. "Do you know how to cook them if I could?" he asked. "I sure don't."

They both fell silent. It was quite dark out by the time Roi said, "I need to think a little. I'll be right out by the rocks."

"Take the light," Flame said.

He sank down where the sand and rocks still held the heat of the sun, leaned back, and turned off the light. As his eyes adjusted to the darkness, the stars seemed to brighten until they filled the skies. He picked out the constellations Ander had taught him, and then tried to find those stars that had occupied planets orbiting them. That was harder, as most of the suns of the Confederation were dim as seen from Central. Palinor's sun, for instance, was so faint he wasn't really sure he saw it, but he was able to locate the triangle of brighter stars that should surround it. Palinor. He had acted as a member of the Inner Council, he realized with some surprise. He had made a suggestion, and they had taken it seriously. Had it helped? He didn't see how he could have made the situation any worse.

He thought about what Flame had said about his advice to Timi, and considered his own reaction to her. He didn't understand himself. But he hadn't understood Derik's frequent insistence on the idea that his father had loved his mother, either. In fact, he realized, he had rather carefully avoided thinking about the details of how he had come to be. Sex, for him, had been a matter of predation and dominance, very much like forcing another person's mind, and he wanted no part of either. But Flame had made a distinction between sharing and invading. Maybe that extended to physical relationships as well?

He hadn't been introduced yet to the complex mathematics that underlay formal conditional precognition, but he understood the basic concept. Fix your mind on a decision, and then look ahead to the possible futures stemming from that decision. There'd be a lot of fuzziness, but if the decision was an important one, there would be a difference in the futures. All right, suppose he refused to be a part of the Inner Council?

He'd learned to look back, in order to Heal himself, so looking forward wasn't too hard. The results were a jumble he lacked the tools to analyze, but he could be a Healer, accepted and loved by the restored Jibeth community.

There was happiness and satisfaction along that road, but also pain as those he cared most about grew old and died, and he did not. He looked farther, and thought he saw a child, one blending Lai and Marna, and caught his breath in momentary relief. But then he was aware that the child was dead, and beyond that death lay chaos and fear, the end of the Confederation and possibly of star-traveling Humans. No. He did not even want to contemplate that future.

And if he accepted being part of the Inner Council?

Very similar, at first. Less satisfaction, and the pain of losing those he cared for seemed to be a part of what he was that he could not avoid. He pressed forward, determined to go as far along this road as he had on the alternative, and found the child again, but an adult now, enmeshed in a time of chaos but not without hope. And if the right choices were made during that time of conflict, this future went on.

Zhaim would never make the kind of choices that were needed.

Roi pressed his back against the warmth of the rock and wiped the tears from his face. He did not want to take responsibility for others. Maybe that was why he had survived slavery so well—he was generally happy to leave the decisions to others, unless he had to do something to keep himself or his friends alive.

He remembered also what Derik had told him. There's always something to do that nobody else can do. He didn't want that. But right now, it seemed, they just wanted him to study and learn. That he could do, he realized suddenly. It wasn't the life he would have chosen, but who got the life they wanted?

"Roi?" Flame called from the cave mouth, her voice anxious.

"I'm here," he called back, and flicked on the light to show her the way. He kept the beam just in front of her feet as she came toward him and eventually flopped down beside him. "If we're out of food," he said after a few minutes of silence, "maybe it's time we went home."

ABOUT THE CONFEDERATION

Calendars

Both Riya and Central used calendars that start with the northward equinox. The lengths of their years and days were similar but not identical in length to Earth's or to each other's. The Central year was slightly more than 364 Central days, and was made up of 12 30-day months plus four days outside the months: Yearday (northward equinox), Northday (northern solstice), Feastday (southward equinox) and Southday (southern solstice.) Of these, only Yearday was tied firmly to the solar calendar, and an intercalary day was inserted as needed at the end of the year to keep Yearday at the longitude of the Confederation administrative complex on the northward equinox (vernal equinox in the northern hemisphere.)

Each 30-day month was broken into six fivedays. One day of each fiveday was a rest day, but which day varied widely. Probably the first day of a fiveday was most often used as a rest day, as was the case at Tyndall. The school year started the first day of the fifth month, 1 month after Northday. The two school vacations started with Southday and Northday and ran for a month each.

At the time of the story perihelion was very close to the northward equinox. This put northern solstice is a few days before Northday and southern solstice a few days after Southday, while Feastday was normally within a day of the southward equinox. At the time of contact between Roi and Marna, northern solstice on Riya was 12 days after southern solstice on Central. Comparison with Earth time doesn't come into this story, but Roi's childhood was assumed to be during the period when the western European countries were well into colonizing the Americas. Think George Washington's birth at about the time the story starts.

You may note from this that the author has ignored the fact that relativity, properly implemented, makes simultaneity impossible. It's not that I don't accept relativity; it just makes plotting on an interstellar scale nearly impossible!

History and legal framework

The Confederation as it existed during the time of the story was roughly ten thousand years old, and dated to the first outbreak of Kharfun. At that time the original R'il'noids, whose R'il'nian genes were derived entirely from Jarn, were wiped out, and the population of the R'il'nai was severely reduced. This left the Human-occupied planets without leaders who could protect their populations from Maung infestation, and with no trusted arbitrators to stop interplanetary conflict. At the request of the Humans, the cross breeding of R'il'nai and Humans was resumed, leading to the modern R'il'noids whose purpose was to protect the Human planets from Maung infestation and from each other, but not to interfere in any way with what Humans did on their own planets. With the passage of time, this evolved into a legal system in which Confederation law applied to relationships among planets and between R'il'noids, while planetary law, which varied widely among the planets of the Confederation, applied to internal affairs on each planet.

Central was originally a R'il'nian planet. As the R'il'nian population declined, increasing numbers of Humans came in as administrators and their support staffs. As the R'il'nian population continued to decline, the R'il'nai eventually handed most of the planet over to Humans, retaining only one smallish continent in the southern hemisphere for their own use. The Enclave in the large sense refers to the entire continent, though by Roi's time many of the R'il'noids had settled on the continent, and the term was also used in a narrower sense to refer to the Confederation administrative complex and Lai's personal home. These were located on the west coast of the Enclave continent, at roughly 35 degrees south.

Pronunciation

L' is a palatalized l, as in the frozen baby mammoth Lyuba.
R' is a palatalized r
Ç is a palatalized c
X is a very breathy kh sound
The apostrophe in words such as K'Zhaim or R'Gal is as nearly as possible silent.